I0772581

CHARMING DEVILS

KATIE MAY

EXPRESSO PUBLISHING, LLC

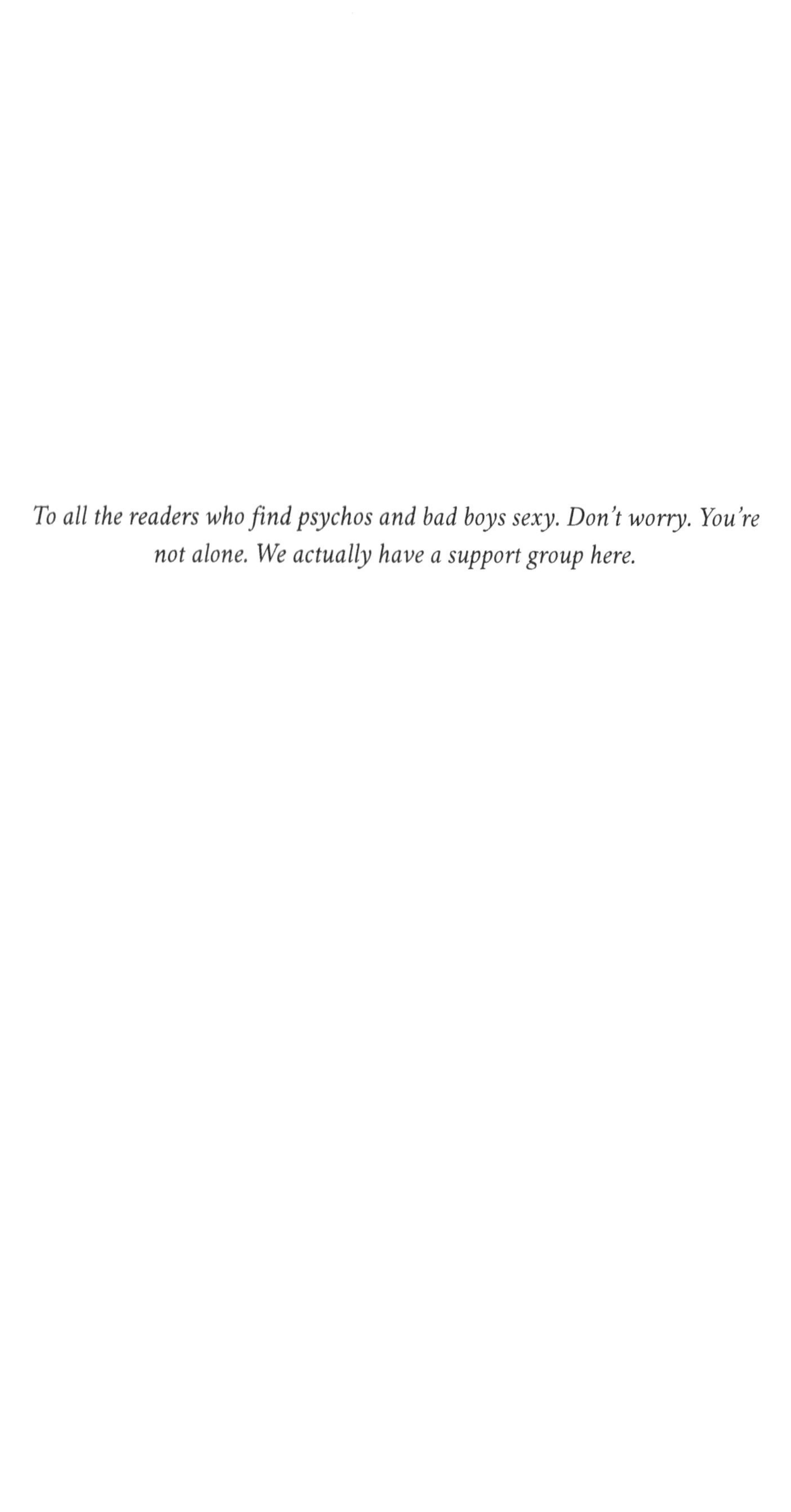

To all the readers who find psychos and bad boys sexy. Don't worry. You're not alone. We actually have a support group here.

CONTENTS

FOREWORD

This is a paranormal revenge/bully reverse harem romance and is not suitable for anyone under the age of 18. It contains strong language, psychotic males, and sexual situations. It does contain triggers of self-harm, depression, and sexual abuse, though everything between the FMC and her men is consensual.

If you don't like a kickass FMC who doesn't need to choose between her love interests…then this book isn't for you. Or if you're in any way, shape, or form related to me. Or if you know me outside of the author world. Put. This. Book. Down. Seriously, Grandma.

PROLOGUE

FIVE YEARS AGO

I stared at the stain on my white blouse. The cranberry color seeped through the thin fabric, highlighting the outline of my beige bra.

Tears of indignation filled my eyes as I spun in a wide circle.

"Hello? Can anyone hear me?"

The last thing I remembered was walking home from school. And then, a car had pulled up alongside me, and four figures bedecked in superhero costumes had jumped out. Their scrawny, childlike frames made me think that they were approximately my age—thirteen. I wondered which of them had stolen his parents' car.

With more force than necessary, they'd wrenched my hands behind my back and shoved a burlap sack over my head. I'd thrashed and screamed helplessly, but only raucous laughter filled the air.

And now, I was here.

They had untied me and removed the sack, but that didn't mean I could escape. One glance confirmed I was in the men's locker room, adjacent to the middle school's football stadium. The pungent stench of sweat and piss barraged my sensitive nose. Lockers lined one wall opposite the showers, with wooden benches spread out before them.

Feeling dizzy, I lunged towards the door and tried the handle. Locked, of course.

"Let me out!" I screamed, pounding my fists against the distressed wood. Panic coursed through my veins as the ramifications of what they had done fully caught up to me.

I was trapped.

Desperate, I raced towards the nearest window and attempted to dislodge it from its casing. Unsurprisingly, it was stuck. I was pretty sure it hadn't been opened once in the last five years. I pressed my fingers beneath the pane, ignoring the blood from my ravaged fingernails, and sought to pry it open. Sweat beaded on my forehead and dripped down my nose.

Fear engulfed me in an icy embrace as a sob lodged itself in my throat. I pressed my forehead against the glass, desperate to soothe my frayed nerves.

Be calm. Be calm. Be calm.

"Look at the little baby," a cold voice sneered from behind me. I spun, unsurprised to find my four kidnappers. Spider-Man had removed his mask, and I found myself standing face to face with my middle school tormenter.

"Let me go," I pleaded, tears blurring my vision. His lips curled up into a cruel, malevolent smirk, though his eyes remained impish. The combination caused the tiny hairs on my arms to stand on end. Rage and fear swarmed through me, like I'd kicked over an angry hornet's nest.

If I was only a few years older…I could blast all of these assholes into oblivion. But for now, all I could do was be the foolish prey to their beasts. The mouse caught in their painstakingly constructed traps.

"Not until you submit." He took a menacing step forward. "Not until you know that we don't accept freaks in our town."

CHAPTER 1

NOW

There's a distinct difference between the California air and Michigan's. For one, it's not nearly as humid, despite being the end of August. For two, it feels almost…cleaner. Less industrialized.

I stare out my window at the busy tourist town. Behind sun-kissed stands, Lake Michigan spreads as far as the eye can see. The sunlight glimmers on the serene surface, making it appear as if it's constructed out of thousands of diamonds. Families are happily playing in the water, sunbathing on the land, and moving from food stand to food stand. The entire atmosphere evokes feelings of love and joy.

"I'd forgotten how beautiful this place is," I whisper, pressing my face against the car window.

"Just wait until it snows," my driver, Charles, exclaims with a snort. "It won't be beautiful then."

"I love the snow." Absently, I lift my finger and trace the outline of a happy family relaxing beneath an umbrella. The wife is sunbathing, a paperback forgotten on her chest. The husband is building sandcastles with two little girls, their faces alight with happiness.

What must it be like to be that carefree? That happy? To know you are loved? Sure, this family probably has some demons—as we all do—but I can't ignore the pang of jealousy that spears me as I watch them.

It isn't long until they're completely out of sight.

I can tell when we leave the tourist hotspot. The once congregated buildings begin to space out, until we're surrounded completely by fields. Interspersed are magnificent country ranches.

"Has Mother called yet?" I ask, turning away from the rolling landscape to face Charles fully. In the rearview mirror, I see his face pinch and eyes shadow over. I know what he's going to say even before he says it.

"No. I'm sorry, Miss Peony."

I swallow down the bitter disappointment, focusing once more on the landscape. We drive through what appears to be a downtown area with cobblestone streets, quaint shops and restaurants, and numerous benches. I remember running down this exact sidewalk...

"You can't run from me forever," a cold voice shouted as my footsteps pounded against the asphalt of the street. Up above, I spotted the bright lights of Mama's House, the local diner.

Just a little farther...

"Found you," he whispered in my ear.

I pull myself out of the memories that threaten to drag me under and consume me. Vigorously shaking my head, I shove them in a steel casket and bury it miles beneath the surface, never to be seen or heard from again.

As we drive out of town, I begin to pay closer attention to my surroundings. The family-owned grocery store in desperate need of repair. The dog park with rusted fences and precariously tilting steel benches.

High Groves Middle School.

My eyes narrow at the unassuming brick building as the car passes it. I know, logically, that I'll now be attending the high school across town, but I can't stop the stab of hate and anger that bombards me.

"Your nana is expecting you," Charles says conversationally. "She set up a room for you in the attic."

"She didn't have to do that," I murmur awkwardly, anxiously chewing on my lower lip. I haven't seen Nana in years, and I can't deny the flicker of self-consciousness that reverberates through me.

We pull up in front of wrought iron gates, and Charles steps out of the car to manually open them. I attempt to peer around the boughs of trees, desperate to catch a glimpse of my childhood home.

It's only when Charles enters the car once more and begins the trek up the curving driveway, do I see the gothic mansion nestled snugly in the middle of a secluded forest.

It's four stories high with numerous gables and turrets. Two gargoyles perch on the roof, their stone faces sending pinpricks of fear racing down my spine. The brown paint on the walls has faded in some spots, though I can't decide if it's from inconsistent weather or time itself. Leaves cover the front steps and porch, already turning hues of black and brown instead of their normal orange and yellow.

My memories of this place depict it as being grand and elegant, plucked straight out of a fairy tale. Was I really that blind to the desolate home towering before me?

"Can I help you with your bags?" Charles asks, already hurrying around the car to open my door for me. His face is weathered by age, deep lines carved down both of his cheeks and around his eyes. When he walks, his back hunches over, almost as if there's a weight pressing down on the middle of his spine.

"I got it," I hurry to respond. "Thank you, Charles." He smiles, showcasing his crooked teeth, and I feel my own lips curve upwards instinctively. Charles has become a fixture in my life. It's going to be hell saying goodbye to him.

I grab my single duffel bag and sling it over my shoulder. The rest of my belongings were sent over earlier.

The pathway leading up to the house is bogged down with weeds, and the air smells like grass and garbage.

Still, there's a skip to my step that hadn't been there prior as I rap my knuckles against the front door. Charles steps up beside me and offers me a reassuring smile. I relish the wrinkled curve of his lips and the sparkle in his eyes. It makes me feel braver, stronger, capable of doing what I'd set out to do in the first place.

Taking another deep, ragged breath, I pound on the door a second time. After a moment of prolonged silence, I hear the patter of footsteps and the jangle of bracelets.

"Peony!" a raspy voice says, even before the door fully opens. "I wasn't expecting you for at least a couple more hours."

"Mom decided to send me off early," I reply dryly. Correction—she practically threw me out of the house.

The door opens the rest of the way, and I get my first good look at Nana, otherwise known as Cardinal Simone. Her naturally gray hair has been dyed a bright violet, the curls cascading to the middle of her back. Despite her age, she has no wrinkles on her face. The only indication that she's above forty is the wisdom emanating from her muddy brown eyes. She wears a silky floral robe over a translucent nightgown, and I quickly look away before I can see something I'll never be able to unsee.

"Nana..." I murmur just as footsteps resonate from behind her. A moment later, three handsome young men—triplets, more than likely—begin pawing at my grandmother. One of them kisses her neck while the other cups her breasts. The final male tilts her chin to the side to kiss her lips. All of them are heavily muscled, with chestnut brown hair and emerald green eyes. They look to be in their mid-twenties, younger than Nana by over forty years.

And they're also butt ass naked.

"Not now, my pets," Nana coos, slapping one of them on the ass. "I have my granddaughter over to visit me."

"For fuck's sake…" I curse, diverting my attention towards a hanging plant. Charles's face turns beet-red as he focuses on his feet.

"I-I'll just be…um…going…Miss Peony," he stutters, finally raising his head to meet my gaze. There's a question flashing in his eyes, one he doesn't dare say out loud.

"I'll be fine," I assure him softly, pulling him into a tight embrace. Fuck, I'm going to miss the old man. A lot. I might actually cry— which is an oddity by itself, considering the fact I haven't cried since middle school.

"Call me if you need anything," he whispers in my ear. "Anything at all. Someone to talk to. Someone to listen to you. Even just someone to raise your spirits."

"I will," I promise, rubbing his back.

With great reluctance, I force myself to step away from the man who has been more like a father to me than my own ever had the chance to. I'm stunned to see tears in his eyes, but he blinks them away before I can comment.

"I need to return to your mother," he announces, already turning back towards the sleek car still idling in the driveway. "Call me when you settle in."

"Will do." I lift my hand in a cheery wave as he begins to back out of the driveway. "Be safe!"

I watch him until he disappears in the twisting landscape of maples and oaks. The farther away he gets, the more it feels as if my heart is physically crumbling into thousands of pieces.

"I always liked Charles," Nana says, seemingly oblivious to the men lathering her body with attention. With a roll of her eyes, she grips the hair of one of the men and pushes him away. He collapses onto his ass, eyes blinking rapidly as if coming out of a daze.

"Enough. This isn't appropriate behavior for my granddaughter to see."

"You don't fucking say," I mumble.

"Ignore them," Nana whispers conspiratorially. "They're just a bunch of horny dogs." Despite her crude words, she stares at them fondly, almost reverently. "That's Polo, Christian, and Gabriel," she introduces, gesturing to each one.

"Um...hi?" Because really, how else am I supposed to greet my grandmother's much younger boyfriends?

"Pleasure to meet you!" the one she introduced as Christian exclaims, extending a hand. All I can do is eye the proffered limb warily. Heaven only knows what he used it for.

"Peony," I answer, lifting my duffel bag helplessly in the air as an excuse not to shake his hand.

Polo, standing beside Christian, smiles warmly and offers me a nod, but Gabriel merely glares and grunts. Oh, boy.

"Let me show you your room." Nana, in her usual dramatic fashion, sashays away from her lovers and towards a grand staircase situated in the center of the parlor. She pauses abruptly and raises one gray brow. "Are you coming?"

With a huff, I begin to trudge after her, ignoring Christian's offer to carry my bag, and my eyes devour the ostentatious interior greedily.

The walls display a hint of color, now faded with time—ghostly mosaics and shredded paintings propped over the pale, orchid-colored walls. Tall marble vases dot the ceramic-tiled floor, each holding clenched buds withering in their bug-riddled refuse and overgrown grass. A five-tiered chandelier hangs from the ceiling, covered in a fine layer of dust. From what I can see, there are no televisions or any modern electronic appliances.

There better be a fucking coffee maker, or else I'm going to riot.

Nana continues to lead me up the stairs until we reach the entrance to an attic, the ladder already pulled down. I eye the dark hole with trepidation, memories once more coming to the forefront of my mind.

The steel walls of the locker seemed to steadily be shrinking like a vise. Each breath I took had my chest constricting. My hands brushed the cold door, currently locked shut.

"Please let me out," I sobbed, pounding my fists against the steel. Through the slats, I could see their grinning faces, nothing but mirth and wicked excitement reflected back at me.

Shaking my head, I reluctantly follow Nana up the ladder, the wood in desperate need of sanding.

"Home sweet home!" Nana cheers once my head finally breaches the hole. She's standing in the center of the desolate room, a wide, enigmatic smile on her face. "Well? What do you think?"

I think...

That this is going to be a long fucking school year.

I can tell that Nana and her men at least *tried* to clean it, but I still catch a myriad of spider webs hanging from the low rafters. It's a large space, at least horizontally, though there are some sections where I'll need to duck down in order to get by. A single triangular window rests against the similarly shaped wall. Ambient sunlight pours through, mixing its light with the single bulb hanging from the wooden ceiling. A bed sits directly beneath the window, with fresh blankets and pillows. Besides that, there's nothing but a dresser, desk, and nightstand. It's cute and practical, but not necessarily homey. There's no mold, fortunately, but the wooden ceiling rafters look like they haven't been dusted in years.

Still, it's better than what it could be, and I know better than to take little things like housing for granted.

"I love it. Thank you, Nana," I whisper, wrapping my arms around her waist. She startles in surprise, a soft noise escaping, before she hugs me back just as fiercely.

"I missed you, kiddo."

"I missed you too."

I don't know how long we stay that way, but it's long enough for Gabriel to clear his throat from down below. At least, I'm assuming it's Gabriel. He seems like an asshole.

"Well…" Nana steps away and fidgets with the tie on her bathrobe. "I'll let you settle in for a bit. Is there anything else you need? Anything at all?"

"No, I'll be fine," I reply, my mind already elsewhere. At this point, there's really only one location it wanders—to them.

"Dinner will be ready in a couple hours. Polo is a great cook. Absolutely divine. If you don't need anything else…"

"Get back to your boyfriends, Nana. I'll be fine," I assure her, my eyes latched on the immense trunk sitting at the foot of my bed.

"I love you, sweet girl. Always remember that." With a tenderness I'm not used to seeing, let alone experiencing, she kisses my forehead. She trots over to perch herself at the edge of the hole and, forgoing the ladder, jumps into one of her men's arms.

Honestly, I don't know if I'm disgusted or proud of her relationship with three significantly younger men. I suppose that I should be happy for her. Love is love, after all, and they're four consenting adults.

But damn, if it isn't strange to see my nana getting her rocks off with three men only a few years older than me.

Once more shaking my head, I drop to my knees in front of the ancient chest before me. The black paint is chipped and turning a rustic red with age. A single lock secures the contents, a green tint surrounding it.

Licking my lower lip, I open my palm and aim my hand at the lock. The entire chest begins to vibrate as I push my magic into it with the intensity of a lightning bolt. After a moment, the lock drops to the ground with an audible clank and the lid flies open.

I peer inside at the contents, a wicked grin pulling up my lips. The first thing I see is a picture, freshly printed. My four tormentors pose for the camera, scowls marring their hideously handsome faces.

With the pad of my thumb, I trace their features before pulling my hand away as if their pictures alone are poisonous.

"School starts tomorrow, boys," I say darkly, removing object after object from my chest. Newspaper clippings. Photographs. Needles. An ancient spellbook. And then, finally, the four dolls I made just the month before. They almost resemble gingerbread cookies in shape, the brown fabric pulled tight over stuffing. Simple black buttons make up their eyes.

But wrapped around each of their necks, distinguishing one from another, are four different colors of hair. Red on one. Blond on another. Black on the third. Brown and purple on the final one.

"Let the games begin," I whisper under my breath.

Come hell or highwater, the Devils of High Groves High School will pay.

CHAPTER 2

I wake up early on the first day of school, sliding out from beneath my covers and stretching my taut muscles. It's still dark outside, the moon a tiny crescent shape in the velvety black sky.

Jumping to my feet, I make quick work of brushing through my white blonde hair. I debate whether or not I want to place it in a ponytail before deciding to leave it down. Nana has hung my dresses from one of the lowest rafters, and I quickly grab a long-sleeved black number with a sweetheart neckline. A splash of pink lipstick and some blush on my cheeks complete the look. As I gaze at myself in the mirror over the dresser, I can't help but compare myself to the old me, the younger me.

I'm still the exact same but…different. I barely recognize the girl staring back at me. The only thing that has remained consistent is my amber eyes, burning like the flames of hell flicker within their depths. They were one of the many things that the students of High Groves Middle School bullied me for.

Freak, they said. Ugly. Unnatural.

For the longest time, those words would cut deep, flaying me open until I stood unloved and unwanted amidst a sea of monsters. But now, they ricochet off my skin, off my armor. I'm stronger because their taunts made me this way. You can only truly understand joy once you've experienced immeasurable pain.

Steeling myself, I blow a kiss at my reflection before grabbing my backpack off the ground.

Polo moving about the kitchen surprises me when I stop there to grab a quick breakfast to go. The smell of bacon sizzling on the stove assaults my senses first, followed immediately by the enticing, addictive scent of coffee brewing.

"Fuck, yes," I breathe, gliding towards the pot.

"Cardinal told us you were a coffee addict," Polo says lightly, scooping eggs and then a few pieces of bacon onto a plate. He slides it across the counter until it rests in front of me. "Gabriel went to pick it up last night."

"Oh," I murmur, suddenly feeling awkward. Still, I can't deny the relief I feel at having the cup of liquid gold in front of me. Fuck, I have an entire arsenal of cheesy nicknames for coffee. Pretty sure I wrote an entire journal of them. "You didn't have to do that."

Unlike the rest of the house, the kitchen is modern with granite countertops and top-of-the-line steel appliances. I half wonder if Nana bought all of these supplies when she discovered I would be staying with her. Wouldn't surprise me in the least, if I'm being honest with myself.

"We wanted to," Polo says firmly. Silence ensues as I sip from my mug and dig into the fluffy scrambled eggs. Nana is right—Polo cooks like a god.

When the man in question begins to wring his hands, I realize he wants to say more.

"Yeah?" I ask, quirking a silvery white eyebrow.

"I know this is weird for you," he blurts out, and I gift him with a dry look. He gulps once before stubbornly forging on ahead. Man has balls, I'll give him that. "We all just want you to feel comfortable.

I know it's not conventional… Okay, listen. We love your nana, and she loves us. It's weird, I know, and not just because of our age difference. Though, technically, it's not as much as you believe. We want you to feel comfortable here with us. We want to be a part of your life in any way you'll allow us to."

That's just a whole bunch of nopes. Honestly, I can't deal with this—*them*—now. What my nana does is entirely up to her, but I can't say it's not fucking weird.

"It's fine," I say evenly, when it appears as if Polo is still waiting for a response. "Just…just don't let me see anything, okay? Like when she answered the door."

Because yeah, the image of Christian groping my grandma is forever burned into my retinas. I might actually need bleach for that, thank you very much.

Polo has the decency to appear sheepish.

"Sorry. That'll never happen again. It's just…Cardinal had just finished a spell…" He trails off again, raking his fingers through his brown hair.

I lift up a hand to stop him from speaking. "Say no more." Please, for the love of all that's dark and gloomy, say no fucking more.

My nana is a sex witch, one of the last of her kind. As such, she requires…err…certain stuff in order to perform her spells. Certain stuff that I shall not name out loud or else risk vomiting everywhere.

Polo chuckles softly, and I have to admit he's handsome. Of course, I'm not attracted to him in any way, shape, or form—ew—but I can see why Nana chose him and his brothers. They're definitely a catch.

You go, Nana.

"Do you need a ride to school?" Polo continues eagerly, as if my acceptance of their unconventional relationship gives him leeway to be a fucking grandfather to me. Honestly, I have no idea what he's playing at.

"Nah. It's only a twenty-minute walk. I'll be fine."

"Are you sure?" he asks, anxiety bleeding through his voice. "I don't want anything happening to you. And it can get cold in the winter."

"Fortunately for me," I pause to stick a piece of bacon in my mouth, holding it between my teeth as I pour my coffee into a to-go mug, "it's *not* winter, and I'm a badass witch who can look after herself." Once I grab everything I need for my first day, I lift my free hand and wiggle my fingers. "Toodles."

HIGH GROVES HIGH SCHOOL IS SIGNIFICANTLY LARGER THAN THE middle school, having been recently updated. It's a single story building that branches in all directions like the spindly legs on a spider. You would think that a small town such as High Groves would have a petite brick building as their high school with a single flagpole erected on the front lawn. Instead, the modernistic school has a single row of windows sprouting down each hallway, showcasing their expensive electronics and appliances. The walls are a mash of brown, red, and even some green bricks, the combination surprisingly easy on the eyes. The main entrance stands taller than the rest of the school, sans the auditorium, with a shingled roof that curves steeply upwards.

While High Groves may be a small community, it's still a rich one. Every kid over the age of sixteen has their own car, and I can't think of one house that doesn't have a heated, outdoor pool.

But these rich fucks are about to get what's coming to them.

With a swagger to my step, I march right through the front doors as if I own the building. At this hour, there are only a few people scattered about. I recognize a chapter of the NHS meeting in the cafeteria, and a male and female couple sitting side by side in front of a stone wall.

I head to the main office and offer a sincere smile to the secretary.

Patricia Brooks had once been the secretary at the middle school before she transferred here. She was my only supporter back in the day, the only one who saw through the Devils' bullshit.

"I don't know if you remember me—" I begin sheepishly. Before I can even finish speaking, her mouth props open and she jumps up from her swiveling chair.

"Peony Simone! Is that you?" she gasps, waddling towards me with her arms outstretched.

"I missed you, Pat," I whisper, accepting her embrace. "And you're pregnant!" I pull back to get a good look at her, surprised to see the generous baby bump pushing at her cream-colored sweater. Her cheeks darken in a blush as she flickers her gaze down towards her belly.

"Met him two years ago," she whispers, her voice taking on that wistful, dreamy quality all new lovers seem to have. "We've been inseparable ever since."

"Good. I'm really happy for you."

When I met her as a hormonal pre-teen contemplating suicide, she told me a little bit about her life. Back then, she'd been in her late twenties and had just gotten out of an abusive relationship. I'm extremely happy that she was able to find someone to love her. Pat's a great woman, and I know she'll be an amazing wife and mother as well.

After all, she saved my life, and she didn't even know me.

"I heard you were coming back, but I didn't believe it," Pat exclaims, moving to once more sit behind her desk. "Are you here to pick up your class information, sweetie?"

"You know it." I lean indolently against the counter before spotting a bowl full of jelly beans. Popping one in my mouth, I wait for her to print out my class schedule. I could've easily looked up this information online...if my mom or even Nana believed in a computer or internet. As it is, I'll have to travel to the local coffee shop with my laptop in order to complete my assignments.

As she passes me the still warm paper fresh from the printer, her hand lingers on mine.

"Are you sure this is a good idea?" she whispers, casting glances in both directions. "Those bullies of yours…"

"I'm better now," I promise, hoping to put her fears at ease. She has a right to be worried, but not for me this time. I refuse to be a victim again. I'm better than that, stronger than that, and the last thing I want or need is to venture back to the dark place that almost killed me five years ago.

"Good. That's good," she whispers, but she doesn't sound convinced. There's a slight furrow between her brows, as if she's attempting to calculate a difficult math equation. "You'll come to me if you need anything, right?"

My heart thumps erratically in my chest at her words. At the sheer prospect that someone actually cares about me in this hellhole.

"Cross my heart and hope to die," I say, using my finger to create an X over my chest. "I'll even pinkie promise if you want me to."

She rolls her eyes at my dramatics before shooing me away.

"Go. Get ready for class."

"Yes, ma'am." With a two-fingered salute, I duck out of the office and into the hallway. It's already busier than it was when I first arrived less than ten minutes ago. Students, like me, are carrying cups of coffee and are rubbing sleep from their eyes.

I understand school. I honestly do.

But why the fuck do classes need to start so early in the morning? It's not even light outside, for fuck's sake.

As I walk through the halls, heading towards the gymnasium, I can't help but notice the appreciatory stares I get from both guys and girls alike. They're not hateful as they had been years ago. They're not even calculating.

It's nice to be the recipient of attention that isn't cruel or domineering.

I stop in front of the wing of the school that houses the three gyms, weight room, and aerobics classroom. If my calculations are correct...

With a spring to my step, I venture into the weight room first, where both the football team and cheerleading squad are hard at work. My eyes survey all of the occupants quickly before landing on my two targets.

Karsyn Alder and Mariabella Stevens.

The quarterback of the football team and his perky, beautiful cheerleader girlfriend.

Karsyn currently has his back to me, deep in conversation with a man I recognize to be his tight end. Mariabella is giggling with one of her friends, blonde hair slicked back into a tight ponytail and perky breasts on display in her skin-tight sports bra.

I chance another glance at Karsyn, but he's still oblivious to my presence. That's okay, I suppose. He'll come to see me soon enough.

With considerable effort, I wrench my gaze away from his sweat-soaked gray shirt and focus on the cheerleading coach, Mrs. Watson. I memorize her face briefly before stepping back out.

My heart hammers a mile a minute as pain—thick and cloying pain—cascades through me. I thought seeing Karsyn would be like eating a bad taco. You feel nauseous for a second, but then get over it. Instead, it's as if every bandage I painstakingly applied to myself has been ripped from my skin. The once scabbed over wounds are now open and bleeding, visible for the world to see.

Fuck!

I press my head against the wall to control my eccentric breathing before willing myself to relax.

I didn't even see his face, and already, it feels as if my world is shattering around me.

Why did I think that this would be easy?

Life, I have come to realize, is never easy. It's a fucking landmine, and one wrong move can send everything into flames.

Hands shaking, I remove my notepad from the side of my backpack. It's spelled so no one will be able to read my words unless I let them.

Next to Karsyn's name, I write, *In weight room, 7:23 AM. With Mariabella.*

The next name on the list is Cassian Jereome.

Where, oh where, will I find my little musician at this hour of the day?

Without preamble, I head in the opposite direction of the gym, towards the auditorium. According to my research, the builders added several practice spaces adjacent to the band room. The first two I find are empty, but the third…

I wasn't able to get a good look at Karsyn, but I am able to see Cassian Jereome. His dark skin glints in the radiant LED lights up above, his eyes closed in pleasure. A guitar droops from his fingers as a girl kneels between his legs, sucking his cock. He moans slightly, tightening his fingers in the girl's rich red hair. I know I should look away. I want to, but I can't prevent my eyes from tracing every contour of his devilishly beautiful face, similar to the person I once knew and despised, yet so, so different. Older. Handsomer. No longer a boy, but a man.

When the girl releases his cock and begins to lick it like a lollipop, I can't help but note how large it is. I'm not even sure my entire hand will fit around it.

You know, for the sole purpose of pulling it off and tossing it to feral dogs.

According to my research, Cassian doesn't have a girlfriend, so this must be one of his groupies. While he's not well-known throughout the world or even the United States, he's a household name in this area. Half the population believes he's going to be the next big thing—bigger than even Queen or the Beatles.

Cue gagging noises.

Struck with inspiration, I remove my phone from where I had stashed it inside my bra and begin recording the two of them. You never know when you'll need leverage to destroy a person's life.

Almost as if he can sense me, his eyes begin to open...

But I'm already running out of the room, the door shutting on silent hinges.

Returning to my trusty little notebook, I write, *Cassian in music practice rooms before class. Getting BJ. Big cock.* With a frown, I quickly erase the last two words.

I hate the asshole, but even I can appreciate a damn good penis.

Lips pursed, I stare intently at the third name on the list. *Elias Briggs.* I don't even bother searching for him. The school records show that he skips school every Monday, and even some Tuesdays, Wednesdays, Thursdays, and Fridays. And if he doesn't skip, he doesn't bother to show up until well after fourth period, AP Lit. Which, conveniently, happens to be my class as well. What are the odds?

Instead, I focus on the fourth name. The final name. Rage crawls up my spine like a set of fire ants have been set free.

Lucas Scott.

Glancing at the clock, I see it's approximately seven-forty. At this time, he should be in the cafeteria with his faithful followers, right after the morning session of student senate ended. Elections for class positions took place at the end of last year, and lo and behold, Lucas Scott managed to snag the presidency. Shocker.

He's exactly where I expect him to be—sitting beside a gaggle of girls and guys, a beatific smile on his handsome face.

His red hair is artfully styled away from his aristocratic face, making him appear even more heart-wrenchingly beautiful. His sea-blue eyes, flecked with gold, are vibrant with laughter. As always, he wears a pressed sweater and skin-tight jeans that conform to his delectable body. And by the smirk on his face, he knows how good he looks and revels in the attention.

Four kings.

Four wicked men.

Four charming devils.

And one witch.

"Let the games begin, boys," I whisper. And this time around? I'm actually gonna win.

Or die trying.

CHAPTER 3

My first class of the day is Biology with Ms. Auperlee. She's a younger teacher with her soul still intact; these leeches haven't sucked it out of her yet. When I enter the classroom, she flashes me a genuine smile, one that reaches her washed-out gray eyes. I'm sure they're a shade of blue, but with the fluorescent lighting overhead, it's almost impossible to discern for sure.

"You must be our new student," she gushes in a saccharine sweet voice. "I'm Ms. Auperlee. We're starting a new chapter today, so I don't think you have anything you really need to catch up on. The first chapter is merely standard lab safety, which I can email you a PowerPoint of. You can take a seat anywhere." She gesticulates wildly towards the various empty desks.

The old me would've been terrified of accidentally sitting in someone's seat, but the new me doesn't really give a damn. I'm no longer the coward that will hide behind my own shadow.

With an imperious set to my chin, like a queen looking down on her subjects, I move towards an empty seat near the back of the classroom.

Directly beside Mariabella Stevens.

This close, she's even more beautiful. Almost ethereal. It's no surprise that Karsyn would date someone like her, someone who seems to physically radiate vibrant light. Her blonde hair has been freshly washed after this morning's workout, hanging in silky, loose curls around her shoulders. She wears a pink sweater that slides off of one shoulder, revealing her porcelain skin. Cognac brown eyes peer back at me beneath a fleet of sooty, ridiculously dark lashes.

I expect to see derision in her gaze, maybe even annoyance at my blatant ogling, but instead, she straightens almost imperceptibly in her seat and smiles at me. It's a...warm smile, one that emanates sincerity. It somehow demotes her from intimidating to approachable.

At the same time, I can't help but wonder why someone like *her* would date someone like Karsyn Alder.

Gag.

"Hi!" Her voice is slightly higher pitched than even Ms. Auperlee's, but it doesn't bother me. There's almost a musical quality to it that I can't help but find endearing. "You must be new. I'm Mariabella."

"Peony," I greet with a timid nod. I have the irresistible urge to bite down on my lower lip and fidget, almost like I'm back in middle school again. But fuck, I'm not that forlorn child anymore. I'm a badass fucking witch, and I don't *fidget*.

But a part of me, a part that I don't think will ever diminish completely, expects her to pour her coffee over my head and then laugh at me like it's my fault.

"Why don't you do the world a favor and drop dead?" Cassian's voice curled around me like an iron vise, gradually tightening until I was clawing at my throat, desperate for air.

"What a loser," Karsyn agreed with his customary smirk.

"A freak." Lucas's face was as impassive as ever, as cold as a marble

statue. There was no inflection in his cruel words. "She's nothing but a freak."

"...excited to show you." Mariabella's babbling pulls me out of my dark thoughts. They continually threaten to drag me under, almost as if I'd gotten stuck in a riptide. Farther and farther away from shore I am pulled, and no amount of kicking and screaming and begging for air will release me.

"I believe you're in my seat," a voice from directly above me states. I whip my head up, startled, only to minutely relax when I see an unfamiliar, friendly face. For a moment there, I thought he was one of the *guys*. One of my tormentors. One of the monsters who lurk under my bed at night, gripping at my ankles with curved claws and jaundice eyes.

The guy slides into the seat beside me, maintaining that flirtatious, easy-going grin.

"I'm Emmett," he introduces, extending a hand. I eye the proffered limb warily, half expecting this to be a trick. I'll be the first to admit that I'm fucking paranoid. Everyone has an angle, and I'll only survive if I figure out what that angle is ahead of time. So far, no one at school has recognized me, but that won't last. Sooner or later, the vultures will descend on my disgusting corpse, pecking away at what little remains of me.

"Peony." Relenting, I place my hand in his, surprised by how cold it is. Goosebumps pebble on my skin as I look at Emmett, really look at him, for the first time.

It's easy to see that he's a jock. Probably on the football team with Karsyn, judging by the letterman jacket covering his shoulders. He exudes a charm and charisma that most women find irresistible. Sandy blond hair, stylishly molded into a fauxhawk, frames a face that could make angels weep. When he smiles, I can't help but notice the dimple on both of his cheeks. Laugh lines surround his jade eyes, almost the color I would associate with a magnificent jungle.

He really is a looker, and if the slightly smug glint in those gorgeous eyes is any indication, he knows it.

"That's a flower, right?" Mariabella interjects.

"Yeah, how do you know?" Most people merely believe it's a strange name my hippy mother picked out. Well, it *is* a strange name my mother picked out, but she's no hippy. That title is reserved for my grandmother.

"I want to be a botanist, actually," she confesses with a sheepish shrug. Almost nervously, she begins to twirl a piece of hair around her finger. "Plants and stuff."

"We know what a botanist is, Mar," Emmett jests dryly, and she sticks out her tongue at him.

One glance at the clock confirms we still have a few minutes until class begins. Already, the seats are three-quarters full, with more and more students trickling in. I don't see any of the *guys*, but I didn't expect to. I specifically made sure that my first couple of hours didn't align with theirs. I figured I'd need a slight reprieve from my revenge, wouldn't you agree?

"Where are you from?" Emmett flashes me another one of his irresistible smiles. He really is a good-looking boy...man. No one with working eyes would ever believe he's a boy. It's too bad that I refuse to date until I'm out of high school. Emmett would've been a fun distraction...but one that I can't afford. I have one goal and one goal only—destroy the men who once destroyed me. Dating can wait.

"California," I blurt after an awkward silence. "I just moved in with my grandma."

"Oh, that's super sweet of you," Mariabella says, resting her elbow on the table and placing her head in her opened palm. "Does she need a lot of help around the house?"

She has three hunks to do it for her, but you know...I'm not complaining. One of those hunks cooks me food.

"Yes," I answer instead.

"What do you think of this place so far?" Almost absently, Emmett drapes his arm over the back of my seat. The initial stab of panic I always feel when someone touches me rears its ugly head, but I shove it inside a reinforced-steel box.

Instead, I focus on Emmett's question, only his question, until the panic abates like wispy strands of smoke. "I like it," I confess, though that's a complete and utter lie. I hate this school and everyone in it.

Half of these students saw what the guys were doing to me, but none of them stepped in. None of them helped.

Even Mariabella, as nice as she seems now, looked the other way when the Devils tormented me.

But I can't focus on the turbulent anger wreaking havoc on my internal organs like a nose-diving plane. I have a plan, and I need to follow it to the T. "I'm a little sad, though, that I missed cheerleading tryouts." I release a heavy sigh, dropping my head into my arms. "I cheered at my school in California, and I'm gonna miss the sport."

Lie.

Complete and utter bullshit lie.

My school was actually a private school with no sports teams—unless you count FireBall, a game designed exclusively for witches.

Mariabella's face lights up as if someone had lit a candle beneath her skin. Her brown eyes, outlined with fireworks of gold, sparkle in the artificial school lighting.

"I'm on the cheerleading team!" she blurts. "I can talk to Coach—"

"All right, class, settle down." Auperlee waves her hands in the air erratically just as overhead, the bell begins to ring. "We have a lot to cover."

The class immediately begins to quiet down, the usual whispers and grumbles all but diminishing, and I can't help the grin that curls up my lips as I watch Mariabella out of the corner of my eye.

Hook.

Line.

And sinker.

CHAPTER 4

When class ends, I half expect Mariabella and Emmett to dismiss me like a child would after she wore down a new and shiny toy. Instead, the two surprise the ever-loving shit out of me by following me out of class.

"I have to go to algebra." Mariabella points farther down the hall. "But come find me at lunch, okay?" Before I can respond, she gives me an awkward, one-armed hug—well, awkward for me anyway, because I'm not a hugger—and hurries in the opposite direction of me and Emmett.

"She's…nice," I muse softly as I reach into the side pocket of my backpack and remove the campus map. I can feel Emmett's sandy blond hair tickling my cheek as he looms over my shoulder.

"She's an energetic Golden Retriever puppy," he snorts, but no ire laces his words. He sounds almost…fond of her. Don't get me wrong, I don't believe he's desperately and hopelessly in love with her or anything, but I detect a strong sense of admiration and respect.

"And what does that make you?" I quip, easily keeping pace with him, despite his significantly longer legs. If I had to guess, I would say he's a wide receiver on the football team. He's lithe but muscular, nowhere near as large as Karsyn, but there's no hiding the six-pack peeking through the gray shirt he wears beneath his letterman jacket.

"Oh...a Husky, maybe?" He laughs lightly, and more than a few girls turn in his direction at the sound.

"A husky." Snorting, I stop at my locker and switch out my biology book for sheet music. It's an instant relief not to have that book weighing me down. Because seriously, how many chapters on mitosis does the school district really think we'll need? How many of us, years from now, are going to be grateful for knowing the lifespan of a cell? Honestly, schools should teach us how to do taxes and finance a house. "I've never heard someone claim to be a husky before."

"Maybe you're just not around the right kind of people," he slyly responds, leaning against the locker and grinning down at me. This close, I can see flecks of golden caramel and agate green in his eyes. He really is an attractive specimen.

And he's really making me reconsider my whole "no relationships while here" rule.

"So, you're new here as well, correct?" I query as I slam my locker shut and zip up my backpack. Surprise splays across his face, and his eyes narrow almost suspiciously. I can't help but snort at his paranoia. "Calm down. I'm not a stalker. I just went to school here when I was in middle school, and I don't remember seeing you before."

"Oh." Emmett relaxes instantly and laughs once more, forking his fingers through his fauxhawk. The strands becoming wild and disheveled, no longer immaculately styled at the top of his head, and his eyes flash with irritation as he brushes at one of the strands grazing his eyes. "I moved two years ago, during sophomore year."

"From?" I unfold my class schedule—from where I had placed it in my pocket—and see that I'm supposed to be on the second floor for my next hour. Emmett once more peers over my shoulder before gently grabbing my elbow and steering me in the opposite direction, towards the now emptying stairwell.

"Minnesota," he responds.

"Why?" I continue my pestering as we climb the curving staircase. I don't know if Emmett has his class up here as well, but I'm honestly grateful for the tour guide. There are so many hallways and so many levels, that I'm sure I'll get lost in record time.

"You're a nosey one, aren't you?" He doesn't sound upset about it, only amused. His jade eyes spark in the fluorescent lighting as we turn down a hallway with only a few students present. Not that I'm surprised. The music department always has significantly less classmates compared to, say, the athletic one.

"Sorry." I shrug nonchalantly. "It's a fatal flaw."

"Nah, it's fine." He blows out a breath as his steps slow, hinting that we may be closer to my destination than I initially suspected. "My mom got remarried."

"And you guys moved to be with him?" I guess.

This time, his laughter is harsh. Cold, even, like a keen icicle falling from a rooftop and impaling someone's heart. "No. The bitch kicked me out." Resentment underlies his words as his eyes harden. "Told me it was time to live with my dad."

My heart hurts for him, because I, more than probably anyone, can relate.

"My mom kicked me out too," I admit with a shrug. "But hey, it's not the end of the world, right?"

Honestly, a part of me was grateful when my mom threw me out the door like yesterday's trash. I knew I would be sent to Nana's... and I also knew that I would return to the town that had once been my personal hell. Only this time, I won't be the one burned by hell's flames. I survived the inferno once before, and now, I'll set the world aflame in the name of sweet, sweet revenge.

Totally fucked up logic? Yes.

Do I care? Nope.

"Yeah." Emmett doesn't sound so sure, but our conversation ceases when he stops in front of my next class. "Room two twenty-six." He taps his knuckles to the wall adjacent to the door. "Maybe I'll see you again later on today?"

Those wide eyes blink down at me, and against my better judgement—against the voice telling me *not* to get involved—I mutter, "Yeah, probably."

Stupid. Stupid. Stupid.

But the beatific smile that erupts on Emmett's face? The one that reveals two dimples on his cheeks? It makes my own hesitation and unease totally worth it.

Flashing him a tentative one of my own, I slip inside of the classroom just as the bell rings, signaling the beginning of class.

Ten pairs of eyes turn to stare at me with varying degrees of confusion and apprehension. Only one appears annoyed, her slate-brown eyes narrowed at me from where she sits with the two other violists.

"You must be Peony." The teacher, a balding man with a protruding belly and a bowtie, hurries forward with a hand extended. "I'm Mr. Tucker, the orchestra conductor."

"Hello." I accept his hand with a soft smile.

"Come. Come." He gestures towards one of the black chairs located near the conductor's stand. "If I remember correctly, you mentioned that you needed to borrow an instrument for the time being, correct?"

"That's correct," I reply. Back at the coven, I had my own violin, an instrument I adored more than anything else. After a particularly brutal fight with my mother, the bitch snapped it over her knee, rendering it impossible to play. I vowed to myself that I would buy a new one…as soon as I came into any sort of money.

"There are some violins you can rent and bring home with you," Mr. Tucker explains as he unlocks a cupboard and procures a black violin case. "But we can discuss those options at a later time. For now, feel free to use this one. You won't be able to bring it home with you, which will impact your grade in the long run, but it should work for now." The man is practically exuding energy, his eagerness almost palpable. It reminds me of the conversation with Emmett a few minutes earlier. If Mariabella is a Golden Retriever puppy, then this man is a full-grown one. I half expect to see his tail wagging back and forth as he hands me the instrument.

This violin has almost a reddish sheen, and when I pluck at the strings, I'm surprised by how in tune the instrument is, especially since the case itself has been collecting dust.

"I heard about you from the middle school conductor," Mr. Tucker gushes, and the rest of the orchestra exchange hushed whispers. There are three boys, none of which I recognize, and two girls I remember from my time in middle school. Sadie and Lauren, I believe? The rest I'm not overly familiar with. The dark-haired violist is still hurling daggers at me as she sits primly in the seat opposite mine. Her black hair hangs in loose curls over her shoulders, and her eyes are a similar shade of obsidian, the brown so dark they're almost black.

"That's Felicia," Sadie whispers from the seat beside mine. I never really had a problem with the petite blonde before. She wasn't necessarily my friend or anything, but she was never openly hostile like some of the other students. And from the confused look in her eyes, I don't think she recognizes me. Though how many white-haired, amber-eyed women she knows remains a mystery. "She's a grade-A bitch, especially when she's not Mr. Tucker's sole focus."

"Kiss ass." Lauren pantomimes barfing from the seat on the other side of Sadie, and the four girls around them—all slightly familiar— giggle. Two are cellists, one's a bassist, and the other one is a violinist, as well as Sadie and Lauren.

"Whenever anyone joins the orchestra, we ask that they play a piece so the other students get a feel for their style. Is that okay with you?" Mr. Tucker's exuberant voice has me whipping my head in his direction. He's once more bouncing on the balls of his feet, rubbing his hands together like the fucking Grinch who just stole Christmas. Honestly, it's kind of adorable.

"Of course." I nod once before procuring my sheet music from my backpack. Sifting through the options, I settle on "Partita D minor BWV 1004" by Bach. It's one of the hardest pieces you can play, but also one of my favorites. There's something beautiful about the music emitting from the instrument, the abrupt change in registers. The movement of your fingers caressing the strings as the bow develops a life of its own. This particular piece isn't as melancholy as some of the other ones I love to play. Instead, it takes you on a journey. You can sense the excitement contaminating the air as the enthusiasm grows and grows.

Putting the violin beneath my chin and the bow to the strings, I begin to play.

I lose myself to the music. For a moment, I forget who I am and why I'm here. I forget about the charming Devils who ruined my life when I was younger. I forget about the pain that accompanied me for years, the sense of failure and resignation that I will never be good enough. The music courses through me, and I squeeze my eyelids shut, no longer needing the sheet music to guide me.

And as the song reaches a crescendo, I feel my body begin to sway.

I play for only a few minutes, allowing the music to taper off when it reaches a natural conclusion, and reopen my eyes, once more joining the land of the living.

The entire class is staring at me with various expressions of disbelief. All at once, like a dam being burst open, excited murmurings drift to my ears.

"That's wonderful!" Mr. Tucker practically squeals...though I feel kind of bad for him. I mean, there's not much he'll be able to teach me that I don't already know. I live and breathe the violin the way some people do dance and others do sports. There's something about losing yourself to the music…

Felicia is the only one who's *not* smiling. It's not quite hatred emanating from her gaze, but it's pretty damn close. Unable to stop myself, I flash her a smug smirk, and I swear smoke wafts from her nostrils.

Orchestra is the one place I don't have to pretend, the one place where I can live without pain and heartache. If this bitch thinks she can take me down, she has another thing coming.

WHEN I'M EXITING THE CLASSROOM, HEADING TO MY THIRD HOUR OF the day, I see Mariabella once more. She's leaning against her locker, laughing at something Karsyn says to her.

For a moment, for a single helpless moment, I allow my trai-torous eyes to linger on one of my childhood tormentors.

He's buffed up over the years. I would've never called him scrawny before, but in comparison to what he looks like now…yeah. The new him could've crushed the old him with one swipe of his hand. From this distance, I can see his muscular forearms, even with the heavy letterman jacket on. His blond hair is a few shades lighter than Emmett's and stylishly tossed to the side. His stupidly pretty face is perfectly proportioned with high cheekbones, lush pink lips, and hazel eyes. At the moment, with laughter dancing in his gaze, the green is more prominent than the brown, reminding me of a swampy pool of water.

I bite my lip as I'm assaulted by yet another memory.

"I'll choose Sweats," Lucas snapped coldly as we stood out on the soccer field. The boy in question—his real name was Markus—ran to join Lucas's team.

Mr. Highland, the Gym teacher, barely looked up from where he was devouring Fifty Shades of Grey *on the bleachers, content with allowing students to run his class.*

"Chubs, you're with me." Karsyn nodded at the only other person besides me still in line, waiting to get picked. Chubs—or Daniel—ran forward with an enthusiastic whoop to join his dodgeball team.

"And what should we do with her?" *Cassian said the word "her" as if it was an unfitting title, as if it would be better to describe me as a hideous monster or something just as degrading. He thrived off of making me feel inadequate and ugly whenever he could.*

"I don't think she should be on any team," Elias mused almost lazily. He never talked much, but when he did, everyone fucking listened.

"Hmmm...so everybody versus the freak?" Karsyn asked with a maniacal glint in his hazel eyes.

"What do you say?" Lucas took a step forward until he was close enough to grab at my chin. His touch was almost bruising as he yanked my head up, forcing me to stare into his ice-cold eyes. "Everybody versus the freak?"

The class erupted into giggles as I felt a piece of my soul wither like a raisin. Pain bombarded me from all sides, and I could barely breathe through the tightness gripping my throat.

"Please, don't do this," I begged, tears pricking my eyes. Desperately, I glanced towards Mr. Highland, but he was too preoccupied with his book to notice what was transpiring right under his nose.

Not that he would care either way. None of them did.

"Begging will get you nowhere," Lucas whispered before abruptly releasing me and wiping his hand on his pants. That was what nearly did me in—the show he made of wiping my germs off, as if the mere thought of my touch made him want to vomit. He was a performer, and this was his stage.

Behind him, Karsyn and Cassian howled with laughter, and even Elias —quiet, subdued Elias—chuckled darkly.

You won't get away with this, *I thought bitterly as I moved to stand on one side of the field and the rest of the class moved to the other. Soon,* I'll be a witch.

And humans wouldn't dare to mess with a witch.

I wrench myself out of my memories just in time to hear Karsyn's throaty chuckle. The large, beautiful man plants a tender kiss to Mariabella's forehead before the two of them separate, heading to their respective third hour classes.

But seeing them together...

Seeing them happy...

It only fuels my blistering rage. Why should he have everything he ever wanted, while I have nothing? How is that fair? Why does the universe have such a sick sense of humor?

I planned to start with Karsyn's football career, but maybe I'm going about this all wrong. Maybe I need to hit him where it actually hurts.

As I stare at Mariabella's retreating back, an idea forms, and I can't stop the demented smile from cleaving my face in two.

Keep your friends close, but your enemies even closer.

CHAPTER 5

There's no Elias in third period, though I'm not surprised. My sources told me that he *never* arrives at school earlier than lunchtime. How he expects to graduate remains a mystery, but I can't find it within me to give any semblance of a damn.

As I slide into a seat near the front of the classroom, my phone pings once. And then twice. And then three then four then five more times. Only one person would have the gall to incessantly message me in the middle of the school day.

Glancing at the front of the room and ensuring that Mr. Milk is still preoccupied talking through an assignment with a group of students, I pull my phone out of my backpack and glare down at the offending texts.

Mom: Hey! The very least you could've done was clean your bedroom completely.

Mom: There are crumbs everywhere!!! Did you even vacuum?

Mom: This is just like you. So disrespectful.

Mom: I told you to take everything.

Mom: I hired a cleaner. Anything of yours, I gave her permission to throw away.

Mom: I'm converting your bedroom into a tanning salon. I'll send pictures! XOXO

Growling, I switch my phone off and shove it face down onto my desk. How to describe my mom…

Well…

She's a fucking bitch who kicked her only daughter out because she's a jealous cunt and terrified that my magic will surpass hers. I always knew I was special. From the very first moment I could conjure up a ball of light, years ahead of my classmates, the coven whispered about me and the plans Mom must have. They thought I was going to take over the coven when Mom eventually retired. But Mommy Dearest? She had other ideas.

The main one being, she'll never retire.

I'm sure if it wasn't frowned upon—wasn't a punishable offense—she would turn into a Blood in order to retain her status as coven leader. But alas, most of the Bloods are hunted down only days after their transitions.

"Why the long face?" Emmett slides into the seat beside mine, flashing me an easy-going smile.

Instead of answering, I merely release an agonized groan and drop my head into my arms where they rest on my desk. He chuckles in understanding.

"The parents?"

"The mom," I correct. "She's killing me."

He snorts as he removes his APUSH textbook from his backpack and sets it on the flimsy wooden desk.

"I feel that. My mom texts me daily just to bitch about something that happened years ago. I can never make that woman happy." He scrubs at his clenched jaw as irritation ripples through him like waves.

"Three cheers for shitty parents?" I ask, not bothering to raise my head. Emmett chuckles darkly.

Class is grueling. And by grueling, I mean that the lesson is slower than molasses and the teacher's monotonous voice makes me want to stab someone. Preferably myself.

By the time he dismisses us, a full minute after the bell already rang, I'm seriously contemplating dropping the class. It would screw up my plans, especially since Elias is supposed to be in this hour with me, but if I have to hear Mr. Milk's growly voice for one more fucking minute…

"You have lunch now?" Emmett queries as he waits for me to pack up my stuff. I shove the heavy textbook into my backpack before sliding my phone into my back pocket.

"Yeah. You?"

"Yuppers." He rubs his toned stomach enthusiastically. "Ain't nothing better than greasy pizza to start your day, am I right?"

I want to snort at his dramatics, but honestly, the man has a point. The timeline of this high school is ridiculous. It's only ten-fifty, and already, we have to eat lunch.

Emmett chats about everything and absolutely nothing as we follow the throng of students towards the cafeteria. He half reminds me of a verbal freight train, charging head first towards a brick wall with no chance of stopping or slowing down. But his enthusiasm is contagious, and I find myself smiling and nodding along as Emmett relays a story about his pet dog.

What can I say? I'm a sucker for cute animals.

When we enter the cafeteria, I pause at the threshold of the main doors, allowing my eyes to travel over the arrangement of tables. There are five ways you can enter and exit this particular section of the school—two doors at the entrance where we stand, two on one side, and one on the other. Directly behind the tables is a pavilion that houses five different buffets, each one manned by a different lunch lady.

The cliques are easy to spot. Without even needing to look, I can tell who is who and what is what.

Near the back of the cafeteria, in the row of booths located flush against the far wall, sit the cheerleaders and footballers. I spot Karsyn chatting animatedly with some of his teammates. I'm not surprised he's no longer friends with Cassian, Lucas, or Elias. I heard that the four of them had a falling out shortly after I left.

Isn't karma a beautiful bitch?

Surprisingly enough, Mariabella isn't sitting with her boyfriend. Instead, she sits at a table behind him with some of her fellow cheerleaders, all of them chatting and giggling amongst themselves. Occasionally, the blonde bombshell will lift her head and glance around the cafeteria, almost as if she's looking for someone, before rejoining the conversation.

On the opposite side of the room, Cassian lounges with a few of the guys I recognize from my Orchestra class. Numerous girls paw at his arms, and he smirks indulgently before pecking first one and then another on the lips. The guys around him hoot and holler, while the girls practically melt into a puddle of goo. I don't see the redhead from earlier, so I figure either he's already tired of her or she has second lunch.

And there, in the center of the room like a king addressing his civilians, sits Lucas Scott himself. With his red hair glinting like garnet stones in the drab school lighting, sea-blue eyes, and form-fitting jeans and gray sweater, it's no wonder he holds the attention of almost every girl in the immediate vicinity. All of the men are a catch, but there's something about Lucas that exudes danger. You'd never expect it from just glancing at him—he looks too much like a preppy fuck-boy—but when you stare into his eyes...

You'll see the devil.

And isn't that the most ironic thing of all?

I made a deal with the devil to get my revenge. And now, he owns my soul.

"Don't be nervous," Emmett whispers in my ear, misreading my silence. "You can sit with me and my friends."

"I'm not nervous," I protest automatically, almost vehemently. And I'm not.

The butterflies in my stomach battering their wings are because I'm excited, right?

Bracing myself, as one would do when faced with a ferocious storm, I step into the cafeteria. Somewhere nearby, a girl plays "A Little Wicked" by Valerie Broussard on her phone, and I can't help but think it's a fitting song for this moment.

Nobody even glances in my direction. No one notices the strange new girl with silvery blonde hair and amber eyes. Nobody, that is, except for the three gorgeous men who each carved out a piece of my soul.

Their eyes hone in on me, as if they're heat-seeking missiles and I'm their target.

Karsyn inhales sharply, and though I can't hear the sound over the chatter in the cafeteria, I imagine his breathing is now stuttered. I can see his wide eyes focus on me as I glide imperiously towards an empty table near the center of the room.

Lucas's lips pull into a tight smile as he nods at something the doting female on his left says. But his eyes…his calming, observant eyes never leave me. They trail after me with unnerving intensity as I pull out a seat and gracefully sit down. Emmett surprises me by sitting opposite, a beguiling grin on his handsome face. Lucas's gaze shoots to him, and his frown tightens almost imperceptibly.

And Cassian.

I'm not even sure he's breathing. His face drains of all color as he shoos away one of the girls tugging at his arm. Unlike the others, his entire head moves to watch me sit down and pull out my lunch.

The rest of the school may have forgotten about me, but these men? These devils?

They remember.

And they know that I'm dragging them to hell with me this time around.

It takes only twenty-two seconds for Karsyn to storm across the cafeteria and plant his large hands on the table. He towers over me, all two hundred pounds of him, but I don't feel any fear or anxiety. There's something near-pleading in his eyes, the softest brown infused with green, a melt of autumn tones.

"Peony." He breathes my name like one would at the climax of a horror story—with heavy trepidation, a hint of fear, and a generous amount of disbelief. "What...? How...?" He trails off, running a hand through his light blond hair.

"Do you know each other?" Emmett volleys his head between me and Karsyn curiously, and Karsyn whips his head to the side to glare down at his teammate.

"Leave," he growls, his guttural voice sending a slight tremor through my body. Lifting his head, he spears me with a heady look, one that almost makes words unnecessary. "I need to talk to you."

"Do you remember," I begin casually, tapping my fingers against the top of the table, "when you dumped a pot of chili over my head in seventh grade?"

Emmett's face scrunches up in horror, while Karsyn's turns grave.

"Peony, please," Karsyn beseeches, and I'm not gonna lie, it feels fucking good to have him beg. Maybe that makes me a little messed up, a little wicked, but I can't deny the burst of light that explodes in my chest like an errant firework.

Ignoring Karsyn completely, I focus on a fuming Emmett. He's glaring at his teammate as if he doesn't know him anymore, as if he can't comprehend what went through his mind. "So, you were telling me about your dog. Roofus, was it?"

Emmett shakes his head violently, as if coming out of trance, and flashes me a tight smile. It doesn't quite reach his eyes, but I appreciate the effort, especially when Karsyn releases a growl of frustration.

"Yeah. Cutest little fucker you'll ever meet." His eyes slide to Karsyn, who remains standing over the table, alternating between glaring at Emmett and pleading with me.

"Is he a Husky?" I tease, and this time, Emmett's lips twitch into something that resembles a genuine smile.

His deep, raspy chuckle pulsates through me, conjuring up images of long, hot nights between the sheets. With his strong body hovering over mine, his lips descending on my own, his hands in my silver hair.

Karsyn's inhuman growl clues me in to the fact that I'm giving Emmett blatant fuck-me eyes. Oh well.

"Peony, please," Karsyn begs again, but Emmett talks over him.

"You'll never let me live the Husky thing down, will you?" He drops an arm onto the table and rests his head on his open palm. It's only then that I realize he doesn't have any food in front of him. Unlike me, he must actually eat the atrocious cafeteria food. I feel bad that I'm keeping him from eating, but when his mischievous grin grows, I know that stale pizza is the last thing on his mind.

"Maybe the Husky is my spirit animal because I'm actually a hussy. Something got lost in translation."

I snort before I can contain the hideous sound. Mortified, I place a hand over my mouth as my core temperature ratchets up one thousand degrees.

Emmett throws his head back in laughter as Karsyn's scowl deepens.

"That was fucking adorable!" Emmett roars, wiping a tear from the corner of his eye.

"Why the fuck are you here?" Karsyn breaks in, but once more, we ignore him.

With a huff, Karsyn throws his large body on the plastic bench opposite me and crosses his arms over his chest, scowling.

Emmett and I exchange a droll look that basically says, "Can you believe this guy?"

Of course, Karsyn makes note of it and begins to mutter something under his breath. The euphoric joy I had seen on his face only an hour earlier, when he was with Mariabella, is nowhere to be seen. It's almost as if I'm staring into the face of a completely different man. And while that one was sunshine and rainbows and glitter bombs, this one is storm clouds and lightning and *actual* bombs. I'm genuinely afraid he's going to explode at any second, decimating the entire cafeteria in the process.

"You can get food if you want," I say to Emmett as I pull out my own lunch. A simple sandwich with turkey, cheese, tomato, and lettuce, an apple, and a bottle of water. I once would've been super self-conscious to eat this in front of Karsyn. With every bite, I would've waited for his smartass quip about my body or weight. I would've wilted under his attention like a flower starved for sunlight.

But now? Fuck him. Fuck all of them. I'll eat what I want, when I want, and if they have a problem with it, they can kiss my slender ass.

Karsyn appears to be in almost physical pain as he watches me lick my lips.

"Nah. I'm not really hungry." Emmett kicks out his feet until they're touching mine, and with a giggle, I press the toes of my foot against his own.

"Here." I offer him the other half of my sandwich, which he accepts with a grateful smile. Those gorgeous dimples make an impromptu appearance as his green eyes sparkle.

"Yum," he moans around a mouthful of sandwich. "This is delicious. Though...I'm sure it's not the most delicious thing you can offer me." His eyes very purposefully roam over my body, and another snort escapes me unbidden. I have no idea if his flirting is genuine or if he's merely attempting to get a rise out of Karsyn, but I don't care either way. Especially when Karsyn's nostrils flare and his muscles tense.

Huh. Apparently even after all these years, Karsyn is still determined to make me a social pariah. I'll never get laid again if he has his say. Maybe I'm just too hideous for his teammate.

"Peony, I really think we need—"

"Karsyn! Peony!" Mariabella's familiar, elfin voice floats to me as she races towards the table like a tornado obliterating everything in her path. She really is a breath of fresh air, this girl, with her warm smile and cognac brown eyes glimmering with jovial mirth and excitement. She throws her arms around my shoulders, squeezing my neck in an iron vise, and I awkwardly pat at her hands.

"Mari," I say, the shortened version of her name slipping out instinctively. Her eyes gleam once more as she giggles, sliding onto the bench opposite me and beside Karsyn. The man in question only grunts, narrowing his gorgeous hazel eyes at me as if it's *my* fault Mariabella decided to join the group. Yeah, no. If he has a problem with our budding friendship, he should talk to his pretty girlfriend about it, not glare at me as if my mere existence acts as a personal slight against him.

"How has your first day been so far?" she asks with a decidedly nervous giggle.

"I've been hearing rumors that you're some sort of musical prodigy," Emmett adds. "You play the cello?"

"The violin," I correct, acutely aware of Karsyn's gaze boring a hole in my head. And now that I'm thinking about it, Lucas and Cassian haven't looked away either. Oh, they're trying to be subtle about it—a flick of the eyes here, a swivel of the head there, a suspicious glance here—but I can tell that I have their complete and undivided attention. Both of them have females hanging off their every word, but they act as if they don't exist, as if nothing in this world exists except for me. And though they attempt to appear impassive, I can see panic radiating in Cassian's gaze and bemusement intermixed with loathing in Lucas's.

Yeah, right back at you, man.

"How long have you been playing?" Mariabella bats her eyelashes at me, and I swear, if it's even possible, Karsyn appears even more annoyed. His eyes practically roll into the back of his head as he spreads out his long, toned legs and steeples his hands together on his chest. How he's able to do this without a backrest remains a mystery. I'd fall on my ass.

"For years now," I admit. "I got…bullied pretty badly when I was younger. Music was my escape from reality." An escape from my pain. From the monotony of my existence. From the dissonant chaos of my life.

I find immense satisfaction in the rapid paling of Karsyn's face. He looks as if he's going to be sick, and I pray that if he vomits, he misses my shoes.

"Really?" Her face scrunches with confusion and sympathy, and I have the urge to snap at her, to remind her that she was around when her precious, perfect boyfriend made my life a living hell. But instead of saying any of that, instead of allowing Karsyn to see how much I actually care, I adopt a nonchalant frown.

"Life happens." I shrug my shoulders. "But it's kind of funny, if you think about it." Glancing in both directions, like I'm about to tell them a secret, I add, "Years from now, they're going to be the ones who suffer. Karma will come back to bite them all in the ass."

Now, Karsyn's face has taken on a green hue, while Emmett throws his head back in laughter. And Mariabella, sweet, innocent Mariabella, appears even more upset, her delicate brows cinched together.

"I'm so sorry, Peony. I had no idea."

I wonder if that's true—if her younger self truly lived a life of blissful obliviousness. But how could she not see the constant torture those boys put me through? How could she not notice that I was falling apart at the seams? That I was the one girl who never joined the cafeteria, in fear of what the guys would do to me?

Maybe she's lived her life in a perfect, little bubble, surrounded by perfect, little people, but that doesn't excuse her ignorance. If you see what's happening and choose not to say or do anything, you're just as bad as those who actually act on their twisted desires.

"Oh, shit." I glance down at my phone, arranging my expression into one of abject horror. They don't have to know that my phone is still currently off. "I need to get to my next class."

"What do you have?" Mariabella asks eagerly.

"AP Literature with Mrs. Town," I reply, and her face falls instantly.

"Oh. I have that sixth hour. But don't you have that class, Karsyn?" She turns towards her boyfriend, who looks as if he wishes to be anywhere else. I bet he regrets coming to talk to me in the first place.

Asshole.

At Karsyn's stilted nod, Mariabella's smile returns, illuminating her elfin face. She's pretty all of the time, but when she smiles, she transforms into something radiant and ethereal. She sort of reminds me of an angel you would see depicted on a stained glass window in church. There's an otherworldliness about her golden hair haloing her cherubic face and her light brown eyes, brimming with an inner purity that's absent in most teenagers.

I really, really don't want to hurt this girl.

But aren't there always casualties in war?

I just need to decide if I'm depraved enough to make her one.

"I have Calculus next period," Emmett grumbles, effectively pulling me out of my inner musings.

Smirking, I rise from my seat and sling my backpack over my shoulder. "Ha. Loser. I tested out of that."

"Oh, you bitch." Emmett sticks his tongue out to show me that he's teasing.

Mariabella's smile curls downwards as she glances suspiciously between the two of us. After a moment, she shakes out her blonde curls and offers another tentative smile, almost like a peace offering.

"Maybe Kars can walk you to class?" Though she words it as a suggestion, her tone brooks no room for argument.

"Maybe," I reply evasively. Before she can press the issue, I wave goodbye and head in the direction of my next class.

CHAPTER 7

Karsyn is a fucking bee.

You know the type—it flits around your head aimlessly, occasionally emanating a buzzing noise, but you're too afraid to swat at it in case it'll sting you.

As I walk to my fourth hour, I'm keenly aware of Karsyn nipping at my heels, but instead of a besotted puppy, I get an enraged, feral, ferocious mutt. More than once, he says my name, but I ignore him.

What can he possibly have to say to me?

Sorry?

It's a few years too late for that, though I doubt the thought of apologizing ever crossed his mind. More than likely, he wants to reprimand me for returning to school after he explicitly told me I could never, not fucking ever, come back. They thought they got rid of the trash once and for all.

By the time I enter the AP Literature classroom, located opposite the cafeteria, Karsyn has resorted to disgruntled huffs and hisses, his scowl firmly etched into place.

Surprisingly, Cassian beat me to class and currently sits near the front of the classroom. That surprises me. He seems more like the back-of-the-class-to-nap type of dude. His eyes narrow when he catches sight of me, and his lips protrude into something that resembles a pout. Oh. My. God. The great Cassian Jereome is pouting like a petulant child.

I can feel his eyes on me like the caress of a spring breeze as I purposely sit in the seat directly behind him. This way, I can keep my eyes on him the entire class period, but he can only stare at me if he goes out of his way to. From the tendon bulging in his neck, I know he's aware of my malevolent plan...and he's not happy about it.

Karsyn sits in the seat beside mine, and I find myself boxed between two sexy as sin, and equally as wicked, men. They don't bother to even acknowledge each other as they pull out their copies of *Pride and Prejudice* by Jane Austen.

Cas is fucking fuming, but that only makes my smile broaden. Why is it so hilarious to see them uncomfortable? What does it say about me that I like watching them squirm?

When the tension becomes almost unbearable, stretching between us like the slime you can purchase in toy stores, Cassian finally spins around and levels me with an inscrutable stare. He always was the easiest to break.

"Why are you here?" he demands, scowling. This close, I can see the minuscule changes that have transpired over the years. Like Karsyn, he's bulked up significantly, filling his long-sleeved white button-down and blue jeans impeccably. His black hair, a shade darker than his onyx skin, is buzzed short, accentuating the harsh planes of his masculine face. It's no wonder women flock to him—he's gorgeous. Even with the hatred I feel for him, I can admit that easily enough. There's something about him that draws you in like a trap hidden beneath leaves. It captures your ankle, propelling you dozens of feet into the air, and you're forced to dangle above the forest ground as you contemplate your own stupidity. And Cassian? He's the definition of "contemplating your own stupidity." He's the type of man you could get lost in.

"Why, I'm here to study classic literature," I taunt as I pull out my own copy of the current assignment. I emailed most of my teachers when I discovered I'd be showing up to the semester a month later than normal. Mrs. Town immediately sent a reading list for me to complete, as well as some sample essay questions.

"That's not what I meant," he growls through clenched teeth. He throws an irritated look in Karsyn's direction, one I can't read, before sitting ramrod straight in his chair. From this angle, I can see every rigid line of his back as anger cascades through him.

It's really fucking funny.

"Do you mean why I'm here, at this school?" I lean forward until my chin rests on his shoulder. He tenses, the action almost imperceptible, and the tempo of his heart increases significantly.

"Yes." He doesn't bother to move his head to look at me, but we're so close, I can discern the smell of his peppermint toothpaste.

Instead of answering, I simply pat his cheek before sliding back into my seat, kicking my legs out far enough to touch his. Keeping my eyes trained on the back of his head, I slowly run the toes of my shoes up and down his ankle. He freezes, hands tightening around his pencil, but doesn't move away.

"Good afternoon," a sultry voice proclaims as the classroom door opens and closes. I can't help but notice that all of the guys—sans Karsyn and Cassian, who are still sitting as if they have poles up their asses—lean forward in anticipation, practically salivating, as the gorgeous teacher enters the classroom.

The gorgeous, *redheaded* teacher.

The gorgeous, redheaded, cock-sucking teacher.

Oh. My. Fuck.

Mrs. Town was the one I saw just this morning, her red lips wrapped around Cassian's dick.

A laugh escapes before I can contain it, and Mrs. Town whips her head in my direction. She really is sexy, though it's easy to see why I initially mistook her for a student. Her red hair hangs around her in shiny, voluminous curls. She's also significantly shorter than a lot of women, coming in at barely five feet. With her clear skin, rosy red lips, and perfectly applied mascara, she could pass for just another one of Cassian's groupies.

But she's not.

She's his fucking *teacher*, and she's a Mrs.

She's his *married* fucking teacher.

"Ms. Simone, do you find something funny?" Her voice carries a husky undercurrent to it that probably makes her irresistible to the male population. I see more than one guy grinning slyly in her direction.

"Nope, not at all." I offer her my sweetest, most innocent smile. Her eyes narrow slightly, almost suspiciously, before she turns towards the whiteboard, stretching on her tiptoes to write in delicate scrawl across the board. The movement causes her blouse to rise up and gives the class a clear view of her perky ass in the pencil-skirt. I see one guy go as far as to adjust his boner.

I lean forward once more—noting from my peripheral how Karsyn's gaze dips to my breasts brushing against the desktop—and place my lips against Cassian's ear.

"Tell me, Cassian, are you hot for teacher?" I whisper breathily, and his head jerks to the side as if I slapped him.

"What?" he demands, voice nothing but a raspy brush of air.

"She must be pretty good at sucking cock... I mean, if she has a student lover and a husband, I would assume she is." I shrug my shoulders and recline back in the seat before he can comment. But his eyes...they're wide and wild with panic. He doesn't even seem to notice Mrs. Town at the front of the room, eyes periodically flicking in his direction and expression growing more and more irate when it becomes apparent he's not paying her an ounce of attention.

At this point, he's not even bothering to hide the fact that he's staring at me so intensely, I feel light-headed. He's almost straddling the back of his chair.

"Peony..."

Before he can speak, before he can conjure up some lame excuse to explain why he would fuck a married, older woman, the door to the room opens and Elias Briggs steps inside. He exudes a nonchalant arrogance, as if attending a class like this is beneath him. His bored, honey brown eyes—a deep, earthy color that reminds me distinctly of autumn leaves—travel across the room almost absently before they pause on me. Then they widen into saucers as his mouth drops open.

Smiling softly, I lift my hand and wave my fingers at him.

CHAPTER 8

Elias looks exactly as I remember him—light brown hair, almost chestnut in color, hanging just beneath his jaw in shaggy waves. Only this time, purple streaks heighten the purple tint in his brown eyes. Of course, I know his eyes aren't actually violet, despite what romance books will have you believe, but there's a decidedly plum undertone to the rich brown. If I didn't know he was completely and one hundred percent human, I would think he was some sort of witch. They're the only species I know capable of having such a strange, enticing eye color. Combined with his leather jacket, black jeans, and combat boots, he's a sight to behold. On anyone else, the different styles would make him look tacky, but it fits him so impeccably that no one would dare question his appearance.

He scrubs a hand across his whiskered chin before moving that same hand to his mane of hair—hair that I once ran my own hands through just the way he did.

His lips moved slowly across mine. Almost teasingly. With every swipe of his tongue against mine, I could taste the chocolate he had just eaten combined with his natural, pine scent.

I can feel his eyes on me—burning me, claiming me, possessing me—as he moves through the aisle and to the very back of the room. He didn't bother to bring a backpack, unlike the rest of the class, so he merely throws his body into the plastic chair, gaze intent on my profile.

I wiggle slightly, unnerved at being the sole focus of his attention, but I refuse to acknowledge him any more than I already did. Unlike the others, I won't give him the satisfaction.

Because Elias Briggs? He destroyed me worst of all.

THE REST OF CLASS IS RELATIVELY UNEVENTFUL. BY THE TIME THE BELL rings, I'm already out of my seat and racing towards the door. I can hear Mrs. Town call Cassian back, but he ignores her, practically running to catch up with me.

"Peony!" he bellows, and I turn my head slightly—in a pathetic moment of weakness—to see him standing shoulder to shoulder with Elias and Karsyn. All three of them stare after me with inscrutable expressions marring their handsome faces.

Fuck you all.

I know that I have fifth hour with them as well, but I'm grateful for the reprieve when I duck into the girl's locker room.

"Peony!" Mariabella squeals as soon as she sees me, jumping up from her perch on the bench. She's wearing a pair of tiny spandex shorts and a sports bra, her blonde hair pulled back into a tight ponytail. "I didn't know you had this class." Quickly, she reaches into a locker—hers, presumably—and grabs a ratty T-shirt, throwing it over her head.

"Gym and Health with Mr. Builder?" I query, moving to stand beside her. There are numerous girls already present, chatting amongst themselves before they have to enter the gymnasium. I spot Felicia, the bitch from Orchestra, watching me with a narrow-eyed glare, seemingly unconcerned that she's both shirtless and braless, her small, pert boobs on display.

Honestly, none of the girls seem self-conscious as they change. I spot more nipples and thongs than I ever thought possible as they switch out of regular clothes and into sporty ones.

Yeah, no. That's not going to work for me.

"Mr. Builder is actually super cool," Mariabella says, a catch to her voice that wasn't there prior.

"Hopefully he's better than my middle school teacher," I murmur under my breath. Still, she cocks an eyebrow at me as confusion dances across her face.

"What do you mean?"

"Never mind." Grabbing my drawstring bag from where I tucked it inside of my backpack, I head towards one of the bathroom stalls. "I'll be back in a second."

I don't have the chance to hear her response before I slide into the nearest empty stall and quickly change into my gym clothes—a long-sleeved gray shirt and a pair of shorts. The last thing I want is for anyone to see me naked and question—

Cutting that thought off before it can solidify, I exit the stall to see that only Mariabella remains. Quickly, so as to not make either of us late, I pull my hair back into a disheveled ponytail, not bothering to comb out the ends.

"Sorry," I whisper to her as we hurry out of the locker room and into the gym.

"Don't worry about it," she replies back as we easily sidle into the line. There are about thirty students in this class, but only a few of them are familiar. Felicia, as I noted before, as well as Lauren. And there, near the end of the line, stands Emmett, who waves and offers me a gleeful smile.

And Lucas, Elias, Karsyn, and Cassian.

They don't stand by each other—hell, they don't even look at each other or me—but I can feel their presence like cobwebs caressing my face in a spooky, dilapidated haunted house. Unease skates up my spine as I remember my last Gym class with them.

And Mr. Builder's next words only cause my irrational fear to increase tenfold.

"...I'll split you into teams for dodgeball. Please remember what team you're on when I assign them."

Logically, I know that the guys won't try anything this time around. I know that. I honestly do. But try telling that to my juddering heart and the sweat beading on my forehead.

As he goes down the line, assigning team numbers, I feel a brief pang of disappointment that Mariabella won't be on the same team as me. Her face falls as well, and she grumbles as she moves to one side of the classroom. With heavy reluctance, and no small amount of trepidation, I move opposite her.

Towards where Lucas stands.

I'm grateful that Lucas is the only Devil on my team. And I'm even more relieved when Emmett joins as well.

The blond football player smiles at me as he saunters forward with all the cocky arrogance a man like him can possess. He *knows* how good he looks in the thin shirt stretched tight over his pecs. And with his hair brushed away, he's practically drool-worthy.

"I'm kind of disappointed we're not on opposite teams," he murmurs when he's close enough to not be overheard by the other students. Well, most of the other students. Lucas lingers only a few inches away from me, his red hair glinting like blood in the gym lighting.

"Why is that?" I question, utterly aware that Lucas's face is becoming graver and graver with every passing second.

"Because I kinda wanted you to catch my balls," he flirts, and I throw my head back in laughter. On the opposite side of the basketball court, Cassian, Elias, and Karsyn watch the exchange with narrowed eyes. Mariabella stands beside them, chewing on her nail uneasily.

I have to give myself a pat on the back. Despite how badly I want to, I don't flip the three of them off. Maturity for the win!

"I hate dodgeball," I murmur as Mr. Builder nods towards the multi-colored rubber balls set in a line in the middle of the gym. Those balls? They fucking hurt when they're hurled at your face, especially when thirty are thrown at one time with no chance of escape…

"Don't worry." Emmett nudges me with his elbow. "I'll protect your sexy ass."

I just barely hold in my snort.

Yeah, good luck with that. Especially since all of the Devils are going to be gunning for me.

I'm pretty sure even Lucas will try to hit me with a ball, despite being on the same team. He's just that wicked.

"When I blow my whistle, you may begin!" Mr. Builder steps backwards until he's on the sidelines, said whistle dangling from his thin lips. The shrill sound pierces the air, and immediately, students from each side—mainly the guys—run towards the balls in the center. I can't help but smile indulgently when I notice that Emmett is one of them, hooting and hollering with his fists raised.

"You came back," a cold voice remarks, and I swear that a gust of icy wind accompanies his presence. All around us, balls fly and whack students, but at that moment, we're in our own separate bubble. No one can hurt us.

"I did," I say dryly. Finally, I pivot on my heel to face Lucas Scott, the king of all bullies. Unlike the rest of us degenerates, he wears a polo shirt and black shorts that conform to his shapely legs. I can't even imagine him wearing basketball shorts and a loose T-shirt. Not Lucas. It's too…beneath him.

Just like my existence was.

Is.

"Why did you come back?" His glacial eyes stay glued to my face as someone next to me releases a whimper of pain. Honestly, I'm surprised that none of the other Devils are aiming at me. Maybe they're already out?

One glance confirms that they're aiming at Emmett, of all people, who merely laughs hysterically, unperturbed at being the target of their ire.

"Why does it matter?" I place my hand on my hip and cock it to the side. "Are you going to tell me to leave? To never come back? Because I've heard that all before, Lucas Scott, and I'm not that petrified little girl anymore. You're not going to scare me this time."

He doesn't flinch at the venom in my tone. Hell, I'm not even sure he blinks. Those cold, cold eyes continue to stare down at me, thousands of secrets lingering in their depths.

"We didn't think you were ever going to come back," he says at last, tone matter-of-fact and...something else. Something I can't read.

I pride myself in understanding these boys better than anyone— better than myself—but I've always known that Lucas would be the hardest to read. He wears his apathetic mask like it's warpaint, like it's the only thing he needs to survive. But he doesn't understand that there are no gunners aiming for him. He's the only monster I know.

Well, him and his three best friends.

Ex-best friends.

"What are you going to do about it, Lucas?" I ask in a surprising spurt of bravery. I take a step closer until we're toe to toe. "Are you going to hit me?"

And for the first time in all the years I have known him, something akin to horror flashes across his face. He looks...stricken, his face draining of all color. Just as quickly, he reconstructs his mask brick by brick, once more making him an impenetrable fortress.

Before he can respond, though I'm not sure I would've even allowed him to, something whacks me in the back of the head. I release a whimper of pain, grabbing at my scalp, as I whip my head in the direction where I felt the ball come from. But instead of the Devils, as I expected, I see an unfamiliar male grinning at me smugly.

Fucking asshole.

With a huff, I stalk to the sidelines, joining the rest of my eliminated teammates. I spot Emmett leaning against the wall, nursing his chin and then his cheek.

The Devils really did a number on him, that's for damn sure.

I've just selected a spot farther down the line when there's a pained wheeze and a loud, agonized cry. Immediately, Mr. Builder blows his whistle and races onto the court, stopping both teams from throwing any more balls.

On the ground, rocking back and forth while fat, ugly tears cascade down his cheeks, is the man who hit me. And standing opposite, expression unreadable, is Lucas Scott. The other Devils stand in a haphazard semi-circle around the sobbing guy, almost as if they were blocking him from escaping.

Surely Lucas didn't hit the guy because he hit me. He was probably just being his normal, competitive self. Or maybe he was pissed that I got eliminated before the real torture could begin.

I watch in wary fascination as Mr. Builder helps the kid off the court before he blows his whistle, once more resuming the game.

And then I watch as three balls—one from each of the Devils—barrel towards Lucas's surprised face.

I think I've died and gone to heaven. All I need now is for the other three guys to be in similar pain, but alas, beggars can't be choosers.

They'll get what's coming to them.

Everyone here will.

CHAPTER 9

The last class of the day is also my favorite—Music Composition with Mrs. Bummer.

I'm practically giddy as I skip through the halls, ignoring the blistering glares I can feel on my back. Nobody, not even the Devils, can ruin my good mood.

My research shows that I have this class with Cassian and Lucas, both of whom eye me with no small amount of suspicion as I slide into an empty seat near the front of the class. I can't help but note that Cassian sits on one side of the room while Lucas sits on the other. I knew that their relationship—all of their relationships—had become strained, but seeing it firsthand sends a surge of primal satisfaction coursing through me. It's ridiculous to believe that I played any part in their falling out, but a girl can hope.

My plans for revenge will prove much, much harder if they're a united front. These boys—these men—are capable of creating fierce, deadly armies if they so desire. They can rule this world and everyone in it with nothing more than a cunning smirk and wave of the hand. You can stare at them and know immediately that they're power. Pure and refined power, the type that kings and queens wield. But their kingdom? It's this school. And their civilians? The unwitting students. I suppose that makes me their prisoner of war. Or maybe just a court jester—someone for them to laugh at and tease.

But revenge can come later. For now, I'm going to enjoy my favorite class.

I refuse, absolutely refuse, to allow the two Devils to ruin my good mood.

Cassian is still sulky as his eyes periodically flick in my direction. Those gorgeous, pouty lips of his are pushed outwards, and I have the strangest urge to bite down on his lower one. To pull it between my teeth until he gasps in pain. The thought is completely irrational, and I shove it away instantly, focusing on Mrs. Bummer as she waddles into the classroom.

She's one of the oldest teachers at the high school, with pure white hair, a heavily wrinkled face, and sea-green eyes. She always wears buttons on her floral dress, each one depicting some weird ass saying or logo, usually in another language.

"I hope you guys brought your composition notebooks, because —" She breaks off abruptly when she lays eyes on me, and the squeal that leaves her mouth doesn't sound entirely human. "Well, praise be! Is that Miss Peony Simone?" She has a distinct Southern accent, one that becomes even more pronounced when she's excited.

With an excited screech of my own, I fly from my chair and wrap my arms around her.

"It's been too long," I say, smiling up at my private tutor.

Mrs. Bummer was a godsend throughout elementary and middle school. She knew about my history with the Devils—every explicit, horrendous detail—and never thought less of me. She loved me unconditionally, even when my own mother discarded me like trash, and was repeatedly a bright spot in the dark abyss of my life. Every weekday, from five to seven PM, I would travel to her music store, located just off of Riley Street. It was she who tended my love for music, fueling it until the flames turned into an inferno. And not just the violin. She frequently set me up with various tutors who were skilled at a variety of instruments, everything from the piano to the drums to the flute.

"Why, you're gorgeous," Mrs. Bummer gushes, pulling back to examine me. "You grew up to be a beautiful young lady."

A blush erupts on my cheeks before I can contain it, and I have the irrational urge to look over my shoulder at Cassian and Lucas, both of whom I can still feel drilling holes into my scalp. I imagine they're scoffing right now at Mrs. Brummer's words. Maybe thinking about how much of a kiss-ass I am.

"Have you been practicing while you've been away?" she asks, a stern scowl on her archaic face.

"Of course. My ex's father owned the music store, Twisted Beats, in California," I admit, thinking fondly of Uriel Griffin. We split amicably a few months before I traveled back to Michigan, and I still text him periodically. I think we just both agreed that the relationship between us wasn't working, at least romantically, but that we could still be friends. The last time he texted me, he mentioned that he was seeing a new girl who worked at the local coffee shop.

I hear what sounds like something snapping, and when I whip my head around, I see Cassian holding a broken pencil as he scowls at me.

"And have you finished that piece you were working on?" Mrs. Brummer queries with a cocked brow. "Charming Devils" was a passion piece of mine when I was younger, but over the years, I've been able to improve my craft until the song wrote itself. It didn't feel like notes on a page. No, it felt like *me*. That song is a story of my life, a story that unravels my soul for the entire world to see.

"I have." I smirk at her, and her eyes light up in understanding. With a nod towards the grand piano, easily worth the price of my car, she moves to sit at the desk I abandoned.

"Let's hear it, child." She waves her hand at me to begin, and I slowly slide across the bench. I move my fingers over the keys, familiarizing myself with the instrument, before I take a deep, reflective breath. I know that when I play this song, I'll be revealing a piece of myself, a piece of my soul, to the two boys sitting attentively in the front row, staring at me with indecipherable eyes. But at the same time, I *want* them to hear it, to know what's coming for them. I want them to question everything and wonder if this is it. If this is the moment I destroy them so irrevocably, they won't be able to pick up the shattered pieces.

I lived in fear for years.

Now, it's their turn.

My fingers glide across the keys as I begin the song I've memorized. Years and years of playing, of writing, of composing, has led to this moment. This single song, played to an audience of seven.

The first half depicts immense, agonizing pain. The notes are lower, louder, to emphasize the fear I felt every day. The panic. The myriad of emotions pounding, pounding, pounding in my head. But then, the piece gets softer, lighter, as I detail my escape from the school and the new life I made for myself in California. And finally, the ending...a mixture of impishness and cunningness, all fleshed together in a fast-paced tune.

When I finally finish, I bow my head over the keys and squeeze my eyelids shut. The emotions roaring through me, demanding my attention, are almost impossible to ignore. They sit on my chest like a fifty-ton weight, pressing down on my ribcage until I'm choking on my own blood. Because pain? It doesn't just go away. I mean sure, there are moments when you forget about it, moments when it doesn't monopolize your every thought, but it always returns when you least expect it.

And it fucking kills you.

"Charming Devils" took years to write, but the funny thing is? It's not done. I just know there's going to be one more section of the song, one more verse, depicting these final moments. And I also know that the ending is going to be written completely by fate, with me as the guiding hand.

I'm vaguely aware of the class erupting into applause and Mrs. Bummer jumping to her feet, but I can't focus on them. My eyes are riveted on the two boys on either side of the room, each watching me with narrowed eyes. They *know* the song was about them...

And that means they also know that the war has only just begun.

CHAPTER 10

Mrs. Bummer fucking saves my ass again by letting class out two minutes before the bell rings.

Before Lucas and Cassian can corner me—I can see in their eyes that's their intention—I grab my backpack and race out of the room, towards AP Literature with Mrs. Town. Then I wait, practically bursting with nervous energy like a bottle of soda that has been shaken repeatedly.

The second the bell rings, I feign a bored, almost nonchalant expression, and walk in the opposite direction of my other classmates…bumping my shoulder into a startled Mariabella, who's just exiting Mrs. Town's classroom.

"Oh, I'm sorry!" I say with fake sincerity as she blinks her long lashes up at me. "Mariabella! Hi! Fancy running into you here."

She blushes, tucking a strand of blonde hair behind her ear.

"This is actually perfect!" I continue, before she can get a word in. "Considering you're the only person I really know, and the only female I talked to today, I was wondering if you wanted to hang out." I offer her a wide smile, one that's so sweet, it's almost sickly. I swear, my cheeks are beginning to ache from smiling so much.

Predictably, Mariabella's face drops and guilt crosses her pretty face.

"I'm sorry. I totally would, but I have—" As I expected, her eyes light up with her grand epiphany, one I not so subtly hinted at throughout the day. "You used to do cheerleading, right?" She doesn't wait for me to respond, barreling ahead while bouncing on the balls of her feet. "I know tryouts already occurred, but I know the coach well. I'm sure she'll allow you on the team!"

"Really!?" I try to infuse my words with the correct amount of enthusiasm. When I get a weird glance from a girl standing opposite me in the hallway, I tone it down a notch. "That would be amazing!"

"All right! Yay!" Quickly, as if she has to stop me from changing my mind, Mariabella links her arm with mine and pulls me in the direction of the football field. "This is going to be *so* much fun. The girls are seriously amazing, and Mrs. Watson—that's our coach, by the way—is incredible. She did college cheerleading all four years and won nationals three times! We're so fortunate to have her here with us."

I nod along, as if this is all new information, but the truth is, I studied Mrs. Watson in depth before I arrived. Not only is she a college national cheerleader, but she's also a damn good coach. Since she took over the program, nearly three years ago, she's made High Groves one of the best cheer teams in the division. My research shows that she married her high school sweetheart at the ripe age of twenty-five, and at twenty-six, she became the youngest coach in the school's history.

She's also a stickler for the rules, fierce and dedicated, and unbending in her belief that hard work is the only acceptable answer to achieve success.

To be frank, she's my kind of person.

Mariabella continues chatting as we head to the locker room, now nearly empty, and change into our workout clothes again. This time, Mariabella forgoes the top, wearing nothing but a sports bra and spandex. I once more hide inside the stall and change into my own pair of spandex shorts and a long-sleeve shirt that conforms to my breasts and arms. Unlike the last one, however, this one cuts off just under my chest, revealing my toned belly.

Back in middle school, my skin had consistently been a pasty shade of alabaster with a splatter of golden freckles from the sun. My time in California has brought about a deep, bronze tan that heightens the white of my hair and the amber of my eyes. It's not dark enough to be considered fake, but it's not light enough to go unnoticed.

And no, I didn't tan for the Devils. This has nothing to do with them. I did it for me and me alone. I wanted to feel good about myself, for once in my life. So I cut my once ass-length hair, developed a natural tan, and started wearing makeup to emphasize my "weird" and "unusual eyes." I embraced all of the things that made me different, and I did so with pride.

We find Mrs. Watson standing on the track of the football field, arms folded over her chest. She really is a pretty woman, with a mane of chestnut hair and gray-blue eyes. She turns expectantly towards Mariabella when we approach before her eyes trail to me. Suspicion clouds her gaze as she glances between the two of us wordlessly.

"What do we have here?" She cocks a single eyebrow as the rest of the cheer team, most of whom I don't recognize, crowds around her.

"Peony," Mariabella introduces. "She's a new student. Apparently, she did cheer back at her old school in California, but she missed the tryouts here."

I'm dimly aware of the football players staggering onto the field. I spot Emmett's sandy blond hair as he races forward, wearing a pair of loose shorts and a wife-beater, before my attention drifts to Karsyn.

The man is a fucking Greek god. From this distance, his blond hair appears to have numerous highlights throughout—streaks of molten gold, rivulets of crimson, and strands of chestnut brown. He's shirtless, the bronze planes of his chest on clear display, and wears a pair of surprisingly tight shorts. Obviously, the team isn't planning on doing any tackling today if they're not wearing protective padding. Though I have no idea if that's something they change into at a later time. Honestly, my limited knowledge of football stems from what I studied a few months before I moved here.

I tune back into Mrs. Watson just as she says, "Call me Helen."

"Helen," I repeat with a small smile and nod. And then, when silence descends, I add, "I understand that it's late in the season, but I just wanted you to know that I'm extremely dedicated to the sport. I'll practice at home to learn the routines—" Lies. There's a muscle memorization spell I can use. "—and I promise to be on my best behavior if you give me a chance."

Mrs. Watson—excuse me, *Helen*—taps her chin in contemplation, and beside me, Mariabella gives her coach the puppy-dog eyes. After a long moment, Helen offers me a crooked smile.

"Would you mind trying out right here?" she asks at last. "We had to cut a lot of good girls, and it wouldn't be fair to them. You can feel free to do a routine that you learned at your old school."

"Oh." Luckily, I prepared for this. "Of course. Do you mind if I use music?"

"Go ahead."

Fortunately, I remembered to bring my phone, and I quickly pull up the song I selected. I hadn't necessarily *expected* to perform today, but I can't say I won't use the opportunity to the best of its advantage.

Next, I pull out a tiny tube that I kept hidden in my bra. Casting a glance in both directions, and ensuring Mariabella is engaged in a conversation with Helen, I down the contents. It's a potion I whipped up a few nights earlier, one that's designed to enhance my flexibility. I also mixed in a healthy dose of an anti-anxiety brew.

Hopefully, it'll be enough to quell the sudden flurry of butterflies erupting in my stomach.

"If you can push play…" I hand my phone to a grinning Mariabella and stand on the edge of the field, my back to the football players. I won't be able to do what I need to do if I know they're watching me. If I know *he's* watching me.

Mariabella hooks up my phone to Helen's Bluetooth speaker, and immediately, "Can't Remember to Forget You" by Shakira featuring Rihanna blares across the field. The muscles in my stomach tighten by the minute as I wait for the first verse to begin.

I spent weeks studying dance and watching YouTube videos for this moment. Honestly, I wasn't sure if it would ever happen. A part of me prayed that it *wouldn't*.

But I tell myself what I told myself thousands of times before. It's music, something that flows through you like a sentient being, something that devours your mind, something that's indescribable. It's no different than losing myself to a violin piece or a piano composition.

Instantly, I begin to move my body to the beat, performing the sexy dance I choreographed with the agility and flexibility of…well, a dancer. I seductively move my hands across my body as I dance with all of the hate and passion burning a hole in my heart. I dance like I'm dying, like the world is falling in crumbles around me, executing each twist and turn and fucking ass wiggle like my life depends on it. To please Helen, I add a few standard cheer moves into the dance as well—a toe touch, high V, herkie, and pike. I also display some of the gymnastic skills the spell helps me perform, including an ariel, round-off back handspring, and front flip.

The result is a seamless routine…and an even sexier dancer.

It's degrading as fuck, especially when someone whistles from the football field, but I push all of those thoughts away. Maybe I'll hate myself down the road for this—for everything—but not today. Not to-fucking-day.

I drop my arms to the ground, keeping my legs straight, and slowly drag them up my body, making sure to keep my ass popped out. I pivot on my heel to see nearly the entire football team staring at me hungrily. The only one who isn't devouring me with his eyes is Karsyn. *He* looks irrationally angry, face beet red. Instead of giving the asshole one ounce of my attention though, I focus on Emmett, who I can see practically salivating.

Offering him a flirty wink, I drop down to the ground, opening up my legs, before rising back up. I think it's called a booty drop or something. Hell if I know. It looked cool on the YouTube video I watched.

I blow Emmett a kiss—one that he dramatically catches, much to the amusement of the other guys and the irritation of Karsyn—before running as fast as I can and performing a seamless back handspring full. It's one of the toughest tricks a gymnast can perform, but with the muscle memorization spell and the flexibility potion, I execute it flawlessly.

When I finish my routine, I'm breathing heavily and a fine layer of sweat coats my skin. Still, it's worth it to see the heat in the guys' eyes.

And, more importantly, the heat in Karsyn's. He tries to hide it, going as far as scowling in my direction, but it's impossible to deny. For a brief moment, there was pure and wanton *need* in his hazel gaze, like he's an addict and I'm his next fix.

"Holy. Shit," Helen breathes, just as the football coach blares his whistle, screaming at his team to get back to work. Emmett flashes me a cocky smile, winking, before he saunters off to join the rest of the disassembling team. Only Karsyn remains behind, his golden chest heaving as he stares at me. His expression is a fine balance between rage and lust. Staring at me for a few seconds like he's never seen me before, he then turns on his heel and stalks away, giving me his back and ass. His rather fine, muscular ass...

"That was amazing!" Helen rushes towards me, Mariabella on her heels. I notice the latter is looking a little flushed, and her eyes are radiant with elation. I imagine she's excited to have a strong gymnast and dancer on the team—though, truth be told, I can barely walk in a straight line normally.

"So…did I make the team?" I pretend to be timid, unsure, going as far as lowering my eyes to the ground in a subservient gesture.

"Did you make the…? Don't be an idiot!" Helen rolls her eyes good-naturedly, though I can see that internally, she's still squealing with excitement. Composing her features, she turns towards the rest of the girls, who are whispering amongst each other, staring at me with wide-eyed wonder and envy. "Now, let's start from the top, shall we, and show Peony what she missed!"

CHAPTER 11

My research proves to be right—Helen is a fucking drill sergeant when it comes to cheerleading. By the time I leave practice, I'm sweating my ass off and my cheeks radiate a bright, hideous red. The face ones, not the ass.

Fortunately, cheer practice got out an hour before football, so I don't risk running into a glowering Karsyn. And I could most definitely feel the evil eyes he directed at me throughout the afternoon. I could practically see the thousands of thoughts circulating in that pretty head of his, but his expression remained guarded. Wary.

Not that I blame him. He most definitely *should* be wary of me. I'm vengeance and hate, anger and rage, pain and suffering. My plot for revenge has been etched into the stars, defining who I am. There's no escaping my destiny.

After saying goodbye to Mariabella and the rest of the girls, I begin the long trek home. While this morning, I'd been enthusiastic with a skip in my step that normally isn't there, this afternoon, it feels like thirty-pound-bricks weigh down my feet. My body aches from the grueling training we just went through and from one of my particularly hard falls.

Helen deemed me small enough to be a flyer. For those of you who don't know cheerleading—like I didn't a mere two months ago—a flyer is the girl who is catapulted into the air. She's usually the smallest and lightest person on the team, but she also must be flexible to pull off some of the stunts required of her. Today, we practiced a simple basket toss, aiming for height. Of course, one of my bases, a girl named Jamie, got distracted by her running back boyfriend and didn't focus on catching me when I came down. My head hit my back spot's shoulder as they struggled to keep me upright. But alas, I tumbled to the ground, nursing a bruised hip and sore ankle.

I seriously regret not allowing one of Nana's boyfriends to drive me as I make the journey back to her house. My backpack suddenly seems to weigh a million pounds, bagged down by textbooks I didn't have earlier.

My phone buzzes in my pocket, and I glance disdainfully down at the screen, unsurprised to see Mom's name. Since school got out, she's been calling me nonstop, never bothering to leave a message. But I don't want to speak to her, especially since I know she'll just bitch me out for no reason. I can never be good enough for her.

The roar of an engine has my head whipping up, just in time to see a sleek motorcycle pull to a stop directly in front of me, the tires leaving skid marks on the asphalt. My heart races madly as I take an automatic step backwards, squeezing the fabric of my shirt in my hand.

"What the—" Before I can continue that expletive, the driver pulls off his helmet, revealing dark brown hair interspersed with purple highlights. Elias Briggs looks like sin personified, like every naughty dream I've ever had. He still wears his leather jacket, this time zipped up, and it makes his muscles appear impossibly larger. He shakes his head from side to side, shaggy hair sprawling in every direction.

Up close, I can see the hint of a stubble on his full jawline. A scar mars his left cheek, directly underneath his eye. I'm nearly positive that it hadn't been there five years prior. He exudes strength and raw masculinity, his entire demeanor screaming, "back the fuck up."

But seeing him makes my heart hurt. Physically hurt. Each heartbeat ricochets through my chest like a pinball machine.

"Elias." I nod my head at him in a curt greeting, knowing that my apathetic tone will piss him off to no end. As expected, his eyes tighten marginally as he leans over the handlebars of his bike.

"Why the fuck are you walking home alone?" he demands, and I'm momentarily struck speechless by the direction of this conversation.

"Excuse me?" I ask, disbelief lacing my tone.

"You shouldn't be alone," he snaps, reaching behind him and procuring a second helmet. "Come on. I'll give you a ride."

I snort before I can rein in the noise.

"Nah. I'd rather walk." Giving him a blistering glare, I pick up my pace and sidestep him and that damn bike.

Immediately, he catches up to me, wheeling his large bike beside him.

I attempt to walk even faster, to where it's a borderline light jog, but Elias's long legs easily keep pace with me.

Anger thrums through me as I shoot him an icy glare.

"What the fuck are you doing?" I seethe.

"Making sure you get home okay," he responds dryly, maintaining pace with me.

"Fuck you, Elias," I snap before I can control my temper. I can feel my magic flare inside of my chest, almost like a lightning bug, before I quell the spark down.

Not yet.

Not yet.

With a completely undignified huff, I continue walking towards Nana's house, attempting to ignore the Elias-sized elephant in the room. What angle is he playing? Why is he pretending to care...or is this some elaborate scheme to humiliate me yet again? My heart judders in my chest at the prospect—at the mere *possibility*—of them pranking me. I wouldn't put it past them. These men are beautiful roses wreathed in thorns, much like the flower Beauty plucks in the classic fairy tale. But I refuse to allow these beasts to own me. They already took away the majority of my childhood, and I'll be damned if they do the same to me now.

I remain silent until I'm through the wrought iron fence and climbing up the twisting driveway. I hear the distinct sound of Elias's motorcycle engine, and despite my body and mind screaming at me to resist, I reluctantly look over my shoulder in time to see him cast one lingering glance of his own at me before zooming away.

What the hell was that all about?

Before I can stop it, before I can reel it in, a memory hits me with the force of a wrecking ball.

"Give it back," I hissed, standing on my tiptoes so I could glare up into Elias's smug face. Instead of looking properly cowed, like I'd hoped for, he granted me a wide smile, one that showed his pearly white teeth.

"Why should I, sweet Peony?" he taunted as he held my short story above his head. This was my final assignment for seventh grade English, and at the same time, I was immensely proud of the story I wrote. There was heartache and pain, love and redemption, hope and regret, all clustered in three hand-written pages.

"'The monsters stare at me, and I meet their stares with a defiant one of my own,'" he read, his smoky voice curling around me. "I refuse to let them drag me beneath the bed, I refuse to let them break me. You see, I might be the only one who knows the truth about the four of them, about how they hide their pain beneath hard masks. These monsters? They're broken. They're...'" Elias trailed off, his eyebrows scrunching together, as he read more of my story silently.

After a moment, he scoffed, purposefully dangling the notebook paper in front of my face before splitting it cleanly in two.

"You're wrong," Elias said, taking a step closer until he towered over me. Almost as if he couldn't help himself, he brushed a strand of my pale white hair behind my ear. "Not all monsters have a reason for being the way they are. Some are just...irrevocably damaged. There's no use trying to explain why they act the way they do." My entire body tensed as he leaned forward, maintaining eye contact the entire time. "And this monster right here?" He pounded his chest. "He just doesn't like looking at a freak like you."

I tug myself out of the memory as I slide into the foyer, glancing in both directions cautiously. The last thing I want to walk in on is my nana have another fucking orgy. Gah.

"Peony!" As if my thoughts conjured her, Nana appears around the corner, her violet hair cascading around her in loose, natural curls. She wears a floral-printed gown that cinches around her waist before protruding outwards. Dangling earrings and numerous bracelets complete the hippy look. "Are you okay? What took you so long to get home? Why didn't you respond to my texts?"

Brows furrowing, I remove my phone and scroll through the messages. Sure enough, intermixed with the missed calls from Mom are numerous texts and calls from Nana—and even some from Polo, Christian, and Gabriel as well.

"What's the matter?" I ask, instantly on alert as I shove my phone back into my pocket. "Is it the coven?" Though I left my home on moderately bad terms, I still care a lot about the witches and warlocks who live there. But I feel like if something had transpired, I would've gotten a call from my ex. Or even his douchebag older brother, Ryan, who is half in love with me. Mom wants me to marry that fucker...but that's a story for another time.

"There was an attack," Nana confesses, just as Polo, Christian, and Gabriel enter from the opposite wing of the house. All of them look relieved to see me, even that asshole Gabriel.

"An attack?" My heart thunders as I once more remove my phone and stare at the calls from my mom. Is that what she called me about? Were we under attack? "Witch hunters?"

Nana shakes her head quickly before capturing my hands in both of hers and giving them a reassuring squeeze. "It's not the coven, sweetheart. It was a town a few hours from here. A Blood attacked a witch this morning."

"A Blood?" I gasp, widening my eyes in abject horror. Bloods? They're dangerous motherfuckers who dabble in the dark arts. They get their power from human—and witch—sacrifices, as well as blood consumption. It's where the mythology of vampires stems from. According to lore, once a witch or warlock partakes in the ritual, they're never able to go back. They'll constantly crave blood, both from unsuspecting humans and witches and warlocks. The power that flows through them is something dark, something *other*, like a malevolent entity that you can't necessarily see but know exists.

Bloods also are immortal.

Sure, they can be killed just like anybody can, but they won't die of natural causes. They don't get sick, they don't wither away with time, they don't grow old. They just remain...stuck, forever trapped in a body consumed by bloodlust.

"I thought..." I swallow around the golf ball sized lump in my throat. "I thought the witch's council had taken care of that problem."

"There's always going to be bad men and women who crave more," Polo speaks for the first time, voice grim. "Some people can't be happy with the hand they were dealt."

Gabriel grunts in agreement, but Christian takes a step closer.

"But stay vigilant, Peony. I think I can speak for all of us when I say that we'd be devastated if anything happened to you." He glances at Nana, who grips my shoulder tightly. "The thing about Bloods... they look human, they act human, but they're not. At least, not completely. They're dangerous fuckers, and years, even centuries of control can't eradicate their desire for blood."

"Especially the blood of powerful magic users," adds Gabriel. "Just...be careful."

Bloods.

I shiver violently at the thought. These...*creatures* are talked about all the time in the coven, used as bedtime stories to deter kids from misbehaving. To know that there's one nearby? Or even a coven of them? It terrifies me. They're the apex predators in a world where *we're* supposed to be. Somehow, they found a way to cheat death.

And I know that if even one Blood catches whiff of me, they will all descend until I'm drained dry.

CHAPTER 12

"Leave me alone." My voice trembled, despite my best efforts to keep it steady. I wheeled around towards the four boys surrounding me, taunting smirks on their ridiculously hand- some faces. "Please." I hadn't meant to plead—witches didn't beg for anything—but the pathetic word tumbled out before I could reel it back in.

Panic burned a hole in my chest, incinerating my heart, as Cassian laughed giddily and grabbed my shoulders, pulling me forward. Before I could react—scream, cry, kick, cuss—a second set of hands grabbed my arms and wrenched them behind my back. I didn't even have to look to know that the cinnamon scent belonged to Karsyn.

Elias merely grinned where he leaned against the far wall. He never really participated when they were all together, preferring to watch his best friends from the sidelines. But that just made him more culpable. Willfully ignorant, but infinitely more dangerous.

But maybe ignorant wasn't the correct word to describe Elias Briggs. It wasn't as if a sick, twisted part of him didn't get off when I was tormented. I could see the excitement in his eyes, the slow curl of his lips, the hunger emanating from his pores. The psycho just preferred to torture me one-on- one instead of in a huge group.

"Don't cry, little witch," Lucas purred as he stepped closer. Lucas Scott. The devil in the flesh. I truly didn't believe in evil until I looked into his sea-blue eyes and saw them devoid of any warmth or compassion. To be frank, I couldn't remember a time I had ever seen him wear anything but an apathetic front. Even around his best friends, a cold glaze remained in his eyes, as if he was hewn from ice itself.

"Lucas." I trembled desperately as he took another step closer, raising a hand that held a pair of scissors. Cassian took a step back and began to laugh gleefully, while Karsyn's arms tightened. "Please, don't."

But my cries fell on deaf ears when he took the scissors to my white ponytail and cut all of the hair off. I watched it pool around my feet as his eyes glowed with satisfaction.

"Whoopsies," he taunted. "My hand slipped."

The rest of the guys broke into laughter as anger burned through me. I could feel it rippling in my veins, wave after wave of electricity, and before I knew what I was doing, I grabbed the scissors out of Lucas's hand.

Before he could scream, I stabbed the scissors into the side of his neck, watching as blood bubbled in his mouth and his jaw slackened in shock. His gorgeous eyes flickered to my face in horror as he tumbled to the ground.

"Whoopsies," I said darkly as Karsyn, Cassian, and Elias began to scream. "My hand slipped."

I WAKE UP IN A COLD SWEAT, MY HEART POUNDING, AS THE REMNANTS of my dream crashed over me like a damning tidal wave. It started as a memory of the time in seventh grade when they cut all of my hair off, but quickly transitioned into…

Into something beyond awful.

Did I really just dream about *murdering* Lucas Scott? Surely I'm not that desperate for revenge.

It feels as if I'm covered in a dark, sticky slime, one that I can't wipe off no matter how hard I scrub. It coats my hands, my arms, my legs, and my face, burning away my skin until I'm scratching at the fleshy meat underneath.

Tossing an arm over my head, I work to control my turbulent breathing as my heart thunders. Logically, I know that it was just a dream, that it doesn't mean anything, that I don't actually want to kill my childhood tormentors, but a tiny voice in my head screams at me, demanding to know how far I intend to go in the name of revenge.

And to be quite honest, it's pretty damn far.

The things they did to me are unfathomable. For years, they tortured and ridiculed me, picking at the scabs, never allowing them to heal properly. Even when I escaped them five years ago, the memory of their torment lingered with me, haunting me. I couldn't escape it.

Shaking my head rapidly to clear the fog residing there, I jump out of bed and grab a dark gray dress with a sweetheart neckline out of my closet. The sleeves run just to my wrists, and the skirt itself cinches around my waist in a tight belt. The outfit as a whole is gorgeous, especially when paired with my white-blonde hair, honey-colored eyes, and a light application of blush and mascara.

I don't bother looking at the clock on the wall. Based on the trickle of light ribboning my room in sheets of golden white, I would guess it's around seven. I'm running slightly behind schedule, but it's no matter. I can easily skip breakfast.

Climbing down the ladder, I dance inside the bathroom and finish getting ready for my day. When I emerge less than ten minutes later, it's to the smell of bacon wafting in the air. My mouth automatically waters as I glide forward, as if in a daze.

Polo is standing in the middle of the kitchen, just as he was the day before. He sings softly to himself as he scoops freshly scrambled eggs and two slices of bacon onto a plate. My to-go cup of coffee is ready as well, filled to the brim with cream, just the way I like it.

"Um…wow. T-Thanks," I stammer as I shove a piece of bacon into my mouth.

On second thought…

Maybe I won't skip breakfast this morning.

"You're welcome," Polo says with a friendly smile.

"Is Nana still sleeping?" I query, just to make conversation. Polo has his back towards me as he slaves over the stovetop, his bronze skin lathered in a light layer of sweat from the heat.

"I swear that woman could sleep through a nuclear explosion," he says fondly, before tacking on, "Another piece of bacon?"

"No thanks." I pick up the fork he placed beside the plate and stab the fluffy eggs. "This is delicious, by the way." I practically moan at the myriad of flavors—a combination of various cheeses, pepper, salt, and something I can't quite name. A secret ingredient, perhaps? "How did you learn to cook so well?"

"I have years of practice," he admits with a teasing wink.

"Oh, come on." I take a tentative sip of the coffee, my eyes rolling into the back of my head when I find the perfect proportion of creamer to coffee. "This is damn good coffee, too. But I'm serious. You can't be older than twenty-five." He raises an eyebrow at me, and I amend, "Twenty-six?"

Another dry look.

"Are you in your thirties?" I gape openly. None of the men look a day over twenty-five.

"A gentleman never reveals his age," he jests as I shovel the last mouthful of eggs.

"That's a lady." I point my fork at him, which he stealthily steals from my fingers. He takes my plate too and puts both in the dishwasher. "Oh, come on. Tell me! Thirty-one?"

He presses his lips into a thin line, as if he's trying to contain a smirk.

"Nope. Not telling. I'm going to let you sweat on it for a little while." He glances over my shoulder, and his eyebrows furrow in confusion. "Peony, are you expecting someone to drive you to school today?"

"No, why?" I follow his gaze out of the kitchen window towards where a strange Jeep lingers in the driveway. I squint, peering through the windshield, until I spot a familiar shock of brown hair with purple highlights. "Oh, come the fuck on."

"You know him?" Polo asks suspiciously, eyes narrowed and hands twitching. A small part of me wants to deny and have Polo race outside and spell Elias's ass to kingdom come. But then I remember my dream, and the urge abates as I scramble to my feet, picking my backpack off the ground.

"Unfortunately," I mutter, too softly for him to hear. Louder, I add, "He's a classmate." I grab my to-go cup and hurry towards the door. "Tell Nana that I have cheer practice and that she shouldn't worry if I get home late!"

"All right. Be safe!"

"You too." Giving him a two-fingered salute, I grab my coat off the hook and hurry outside.

My irritation exacerbates when Elias rolls down the window of his Jeep—a Jeep *and* a motorcycle? Really? Fucking rich kids—and leans his head out.

"I thought I would give you a ride," he calls, but I wave him away without actually speaking.

Honestly, I would rather eat shit than ever accept a ride from Elias fucking Briggs. Hell would freeze over first.

Ignoring him completely, I begin the long walk towards school, periodically checking my watch to make sure I'll still get to class a few minutes early.

"Peony, please. It's freezing." Elias's car has slowed to a crawl as it idles beside me. His gaze flickers from my face and then to the empty street. Damn Nana for living in the middle of nowhere. I would much prefer for there to be lots of traffic, forcing Elias to drive the speed limit.

I continue to ignore him as I grab my phone from my jacket pocket and thumb through the texts. Seven missed calls from Mom, of course, and a single text from Uriel.

Uriel: How's the new town? Hating life yet?

Me: Always.

Uriel: The Devils there?

Uriel is one of the few people who knows the truth about what happened to me five years ago. He hates the Devils almost as much as I do.

Me: Yup. There's one currently stalking me.

Uriel: WTF?!?

Me: Yup. Don't worry. I'm being smart. Miss you, loser.

Uriel: Miss you too.

Me: Tell Yoselin I said hi!

Uriel: Will do. Be careful. I don't trust them.

Some people might find it weird to be close friends with your ex's new girlfriend, but that's never been the case with us. I've known Yoselin since we were in diapers, and if anyone was a perfect match for Uriel, it's her.

Out of the corner of my eye, I see Elias's jaw clench as he focuses his gaze completely out the front windshield. But despite no longer glaring at me, he still doesn't drive away.

The next twenty minutes are fucking grueling as Elias continues a leisurely speed, easily keeping pace with me. I try my hardest to ignore him, but no matter what I do, where I look, I can sense him like a bug that sits on my skin.

Finally, after what feels like hours later, we arrive at the school, and I'm immensely grateful when Elias has to veer to the right in order to park his Jeep in the student lot. It allows me time to slip into school undeterred.

What game are you playing, Elias Briggs?

And how do I beat you at it?

CHAPTER 13

"Peony!" Mariabella's voice reaches me before I even touch my locker. I turn around to see her barreling towards me, golden blonde hair cascading around her in perfect ringlets. Today, she wears a gorgeous white sweater and skin-tight jeans, and though I know the temperature will increase during the day, reaching the upper seventies, I have to admit she looks stunning.

"Hey." I smile as I enter my combination, open my locker, and sort through my textbooks. I'll need my biology one, but I'll also need the sheet music Mr. Tucker gave us for Orchestra. Hopefully, I'll be able to stop at my locker after second hour and switch out my books for AP U.S. History.

"So, I was talking to Helen," she begins, leaning against the locker beside me and tucking a shiny strand of hair behind her ear, "and she mentioned that we're going to work solely on tumbling today." Her voice raises to a deafening squeal, garnering the attention of a few classmates nearby. But instead of being an excited screech, as I initially thought, I realize it's a terrified one when her face drains of all color.

"I take it you don't like tumbling," I muse as I slam my locker shut and lean against it.

"I'm horrible at it," she admits, blushing. "Absolutely awful. I've been trying to do a back handspring since freshman year." She leans closer to whisper conspiratorially. "I'm afraid Helen will cut me from the team if I don't get my shit together."

"No." I shake my head adamantly. "No way in hell. Helen loves you."

"As a person, yes. As a cheerleader, not so much." Mariabella's voice is laced with such self-loathing and pain, that my heart breaks for her. "The only reason she's keeping me on the team is because—"

"Because you're a damn good base," I finish for her, placing a hand on her shoulder. I give it a tight squeeze as her eyes flicker to my face in shock. "But if you're seriously worried about tumbling, I could spot you."

It shouldn't be too hard...right?

Mariabella's eyes light up as if I told her she won the lottery. "Do you mean it?" she whispers, breathless.

"I mean, yeah—" Before I can even finish speaking, she lunges at me with a squeal, wrapping her thin arms around my waist and jumping up and down. She rests her head on my breasts as she rocks us.

"Thank you, thank you, thank you, thank you, thank you—"

"I'm not gonna lie." Emmett's voice comes from directly behind me, and a moment later, I feel his chin on my shoulder. Flicking my eyes in his direction, I see a lazy grin playing on his lips, making him look like an overgrown house cat. "I totally imagined this moment last night when I was jerking off. But the only difference was that in my dream, you two were naked."

Mariabella pulls away from me as if I'm on fire, a scowl distorting her pretty features, even as her skin turns red.

"You're disgusting, Em."

"But you love it." He gives my cheek a chaste kiss, one that causes butterflies to take flight in my stomach, before pulling away and moving to complete our misshapen triangle. "Now, what are you thanking Peony for?"

"You're rather nosey today, did you know that?" Mariabella huffs with a small grin.

"Nosey? That's rather rude, wouldn't you say, Peony?" He bats his ridiculously long lashes at me. "It's perfectly acceptable to be curious about my best friends' lives."

"Best friend?" I snort in disbelief, giving his shoulder a half-hearted shove.

"Fine." He releases another petulant sigh. "I meant to say future girlfriend."

A snort of laughter escapes me unbidden as I roll my eyes to the heavens. "Mariabella's right—you are disgusting. And nosey."

"Hurtful!" He places his hand over his heart and adopts a slightly adorable frown.

But before I can tease him about it, I become aware of a figure rapidly approaching. The crowd parts for him instinctively, as if he has an electric force field around him that propels others away.

Lucas Scott looks handsome today, with his red hair slicked back and a comfy, dark green sweater clinging to his muscular frame. He even wears an easy-going smile, as if his beautiful face doesn't hide a monster. He's a psychopath made flesh, his perfection belying a dark and twisted soul.

"Lucas," I say curtly as he stops in front of me, shoving Emmett out of the way.

"I need to talk to you," he growls, the noise practically wrenched from his throat. It's primal and possessive, and for some odd reason, it sends a thrill shooting through me like a fallen star.

Flashing him a saccharine sweet smile, I step away from a frowning Mariabella and a scowling Emmett. "Of course," I all but purr, crooking my finger in a come-hither gesture. Lucas appears confused, a crease forming between his eyes, before he blanks his expression, steps in front of me, and leads me towards a nearly empty stairwell.

When we're alone, and he whirls towards me with the fires of hell in his eyes, I offer him another sugary smile, one guaranteed to give you toothache. "What can I do for you, Lucas?" I ask pleasantly.

"Why are you here?" he demands. He doesn't cross his arms over his chest. He doesn't take a step closer. Hell, he doesn't even blink as he stares down at me with his icy blue eyes. But he doesn't need to do any of that to make me terrified.

I try not to be intimidated, but a sliver of fear snakes down my back before I can contain it. Everything about Lucas is just so much...*more*. He might not be the largest in the room, he might not even possess any supernatural powers, but there's no denying that he's by far the scariest monster that ever walked this earth.

"Why. Did. You. Come. Back?" He says each word slowly, curtly, as if I'm hard of hearing or an imbecile. His condescending tone only makes my hackles rise, but I keep my smile firmly plastered on my face.

"To destroy you," I answer bluntly, and I have the brief satisfaction of seeing surprise flicker in his eyes, there and gone in less than a second. His lips don't even twitch as he meets my stare with a toe-curling one of his own.

"Excuse me?"

This man...he's the fucking Grim Reaper come to collect my soul and bring me to hell. I have no doubt about that. And maybe when this is all over, I'll be okay with selling my soul to the devil. I know I won't be the same girl I started as, because so many pieces have been carved away.

Maybe there will be nothing left of me at the very end for hell to even take.

"I think you heard me perfectly fine, Lucas," I say softly, almost smugly.

Like before, another emotion breaks through the cracks in his mask, and I see pure rage reflected back at me. I wonder if I look at him like that—like I want to put my hands around his throat and strangle the life out of him. Watch it bleed from his eyes.

Because I'll never hate anyone more than I hate Lucas Scott.

"You think you can destroy me?" He releases a harsh bark of laughter before dipping his head down, his lips a hair's breadth away from my own. "You don't have the power to do that, little witch. You're nothing to me, and you'll never be able to break me."

Despite his sincere words, I maintain my smile, knowing it'll only infuriate him more. "You sound scared, Lucas, and you should be. Because mark my words, I *will* destroy you. I'll make you wish you never met me." Pressing up onto my tiptoes, I place my lips directly to his ear. "I'll make you wish you never teased this *little witch.*"

His eyes darken as he glares down at me before he quickly replaces it with a smile of his own. He doesn't even bother to hide the insanity in his gaze, the cutting edge of his lips, the cruelness evident in the harsh planes of his face. He's beauty and death, and his eyes ensnare me as effectively as a knife slamming into my chest, rendering me immobile.

"Game on, little witch," he purrs, his tone reminding me of the forbidden fruit Eve ate. Something decadent and wicked. Something you know you shouldn't covet but do so anyway.

"Game on, asshat," I reply back, spinning on my heel and leaving the stairwell. I can feel his eyes on my skin as the door slams shut, effectively severing the pull he had on me. The intoxicating, insufferable pull.

Lucas Scott will be the hardest of all the Devils to break.

But it will just make his demise that much sweeter.

CHAPTER 14

For second hour Orchestra, Mr. Tucker sent us all to the private practice rooms. In his mind, we can't play as a cohesive unit if we're unable to perform individually.

Personally, I'm grateful for the reprieve from Felicia's constant sneers and scowls. The girl *really* doesn't like me much, which is odd because we play two completely different instruments. It's not as if we're competing for solos or anything, so what's her deal?

Ignoring the lingering stares I can feel piercing my spine, I hurry towards an empty practice room a few doors down. The first room I step into is already occupied, so I settle for the one beside that.

Which happens to be the same room I witnessed Cassian getting a blowie from our married English teacher. Oh, I really shouldn't laugh, but it's too damn funny not to.

Smirking slightly, I settle myself into the black chair and get comfortable before removing my instrument from the case. Well, not technically *mine*. I still have to borrow a violin from the school until I can afford to pay for my own. I've searched online, but even a used one is way out of my price range until I can find myself a paying job. I do have some money saved up from my time in the coven, but I'd planned to use that for college. It's not like I'm going to get financial help from Mommy Dearest. Hell, I'm not even sure if my grades are good enough to receive even a partial scholarship.

Frowning at the direction of my thoughts, I set the instrument beneath my chin and grab the stringed bow, content to lose myself for the next fifty minutes.

My body trembles with the need to play, to express myself. The confrontations with first Elias and then Lucas play on a continuous loop in my head as I disregard the sheet music and begin to play from my heart.

The song starts off slow, sad, almost melancholic as the bow dances across the four strings. And then, in tandem with my festering anger, the notes turn harsh and clipped. I can feel my lips curling into a scowl as I brutalize the instrument, pouring all of my pain into the instrumental song.

Pain. Heartache. Anger. Vengeance.

They all mesh together as I move my fingers rapidly over the strings. It feels almost euphoric to lose myself to the music, to the anger physically manifesting itself in each consecutive note.

Finally, I reach a crescendo moments before the song reaches a natural ending, the music ceasing as abruptly as it began. Just like my time here with the Devils. I've come in as an avenging angel, and then I'll disappear soundlessly into the night.

Slow clapping has me dropping the instrument and blinking wildly at the intruder.

Cassian fucking Jereome.

"You've gotten better, baby," he purrs as he grabs a second chair and sits on it backwards. He drapes his arms lazily over the back of the chair as he flashes me a singularly beautiful smile, one that reveals the dimples on both of his cheeks.

"Don't call me that," I huff as I lower the violin into my case, trying to pretend that I don't feel his eyes grazing every inch of exposed skin.

"Why? I remember hearing you play once in middle school, and you guys all sounded like a pack of dying hyenas." He chuckles gruffly, but my mind is struck on what he just confessed to. When did he ever hear me play? We didn't perform for the school, sans a family-only event in the spring. Had he planned something nefarious that day? Had he been there in the audience? Why didn't he do anything?

"Why are you here, Cassian?" I ask snidely as I clasp the locks on the case closed.

"I could be asking you the same thing." I hear the sound of his footsteps, and suddenly, he's hovering over me, those dark brown eyes of his drilling a hole into my scalp. One of his fingers touches my cheek, trailing from the corner of my eye, across my lips, and then to my chin. I can't help but notice that his hands are rougher than I would've guessed them to be. It's apparent that he uses these hands daily, the callouses clearly from a guitar. "What do you want, baby? Because I can give you everything your twisted heart desires." He leans down until his dark face is all I can see.

"What the... Are you trying to fucking seduce me?" I squeak, practically falling off the chair in my attempt to escape.

Abruptly, his eyes harden, and the lust that darkened them only a moment earlier dissipates. His plush lips curl downwards as he scowls at me.

"What you said before...in AP Lit..."

"About you fucking your married teacher?" I ask nonchalantly, enjoying the way he blanches. "What about it?"

He places his hands on either side of the chairback, leaning forward until he's caging me in. The hard planes of his chest brush against my pebbled nipples as I meet his glare with a defiant one of my own. I refuse to let him scare me. Fucking *refuse*.

"I don't know what you're talking about," he seethes. "That's a pretty serious accusation, baby."

"Huh?" I feign confusion, tapping a finger to my chin in mock contemplation. "So the video I have is of a *different* redheaded teacher sucking your cock? Hmmm. Interesting."

His eyes flare brightly, golden sparks interspersed in the rich mahogany brown.

"How the fuck...?"

"I'm a creepy freak, remember?" I say with a teasing grin. Maintaining eye contact, I press the tips of my fingers to the side of his cheek and slowly, almost seductively, trail them down to his neck. His eyes close as if he's in physical pain, his Adam's apple bobbing, but he doesn't pull away from my tantalizing touch.

"You don't understand what you're talking about," he breathes at last, and out of my peripheral vision, I can see goosebumps dotting his muscular arms.

"I think you know *exactly* what I'm talking about," I murmur as his eyelids flutter open, his eyes spearing me to the chair.

"Did you like it, baby?" His voice is husky, almost a growl, as I continue to rub my fingers up and down his face.

"Like what?"

"My cock," he breathes out, his tongue snaking out to lick his lower lip. "Do you want a taste of my cock, baby? I can give it to you, if you want. All I need—"

A breath of laughter escapes me before I can contain it, and I drop my fingers from his face. Another string of giggles follows as I clench my stomach, and Cassian pushes away with a huff.

"Are you...ser-seriously...trying to...se-seduce me again?" I brush away a tear as laughter continues to reverberate through my body. "Your cock in exchange for the video? What the fuck is wrong with you?"

He straightens to his full, impressive height, nearly a full foot taller than me, and scowls, looking every inch the dark, seductive prince.

"You can't show anyone that video," he says seriously.

"Why? Because you won't be able to sneak around with your perverted lover?" I ask, still trying to get my laughter under control.

Cassian shakes his head vehemently as tension causes his shoulders to tighten. "No, I don't give a fuck about that. Peony, please. You can't show anyone that video."

"Didn't I say the same thing in middle school when you guys posted the video of my first kiss with Elias?" I query thoughtfully.

"Peony…"

I jump to my feet and tilt my head up until I can see into his damning eyes—the eyes of a demon. Not the devil—that spot is reserved for Lucas—but one of his evil minions content to destroy the world and everyone in it.

"You made your own bed, Cassian. I'm just helping you lie in it."

His eyes harden into chips of obsidian as something undefinable flashes across his face.

"You're different, aren't you?" he muses. "You're no longer that scared girl anymore."

Anger hardens my features and my heart. "You killed that scared little girl," I retort venomously. "And this is what you're left with."

For a brief, brief moment, I swear I see pain and something akin to regret flicker in his eyes. But it's there and gone before I can know for certain.

"You don't know what you're doing," he warns as his hands clench into fists at his sides.

"I know *exactly* what I'm doing," I purr as I place my hands on both of his shoulders and slowly slide them down his bare arms. Once more, he doesn't push me away, but his eyes remain as cold as ice. "Now, go find your actual 'baby' and leave me the fuck alone."

"No can do, baby," he mocks, reaching down to open his guitar case. "All of the other practice rooms are full, and I need to work on this piece."

"This room's full, too," I hiss through gritted teeth, resisting the urge to deck him over the head. He merely smiles, flashing those blindingly white teeth in my direction, as he grabs his guitar and begins to pluck absently at the strings, moving to return to the chair he pulled up.

"I always thought we could make pretty music together, baby," he confesses, and I can't tell if he's mocking me or not. Probably, because he's calling me "baby" again, the fucker. I hate that endearment, and if his smug smile is any indication, he knows it. Which only means he'll use it more often.

For a long moment, I simply stare at him in silence as he focuses on the strings of his guitar, tuning the instrument. My eyes track his long, slender fingers as they twist the knobs and then strum the strings. "But that instrument you have there is a piece of shit. Is that a chip I see in your violin?"

"You're such a jackass." With a huff, I throw myself back into my chair, prepared to ignore him the entire hour. Or else I just might be liable to kill him. Why does he have to infiltrate my life like an annoying gnat that won't go away no matter how many times you swat at it? Why does he insist on staying and annoying the shit out of me? The answer's simple—he's a sadist.

"I have a nice ass," he corrects immediately. "Super hard. Could bounce a penny off of it. Actually..." He puts down his guitar, stands, and then reaches into all of his pockets until he procures a penny. "Throw it at me." He then proceeds to stick his ass out at me and shake it.

"I'll ram it up your asshole," I threaten, but my eyes are automatically drawn to those granite cheeks, emphasized by the tight jeans he wears.

"Wow, baby. How'd you know I like anal play?" He whirls towards me, one hand over his mouth in mock horror.

I bite down hard enough on my lower lip to draw blood as I bring the violin back to my chin.

But I can't. Fucking. Play.

Not with him watching me.

Not with those golden-brown orbs traveling across my body as if he wishes to undress me and fuck me over the top of my music stand.

Kinky motherfucker.

"You gonna play or just sit there looking murdery?" Cassian quips.

"I prefer the term 'stabby,' as in, 'I'm mentally planning to stab you a thousand times,'" I quip, my dry sense of humor making an impromptu appearance.

His damn smirk remains in place. "If it's a knife up my bumhole…"

"Oh my god. You're ridiculous!" I throw my hands up in the air, one still holding the neck of the violin and the other the bow.

"I'm an insatiable asshole," he admits with a shameless shrug. "Literally. I'm insatiable…about having stuff in my ass."

I physically bang my head against the music stand.

"I'm going to pretend you don't exist for a few minutes, okay?" I snap, bringing my violin up to my chin for the *billionth fucking time*.

But before I can continue the piece I've been practicing, Cassian begins to play. Only my eyes move to watch him, hypnotized.

His fingers slide across the strings as he lowers his head, eyes fluttering shut. For the first time, there's no mocking mirth in his eyes. No wickedly sinful smile pulling up his lush lips. He looks… vulnerable. Sincere. The harsh planes of his face appear softer, if that's even possible.

I recognize the song as "Hallelujah" by Leonard Cohen. It's one of my favorites to play on the violin, one that I don't even need sheet music to play.

As if my hand is being moved by some unseen force, I lower the bow to my instrument and begin to play the melody. I allow the music to rush through me as the familiar notes fill the air. Cassian immediately switches to the harmony, our notes joining together to create the most beautiful masterpiece I've ever heard.

I want to hate the music we make together, I honestly do, but I find myself lost in the mesmerizing combination. My violin's high-pitched notes juxtaposed by his low ones.

And for a brief, brief moment, I feel as if our souls are merging. As if our music is screaming at us to stop this incessant fighting and be at peace. It's stupid, I know, and entirely irrational, but I can't help but feel that we're perfect duet partners.

I'll never find someone like this to play with again.

As if they have a life of their own, my eyes open and clash with Cassian's dark, smoldering ones. I don't know how to describe it, but it feels as if my soul is physically crawling out of my body and into his. I can't tell you for certain where he ends and I begin. All I'm aware of is the music pulsing through my veins, stealing the air from my lungs and leaving me breathless. My heart pounds in my chest as my fingers move across the strings.

As the song tapers off, we both bow our heads, allowing the music to pulsate through our very bones. At least they do in mine. The moment is beautiful and perfect and slightly ethereal.

"You're even better than you were before," Cassian whispers, sounding awed.

"Thanks." Heat enters both of my cheeks as I lower my head. "You sounded pretty good yourself."

"I should be," he states, his tone for once devoid of his usual teasing. "I've been playing for years."

"I remember that." Even at a young age, Cassian always found an excuse to play music. He lived and breathed it the same way I did. Honestly, if he wasn't my enemy, we could've even been friends. There's something about music that propels two individuals together, like a ponytail around your wrist being pulled tightly and then snapping back into place. "You still play in that one band?"

He chuckles softly, the low noise reverberating through me just as effectively as his music did. "The Rockets? Yeah, no. Ended that band my sophomore year. There's a band I sometimes play with, but

I'm not truly a member. Now, I just play for me." He absently plucks at a few strings, his mind seemingly a thousand miles elsewhere.

"That's the same for me," I confess, the words tumbling from my mouth before I can think better of it. I shouldn't be talking to Cassian like this. I'm supposed to hate him, destroy him. So why don't I want to leave? "Music is… It's an escape. A way to forget about everything wrong in life, you know?"

He nods seriously, those golden-brown eyes drilling a hole into my scalp with their intensity. "I do." A wry smirk pulls up those thick lips of his. "I wanted to stop playing when my dad left, but you want to know what my mom told me?"

His dad left? I don't remember the man well, but I do recall an older gentleman with similar chocolate skin and sparkling brown eyes.

My heart aches for Cassian, because absentee parents? That… that I can relate to.

"What did your mom say?" I query, even as the small niggle in the back of my mind becomes a large, battering ram against my subconscious. Every instinct shouts at me to leave, to remember what he did to me, but I can't get my feet to move. I *want* to hear what he has to say. I want to hear everything.

He licks his lips, the movement almost reflexive. "That you don't play music for others. Fans. Agents. Crowds. You don't play for them. Sure, they hear it, and if you're a good enough musician, they can understand why you play, but they're not your target audience. You only truly play for yourself. That…" He swallows heavily. "That stuck with me. And it made me realize that my dad may have brought me into the music world, but I'm staying in it because I want to. I'm staying because I love playing. I don't need a band or anything to do what I love. Maybe in a few years, I'll be the next Santana."

We exchange soft smiles that aren't laden with years of pain and hurt. No animosity pings between us as we stare at one another, his brown eyes locked with my amber ones. For a brief moment, I allow myself to imagine a future where we don't hate each other. Where we, dare I say, have a chance of being friends.

Until Cassian has to open up his big, stupid mouth and ruin everything.

"Anyway, I told you we'll make beautiful music together, baby. I'm compatible with just about everyone." He chuckles darkly, even as his eyes turn guarded. Cruel. It's almost as if…

Almost as if he's afraid of the moment we just had. As if he felt the electrical pulse between the two of us just as I had and now wants to run from it.

"Just ask Mrs. Town," he finishes with a sideways smirk.

The warm fuzzies I felt earlier dissipate, only to be replaced by something much, much colder. I mimic his cruel smile, even as my heart twists into a pretzel. At the same time, I refuse to believe that our interaction only meant something to me. He stared at me *tenderly*. Those brown eyes, flecked with gold, sparkled with a light I've never seen before. He wouldn't do that if he really hated me.

But a tidal wave of unbridled anger quickly brushes those thoughts away.

"Then maybe you should go to her," I suggest, trying not to feel hurt by his words. There's no fucking reason for me to be. I hate him, after all. *Despise* him.

Even if we do make beautiful music together.

"Maybe I will," he responds gruffly.

"Goodbye, *baby*," I snap.

With a mocking smirk, I give him my back, a slight I know will piss him off. It shows him that I'm no longer afraid of him, that his words don't hurt me, that I don't perceive him as a threat. Not anymore.

I hear the sound of the door opening and closing as he leaves, and my grin widens.

I meant what I said.

Their downfall will be their own doing, but that doesn't mean I can't have a little fun along the way.

Smirking at my sudden epiphany, I check to make sure I'm alone before reaching into my backpack and grabbing the voodoo doll with black, coarse hair wrapped around its neck.

Cassian apparently can't keep his cock out of women.

Maybe I can help him with that…

CHAPTER 15

The rumors reach me at lunchtime.

Even before I sit down, whispers surround me, causing my grin to broaden even further.

"...so *big*."

"You saw it, right?"

"I wonder what happened."

I'm feeling pretty damn smug when I throw myself into the chair opposite Emmett, who's currently bent over his textbook to prepare for a test later today.

"What's the smile for?" he asks with an easygoing grin. "Did you commit a murder? Because I'll have you know, I already hid one body this week. I don't think I want to hide another one."

"No murder. No body." My smile turns fucking dopey as he leans across the table, his arm muscles bunching enticingly.

"What's up?"

"Did you hear?" Mariabella hurries to our table like a whirlwind of sleet, pelting and destroying everything in her path. Karsyn stands behind her, resembling a grumpy, scowling bodyguard. His eyes dart to me as he moves to take the seat beside her. When I meet his gaze point-blank, he quickly glances down at his tray of noodles and his carton of milk.

"Hear what?" Emmett asks eagerly. I'm beginning to believe that Emmett enjoys gossiping more than most girls. And no, I'm not saying that to be sexist or anything—I know guys are big gossips too—but I swear Emmett's going to have a profession as a paparazzi or something. He needs to know *everything.*

"About Cassian Jereome," Mariabella says simply, and Karsyn's head snaps up in surprise.

"What about him?" he queries.

And honestly, I sort of want to punch him in the face. There's literally no reason except for the fact that his voice only makes me hate his guts more.

"Apparently," she lowers her voice to a hushed murmur so as to not be overheard, "he's been walking around with a raging boner since second period. Like, it's so big that he literally looks like he's in physical pain. He went home a little while ago."

I bring my water bottle to my lips to hide the snort that threatens to escape.

Because that boner?

Yeah, I take credit for it. It's surprisingly easy to spell a voodoo doll to have resting cock face.

And the best part is that he'll not even be able to relieve himself until I say so. I'm not a sadist or anything—I won't make the man suffer for *too* long—but it's only fitting that the manwhore spends a few hours with a painful boner, wouldn't you say?

Hell, he might even seek out little miss teacher in a failed attempt to relieve...

I tighten my grip on the water bottle as the thought crosses my mind.

Why does that thought bother me so fucking much?

Maybe it's because she's a predator taking advantage of someone significantly younger than her and in a subordinate position. She's supposed to be someone kids can rely on and talk to. Confide in. And what does she do? Exploit her position.

A memory creeps at the edges of my vision, threatening to consume me, but I shove it down with a vigorous internal shake of my head.

Now is *not* the time. I should be enjoying my victory, dammit, not reminiscing on the painful past.

"So you're saying that Cassian went home," Karsyn begins slowly, carefully, gauging our reactions, "because of a boner?"

"That's *exactly* what we're saying," Mariabella exclaims triumphantly.

I really, really need to tone down my smug grin. It might give people the impression that I'm the cause of the boner. Which I am, of course, but not for reasons they'll assume.

"Enough about boners and penises," Emmett drawls, and Karsyn wrinkles his nose like a fucking prude. Honestly, I remember him being the jokester of the group back in elementary and middle school. Always quick-witted and smart-tongued. There was constantly a sly retort dripping from his lips like honey, trapping us helpless flies in an unbreakable trap.

When did he become such a boring fuck?

"What's up, Em?" Mariabella asks sweetly, placing her cheek on her open palm and twisting to face him. He smiles mischievously, those gorgeous dimples making an appearance, before he focuses his jungle-green eyes on me.

"So, the homecoming party is coming up…"

"The homecoming dance?" I query, and this time, it's me who wrinkles her nose. Because yeah, dances and me? We don't really go together. The only dance I went to was in middle school, and it was one of the worst days of my fucking life.

"You look beautiful," Elias's raspy voice curled around me as I gazed into his honey brown eyes tinted with purple. Some of the girls in the class gossiped that he wore colored contacts, but I believed them to be his natural

eye color. The shade was so exotic, so Elias, that I refused to believe anything else.

"I-um...thanks," I replied shyly as his hands landed on my waist and we began to sway. The dress I wore was azure in color, stopping just below my knees. Nana had driven to my house earlier in the day to curl my white-blonde hair so it fell around me in shiny waves.

I had to admit that Elias looked stunning in his khaki brown pants and his blue polo shirt. His brown hair was pushed away from his smooth-shaven, arresting face.

At the edge of the gymnasium, I could see numerous teachers milling about, watching the proceedings unfold. My eyes latched on Mr. Gurrel before I quickly looked away, shame threatening to consume me, filling me like water in an over-inflated balloon, mere seconds from bursting.

"You okay?" Elias asked gently, lifting his right hand from my waist to run his fingers through my hair. After they cut it off, it had taken months for it to grow to the length it was now—nearly to my shoulders. But it was okay. Elias apologized and told me that he was sorry.

Everything was going to be okay.

I pull myself out of my memory, shaking my head vehemently.

Younger me was such a fucking dumbass. How could she have seriously believed the Devils? Did she take too many hits to the head during dodgeball?

Sometimes, I wish I could go back in time and shake my younger self. And zap the Devils to kingdom fucking come.

"...no!" Emmet's saying now around his laughter. "The homecoming dance is fucking lame. I'm talking about the party Karsyn always throws. He invited you, right?"

Karsyn's throwing a party?

I turn towards the football player in question, who's glaring at me with vitriol in his eyes. He shakes his head subtly, a clear indicator that I should decline, but a wicked idea occurs to me.

I mean, I *could* tell them that I haven't heard about the party, that

Karsyn hadn't invited me, that I'm just the poor new girl struggling to make friends.

But pity has never been a component of this game.

So instead, I smile brightly, ignoring Karsyn's searing warning look. "Of course I was invited! After the football game, correct?" That's just an educated guess, but when else would they have the party?

"It's going to be so much fun!" Mariabella gushes. "You're coming, right?"

Karsyn growls, the low noise erupting from his chest and causing goosebumps to pebble on my skin. There's something decidedly carnal and primitive about it that calls to me. Something that screams of dark nights between the sheets and hunts in the woods where he chases me and I willingly give myself over to him.

"I'll go." I place a strawberry in my mouth and wrap my lips around it, my tongue darting out slightly. Karsyn's eyes drop to the fruit, and his breath hitches as his hands grip the edge of the table. Maintaining eye contact, I slowly bite off the tip of the strawberry and lick the juices from my lips. "It'll be fun."

It'll be very, very fun.

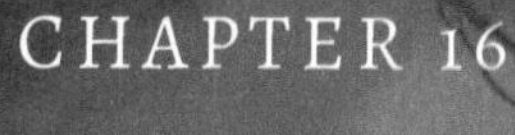

Once class ends for the day, I make quick work of changing into my standard cheer attire. Unlike the movies and television shows depict, we don't wear our uniforms to practice. Instead, most of the girls wear ratty T-shirts and shorts that don't hinder their ability to move. I choose to wear my standard long-sleeved shirt, this one a bright blue, and a pair of spandex shorts that, in all honesty, make my ass look great. I quickly tie my white hair back into a high ponytail, making sure to secure all of the wayward strands, before heading out of the locker room.

Believe it or not, I'm actually *excited* for cheerleading practice. Though Helen is a hard-ass, she's a damn good cheerleading coach. And I actually like the twelve other girls on the team. After I proved myself to them, they opened up to me and welcomed me into their fold. I'm not used to having female friends. To be completely honest, I'm not used to having *any* friends. People in middle school steered clear of me, especially when the Devils honed in on me and declared me public enemy number one. Back at the coven, I stayed mainly to myself, too afraid that every kind gesture would have a malicious intent behind it. How could I not be paranoid? My entire childhood was built on lies and deceit. When it wasn't the charming Devils terrorizing me and making me afraid of my own shadow, it was my own fucking mother demanding more than I could ever give.

I don't trust easily.

Come to think of it, I don't trust at all.

Why would I willingly hand out trust when everyone in my life inevitably betrays me?

Shaking my head to clear the macabre thoughts, I exit the locker room and walk down the hallway. Unlike the guys' locker room, the girls' is on the opposite end of the hall and does not lead directly to the football field or even the gymnasium. Instead, we're forced to walk past the cafeteria and to a second hallway that ends with a door to the fields.

I've just reached the end of the hall when I feel a pair of eyes on me. I don't know how to describe it. Except it's like someone is physically running the pad of their finger up and down the nape of my neck, and then that same finger travels the length of my bare spine in an icy caress. It's the feeling you get when you're in a crowded room and every eye fixates on you.

Someone is watching me.

Every hair on my body stands on end as I glance inconspicuously in both directions, ensuring the hallway is empty. But it's when I turn around, towards the direction of the cafeteria, where only a thin plate of glass separates me from the dozens of tables, that I see him.

Cassian has his arms crossed over his broad chest, a scowl etched firmly in place.

What...? How...?

How is he here?

I try to keep my shock off my face as I stare into his obsidian black eyes. I know that they're actually a deep, mahogany brown, but from this distance, they appear to be endless abysses. Black holes you could become lost in, swept away in tidal wave after tidal wave.

His muscular forearms flex as he glares at me, and unwittingly, my gaze slides to his crotch.

And his limp dick.

What the ever-loving fuck?

There's no way in hell he should've been able to break my spell. It's unheard of.

Cassian Jereome is still supposed to have blue balls.

So where the fuck is his erection?

I could almost laugh at the direction of my thoughts. How has my life come to this? Staring intently at the penis of my bully as I wait to see if he has a boner? Not for the first time, I wonder if I'm taking this whole revenge thing too far, but a flood of incandescent anger sweeps away any hint of trepidation or remorse. They *tortured* me. Locked me in the middle school locker room over the weekend. Shoved me in a locker. Broke my heart.

What I'm doing is only cosmic justice.

Karma is a bitch, my friends, and she just so happens to go by the name of Peony Simone.

When he crooks his finger in a come-hither gesture, beckoning me towards him, I turn on my heel and promptly step away, pushing open the heavy doors to exit the building.

His attention leaves me feeling dirty and disheveled, almost as if I'd rolled around in a mud pit. I desperately scrub at both my arms, hoping to dispel the nauseating aroma permeating the air and clogging my nostrils, but it proves to be hopeless.

How can Cassian, even after all of these years, still affect me like this? Why does one tiny stare from him brand my skin as if he has taken a cattle prod, dipped it in molten lava, and then stuck it to my forehead?

Because even after all of these years, you still—

I shut that thought down quickly. No, not just shut it down. I close all the doors, flip off the lights, switch the sign from open to closed, and then scream at the top of my lungs, "I'm not home!"

"...asshole!" The familiar voice causes my feet to stagger slightly, and I brace one hand against the brick siding for support. Quieting my footsteps, I peek around the corner to see Mariabella and Karsyn huddled together. Tears brim in my friend's eyes as she glares up at him, fury like I've never seen before engraved onto her beautiful face. Karsyn appears tired, almost discouraged, and his head hangs forward, shaggy blond hair concealing his eyes from view.

From this angle, I can only see their profiles, but it's enough to send a sharp stab of...of...something straight to my chest. I can't identify or define the emotion, but seeing the two of them together has me rubbing absently at my chest, as if I could somehow fix the organ currently crumbling to dust inside of it.

"I can't keep doing this," Mariabella whispers, voice hoarse. She shakes her head slightly, wispy blonde hair framing her angelic face. "I don't—"

"It's your decision, Mar." Karysn's voice is softer than I've ever heard it before. And once more, that pesky pang returns with a damning vengeance, threatening to drag me straight to hell. It's obvious that he cares about her. A lot.

And why the fuck do I care so much?

"Just...just leave, please," Mariabella chokes out, and before I can duck away and pretend that I haven't been blatantly eavesdropping, Karsyn turns in my direction. Fury dances in his eyes as he levels me with a glare capable of dropping a lesser man dead on the spot. But instead of cowering in fear, instead of apologizing profusely, I hold my chin up stubbornly as if I had every intention of getting caught.

Fake it til you make it. Or however that saying goes.

"Eavesdropping much?" Karsyn snarls, and Mariabella's head jerks up. She quickly wipes at her blotchy eyes, but tears fall faster than she can catch them.

"Don't be an ass," Mariabella and I snap at the same time.

And it brings me great satisfaction when Karsyn's scowl deepens even further.

With a disgruntled huff, he stalks away from his girlfriend, purposely ramming his shoulder into mine when he passes.

"Watch it, Simone," he hisses through gritted teeth.

"Back at you, Alder," I reply, ignoring him completely to give Mariabella a tight hug. She immediately collapses in my arms with a pained sob and heart-wrenching whimper. I'm momentarily at a loss of what to do, so I settle for awkwardly patting her back. "There. There."

Over her shoulder, I level my own glare at Karsyn, who is already retreating, his hands shoved into his pockets and his head hung.

"What the fuck did the asshole do?" I hiss.

"I don't want to talk about it." She sniffles.

"Well…whatever it is, I'm sorry." It feels like such an insignificant word, but it's the only one I can think of to use. "I don't know what happened between the two of you, but I'm sorry you fought."

"I…I just…" She squeezes me tightly once before reluctantly releasing me. Bringing both hands up to her face, she begins to flick away tears as if they're pesky inconveniences. "You're a good friend, Peony."

"If you ever need to talk…" I allow the offer to linger in the air, not bothering to say more. We don't know each other very well, but I'll be there for her if she needs an ear to listen to or a shoulder to cry on. Or a fist that can be used to punch Karsyn Alder in his stupidly handsome face.

And I also vow, right then and there, that no matter what happens, I won't pull Mariabella into my revenge scheme against the Devils. Originally, I wanted to get close to her in order to harm Karsyn, but that's not fair. It only makes me hate myself a little bit more. She's innocent in all of this, and so far, she's been one of my only friends.

I *will* make the Devils pay, but I refuse to drag Mariabella into hell along with them.

CHAPTER 17

The next morning marks the day of my first ever football game—and also homecoming. Per our coach's requirements, I'm wearing the standard cheerleading uniform we were issued the day before. Fortunately, the black sleeves are long, stopping just at my wrist. It's actually pretty damn comfortable, the material both soft and flexible. The dark red, almost burgundy in appearance, of the shirt contrasts nicely against the onyx black of the sleeves and skirt. I've braided the front of my hair away from my face and clipped it at the back, allowing the rest of my white hair to cascade in loose curls.

When I step into the kitchen, it's to see Nana at the dining room table, bent over a spellbook. There's a diagram stenciled into the table, but from this angle, I can't tell for certain what it is. All I can see are sharp angles and numerous candles. An ancient grimoire rests in front of Nana as she closes her eyes and begins to speak softly in Latin.

A witch can perform a spell in a few different ways. Some can use their natural magical abilities and simply call upon their magic. It takes years and years of training to master that particular skill. And of course, there are the physical objects and hex bags that you can spell. Say, for instance, voodoo dolls? These usually require incantations and intricate spellwork, but it's less taxing on your internal magic reserve. And finally, there's the old-fashioned, recite-from-a-grimoire magic. Usually, these magical books are passed down from generation to generation. When Nana dies, she'll gift the book to Mom as her last act before the ancestors accept her into the afterlife.

"Whatcha doing?" I ask cautiously, and Nana whips her head up so fast, I'm honestly afraid she broke her neck.

"Nothing," she says quickly. Too quickly. She slams the spellbook shut and moves to stand in front of the table, obscuring the strange, chalk markings from view. Honestly, if she's trying for subtlety, she's failing at it epically. My curiosity now piqued, I attempt to look behind her.

"Seriously, Nana. What's going on?" She doesn't stop me as I peer over her shoulder at the pentagram etched in chalk across the table. The smiling photograph of an unfamiliar woman lies directly in the center. She appears to be around twenty, maybe a year or two older, with wheat-colored hair and sparkling eyes. "Who's this?" I query as I pick up the picture.

And why the hell is my nana performing a spell on her?

"She's a young witch. Ali." Nana sighs tiredly, moving to take the photograph from my hand. Her features soften as she stares at the young girl's face. "She went missing last night."

Understanding dawns on me with the force of a freight train barreling me over at one hundred miles per hour.

"And they think the Bloods took her," I surmise, and she offers me a barely perceptible nod.

"The witch's council asked me to do a tracking spell to find her," she confesses, and I just barely rein in my grimace. Because that type of magic? It's powerful. And though Nana is immensely powerful in her own right, to garner that much magic as a sex witch would mean...

Things I don't want to think about. Ever. Bleach from mind.

"But this spell would only work if she's—"

"Still alive, yes." Nana nods sadly as she lowers the picture once more onto the table. "And unfortunately, the spell failed. Again. This is my fifth time trying."

My heart hurts at the realization that this girl, this witch, is probably dead. No, not probably. The only reason Nana's magic wouldn't find her would be because she's already dead. Poor Ali.

"Is there anything I can do?" I ask meekly, swallowing the tennis ball-sized lump in my throat.

"Stay safe." A wide smile suddenly blossoms on her face as she gives me a once-over, the morose expression disappearing completely. "And you look adorable! Is today really your first game?"

"Yeah." I tug self-consciously on the hem of my shirt. Is it too tight? Too thin? Does it make me look fat? All of my insecurities play on repeat in my mind as I shift awkwardly from foot to foot. "We're playing the Hawks tonight."

"Oh! We'll be there!" She raises her voice to be heard upstairs. "Christian! Grab my camera! I want to get a picture of Peony!"

"God, Nana, no…" My protests fall on deaf ears when Christian enters the kitchen a minute later, smiling brightly and carrying a camera.

"Don't you look cute!" he practically coos, like one would when staring at an adorable dog. He continues to offer me that infectious smile, one that even the grumpiest person in the world can't resist. "Smile for the camera!"

I awkwardly flash my teeth, cheeks burning one thousand degrees, before I grab my packed lunch from the fridge.

"Stop it," I murmur, blushing.

"Another one?" Christian asks Nana seriously. "Maybe this time a photo of the two of you?"

"Oh my god. I'm leaving. Bye." Still keeping my head lowered, I hurry towards the foyer to grab my light jacket. The weather in

Michigan ranges from sweltering hot to miserably cold. There is no in between, and you never know what the bipolar weather will do next.

"Perfect timing," Gabriel says, just as I slip my hands into the sleeves of my coat. A cigarette dangles lazily from his mouth, and he removes it to blow a puff of smoke out the opened window. "Your stalker is here."

"My stalk—Oh fuck."

Sure enough, when I glance out the window, Elias's Jeep is idling in the driveway. His features are shadowed, but I can see his fingers tapping against the steering wheel.

"Ugh." Groaning, I rub a hand down my face, grab my backpack from where I discarded it on the floor the night before, and hurry out the door. "Bye, Nana!" I call out as I exit, hurrying away before I can hear her reply.

Like it's becoming our new routine, I ignore Elias and begin my trek down the long, curving driveway. And like before, he slows his Jeep to a crawl as he keeps pace with me.

"My stalker returns," I deadpan, and his lips twitch ever so slightly.

"Stalker is such a strong word," he muses as he puts on his hazards, allowing a car to pass him.

"Is creeper a better description?" I quirk a brow at the stunning man, malice lacing my tone. But instead of being offended, Elias throws his head back in laughter. The sound does strange things to my body, things I refuse to look at too closely. I remind myself that this is the same man who laughed when I was completely and utterly humiliated in front of the school, and some of my lust abates.

But not all.

He doesn't respond to my inquiry. Instead, he taps his fingers against the steering wheel, his eyes flickering to me every few seconds. Elias and silence…they go together. He doesn't usually have anything to say, so when he does speak, you just know it's going to be important. He was that way in middle school too. The silhouette behind his friends, constantly observing but not always participating. I don't know if that makes him even more culpable for what was done to me or less.

I continue walking until it feels as if I might burst from the silence. "If you're going to shadow me, the least you could do is speak, instead of just acting like a weird, creepy mouth-breather," I huff, whirling on him. He slows his car down even more until it's practically stopped in the middle of the street. There's a tiny smirk on those delectably wicked lips, one that makes the tiny scar on his left cheek appear even more pronounced. But instead of hindering his appearance, it only adds to his appeal. It makes him seem rugged and unattainable. Hard and gruff and dangerous.

"Words are strange," he answers simply, fiddling with a dial on his Jeep. A second later, soft classical music drifts from his speakers. He nods his head at the radio, as if pleased with the song selection, before turning to face the road once more. "You're supposed to string them together to create some type of meaning. You do this for monologues, for novels, for songs, for normal, everyday conversations. But look at the English dictionary. There are dozens of words that mean joy. So which one will you use to describe yourself, if you had to? Jovial, enthusiastic, happy—"

"So you don't talk...because there are too many words?" I ask bluntly, and those violet-brown eyes of his glimmer in the morning light.

"I don't talk because there's usually nothing to say," he counters immediately, and then he pauses, eyes turning contemplative he taps his fingers in time to the grand piano. "Except...except for when I'm talking to you."

I try to ignore the surge of butterflies that take flight in my stomach as I peer out of my peripheral vision at the striking, evasive man. Currently, his brown and purple hair is pulled into a loose bun at the top of his head. A few strands frame his face, but it doesn't make him look any less masculine. I'm pretty sure Elias could wear a tutu and a sparkly headband and still look like something out of a magazine.

"Is that why you've been showing up at school?" I blurt, and when he turns to stare at me, one eyebrow quirked, I realize my slip. "I mean, I heard from some of the other cheerleaders that you usually skip the morning classes."

But not now.

I'm pretty sure since I arrived, he's had a perfect attendance record.

"I told you," he evades with a small smirk. "I don't like talking to people."

"That doesn't answer my question," I point out, but his smile simply grows, turning almost smug, as we turn onto the road that leads towards our school. "What do you even *do* when you skip?"

"What do you *think* I do?" he counters immediately. Amusement dances in his eyes before he focuses once more out the windshield. "Let me guess…have illicit affairs. Partake in drug deals. Rob convenience stores. You know, the stereotypical 'bad boy' thing." He gives me a glance that makes me feel indignant.

"Well, you *do* feed into it—riding a motorcycle, wearing a leather jacket…" I protest, gesturing towards him. "And you have this whole…" I trail off once more, unable to articulate my thoughts without sounding like an imbecile.

Of course, Elias won't let the conversation drop.

"Have that whole what?" He bites down on his lower lip to keep from laughing at me.

"That whole… Ahhh!" I wave at him in dismay.

"Are you saying that my face makes you scream? I'm hurt." He places one hand to his chest in mock offense, while his eyes alternate between me and the road. Through it all, that damn smirk remains firmly in place.

"You know, that whole 'stay the fuck away from me or else I'll cut you' thing going on," I confess in a rush. He stares at me for a long moment, his jaw slack, before he breaks into raucous laughter. Tears stream down his face as he slaps at his knee.

"You have me pegged," he chortles.

"Stop it." Embarrassment burns my face as I pick up my speed. "It's not funny."

"It *is* pretty damn funny," he protests around another laugh. "Maybe that's what I need to do with my spare time when I decide to skip again…cut someone." He throws his head back once more, and I can't decide if the noise irritates me or…arouses me. Definitely the former.

Definitely.

"Whatever," I huff.

"And if you must know, I usually do exactly this," he says simply.

"Terrorize innocent females?" I mumble under my breath, but he still manages to hear.

"Sit in my Jeep. Listen to music. Smoke a few joints. Forget about the world," he answers, and I have a feeling he's being sincere. Which is strange. If what he said is true, then words are special to him.

So why did he waste them on me?

And why do I care that he did?

When we arrive at school, Elias once more branches off to park in the student lot while I head into the building. I don't know why I'm so reluctant to let him go, but I find my eyes trailing after the Jeep until it disappears around the side of the building.

As the wise Taylor Swift once said, shake it off, Peony.

The hallways are already full when I enter, and a few heads turn my way as I walk towards my locker. Self-consciousness pierces me like an arrow shot from a bow, and I have the sudden, irrational need to duck my head. To hide my face and pretend that everyone isn't staring at me.

Is my skirt too short? Can they see my scars? Do I look weird? Ugly? Different? Do I look like a freak?

I try to shove those insecurities and fears in a steel coffin and bury them, but they continue to pop to the forefront of my mind like a damn jack-in-the-box. Even after all of these years, I'm still riddled with one lone, pesky thought—I'll never be good enough.

"Damn!" a boisterous voice carries over the bustle of the hall. I turn from where my head is buried in my locker to see Emmett swaggering forward, his football jersey emphasizing all of his delicious muscles. "You look hot."

"Thanks, Em." I smile softly. "And you don't look too shabby yourself."

He looks the exact opposite of shabby, if I'm being completely honest with myself. He looks hot as hell. Like, if my vagina hadn't just dried up like a desert from my interaction with Elias—denial is my close friend—it would be gushing right about now.

When the fuck did I get so horny?

"You excited to cheer tonight?" he asks, leaning against my locker and gifting me an incredibly effective smolder. Seriously, Emmett smolders with the best of them, easily surpassing Prince Charming in the rankings.

"Are you excited to football tonight?" I retort immediately, and he quirks one eyebrow.

"That was…honestly adorable. But to answer your question, yes. I'm super excited 'to football' tonight." He flashes me a teasing smile. "But I'm more excited to see your tight ass in that little skirt doing the splits."

"Oh my god!" I exclaim, laughing and shoving at his shoulder. "You're a big horn dog."

"I would take offense to that if it wasn't true." He shrugs, unashamed as his languid gaze continues to undress me.

"Oh. Em. Gee!"

Mariabella races across the hall and practically tackles me with her hug.

"Mar…" I say with a laugh as she pulls away, an undefinable gleam in her eyes.

"You look sexy as fuck!" she breathes, dropping her gaze to my legs. She instantly blushes and meets my eyes. "Sorry. That was blunt. But damn, cheerleading looks good on you."

"You too," I respond, and I mean it. Mariabella looks completely in her element in the skin-tight uniform, one that showcases her luscious curves. Karsyn really is a lucky man. It's a shame I have to destroy him and then eat his insides.

She giggles slightly, another blush erupting in her cheeks, before she turns towards Emmett with an enigmatic grin.

"So…"

"So?" Emmett raises an eyebrow as he stares down at her fondly.

"What are your chances of winning tonight?"

"With Alder as QB, I'll say pretty damn good. It's really going to be a defensive game, since both of our offenses are evenly matched and—"

His words go through one ear and out the other.

Football stats? Not my thing.

Mariabella, on the other hand, nods endearingly as he prattles on and on about how close the game is going to be, especially if they don't work as a coherent unit. She interjects once or twice to ask for clarification, but overall, she's attentive and genuinely interested.

Once again, a pang explodes in my chest when I think about how perfect she is for Karsyn. Sweet. Funny. Beautiful.

It's no wonder he loves her.

And it's no wonder he never bothers to give me the time of day, unless it's to remind me that I don't belong.

I scratch absently at the skin on my arm, ignoring the pain that detonates inside of me like an atomic bomb. Now is not the time to fall in an endless pit of despair and misery. I refuse to allow my past depression to drag me under, stealing the remaining air from my lungs. Not again.

Movement out of the corner of my eye clues me in to the new arrival a moment before his hands are on my ass, wrenching my skirt up and bearing my black panties to the entire hallway.

I gasp as mortification fills me, tears pricking my eyes. Immediately, I jump away from the asshole and smooth down my skirt.

"Sorry," the guy says unapologetically. "My hands slipped."

From the hoots and hollers of his friends a few lockers away, I have a feeling that was not the case. At all.

I recognize him vaguely as Simon…something. I can't recall his last name. He's been in all of my classes since fourth grade, and he reveled in the Devils' treatment of me. I think he secretly wanted to join them, so he always laughed the loudest at their crude jokes. Watched as they tortured and tormented me. Smirked when I sobbed.

And apparently, he's one of the few students who remembers me, even with my stylish haircut and toned body.

"What the fuck, asshole?" Emmett seethes, stepping forward with his teeth bared and hands balled into fists. Mariabella places a hand on his chest to stop him, though her eyes are colder than I've ever seen before. They're practically hewn from ice.

"I'm going to report you," she hisses, and the venom in her voice takes me by surprise. She's usually so sweet and calm, so the change from an innocent angel to an avenging demon sort of terrifies me. Her eyes narrow into thin, unforgiving slits as if daring Simon to try something else.

"It was just a joke." He holds his hands up placatingly as he begins to slowly step away, rejoining his group of assholes. They're not wearing the red and black football jerseys, so that means they're not on the football team. I don't recognize them from any of my classes either. But then again, the school is so big that I don't have classes with half of my grade.

"Fuck you!" Emmett bellows, garnering the attention of a few classmates lingering nearby. I receive a few pitying looks from students who no doubt saw my underwear, but no one outwardly laughs or even leers. Even the guys nearby look disgusted at Simon's behavior.

"Let's just go," I tell Emmett and Mariabella firmly, taking both of their hands in mine and tugging them towards our first hour. "He's not worth it."

"I'm going to rip his fucking head off," Emmett continues, struggling against me. I can tell he doesn't actually want to get away—if he truly wanted to break free of my weak grip, he could in a heartbeat.

"That's sexual assault," Mariabella adds with a frown. "He should be expelled."

"It's fine."

I dealt with worse.

But maybe Simon should find himself at the end of one of my voodoo dolls?

I smile coldly at the thought as I quicken my pace. But that smile fades when I spot the figure standing ramrod straight at the end of the hall, expression utterly unreadable. He's close enough to have no doubt witnessed the entire incident, but instead of the glee I expect from the devil himself, I see nothing but carefully constructed impassiveness.

Except for his eyes.

Lucas meets my gaze once, eyes stony and almost incandescent in fury, before he turns and walks away.

CHAPTER 18

We arrive at our first hour without any additional issues. I don't know if it's because word hasn't yet traveled this far, or if Emmett's "don't fuck with me" look deters anyone from saying anything. Either way, I'm grateful when I slide into my seat nestled between Mariabella and Emmett without anyone commenting on what I dub the "panty incident."

"I can't fucking believe that prick," Mariabella seethes, and the vitriol in her voice has me spinning towards her. And to hear her cursing? That's a feat in and of itself. I haven't known her very long, but I can't think of one time I ever heard her raise her voice in anger before our confrontation with Simon. Sadness, maybe, like when she spoke to Karsyn before cheerleading practice. But never anger. Never this toe-curling, stomach-clenching anger that makes me fear being on the receiving end of her wrath.

And Emmett…

He hasn't stopped glowering since the incident. His hands are balled into tight fits, and he's radiating a decidedly "steer clear of me or die" vibe. More than one person glances at the normally jovial football player before darting their eyes in another direction. He's fucking livid on my behalf, and it only endears him to me more. I can't remember the last time I had someone in my corner, someone angry on my behalf. Maybe Uriel, but that's about it.

Ms. Auperlee is pulling up a PowerPoint when the door to the classroom slams open, careening off the wall. Every student whips their head in the newcomer's direction, mouths agape in shock.

Standing in the door frame like an avenging angel—one that's been plucked from hell and not heaven—is none other than Lucas. He absently brushes at the top of his red hair, smoothing down the wayward flyaways until it returns to its immaculate style. Then, his sea-blue eyes roam over the students before settling on me.

Like in the hallway, his face is devoid of any expression whatsoever. But his eyes...

Back at the coven, we were forced to hang our laundry on a string connecting our home and the next. I would sometimes watch from my bedroom window the articles of clothing blowing in the light breeze, weightless and ravaged by the elements. One look into Lucas's eyes feels as if he is plucking me off that thin rope and holding me tight, protecting me from flying away and drifting aimlessly. I no longer feel as if a sharp gust of wind is going to completely obliterate me. I no longer think—

What the fuck am I doing?

Thinking poetic thoughts about Lucas fucking Scott, of all people? He's the most dangerous Devil of them all, one that exudes pure malice. He looks like an angel with his studious good looks, but it only belies something infinitely darker and more dangerous.

And now, the metaphor has changed. He's the tornado hurtling towards me at one hundred miles per hour, destroying the entire laundry line...as well as every house nearby. He's destruction and pain and misery, all wrapped in an enticing package complete with a pretty bow.

"Lucas? I thought I didn't have you until later today," Ms.

Auperlee states, sounding flustered. There's just something about this ice-eyed boy that does that to a person.

"I transferred in," he states blandly. Without taking his eyes off of me, he removes a pink slip of paper from his pocket and hands it to the frazzled teacher. She scans over what I recognize as an administrative note, before nodding once at the empty seat opposite me in the classroom.

"Please have a seat, Mr. Scott."

But he ignores the direction she indicated. Instead, he heads straight towards me.

The guy sitting directly in front of me looks as if he's going to piss himself when Lucas hovers over his desk. He doesn't frown or even scowl. He doesn't lift a finger at the boy, nor does he raise his voice. Instead, he just stands there, a bored, almost apathetic, expression on his too-beautiful face.

And the guy all but jumps out of the seat, running towards the empty desk on the opposite end of the room.

Motherfucker.

Lucas's back remains ramrod straight as he slides easily into the now vacated seat. Unlike the other students, he doesn't slouch or take out his phone or even lean forward on his forearms. He sits like he does everything in life—with a giant stick up his muscled ass.

"As most of you already know, we have a project coming up that will last the remainder of the semester." She moves to sit behind her desk, rifling through notebooks and loose paper. "At the end of the semester, we have an anatomy unit. Your assignment is to build a creative human skeleton using everyday items you have lying around your house. It can be paper clips or remote controls or even shoes. But it *must* be anatomically correct, and it must be at least five feet long." After she finishes her spiel, she stands, once more moving to pace at the front of the room. "Now, most teachers would assign partners—"

There's immediate grumbling from some of the classmates, while others exchange wistful looks. The corners of Ms. Auperlee's lips twitch, and I decide that she might be one of my favorite teachers.

"—but I'm not like most teachers. I'm allowing you to choose your own partner. But!" She raises her voice to be heard over the sudden onslaught of noise. "Make sure it's someone you'll actually get stuff done with." At that, she swivels her head until she's narrowing her eyes at two unfamiliar football players sitting near the back of the classroom. They chuckle at her good-naturedly and shrug their broad shoulders sheepishly.

A few things happen at the exact same time.

Lucas begins to turn around in seat, still sitting like a fucking king overlooking us lowly peasants. All he needs is a crown in his meticulously-groomed hair. Emmett begins to turn towards me as well, a mischievous smile replacing the anger I'd seen in his eyes when class began. And Mariabella grips both of my hands with a delighted squeal.

"We totes have to be partners!" she gushes, rubbing her thumbs across the tops of my hands.

And Mariabella? She's the safest option by far.

If I choose Emmett, I might forget about all of my carefully constructed plans and my vow for "no romantic entanglements." Something about the cheeky boy reels me in, hook, line, and sinker.

And if I choose Lucas…

I'll lose myself to the darkness pulsating just beneath my ribcage.

"Of course," I say immediately, ignoring the probing eyes I can feel drilling a hole in the side of my face. Those cold, cold eyes…

"I guess that leaves you and me, fucker," Emmett grumbles, but Lucas ignores him completely, turning back towards his notebook and scribbling in the margins. His red sweater is pulled tight over hard, sinewy muscles. How is it possible that someone so…nerdy could have such delectable muscles? It's not fair.

"Or just me," Emmett relents at last with a disgruntled sigh.

Mariabella giggles and sticks her tongue out at him. "You snooze, you lose."

"Obviously." He rolls his eyes as his dimple makes another appearance. "If you fall asleep after sex, you're always losing."

"You're disgusting," I say with a grin as I flick an eraser at his head.

Instead of answering with words, he simply wags his tongue like a dog and shakes his head from side to side enthusiastically.

Disgusting, yes.

But also very tempting.

We don't talk more about the project for the rest of the class period. Instead, Ms. Auperlee continues her PowerPoint presentation while I pretend that I'm *not* staring intently at Lucas's broad shoulders and his perfectly sculpted back. That I'm not noticing the one hair slightly out of place near the back of his scalp. That I'm not paying attention to the way his long, elegant fingers wrap around the pencil as he writes perfect notes into his notebook.

"Who are you writing to?" I asked softly as I moved to sit next to the red-haired boy. The rest of the kids were playing on the playset, running through the field, or shoving each other off the swings. But not Lucas. Never Lucas. He always spent his recess by himself.

He smiled up at me, revealing a gap between his two front teeth, and I felt my heart flutter.

"You," he answered simply, thrusting a piece of notebook paper into my hands.

Gingerly, I smoothed the paper out on my knee before reading the words he wrote in his small, albeit sloppy, print.

Peony. I thank u pretty. Will u b my girlfrend?

I hugged the letter to my chest as I stared at the shy, skinny boy. A tentative smile curled up my own lips as I resisted the urge to squeal. The other girls in my class were going to be so jealous.

"Do we get to hold hands?" I ask, slightly breathless. Lucas grinned timidly as he reached forward and took my hand in his.

"I'll be the bestest boyfriend ever," he vowed. "For now and always."

When the bell rings, signaling the end of class, I'm out of my seat like a bolt of lightning, practically racing to the door. I can hear Emmett and Mariabella calling my name behind me, but I simply wave my hand in the air and give a muffled, "Bathroom."

My heart is running a marathon in my chest when I arrive at Orchestra, throwing myself into the uncomfortable black seat before remembering I need to grab a violin from the storage closet.

Why does Lucas affect me the way he does? Am I one of those heroines you read about in books who falls for one of her tormentors? The mere thought is laughable. Been there, done that with Elias. I learned my lesson once before. Never again.

And I hate Lucas more than anything in this world. Maybe even more than I hate the other Devils.

Even I can admit, though, that he's a fine specimen. When I look at him objectively, like one would when ogling your favorite celebrity on a magazine cover, it's easy to disassociate the bully from the man. The bully is a horrible human being who deserves to be mauled by apes and then chewed on by rabid bats, if bats can even be rabid. But the man? He's sexy, in a fifties-vibe, nerdy way. If I was simply a new student starting a new school, he would be the ideal, crush-worthy guy for me. Handsome, class president, smart. And I'm sure he's charming to some people, when he's not planning their demise.

But all I can think about when I see his face is those cold blue eyes glaring down at me as I stand in the middle of the gymnasium in my pretty dress.

"You're nothing," he'd said.

But now? Now this "nothing" will become his worst nightmare.

"How did you do it?" a sly voice asks from beside me. I turn, startled, to see Felicia standing with her hands on her hips, eyes narrowed.

"Do what?"

I honestly don't understand her animosity towards me. Seriously, did I shit in her Cheerios or something and forget? Or is it simply jealousy that Mr. Tucker showed an interest in me?

"Get Lucas to beat up that guy for you."

Her words have me freezing in place, and the violin case would've dropped from my clammy fingers if I hadn't caught my bearings at the last possible second, retightening my grip.

"I don't—"

"Don't lie." She tosses her silky black hair over her shoulder before stalking away. "I saw him beat up Simon at the beginning of first hour."

Her words are the equivalent to a literal bomb exploding in my face, the blast sending me spiraling dozens of feet backwards.

Lucas beat up Simon?

Why the fuck would he do that?

Is he some vigilante warrior who beats up every bully who walks these halls? Or is it because of me?

Is Lucas mad that someone else messed with his favorite toy?

Those thoughts continue to circulate in my head as Mr. Tucker ambles into the room, his arms full of sheet music he more than likely illegally printed from the internet.

But all I can think is why?

Why would Lucas do that for me?

Unless…

Unless this is just the start of something bigger and badder. Maybe Lucas has finally seen the chess board I'd laid out in front of him, and he's only now moving his piece.

I'm not scared. If there's one thing I learned from playing chess with Uriel, it's that there's nothing more important than the queen. And this queen will get the kings to fall for her, one pawn at a time.

CHAPTER 19

I decide to go to Mariabella's house to get ready for tonight's game. She rattles off the address which I plug into my phone, before she skips away with a cheery wave, promising to meet me there.

The poor girl thinks I own a car.

But honestly? I don't mind the short walk to Mariabella's house, though I feel guilty that she's no doubt waiting for me to arrive.

Before I leave, I change into my normal clothes so I'm not forced to walk miles in a short skirt and skin-tight shirt.

Like the last couple of days, Elias keeps pace with me in his Jeep. He doesn't even question the change in direction, continuing to slowly roll along beside me. I huff, quickening my pace, but that doesn't deter the relentless fucker as he continues to drive alongside me, classical music blaring from the speakers.

"Fucking hell, Elias," I pant. "My short legs can't run this fast."

"Then don't run," he answers simply.

"I wouldn't need to run if I wasn't being stalked," I point out, and I swear his lips thin ever so slightly.

"How many times do I have to tell you? It's not—" He pauses abruptly, and his frown deepens. "Fuck, it *is* stalking."

A laugh escapes me unbidden. "You just now realized it, Sherlock?"

"Hey, cut me some slack," he jests lightly. "This is the first time I've ever done anything like this before."

"Stalk a girl?"

"Attempt to woo one," he answers bluntly, and when his eyes slide to mine, I find that I can't look away. I don't *want* to. His square jaw is clenched, the stubble on it more prominent than I remember it being, but I find that it suits his unapologetic, forceful personality. There's such raw power held in his tightly compacted body. Fiercely strong and primal, and at the same time, exceedingly gentle. He always seems to hesitate when he's with me, as if he's choosing each and every word carefully. Considering what I know about him, I imagine that he is.

So when he claims he's trying to woo me, he means it.

I push down the eager butterflies trying to crawl up my throat as I force my gaze away from his. I can never seem to think straight when he stares at me like that—with eyes that reflect desperation and need. I have only so many defenses around my heart, and they're already beginning to crumble. With one eloquent look, he's bombing the carefully constructed walls and slaying the fire-breathing dragon guarding the entrance.

"I think you're doing it wrong," I manage to choke out, quickening my pace.

He doesn't speak the remainder of the trip.

When I pull up to the address Mariabella gave me, Elias waits until I'm through the front gates and knocking on the door before he pulls away.

I'm still confused over my interaction with Elias when Mariabella opens the door, one hip cocked to the side. Like me, she changed into a pair of loose sweats and a sweatshirt, her blonde hair still hanging around her shoulders like molten gold.

"Hey, what took you so long?" she demands as she pulls on my arm, dragging me inside.

"Sorry. Don't have a car," I mutter absently as I glance around the foyer with wide-eyed wonder. If I thought Nana's house was big, this is something else entirely. I didn't get to see the exterior—given that I was so eager to escape Elias, I barged right inside—but I can tell that Mariabella's family isn't lacking in the money department.

The white tiled floor is polished so meticulously, I can see my reflection. A three-tiered chandelier dangles from the ceiling, illuminating everything in a white-gold light. Numerous vases rest on small, decorative tables that sit against the walls, all lined with framed portraits. Two staircases connect above in a gorgeous mezzanine overlooking the foyer. Everything appears modern and new and so incredibly shiny, my head hurts just looking at it. I'm afraid my mere *presence* will tarnish it.

"You don't have a car!" Mariabella's shrill voice pulls me out of my musings as I turn towards her in alarm. She has one hand on her hip as she glares at me. "You bitch! I could've given you a ride. Why didn't you…? Ugh! I'm mad at you right now."

I smile sheepishly and take a step forward, before stopping myself and glancing at my shoes in dismay. Is this the type of place I have to walk around barefoot in? I'm pretty sure I didn't step in a mud puddle or anything, but I don't dare bring even a grain of sand into this perfectly cleaned house.

"Sorry. But I don't mind the walk."

Mariabella huffs before stalking towards the left staircase, her Mary Janes clacking against the floor. Well, I suppose that answers that question.

"Well," she begins, "if you need a ride, I'm always free. Don't ever hesitate to ask." She pauses abruptly on the staircase, drilling me with a look over her shoulder. "Seriously, P, I mean it."

I wrinkle my nose. "Don't call me P. It makes me think of taking a whizz."

"That's gross," Mariabella deadpans as we walk down a creepily-pristine hall. Seriously, how does a house even become this clean? She pauses at a door on her right, poking her head into a tiny office where a small woman sits at a desk. "Mom! I'm home. And I'm with a friend."

"Karsyn?" her mother asks, turning to face us. I can see where Mariabella gets her beauty from. Her mother is a petite thing, with golden locks framing a delicate, almost elfin, face. "You know the rules—leave your bedroom door open at all times."

"It's not Karsyn," Mariabella says with an eye roll and a blush, giving me a look that says, "can you believe her?"

But inside, my stomach muscles clench together like I've just run ten miles without stopping to drink water. It's a painful sensation that has me rubbing at my abdomen absently.

Because the thought of Mariabella and Karsyn alone in her bedroom together...

I shake my head, attempting to violently clear the images that thought evokes.

"Oh." The woman removes a pair of glasses and offers me a warm smile, standing from her chair to extend her hand. "I'm Lydia."

"Peony," I introduce.

"Peony...that's a strange name," she muses, and Mariabella groans.

"Mom! That's so freaking rude!"

"It's okay," I say around a breath of laughter. To Lydia, I explain, "My mom went through a...phase."

Nothing else needs to be said.

I'm pretty sure if I had siblings, they would've been named Daffodil, Sunflower, and Tulip.

Not normal flower names like Daisy or Rose. Oh no. Even when I was a baby, Mom harbored resentment for me.

"Well, have fun, girls! I'm just going to be getting some work done in here." The last sentence is said pointedly at her daughter, a reminder to remain quiet. Mariabella pantomimes zipping her lips shut and throwing away the key, and a wry smile curls up Lydia's mouth.

"Come on," Mariabella says to me, pulling me away from her mother. I wave goodbye at the friendly woman, who once more closes the door to her office. "Let's get ready in my room."

Mariabella's room is exactly what I would expect from her—an explosion of pink. The walls are painted a creamy white, decorated with Polaroid pictures, and more pillows cover the pink bedspread than I'm sure she knows what to do with. Besides that, there's nothing that really tells me who Mariabella truly is. Sure, there are numerous pictures of her and her friends, but where are the embarrassing stuffed animals? The tattered baby blanket she kept since she was young? The clothing she hadn't bothered to place in the hamper? The room seems too clean to belong to a teenage girl.

As Mariabella moves to place her backpack on the bed, I peruse the pictures taped to the wall. There are dozens of her and her cheerleading friends, a few of her and her parents, but only one of Karsyn. It's that one I focus on, seeming to be taken when he wasn't looking. He's wearing the red and black letterman jacket required of all football players, but his face appears younger. Sadder, almost. Pensive. His gaze is faraway and distant, and his hand is lying loosely on his knee. I can almost hear the staccato as his fingers thrum against his jeans, belting out an unfamiliar tune.

"So, do you want to get any homework done, or do you just want to hang out?" Mariabella asks, pulling my attention away from Karsyn's photo. I move to stand beside her, shrugging off my backpack and placing it by my feet.

"No homework." I shake my head once. "It's the weekend, and I'm schooled out."

She chortles. "Ugh. You're right. We can work on our project for

Bio another time." Her eyes glimmer suddenly, and she pats the spot next to her on the bed. "Sit. Let's talk."

"How much time do we have before we have to get to the game?" I move to do as she instructed, perching awkwardly on the bed beside her. At the coven, I didn't have a lot of girlfriends. No one to braid my hair or do my nails or gossip with. It was just me and Uriel, but we were never the type of friends who did any of that stuff. Instead of braiding hair, we pulled it. Instead of doing our nails, we scratched them down each other's backs. And our mouths were used for more important things.

I probably tasted every inch of that fucker's skin, but I can't remember if we ever truly sat down and just talked.

"So..." Mariabella purposefully drags the word out, and I can feel my brows tilt downwards.

"So?"

"First week. Spill. How was it?"

"It was exactly how you would expect the first week to go in a new school." I attempt to choose my words very, very carefully. So far, I don't think Mariabella remembers me from middle school. But then again, I don't remember her that well either. She was always just *there*, with a gaggle of laughing girls, never joining in on the bullying but never stopping it either. It's not a complete surprise that she wouldn't remember me. I don't think we ever said more than two words to each other.

"You and Emmett seem to be getting along really well," she presses, and despite her light tone, I can hear the curiosity brewing like a kettle seconds from boiling over.

"Are you asking me if we're fucking?" I jest teasingly, and she immediately makes a face.

"Ew. Don't need that visual, thank you very much, but yes. I suppose that's what I'm asking."

I shrug my shoulders once. "He's cute. And funny. And entertaining. But..."

"But…?" she queries.

"I don't want to date," I finish firmly. *Because I would much rather spend my time planning ways to destroy your boyfriend and his ex-best friends.* But you know, semantics.

"Ever?" Mariabella asks, sounding genuinely disappointed, and I can't help but smirk. I have no doubt Emmett put her up to this line of questioning. Those two seem really close, despite the apparent animosity between Emmett and Karsyn.

"I just got out of a long relationship," I fib…at least, half-fib. That *is* true, but it's not the reason why I'm swearing off dick.

"Oh." Mariabella places a manicured finger against her pink-painted lips. "What happened?"

"Enough about me," I say with a nervous laugh. "Let's talk about you. And Karsyn." I nod towards the lone photograph on the wall. "How long has that been going on?"

Now it's *her* time to look awkward, and I watch with macabre glee as she fidgets uncomfortably. "About a year or so."

"That's a long time for a high school relationship." Is my heart pounding in my chest? Are my hands sweaty? What the hell is going on with me? For a brief moment, I legit fear that Mariabella poisoned me somehow. That's the only explanation for the crippling pain that rushes through me at her innocent statement. A pain that steals the air from my lungs and makes my heart stutter to an abrupt halt.

"Yeah." Her voice is intentionally vague, and I have a feeling she doesn't want to talk about it anymore. My mind plays back the fight I witnessed between the two of them. Did they breakup? No, that can't be it. Karsyn sat with her at lunch again today.

But maybe they're no longer the fairy tale couple they'd have everyone believe.

"Is your hair color natural?" she asks, and I'm honestly not surprised by her abrupt change in topic. She begins to comb her fingers through a strand of my silky white hair. "Because I'm so freaking jealous."

"All natural," I admit. "And it's funny, too, because my mom has black hair and my dad was a redhead."

"No way! Really?" She wraps a strand around her finger before releasing it with a heavy sigh. "I hate my hair." She pulls disgruntledly at one of her blonde ringlets, watching as it straightens out before bouncing back into place, stopping just beyond her shoulders.

"I love your hair," I say quickly, grabbing the brutalized strand and giving it a slight tug. "It's super pretty."

She blushes, ducking her head and staring up at me through a fringe of thick lashes.

"Really?" she asks, and I detect a hint of self-consciousness in her voice.

"Cross my heart and hope to die," I promise, drawing a X with my finger over my chest. She flashes me a brilliant smile before clapping her hands together gleefully.

"I'm going to have Marsha put a pizza in the oven for us, so we can stuff our faces while watching *Vampire Diaries*." Mariabella pauses. "You like VD, right?"

"Damon is…" I fan myself dramatically as she queues up Netflix on the television in her room.

"You can have him," she says dismissively, and I stare at her, affronted.

"Don't tell me you're a Stefan fan? I don't know if our burgeoning friendship can survive this."

After binge-watching the show and debating which brother is better for Elena, Mariabella turns off the television with a yawn, dumping her empty pizza plate onto the floor in the process as she stands.

"We have to get ready for the game. You still have your uniform to change into, right? Those things are so fucking uncomfortable. Honestly, I hate having to wear them to school. Can we talk about chub rub?" Mariabella says now, unashamedly wrenching her sweat-shirt over her head so she's standing in nothing but a thin white bra. I eye the connecting bathroom warily. I'm beginning to trust Mari-abella, I honestly am, but there are some things I'm just not ready to share.

The scars on my arms being one of them.

"Can I use…?" I point towards the open door, and her brows furrow in confusion as she finishes pulling off her pants.

"Oh shit. Did I make you uncomfortable?" She stares down at her scantily-clad body with a blush darkening both of her cheeks. "Sorry. I tend to not really think things through."

"You're fine," I rush to reassure her, not wanting things to already be weird between us. If I were any other girl, changing in front of my friend wouldn't be an issue. But I'm not any other girl. I'm a bag of jagged glass, each shard repeatedly drawing blood until I'm nothing but a husk of who I once was. "It's me."

"You're self-conscious," she muses, and I suppose she's half-right. "I don't know why. You're freaking gorgeous." The last part is said almost as a grumble, as if she's pissed at me for it. "But sure. You can use the bathroom." She slides her bra off as she reaches for the top of her cheerleading uniform, and I feel another pang of that dreaded self-consciousness she mentioned as I stare at her breasts. Mine are big, a size D, but hers are so fucking perky and perfect, it's just not fair. They're literally a perfect pair of breasts, and the sudden image of Karsyn leaning forward to kiss one of her rosy pink nipples pops in my head.

And I want to fucking gag.

I tell myself it's because Mariabella is my friend and Karsyn is a trashy human being. That I hate Karsyn with a passion capable of setting this world on fire. I tell myself that until I'm blue in the face, but I'm not sure if I believe it.

"Peony?" Mariabella asks with amusement, and I realize that I'm staring at her boobs like some sort of creeper. This time, it's my cheeks that turn crimson as I all but run into the bathroom, slamming the door shut.

I need to get over this…this infatuation I have with Karsyn Alder. It makes no logical sense whatsoever. But then again, my reaction towards all of the Devils doesn't make a lick of sense. I should hate them—and I do—but my body wants them in a primal, carnal way.

My hands clench into fists as I take a deep, fortifying breath.

I'll get over this…whatever this is. And then, I'll destroy the charming Devils once and for all.

WE HAVE TO ARRIVE AT THE HIGH SCHOOL AT FIVE-THIRTY PM FOR check-in, despite the game not starting until seven. We leave the locker room as a team, walking the paved pathway until we reach the stadium.

Like everything else at the high school, it's rich and superficial, with a parking lot easily able to hold five hundred cars. The stadium has four concession stands, two on either side, and the football field itself consists of artificial green grass. When we arrive on the track field, a level below the bleachers, I'm shocked by the crowd already in the stands. It seems that football is a popular sport here.

As the rest of the girls huddle together around Helen, I allow my eyes to drift over the assembled students and parents. Almost all are wearing our school's colors and waving ridiculous flags around their heads as they cheer for a team that hasn't even arrived on the field yet. Seriously, who comes to a high school football game two hours early? These people do, apparently.

My gaze lands on Lucas sitting in the center of the bleachers, his eyes intent on me. It feels as if he's put me between two panes of glass and is studying me beneath a microscope. I feel naked and vulnerable and, honestly, a little frightened. I can't help but think that he's here for a specific reason—to destroy me.

Girls surround him, each one more beautiful than the last, but he doesn't pay them any attention, despite their repeated attempts to claim it. His eyes remain fixed on me. Only me. That ice-blue gaze almost feels searingly hot, and the irony of that statement isn't lost on me.

Cassian sits a few bleachers away from him, hands curled into fists and looking unbelievably sexy in his leather jacket. Back in middle school, he always wore Ray-Bans and skinny jeans—whatever was in style at High Groves Middle School. But just now, he looks like a rocker bad boy with his buzzed black hair, dark skin, and penetrating gaze.

And two rows behind *him* is none other than the teacher slut herself. Mrs. Town is cuddled into the side of a thirty-something-year-old man who looks to be the size of a NFL linebacker. Despite her attractive husband, Cassian's broad back holds her gaze, as if she's wishing for him to fuck her even now, in direct view of her oblivious husband. A husband who's currently smiling at her as if she holds the moon and stars in her tiny, cheating hands.

With a wicked grin pulling up my lips, I glance pointedly from Cassian, to Mrs. Town, and then back to Cassian. When his eyes narrow, hands balling into even tighter fists on his dark blue jeans, I wink. And I swear something akin to heat flares to life in his eyes, and he stares at me like Mrs. Town stares at him—as if he wishes to devour me whole.

"He never comes to games!" A hushed whisper rips my attention away from Cassian and towards a group of cheerleaders huddled in a makeshift circle, Mariabella front and center. Her brows are scrunched together as she stares at something over my shoulder.

"He's looking right at us," another girl exclaims with a nervous giggle. I think she introduced herself as Brianna.

Are they talking about Cassian? Or Lucas?

I pivot on my heel, following Mariabella's line of sight, until I see Elias Briggs leaning languidly against the waist-high fence separating the field from the bleachers. He leans forward on bent elbows, and the cheerleaders are right. His eyes *are* fixed intently on our group. Or more specifically, on me.

"He's so cute," someone giggles, and I have the irrational urge to remind them that Elias is *not* cute but a predator in seductive clothing. The steadily setting sun is still bright enough for me to see the streaks of purple in his brown hair, flying around his chiseled face. Thick, curled lashes frame those violet-tinted brown eyes and give him an almost innocent appearance. But Lucifer was beautiful, even when he fell, wasn't he?

He's close enough that if I were to take five steps, I would be able to reach up and run the tips of my fingers over his hands.

But instead of giving in to that horrific desire, I ball my hands into fists and focus on Helen, who, as if hearing my mental plea, calls for the girls to circle her.

"Mariabella, I want you to take the lead this game," she begins, and my friend positively beams as if she's been offered an award constructed of pure gold. "Girls, Mariabella will start all the cheers and will be in the center of the formation. If you forget any of the movements, follow her."

Everyone nods in understanding before Helen turns towards me.

"And, Peony, since you don't know all the cheers yet, I'm going to have you sitting out the first half of the game. Just to watch and get an idea of what to expect. I'll consider putting you in the second half if you feel up to it."

I nod once to show her I'm not offended or upset. Despite working with the team for about a week, I still struggle with remembering a lot of the cheer moves. And besides, I'm not sure I brought enough flexibility potion to last the entire game.

I move to sit on the sidelines, resting my back against the wall that houses the raised bleachers. From this angle, I can't see anyone in the stands, and hopefully, they can't see me. I can, however, see the football team race out of the locker room, to the whoops and cheers of the adoring fans. They proceed to do pre-game warmups while the cheerleaders talk amongst themselves and work on some tosses and lifts. When seven rolls around, I'm actually excited for the game to begin. I'm not the biggest fan of football, but there's something infectious about the screams from both sides of the stadium.

And of course, there's Karsyn.

I try not to admire the way his broad muscles fill out the tight jersey and knee-high pants. I know that football players wear tighter than normal clothing to keep their opponents from pulling at it, but damn. Karsyn looks like a Greek god plucked straight from history. With his helmet off and blond hair askew, he's breathtaking.

Emmett materializes next to Karsyn and flashes me a cheeky wink. He then sticks out his tongue and pantomimes licking an...ice cream cone. Let's go with that. The crude gesture causes goose-bumps to pebble on my skin as I roll my eyes at the sheer ridiculous-ness of it. Karsyn whips his head in Emmett's direction, face scrunched in confusion, before he follows the other man's eyes to me. Then his gaze darkens considerably, and he offers me a menacing scowl before slamming his helmet over his head.

Emmett rolls his eyes at his teammate's antics, tossing me another wink, before he shoves his own helmet on and jogs towards the coach and the rest of his teammates.

And then the game begins.

When I say Karsyn is good, that would be the understatement of the damn century. He's not just good. He's fucking phenomenal. He plays football the way I play the violin—like each play is a separate note that has to be plucked. The anger from his eyes diminishes as he gets sucked into the void of the game, losing himself to each play.

By only the second quarter, our team is up thirty-five to zero.

They call Karsyn and Emmett back to the sidelines when the other team is set to receive the ball.

At this point, I'm standing at the edge of the field, slightly away from the cheerleaders to get a better view of the game. I don't think I could sit even if I wanted to.

Maybe I actually *like* football. I know. The horror.

Uriel would piss himself laughing if he ever heard.

The running back from the Hawks begins to return the ball, running down the edge of the field near where I'm standing. The visitor's side of the stadium cheers raucously, still hopeful that their team can win, even when they're behind by five touchdowns. I can see our defensive players racing forward as well, hoping to tackle the dude before he can score. I'm bouncing on my toes, a wide grin on my face, when the Hawks' player veers in my direction, hoping to get out of bounds before he can be tackled.

I squeal, attempting to run to the side, but I'm not quick enough.

The next thing I know, a two-hundred-pound man barrels into me, knocking the air from my lungs and forcing me to the ground. My head careens against the grass as stars dance in my vision, pain reverberating through my scalp from the impact. I'm dimly aware of the ref blowing his whistle and Mariabella's startled scream. I can see Helen's shoes in my peripheral vision as she jogs towards me, but I can barely breathe.

"Get the fuck off of her!" I hear Karsyn shout, and a moment later, the heavy body is all but ripped away from me. The ref once more begins blowing his whistle, but Karsyn ignores it as he kneels beside me, panic etched onto his handsome face. "Are you okay? Peony, are you okay?"

I try to manage a weak, feeble nod, but my body feels as if it's been run over by a semi-truck. Or just a very big and muscular dude.

"I'm sorry," the football player begins, but Karsyn throws him a look so frosty and full of loathing, that the guy immediately turns and jogs back towards his team.

The athletic trainer races forward and very gently begins prodding my body for injuries.

"I don't think anything is broken," she murmurs to my coach.

"Karsyn!" someone shouts, yanking at the quarterback's shoulder. Karsyn quite literally growls at the man who I now recognize as the head football coach. "Get your ass away from them, and let them work."

Face contorted in pain, as if leaving me is the last thing he wants to do, Karsyn allows his coach to steer him back towards his team, though his eyes refuse to leave mine.

"Can you sit up?" the athletic trainer asks, pulling my attention away from Karsyn. I nod once, feeling like a giant, nasty bruise, and both she and Helen help me into a sitting position. I twist my neck from side to side, attempting to alleviate some of the pain that radiates there, as tears prick my eyes. Fuck. I hate crying.

Helen slings one of my arms over her shoulder and helps me limp away from the field. As we turn, facing the bleachers, I see that almost everyone is now sitting, except for three people. It's almost as if they jumped to their feet when I first got hit and haven't been able to move a muscle since.

Lucas's jaw clenches tight as he stares from me, to the Hawks' football player who tackled me, and then back to me. Dozens of emotions dance across his face, like he can't decide which one he wants to settle on. Cassian is standing as well, hands balled into fists and teeth clenched as he watches me like a hawk. Mrs. Town is staring at him with a tiny crease between her red brows, jealousy distorting her features. But he doesn't pay any attention to her, focused on me.

And then there's Elias. He's still standing at the fence, still leaning lazily over the top of it, but his hands are extended as if he wishes to reach for me. His eyes are wide with fear, and I swear his chest doesn't move, as if he's not even breathing. When we make eye contact, he releases a noticeable exhale, muscles slumping with relief.

Why is he staring at me like that? Like I'm the only person he sees?

Confusion swirls in my gut, causing bile to rise up my throat, before I force myself to look away. Isn't that my go-to answer? *Look away.*

I just don't know if I want to anymore.

"Peony!" Nana bypasses two security guards with a wave of her hand, racing towards me. "Are you okay, darling? We saw what happened in the stands..."

"I'm fine," I say through gritted teeth as another stab of pain shoots through me. I don't think my ribs are broken, but I do believe they're bruised.

"I'm going to take her home," Nana says to Helen, and my coach nods once.

"Take it easy, okay?" Helen tells me with a soft look.

"I'll be fine," I assure her. "I just need to rest."

And perform a few healing spells.

I accept Nana's arm gratefully and allow her to lead me off the field to the polite claps of the audience. I can hear the game resume before we've even left the stadium. Isn't that the way things always go? Someone gets injured and life goes on as normal.

But something changed in those last few minutes. Something that I can't put into words. Something that will make it so life can *never* go back to normal.

Because beneath the hate, the anger, the burning fury I feel towards the Devils...

I feel the embers of something else, too.

CHAPTER 20

"How do you feel?" Nana demands, fussing over me. She attempts to fluff the throw pillow propping me up on the settee in the living room, her muddy brown eyes even darker with worry, but I shoo her hands away.

"Like someone plowed into me," I respond dryly, my eyes flicking to the three triplets kneeling in front of the coffee table. Christian stirs a cauldron of a pink, bubbling liquid, while Polo tosses in a teardrop preserved inside a crystal tube. Gabriel watches the proceedings with a scowl marring his handsome face. Unlike the others, he chose not to attend the football game, so he's shirtless instead and wearing a pair of loose pajama bottoms, the broad planes of his bronze chest on display.

"I think we're just about done…" Christian murmurs, for once, his jovial smile nowhere to be found. He blows out the candle currently resting beneath the cauldron and then pours the liquid into a coffee mug for me to drink. Immediately, the pungent stench of sulfur combined with vomit contaminates the air, causing me to gag. I wrinkle my nose in disgust as I stare at the potion in distaste.

Most potions taste like shit. Some witches, like my mother, place flavorful additives into their potions. Strawberry, raspberries, bananas, and even chocolate.

But we don't have time for such frivolous things, not when it feels as if my body has been through the meat-grinder. Pain explodes throughout my body like errant fireworks as I bring the disgusting liquid to my lips, the sour scent barraging my senses.

"Drink it all," Nana instructs sternly, and despite my grimace, I do as she says, chugging the liquid in one go. The taste makes me gag, and wanting to vomit, I bring my hand to my lips to quell the almost painful urge to do so. But when the nausea fades, I can feel the potion traveling through my body like the rapids in a river. It cascades all the way from my head to my toes, branching out to my fingers and shoulders, my stomach and my back. It's almost as if my body is made up of thousands of train tracks, each one traveling to a new location. Warmth explodes in my stomach like bottled sunshine, and I squeeze my eyelids shut against the almost euphoric feeling.

"Fuck..." I curse as the aches and pains flare once, then begin to ebb as if they never existed in the first place. If anything, it feels as if I fell asleep in an uncomfortable position and am only now able to stretch out my taut limbs. Thousands of pinpricks dance on my skin as I flex first one foot and then the next. I bring my hand to my stomach, tentatively pressing on my once bruised ribs, but I feel no pain.

I have made and used healing potions before in my life, but never one like this. Never one that almost instantaneously healed something that should've taken hours with a normal potion and weeks without one.

"Christian here is a skilled potion-maker," Nana explains when I stare at the three triplets in wide-eyed wonder. Christian blushes from the roots of his hair down to his neck.

"Sorry I couldn't make it taste better," he says before once more flashing me his easy-going grin. "I usually add a dash of caramel."

"I'll show you where you can put your caramel," I hear Nana mutter, and his eyes turn heated when he stares at her.

Ohmygawd.

Stop.

Please.

"Well, now that I'm feeling better…" I say, voice laden with disgust. That vomit I mentioned earlier? It wants to make another appearance.

Before I can make my stealthy exit, the doorbell rings. I exchange a confused glance with Nana, even as Gabriel pushes off the wall, stalking into the foyer.

"I'll get it," he murmurs in his growly, raspy voice.

I hear the door opening, followed by a familiar voice. "How's Peony doing?"

Karsyn.

What the hell is he doing here?

On silent feet—and ignoring Nana's amused expression—I patter to the foyer, placing my back flush against the wall to eavesdrop on their conversation.

"Who are you?" Gabriel asks coldly, crossing his muscular arms over his chest and staring down his nose at Karsyn. From this angle, I'm able to see both of them, but they still have yet to glimpse me. I watch as Karsyn's eyes survey Gabriel from head to toe, noting his young age, his bare chest, and his mussed hair. If I'm not mistaken, jealousy flares to life in his hazel eyes, and he stands even straighter, puffing out his chest.

"Karsyn Alder," he says, as if he thinks that name will mean something to a frowning Gabriel.

I can see the cogs and wheels turning rapidly inside Gabriel's head as he tries to recall where he's heard that name before. And I can also see the moment he pieces it together, when he remembers the numerous stories Nana must have told him about Karsyn Alder and the rest of the Devils.

I'm unable to see his eyes, but his entire body stiffens, and he stands taller, almost vibrating with animosity and tension.

"I think you should leave," Gabriel says tersely, and I choose that moment to make my appearance.

Immediately, Karsyn's eyes flicker over Gabriel's shoulder and focus on me, roaming the length of my body and inspecting me for injuries.

"Simone." His tone is unreadable.

"Alder."

An awkward silence ensues as Gabriel volleys his gaze between the two of us. After a moment, he takes a step towards me, giving Karsyn his back, and places a large hand on my shoulder. I watch Karsyn's gaze zero in on the menial touch, hatred and jealousy emanating from his eyes.

"Will you be okay?" Gabriel queries, soft enough to not be overheard. Of course, that only pisses Karsyn off further, if his clenched hands are any indication. For all he knows, we're whispering sweet nothings to each other. The thought of him being upset, of him being *jealous*, causes a wicked grin to curve up my lips as glee sparks inside of me.

"If I'm not, I'll just zap his ass," I assure him, and I swear the corners of his lips twitch. But before it can blossom into a full-blown smile, he gives my shoulder another squeeze before stalking off to join Nana and his brothers. I have no doubt that all four of them will eavesdrop from around the corner. After all, it's what I would do.

I take a moment to study Karsyn as he does the same to me. His blond hair is freshly washed, as if he's just come out of the showers, but it hasn't been combed. Clumpy strands stick up in all directions. He's wearing a faded T-shirt and low-slung blue jeans, and I can't help but think how great they make his thighs look. I'm sure if he turned around, his ass would look even better.

"I thought you had a party tonight," I blurt out, attempting to sound nonchalant.

"Canceled," Karsyn says through gritted teeth, his gaze almost unnerving with its intensity. Finally, his eyelids flutter shut and he releases a heavy exhale, shoulders drooping. "Peony, how are you feeling? When I saw you get hit, I thought I—" He cuts himself off abruptly, reopening his eyes to meet my own.

"I'm fine," I say quickly. "Don't feel a thing. He must not have hit me that hard." I shrug my shoulders, trying to act casual, but confusion and suspicion causes Karsyn's eyes to narrow.

"You were tackled by a guy three times as large as you."

"But I'm fine. See?" I punctuate the last word with a tiny shimmy of my hips, ending with a high kick. Instantly, my cheeks burn when I realize that I looked like a complete and utter dork.

Karsyn's lips twitch before straightening into a thin line.

"I'm glad you're okay." Almost as if someone put a match to his ass, he turns on his heel and practically sprints outside.

But I'm not having that.

For some reason, Karsyn decided to cancel his homecoming party, show up at my house to check on me, and then leave only a few seconds later? Not having that.

"Karsyn Alder!" I race outside, ignoring the slight tug at my midsection, and hurry down the steep staircase until my bare feet touch gravel. He freezes only a few feet in front of me, every muscle in his body locked tight. "Why did you come?"

He continues to stare stubbornly ahead, but I see his hands ball into fists.

When he doesn't respond, I take another step closer, ignoring the pain in my feet from the tiny rocks and pebbles. My voice sounds desperate even to me, almost a plea, when I say, "I need to know why you came."

Finally, he turns around, and I'm struck speechless by the expression on his face. For a brief moment, Karsyn lets his walls down, his expression unguarded. My breath catches at the tender vulnerability reflected in his gaze. But like theater curtains being drawn closed, he tenses up, eyes flickering to something over my shoulder.

Or, more accurately, the three men hovering on the porch, not even bothering to pretend they aren't eavesdropping. They glare at Karsyn with varying degrees of hatred and annoyance. Even carefree Christian and sweet Polo stare at him like he ate their candy.

"I don't know," he says curtly. Meanly. "I shouldn't have." He wrenches his gaze away, almost as if it pains him to stare directly at me. It sort of reminds me of when you stare intently at the sun, the glow blinding you. You can never stare for too long without suffering repercussions.

"Karsyn—"

"Fuck you, Peony," he seethes, and without another word, he turns on his heel and stalks to his car, slamming the driver's side door shut behind him. He doesn't bother to glance my way once as he backs away, despite no doubt feeling my glare drilling a hole into his head.

I want to scream at him to come back, to talk to me and tell me the truth...

And at the same time, I want to demand that he leave me alone and never come back. That I've done nothing to warrant his vitriol, that I've *never* done anything to deserve how he's treated me. This toxic cocktail of emotions tangles up my insides, steadily cutting off my air supply until it feels like I'm choking. Drowning. Dying.

I don't know how long I stand there, staring down the driveway, but it's long enough to cause Nana to hurry forward in concern.

"You should—"

Not giving her the chance to finish, I storm away from her—away from the triplets' pitying glances—and climb the ladder to my attic bedroom. I want to break something. Smash something. Destroy this entire fucking room.

But I don't.

Instead, I reach into my backpack and grab the brown voodoo doll with Karsyn's blond hair wrapped around its neck like a noose.

My stomach muscles clenching uneasily, I begin to chant.

CHAPTER 21

I take the weekend to recuperate. At least, that's what I tell Mariabella and Emmett when they incessantly text me, demanding updates.

Mariabella: u sure ur ok?

Mariabella: I can come over and check on u

Mariabella: text me back bitch!!!!

Snorting at my persistent friend, I roll back on the bed and type back a hasty reply.

Me: sorry. Sleeping.

Lies.

But how can I tell Mariabella that I was thinking about her boyfriend? That I was envisioning his face a moment before he stomped away, the hurt and anguish and something akin to need reflecting in his eyes? I can't, that's for damn sure.

Mariabella: how are u feeling? The girls r worried.

I stretch out my taut muscles, pleased when I only feel a slight tug of pain. Christian's potion worked miracles. Most witches and warlocks spend years perfecting such a spell, sometimes even decades.

Me: I'm fine. Pinky promise.

I send Mariabella a picture of my pinky to emphasize the point, and she replies with three laugh emojis.

As I wait for her to respond back, I scroll through my other messages.

There are a few from Emmett, demanding to know I'm okay. As I scroll through our text thread, my breath catches when I spot a picture of him lying on his bed, one arm behind his head while he uses the other to hold up the camera. He's shirtless, the golden, chiseled planes of his chest on display.

Emmett: Thinking of you.

Quickly exiting out of his messages, heart racing, I pull up one from Uriel. Disregarding it completely, I settle on calling him, clenching the phone between my ear and shoulder as I lean forward to mute the television in my room.

Uriel picks up on the third ring.

"You rang?"

"SOS. Send wine," I deadpan, and he snorts.

"That bad, huh?"

I collapse back on my bed, my legs extending in both directions like a star.

"Remind me again why I want to do this?"

There's a pause, and a second later, Yoselin's feminine voice greets me. I can picture Uriel's girlfriend perching on the edge of his bed, her auburn hair meeting the middle of her back in luscious curls.

"Because they're evil," she says without preamble, and I hear Uriel grunt his assent. "Because they once locked you in the locker room for an entire weekend. Because Elias asked you to the middle school dance, kissed you, and then *Carrie*-d you. Because they're egotistical, nasty, horrendous—"

"Okay, I get the point," I say with a light laugh, twisting my head to the side to stare at a strand of my white hair. Hair that Lucas told me was beautiful...and then immediately doused with tomato sauce.

I want to tell my friends about last night, when Karsyn came to check on me. I want to pick apart every emotion that distorted his features. I want them to tell me I'm crazy, that I'm imagining things, that it's impossible for me to truly believe that he has...feelings for me.

He can't, not after all of the things he did to me. I wonder if it's misplaced responsibility and guilt, like he's trying to make amends for the things he did five years ago.

Peony, forgive me, for I have sinned.

"Is Stalker still there?" Uriel chimes in, and I bite my lip to contain my groan. The triangular window in my attic allows me an unrestricted view of the driveway...and the Jeep currently idling at the very end.

"Yes," I grouse, pulling the phone away from my ear to set it on speaker. My finger hovers over Elias's name that I reluctantly plugged into my phone last night when he first texted me, asking if I was okay.

When I refused to respond, he drove to my house.

And he's only left three times since then, to go to the bathroom and eat. Almost every time I look, he's sitting in that damn Jeep, eyes glued to the attic window, as if he can sense my presence. Which is ridiculous. Elias doesn't know which room in the house belongs to me, and he definitely can't see me this far away.

But it almost feels as if his eyes are physical hands, lightly caressing my shoulders and then cascading down the length of my arms to interlock our fingers together. It's not technically an embrace, but somehow, it feels even more intimate.

"Isn't that creepy?" Yos gripes, and I can already picture her petite nose scrunching.

"It's..."

Confusing.

Infuriating.

Sweet.

The last thought causes me to wrench my gaze away from the window, focusing once more on my phone.

"Enough about that," I say quickly—too quickly. I pray that Uriel doesn't hear the hitch in my voice. "Tell me about what's going on in the coven."

For the next half hour, Yoselin and Uriel regale me with stories of all the people I left behind. Amanda Gray accidentally set off an explosion in the training lab. Jacob and Ryan broke up after Jacob was caught fucking Mr. Leif, the Magic History teacher. And Mom's still being…Mom. Bossing people around and being an all-around bitch.

I want to ask if they heard about the recent attacks by the Bloods, but I don't know yet if it's common knowledge. Besides, I don't want to worry them, especially since the attacks seem to be relegated to Michigan.

So instead, we keep conversation light, and I tell them a little bit about my revenge scheme on the Devils. When I tell them about Cassian's boner, they break into raucous laughter, with Uriel pouting because I failed to take a picture. At this point, they know the Devils nearly as well as I do. The three of us stayed up numerous nights, stalking them on social media and discussing different revenge tactics. They know almost everything the Devils did to me when I was younger, and they never once told me to "get over it."

Because you can't just dismiss years and years of pain as if it never existed. That's like hastily placing duct tape on an opened wound and hoping you don't bleed to death. I'm not saying I want to prolong the pain, but in order to heal, you need to stitch the skin back together carefully. And that's what I'm doing right now—stitching myself back together, one Devil at a time.

When I hang up the phone, I feel infinitely lighter, like a weight has been lifted from my shoulders. I'm actually smiling when I climb down the ladder and enter the kitchen. But that smile fades when I notice the somber expressions of Nana and her men. Tears wet her cheeks as she stares up at a frowning Gabriel. Polo and Christian seem just as distressed, their arms folded over their chests and their lips curled into severe-looking scowls.

"What's going on?" I ask, causing their attention to divert to me. Nana hastily brushes at the tears which have escaped her eyes, attempting a nonchalant laugh, but Gabriel's frown remains.

"I've been called away by the witches' council," he states without preamble. "There's been another death."

"By Bloods?" I query anxiously, now understanding why they all look so upset.

"Gabriel is an expert on Bloods," Nana explains tiredly, raggedly. She sniffs once, attempting to plaster on a feeble smile, but it slips off her face almost instantly.

"You are?" I eye the man with newfound wonder. "I didn't know that."

"No one does." Polo offers me a kind smile, though his eyes remain worried as he stares at his brother. "But the council asked Gabriel to travel to the various sites and investigate."

"You know I have to do this." Gabriel addresses this to a frowning Nana, whose lips are so thin, they're practically nonexistent. "For you. For my brothers. For Peony. These Bloods..." He shakes his head in disgust. "I have to do this."

Nana's knuckles are white from her harsh grip on the tabletop, but she manages a weak nod. It's barely a tilt of her chin, but her eyes spark with steely determination and resolve.

"I know you do, my beloved," she says. "But..."

"I'll be careful." He tentatively places a hand on her cheek, smoothing his thumb over her lip, and I turn away, unwilling to intrude on their personal moment. Less than a second later, Gabriel stands directly in front of me, eyes cold and assessing.

"You need to be careful, Peony," he warns. "Don't walk home alone at night. Don't get into cars with strangers. Don't—"

"I understand." I take his hand in mine and give it a reassuring squeeze. I only saw pictures of my dad and I never had a brother, but I imagine if I did, they would be like Gabriel, Polo, and Christian. I may not know them that well, but I believe they'll go to bat for me if I ever needed them to. We're family, after all, and family sticks together.

And despite only being five to ten years older than me, I feel centuries younger beneath their archaic gazes—gazes that have seen too much. Survived unspeakable horrors. "Don't be a dumbass."

The corners of his lips twitch. "Right. Don't be a dumbass."

"You know, someday, I'm going to get you to actually fucking smile," I vow, attempting to alleviate the tension ratcheting up ten octaves in the room. I hear Christian release a strained laugh from somewhere behind Gabriel, and even Polo chuckles softly.

Gabriel continues to stare at me with a weird combination of fondness and annoyance.

"Be safe. And protect your nana."

"You be safe too, old man," I tease, and he rolls his eyes at me before turning back to face Nana and his brothers. The looks they give each other makes me want to run from the room...run from the *house*...as fast as humanly possible. Vomit climbs up my throat as I turn on my heel, all but stomping back towards my attic bedroom. The one good news about living in a hole in the ceiling—I don't hear anything. Thank fuck.

The second I'm back in my room, I make a beeline towards the window. Unsurprisingly, Elias's Jeep is still parked in front of my house. I can see his broad silhouette in the front seat.

Elias: I just want to know you're alright.

Elias: I need to know you're alright.

Maybe it's the fear for Gabriel leaving. Or the heartbroken

expression on Nana's face. Or my conversation with Uriel and Yoselin. Or my confrontation with Karsyn the night before.

Either way, I find my fingers moving rapidly over the keyboard on my phone as I type out a reply.

Me: I'm fine. You can go now.

I watch in rapt fascination as Elias's shadowy head bends over, reading my text message. His reply is instantaneous.

Elias: thank you.

I swear my heart shreds into thousands of pieces smaller than confetti as he finally backs away from my house. I don't know why. I wanted him to leave, right?

Then why am I mourning his departure? Why did my text message seem so…final, like the last nail being drilled into our coffin, sealing our fates?

Ignoring the pang in my chest—the throbbing of my heart demanding me to call him back—I dial the only other number I have in my phone. I wait with bated breath as it rings, rings, rings, rings, rings. At first, I think she's not going to answer, but after the tenth ring, my mother picks up the phone with an annoyed, "What?"

"Did you know?" I don't bother with pleasantries. Neither of us can be bothered with it.

"Know about what?" she huffs, and I hear muffled chatter from behind her. "Can we hurry this call up? I'm getting my nails done."

"About the Bloods. And their attacks. Did you know?" I scarcely breathe as I wait for her to respond. Her sudden silence is so pronounced, that it's almost answer enough. I bite down on my lower lip, abusing the tender flesh, as I nod my head slowly. "You did, didn't you? You sent me to live with Nana, knowing that Bloods were targeting humans and witches in the area."

"I didn't send you to live anywhere," she snaps, some of her original ire returning. I can literally hear her take a deep breath as she attempts to moderate her volume while in public. "You chose to go there."

"After you chose to kick me out." I try to keep the confrontation out of my voice, but it seeps in unbidden. The hurt and anger I've kept locked up oozes from my pores, contaminating the air with its sickly scent. I can feel my power fizzle and spark beneath my skin, demanding an outlet, and I have no doubt that if Mother was directly in front of me, I would zap her to hell.

"Don't be so dramatic." She attempts a light, carefree laugh. "You're perfectly safe."

"What else do you know?" I demand, heart juddering in my chest.

"You're trying to find connections where they don't exist," she snaps. "Stop it."

"Mother…"

"I need to go now. Fabian is here to give me my afternoon massage." She doesn't bother to say "I love you" or even "goodbye" before she hangs up the phone. Instead, only static greets me, and though I expected it, it still feels like lemon juice is being squeezed into a particularly deep cut. I'm bleeding out, and I don't know how to make it stop.

First Karsyn, melting down my walls when I want nothing more than to keep them impenetrable.

Then Elias, checking in on me when I thought he still hated me.

And now Mom, with her blatant dismissal of me.

I don't know what to think anymore. I don't know what's right and what's wrong.

With a roar, I throw my phone against the wall, watching it drop to the floor with a loud smack. I don't bother to see if I cracked the screen. All I can do is collapse onto my bed and bring my knees up to my chest. Pain bombards me from all directions, squeezing at my heart like a steadily shrinking iron vise.

Everyone in my life always hurts me, always leaves me.

People say you can't die from a broken heart, but what they don't say is that it may just make you want to.

CHAPTER 22

The next week is relatively uneventful…if you don't count Karsyn's haircut as "eventful."

On Monday, he arrived at school with his normally unruly blond waves shorn in a buzz cut. On anyone else, the hairstyle would make him look hard and severe, almost like a drill sergeant, but on him, it only serves to accentuate his masculine features. His cupid bow lips. The dimple in his right cheek, normally hidden by his scruffy hair. His prominent forehead and honey-blond eyebrows. The strong dip of his jaw.

Rumor circulated that Karsyn woke up on Saturday morning—the morning after I completed my spell—with his hair on fire.

I still can't stop the sly smirk from overtaking my features at the thought. I initially feel a stab of guilt whenever I see the current state of his hair, but I dismiss those pesky thoughts like one would an annoying fly. I remember how he talked to me at my house, the anger emanating from his eyes, and I know that whatever that "moment" was had only been one-sided. He still resents me for coming back, and honestly, I can't even blame him. I'm planning to make his life hell, and he doesn't even realize it yet.

By Friday, I've fallen into the same routine as the week before—meet up with Emmett and Mari at my locker, walk to first hour together, have lunch with the two of them plus a freshly-shaven Karsyn, and then head to cheerleading practice. Through it all, Elias continues to follow me to and from school. Sometimes, he drives his Jeep. Other times, like this morning, he rides his motorcycle. But no matter what, he always plays that damn classical music as he hums softly beneath his breath.

The weather this morning is humid, a warm mist permeating the air, causing my clothes to stick to my figure. The end of September draws near, and the elements are beginning to reflect these changes. Auburn leaves now grace the trees, and already, I see Halloween decorations dotting the driveways and front porches. I spot a jack-o'-lantern displaying a serrated mouth of square teeth, a tiny triangular nose, and two rectangular eyes. On another house, an eerie skeleton dangles from a tree, its plastic bones swaying in the light fall breeze.

I firmly believe that it's too early to decorate for Halloween, but apparently, I'm in the minority. Maybe my distaste stems from being a witch. It gets redundant to see sexy witch costumes and pointed hats every damn year.

Real witches are much more terrifying.

The motor of Elias's motorcycle revs as he crawls along beside me. Since he's driving this time instead of walking, he's forced to go slightly faster than I can walk. He'll make it a few blocks ahead of me, stop, and then wait for me to catch up.

After the tenth time, I blow out a raspberry and give him the side-eye. "Don't you have somewhere to be?"

His gorgeous mouth twitches, eyes sparkling with mirth behind the translucent helmet, almost as if he's been waiting for me to say exactly that.

Or...

As if he was just waiting for me to acknowledge him.

"Nope," he says calmly, putting the bike into neutral and jumping to the side. He removes his helmet, shaking out his purple-high-lighted hair, and begins to walk beside me.

"This isn't permission for you to join me," I huff stubbornly, but his grin only broadens. Unlike Emmett and even Karsyn, he doesn't have any dimples. However, his smile extends to his eyes, causing them to glow in the darkness. At this hour, the sun still hasn't quite set, and dark, oppressive shadows sheath the entire neighborhood. The only saving grace is the street lamps lining the length of this street.

I won't admit this to anyone, let alone Elias, but his presence every morning serves as a comfort. I feel...protected. Safe. I don't know if I would feel as comfortable walking to school at seven in the morning if he wasn't beside me.

But the mere thought of admitting that out loud sends cold fear trickling down my back, almost as if someone is squeezing out a sponge above my head.

I *shouldn't* feel comforted. I know that. Being with him is the equivalent of standing on a tightrope and having the rope suddenly cut. You don't have enough time to grasp the building's edge before you fall, fall, fall.

Isn't this just like before?

He made me feel safe then, too.

A memory sweeps through me before I can shove it beneath the proverbial rug.

Elias's kiss was like a soft spring rain. It feathered across your bare skin, but you weren't cold. Instead, you wanted to open your arms wide and embrace the rain like you would a long-lost friend.

"Attention, everyone!" Lucas called from the makeshift stage erected in the school's gymnasium. "We have an important announcement." Even with hundreds of kids pressing in on all sides, obscuring me from view, I could feel his eyes searing my skin. Somehow, someway, he found me in the crowd. "Can Peony Simone come up here, please?"

I turned towards Elias hesitantly. He had apologized, but his friends? Not so much.

Elias offered me a tentative smile that didn't reach his eyes. Looking back, I should've seen that smile for what it was. I should've noticed the way it twitched ever so slightly, transforming it into a grimace.

"Go," he whispered with an assuring squeeze of my shoulder. "Maybe they want to apologize."

Apologize.

The thought sent my heart into overdrive.

All I had ever wanted was to be a part of their group. One of the Devils. And then they had begun their incessant bullying, destroying piece after piece of me until I feared there was nothing left.

Until last week, when Elias stopped me in the hall and apologized profusely. There had been tears in his violet-tinted eyes as he begged for me to forgive him. He told me he always had feelings for me, and he was afraid of them. He didn't think I was a freak or weird or any of the other deroga-tory terms they'd called me.

I hadn't believed him.

But then the next day, he had sidled into a seat beside me during first hour. And at lunch, he offered me a bouquet of gorgeous peonies. Ignoring the weird looks he received from my other classmates, and the hostile ones from his fellow Devils, he'd befriended me, eventually inviting me to the end-of-the-year dance.

It made me realize that maybe I never hated the Devils as much as I pretended to. After all, emotions were like a pendulum, swinging from hate to love in the blink of an eye. I'm not saying I was in love with the Devils or anything like that, but maybe I didn't hate them. Maybe.

"Are you sure?" I asked Elias, staring once more at the stage. Karsyn and Cassian had joined Lucas, and all three of them were staring intently at me, almost as if there was a spotlight I couldn't see.

Where were the teachers? Shouldn't they say something?

Hope was a fickle thing. When it faded, it left you feeling empty and bereft, as if you had nothing inside of you anymore. It constructed impene-

trable walls around your heart that no one could remove, not even an
army.

Elias smiled tightly and nodded towards the stage.

"Go."

I pull myself out of my memory, having not realized that I stopped in the middle of the sidewalk. Elias stands directly in front of me, worry clouding his features.

"Peony? Are you okay?" he breathes, his hands warming my arms as they brush up and down and back again.

But all I can see is his face at the dance, when he plunged his hand into my rib cage and grabbed what little of my heart remained. All of their torment, all of their cruel jokes…

It all paled in comparison to what Elias did to me that night.

"Why?" I whisper. I can't hear anything over the erratic pounding of my heart.

His brows crunch together in confusion.

"Huh?"

"Why me?" Tears well in my eyes before I can contain them, and I mentally curse myself for showing weakness.

I can see the exact moment understanding dawns. A myriad of emotions crosses his face—pain, regret, anger, and then finally, guilt. So much guilt, even I'm choking on it.

And then I realize why Elias has been following me to and from school. It's not because he likes me or even cares about my wellbeing.

It's because he feels guilty.

Uriel warned me that the Devils might have changed. He told me that they'd likely grown up and reformed.

Elias wears his guilt the same way he dons his leather jacket. He doesn't actually want to spend time with me, the freak. He just wants to alleviate his guilty conscience.

"I need to go." I practically shove him away and race down the sidewalk.

"Peony!" he calls, but he doesn't follow me.

None of the Devils have ever physically hurt me, but they're the ones responsible for every scar on my soul and each cut on my arms and thighs.

Even now, years later, my skin tingles at the memory.

Freak. Weirdo.

Those words haunt me, just like the ghost taped to our school's window.

MARIABELLA AND EMMETT ARE WAITING FOR ME AT MY LOCKER WHEN I arrive. They take one look at my dour expression and then exchange anxious looks.

"Peony? Are you okay?" Mariabella asks softly, like one would when cornering a rabid dog. But all I can hear in her voice is pity.

Pity. Pity. Pity.

Pity for the poor, broken soul who's been through hell.

I hate that simple word and the numerous connotations behind it. There's an underlying assumption that a person *wants* to be pitied, wants to have people fret over them. And maybe that's true for some, but it's not true for me.

I don't want people to look at me like I'm some sort of victim.

Mariabella nudges her elbow against my side and offers me a reassuring smile. I attempt to give her one in return, but I'm afraid mine comes across more as a grimace.

When we arrive at our class, I'm still in an extremely sour mood. No amount of teasing from Emmett or compliments from Mariabella can pull me out of it. I slide into my desk feeling like complete and utter shit. Worse than shit. Like the gum that has gotten stuck to the bottom of your shoe. You go about your day normally, repeatedly stomping on and smearing it, until you realize you have a pesky tag along. Then you take a knife and you cut the gum from your sole, all the while grimacing in disgust.

I'm that gum.

I can tell the two of them are uneasy around me, despite their best attempts not to show it. Emmett continues his relentless flirting, and I try my best to smile. I honestly do. But it almost seems as if the muscles around my lips are incapable of working. Instead, they sag downwards.

Lucas arrives then and moves to sit in the seat in front of me once more. Like always, he's wearing a form-fitting sweater that clings to his muscular but lithe form. His red hair is slicked away from his cold, critical face. He spins around in his chair until he's facing me, his sea-blue eyes meeting my own until I hastily look away. I don't want any of the Devils to see me like this. I'm afraid they'll see too much, see the demons I wish to remain hidden.

His red brows scrunch together, and something akin to concern flitters across his face. He opens his mouth before snapping it closed, the concern diminishing like it was never been there to begin with.

"I want to take you out."

Mariabella sucks in a breath in the seat beside me, and I wrench my attention off of Lucas to meet Emmett's imploring gaze. He's smiling, displaying those mouth-watering dimples, but his hand anxiously twists his pencil through his fingers. I watch, mesmerized, as the silence turns pregnant and pronounced.

"What?" I finally pterodactyl-screech.

Out of the corner of my eye, I watch Lucas stiffen ever so slightly. It's so miniscule that I almost think I imagine it.

"I want to go out with you, Peony Simone," Emmett declares without preamble, using the hand currently not destroying the pencil to run through his blond hair. "I think you're sweet, funny, sexy as hell, and I want to go on a date with you. Tonight."

"Oh my god!" Mariabella gasps, and I can't tell from her tone if she's excited for me or upset.

"I...um..." Almost unwittingly, my eyes flicker to Lucas's face. As usual, it's carved from stone, giving no hint of what he feels. But his eyes tell an entirely different story.

They seem to *burn* like a blistering hot flame.

He's positively livid, and the thought sends a surge of *something* through me. Satisfaction? Contentment? Something else entirely?

Either way, it's not Emmett's face I picture when I reply, "Yes. I'd love to."

CHAPTER 23

He corners me the second first hour ends. His huge body seems to block me in from all sides as he towers over me, eyes spewing vitriol and something I would almost describe as jealousy.

"Tell him no." His words are as monotone as everything else in his life, devoid of any inflection or emotion. He could've been reciting something as mundane as the newspaper. But that same fire flashing in his eyes from class remains as he glares down at me.

"I don't think I will," I huff, purposely giving him my back as I change out my books in my locker. Lucas releases a disgruntled huff, standing so close that his hot breath stirs the hair by my ear. Goose-bumps ripple across my flesh, and I try to quell my body's automatic, visceral reaction to his nearness.

"You don't want to go on a date with him," Lucas continues as I slam my locker shut and stride briskly towards the staircase. I know that his next class is on the opposite side of campus, but despite that, he follows me into the stairwell.

"Don't tell me what to fucking do," I hiss, whirling on him. Instantly, I become lost in his ice-blue eyes. Not in the "I'm so captivated by your beauty" way. Something about Lucas seems to innately command my attention. I think it's the power he exudes in seemingly tangible waves. You could never mistake him for anything less than the predator in this situation.

But I refuse to be his prey.

Maybe this is the moment when two lions meet in the middle of a jungle, and a fierce battle ensues. Only one of us will emerge victorious. Sooner or later, either Lucas or I will have to submit and bow down willingly to the other.

And it's not going to be me.

A few last-minute stragglers shove us apart as they hurry up the stairs, the bell ringing overhead, but we continue our standoff. His chest rises and falls with every consecutive second, and my attention can't help but drop there. Some demented part of me, a part that I hate more than anything else, wants to place my palm directly over his heart and feel if it's beating as rapidly as my own. That same part wants to run my fingers across the smooth planes of his chest and stomach, memorizing his muscles through touch alone. Would he have scars? I imagine not. Lucas seems too…perfect for something like that. Too ethereal.

"Tell him no." Lucas's cold voice drags me out of my wistful fantasies, reminding me of what, exactly, we're fighting about.

"Why the fuck would I do that?"

Lucas doesn't answer; he simply takes a step closer. I have to crane my head back to maintain eye contact.

His hand moves to touch a strand of my white hair, pulling it between his fingers. I scowl, attempting to pull my head away, but he doesn't let go of my hair.

"When you got hurt at the football game…" Lucas trails off.

"What?" I ask dryly when he doesn't continue. "Did you forget what you were going to fucking say? It's a good thing you're pretty, you fucking prick, because you don't have a lot else going for you." I rap my knuckles against the side of his head, and his scowl deepens.

"Such a bad girl. Such a filthy mouth." He takes a step even *closer* until my heaving chest touches his muscular one. "Do you know what I want to do when you sass me like that?"

"Lock me in my locker?" I hold up my hand and begin to tick off the various offenses. "Pour tomato sauce on my hair? *Cut* my hair? Call me a freak? A weirdo? Torture me in gym class? Trip me in the halls? Oh wait, you've already done all of that!"

"You hate me," he says simply. It's not a question, but I take it as one.

"I fucking *despise* you," I seethe, allowing all of my loathing to spew from my lips like a sickly poison. "I hate you and everything you stand for. How can you stand here and think that you have the right to tell me what to do? How can you stand here at all, after what you did to me?"

"Peony." His voice is harsh, a warning, but I continue on.

"I want you to bleed, Lucas Scott. I want you to burn at the stake the way you made me burn."

"I'm not a good guy, Peony," Lucas says gravely, and I see in his eyes that he's thinking about all of the things he's done to me. All of the things he will continue to do. I truly believe there's something irreparably broken inside of him. Something dark and twisted and laden with shadows. Maybe that's why he's so obsessed with breaking me—he's already fundamentally broken himself. A man like him can never love, can never find true happiness. In ten years, he's going to end up in rehab or dead. That need for control...

It's going to kill him.

And while one part of me wants to dance on his grave, another twisted part of me rebels. Screams. Cries. Her agony is almost palpable.

"You'll never forgive me," he continues on, and this time, his voice is high-pitched in wonder, as if the thought that I could hate him forever never crossed his mind. Those eyes of his become guarded, almost cautious, as they narrow on me. "Even though that was five years ago."

"You don't just forget about years of torture," I hiss.

"I've never forgotten."

"What?"

His voice is quiet, a breath in the wind. "I never forgot you, Peony. I never stopped thinking about you."

"And you won't forget me." I stand up on my tiptoes so our faces are mere centimeters apart. "I'll make sure of that, Lucas Scott. I can't—"

His lips collide with mine before I can even finish my sentence. Before I can even catch my bearings. Before I can even blink. His lips feel softer than I would've thought, lighting up everything inside of me like a wildfire. A tiny voice, almost muffled, sighs in contentment, as my body arches towards him like a flower seeking sunlight.

I want to run my fingers through his dark red hair until the strands stick in all directions. And then when he leaves this spot, I'll be on his arm, a queen to his king. Everyone will then know who's responsible for his disheveled state, and a surge of possessiveness cascades through me.

The taste of mint invades my mouth as my lips part instinctively, granting his tongue entrance. I feel my hands move to his chest and clench his shirt, squeezing the fabric as he makes a low, dangerous noise in the back of his throat. His massive frame pins my much smaller one against the wall, and I've never felt more petite. He holds so much power in his lithe, muscular frame. So much anger and energy. He could snap my neck as easily as he can caress it and shower it with kisses.

What are you doing?!? Why are you kissing Lucas fucking Scott? Why are you enjoying it, panting for more?

Coming to my senses, I jerk my head away from him, lift my hand, and slap him as hard as I can across the face. I don't care that there might be a camera in the stairwell, capturing this on film. I don't care that Lucas could make my life even more of a living hell.

All I know for certain is that a tiny piece of my anger incinerated with my slap. And at the same time, I never felt more empty and broken.

His eyes flare brightly as he rubs a hand across his red cheek. That apathetic expression remains on his face as he stares at me blankly.

"Go fuck yourself," I hiss, storming up the staircase. I'm to the second level when I realize that he hasn't followed me...but he also hasn't left. I would've heard the sound of the door slamming shut.

Curiosity getting the better of me, I tiptoe towards the railing and peek my head over the side.

My breath leaves me in a whooping exhale, and my body's internal temperature ratchets up one thousand degrees.

Lucas still stands at the bottom of the stairwell, now leaning against the wall, out of view of the lone camera. His jeans are unzipped, his long cock squeezed between his fingers as he strokes himself. Fuck, he's big. Not wide, but long. And is that... Is that a piercing?

I bring my fingers to my mouth to quell the gasp that wants to escape as he throws his head back in pleasure, stroking himself. His hand fondles the mushroom tip before stroking back to his base. His other hand begins to fondle his balls as a breathy exhale leaves his parted lips.

The scene is so erotic, so enticing, that I find my hand drifting to my own crotch without conscious thought. Through the material of my jeans, I begin to rub myself. I wish desperately I was brave enough to place a finger in my pussy. I imagine it's already soaking wet.

But then that image changes, and instead of my finger, it's Lucas's cock. I envision it impaling me as his slender fingers tweak at my breasts.

The vision transforms a third time, and instead of Lucas sheathing his length into me, he's pushing it inside Karsyn's ass. The quarterback groans, muscles clenching, as Lucas enters him inch by inch. And then Cassian's there, his thick cock on display as he fists Karsyn's hair, bringing the other man's lips to his twitching dick. As Lucas fucks Karsyn's ass, Cassian fucks his mouth. Behind Cassian, Elias places his lubed cock into the crease of the dark man's ass, his hands flicking Cassian's nipples. And then there's me, sitting over them all, naked. Like a ruler supervising her court. I'm their fucking queen.

As if my mental imagery wishes to reflect that, all of a sudden, all four men are surrounding me. Cassian kisses one breast, and Karsyn sucks my other nipple. Elias pulls my lips into a heated, passionate kiss, while Lucas's pierced cock lines up with my entrance...

Oh. My. God.

My orgasm explodes through me, soaking my jeans and panties, as I squeeze my eyelids shut.

That image...

I force my eyes open, only to meet a pair of blue ones down below. I watch in rapt fascination as Lucas's cock twitches once, twice, three times before shooting cum. His eyes never leave mine as a low, predatory groan leaves his mouth.

What the hell did I just do?

Feeling flustered and embarrassed, I run as fast as I can up the remainder of the staircase.

I'll repeat—*what the fucking hell did I just do?*

CHAPTER 24

Thank fuck I always have a change of clothes to wear after cheerleading practice everyday. Because walking around in cream de pants? Not my cup of tea.

There's not much I can do about my panties, though, so I choose to go without them. I toss the wadded up underwear into the bottom of my backpack, remove my jeans, and then slip into a new pair. This one is a shade or two lighter than the previous pants I wore, so I can only pray no one paid me enough attention to notice.

In the bathroom mirror, I purse my lips and stare at myself intently. My cheeks are flushed, the red noticeable even from a distance, and my white hair is unruly from how many times I ran my hand through it. There's not much I can do about the cheeks, but I did bring a brush.

Quickly, I sort through the tangles until it once more hangs around my shoulders loosely.

But despite my immaculate physical appearance, my insides are in tangles. Thousands and thousands of intricate webs, pulling and tugging at the organs like iron chains.

I hate myself.

How can I not?

I fucking came envisioning the *Devils*. It's dark and sinful and so damn disgusting, I feel sick just thinking about it. How weak must I be for that to happen? How pathetic? The familiar tendrils of self-loathing circle around me before grasping both wrists and pulling tight, extending me like some fucked up sacrifice on a stone altar.

The thing that pisses me off the most? It's the fact that I can't stop thinking about it. Whenever I close my eyes, I see Lucas's hand on his cock, pumping. I see his face contorted into a mask of euphoria. I see those curled lashes of his, lashes capable of making most girls jealous, flutter against his cheeks as sticky cum squirts from his tip.

Arousal once more settles in my core, percolating like molten lava, and I rub my thighs together like some sort of hussy.

No, Peony! Stop!

Taking a deep breath and reminding myself of all the reasons why I hate the Devils, I swing my backpack over my shoulder and head into the hallway. I'm already twenty minutes late for Orchestra, but I doubt Mr. Tucker will reprimand me. I'll just lie and say I got lost or something; despite this already being my second week, he'll believe me.

It's only when I'm passing a hallway of practice rooms do I hear the voices.

"I said no." I'd recognize that low, husky timbre anywhere. Cassian. But even in middle school, when he hated me almost as much as I hated him, I've never heard such rage before. It changes his sultry voice to something dark and almost unrecognizable.

"Honey," a second voice coos, and my footsteps falter when I realize it belongs to Mrs. Town. Anger momentarily darkens my sight, almost like a tarp being tossed haphazardly over my head, and my hands clench into fists. "Come here."

Against my better judgment, I tiptoe towards the door. Unlike the first practice room I found him in, this one has a small, rectangular window facing the hall. Risky, but I figure they believe no one would be coming this direction at this time in the hour.

The black rage transitions into something red-hot when I see Cassian standing against the wall, scowling, and Mrs. Town cupping his junk through his pants.

"I don't want to do this anymore." He attempts to step away from her, but she only tightens her grip on his cock. Pain flashes across his face, one he covers up by gritting his teeth.

"Come on. I'll suck you." Without waiting for him to respond, she unbuttons the top of her shirt, pushing her bra cups down until her massive breasts spring free. They're definitely fake, probably the size of a modest watermelon. She begins to pluck at her nipples as she gives Cassian what she probably thinks is a seductive look. Honestly? It makes her appear slightly constipated.

As she falls on her knees before him, those massive breasts of hers bounce in a way that's designed to draw the eye. Her manicured hands run up Cassian's thighs until they reach his zipper.

He's...trembling. Not in desire as I originally suspected. Not even completely in anger. It's fear.

Horror rushes through my veins as I take in the image before me with new eyes.

When Mrs. Town removes Cassian's cock from his jeans, that horror turns into anger, so thick and pronounced, I'm choking on it. My magic sparks before I can contain it, and then it floods from my pores in a sudden surge of power.

Mrs. Town's screech is music to my ears, and all I can do is grin as she's suddenly propelled backwards by some unseen force.

Cassian looks alarmed, but does not lift a hand to help the bare-chested teacher back up.

"I think I was electrocuted," Mrs. Town breathes in horror, staring up at the fluorescent light above.

"Oh, really?" Cassian's tone makes it sound like he couldn't give a damn anyway. Slowly, he tucks his flaccid dick back into his jeans and levels her with a look capable of curdling milk.

Mrs. Town staggers to her feet, appearing flustered, and says something too low for me to hear. Without another word, she pulls her bra back into place, rebuttons her shirt, and then sashays towards the door, red hair swaying.

I have just enough thought to duck to the side, using the shadows as coverage, before she glides past me.

My breathing is choppy as I suck in lungfuls of air, grateful I wasn't caught. But my relief is short lived when Cassian's dry voice queries, "How long have you been here?"

He leans against the opened door of the music room, attempting to adopt a nonchalant, "cool guy" expression. But I can see the tightening of his eyes, the clenching of his jaw, the dimness in his normally radiant eyes.

There's no use lying. I have no doubt he saw me through the window.

"A bit," I say vaguely, backing up a step. He immediately counters my retreat with two quick strides of his own.

"What exactly did you see?" he demands in a dangerous tone.

I hold my chin up stubbornly, refusing to cow beneath his dark, penetrating gaze.

"What she did was assault," I settle on at last, and I hear his teeth physically grind together as he glares down at me.

"You don't know what the fuck you're talking about."

"I know what I saw," I counter. He's trying to intimidate me, trying to use his massive size in order to get me to cower, but I simply straighten my shoulders and meet his gaze dead-on. I always feel as if I'm walking on eggshells around this devilishly handsome man, as if every word I say only serves to poke the beast.

But I can't ever seem to stop myself.

"So you saw me begging for it?" he asks darkly, continuing to use his impressive height to tower over me and make me feel small. I think out of all the Devils, he's the biggest. It's surprising, considering Karsyn is the football player and Elias is known for his kickboxing. But Cassian? He's massive. "You saw me begging for my teacher to suck my cock?"

There's a threat in his words, an underlying warning to "back the fuck off," but I choose not to heed it.

"I saw you shaking," I confess. "I saw that sliver of fear in your eye as you told her no."

"You don't know what you're talking about, baby," he purrs, trailing a finger down my cheek. He stands close enough for me to feel the hard planes of his chest against my delicate curves. "I wanted that bitch to fuck me."

"Cassian…"

"Besides," he shrugs his broad shoulders, "it's a mutually beneficial arrangement. She gets my monster cock, and I pass Lit. A win-win. And I *need* to pass my English class this year."

"It's assault," I stress again, feeling my heart rise in my throat until it becomes lodged there. *Ba-dum. Ba-dum. Ba-dum.*

"Not if I wanted it," he counters, smirking arrogantly back at me.

"But you didn't." I can feel tears well in my eyes, and Cassian appears momentarily taken aback. He drops his finger from my face as if my skin burned him. "Cassian, I understand."

His dark brows furrow.

"Huh?"

"And I know you think that you can't do anything, that no one will believe you, that it's your fault…" My voice hitches, and whatever Cassian sees in my expression causes his own to darken exponentially.

"Who hurt you?" he rages, baring his teeth. "Who the fuck hurt you?"

You did, I yearn to say, but I know that's not what he's asking.

"It doesn't matter."

"Yes, it fucking does!" he bellows, and I cast a glance in both directions, worried someone will overhear. Fortunately, this section of the school is separated from the academic classes on the lower level. And most of the music classes are a few halls down. Cassian, seeming to realize where my thoughts have gone, takes a calming breath, attempting to moderate his volume. I don't think it works, though, when I see the pure venom spewing from his eyes. "Who was it, baby?"

"I understand, Cassian," I say instead, willing him with my eyes to...to what? Stop his illicit affair with our teacher? Turn her in to the authorities or even just the principal?

"But you don't, baby. You really don't." He squeezes his eyelids shut, and before I can even respond, he smashes his fist into the wall. It does nothing to cement, but his fingers come away bruised and bloody.

"Fucking hell!"

"If I fail her class, I don't get my scholarship," he whispers, and I remember from my research that he got accepted into Juilliard for guitar. "And if I don't fuck her, I don't get my A. So no, you don't understand."

I understand more than you can possibly believe.

Cassian's face closes down when he sees the rebuttal on my face. With an enraged roar, he kicks at the nearest wall before stomping away, cradling his injured hand to his chest. I watch him go, feeling my heart shatter into thousands of pieces, all of them smaller than the sprinkles you would put on ice cream.

What Cassian is doing destroys something inside of you. Destroys a tiny portion of your soul you can never get back.

And if anyone is going to destroy Cassian, it's going to me, not that bitch.

Trembling slightly, I pull my phone out of my pocket and swipe to the video of Mrs. Town and Cassian on that first day. And then, I head towards the principal's office.

Cassian might never forgive me for what I'm about to do, but I didn't come here wanting his friendship.

I came here to destroy him.

But maybe this time, my method of destroying him might actually save his soul.

CHAPTER 25

I have a date.

Tonight.

With Emmett.

My heart gives a girly little scream, throwing confetti in the air and writing his name and mine repeatedly in my internal notebook. But then that confetti turns into bouts of blood and our names contort, transforming into some demonic summoning ritual.

And though I should be focusing on Emmett, and only on Emmett, my mind repeatedly drifts back to my confrontation with Cassian, followed by my trip to the principal's office where I showed him the video.

My hands are slick with sweat as I think about what I did. He's going to hate me. I know that. I accepted that. But…

"Peony?" Nana's head appears at the top of the ladder, her vibrant violet hair visible in the dim light. "Mariabella is here."

"I'll be right down," I say as I peruse my selection of dresses for the hundredth time. Do I go casual? Flirty? Fun? According to Emmett, after dinner, we're heading to a party at Jessica Simmon's house. What would someone wear to a house party?

When Nana doesn't immediately retreat, I turn towards her with an eyebrow raised. "Yeah?"

"Why didn't you tell me you're going on a date?" she demands, sounding genuinely upset.

"Because it just happened today." I grab a few different outfits at random, slinging them over my arms, before grabbing my makeup case and curling iron out of my trunk. The rest of my supplies are already in the bathroom.

"It's with that one boy, isn't it?" Nana gushes as I gesture for her to climb down the ladder. I follow after her, dropping my clothes and items unceremoniously onto the ground so I don't need to carry them as I descend.

"What boy?" I query once my feet land on the wooden flooring.

"The one with the purple highlights." Nana grins mischievously. "I see the way he looks at you, Peony. I always knew it was a matter of time."

I swear my body's internal temperature ratchets up a billion degrees. I can feel flames fan my cheeks as I bend down and grab my discarded items.

"No," I protest. "It's not him."

"Oh." Nana frowns. "Well, I guess...have fun tonight?" Her words turn into a question, and I just barely resist the urge to roll my eyes. "And don't do anything I wouldn't do."

"That's a pretty short list," I tease as I move down the hall and towards the foyer where I see Mariabella's sheet of golden hair. "I might need a microscope to read it."

"Oh, ha. Ha." Nana swats my arm playfully. "You can be such a brat sometimes, you know that?"

"And you're a wrinkled, old hag," I retort, and she gasps, placing both her hands over her cheeks.

"I am no such thing!"

Mariabella turns towards us when we enter, a wide smile unfurling on her face.

"Peony!" She races forward and grabs me in a tight hug, before releasing me and turning towards Nana respectfully. "You must be Mrs. Simone."

"Please, call me Cardinal." Nana extends a hand, but Mariabella ignores it and pulls the older woman into a hug.

"It's so good to meet you!" she exclaims, and Nana chuckles good-naturedly, patting my friend on the back. To me, she adds, "When is your date going to be here?"

I glance at the archaic grandfather clock with vines and various types of flowers carved into its woodworking. "About an hour." I grab Mariabella's hand and pull her towards my bathroom. "So let's make me look beautiful."

Mariabella laughs lightly. "You're always beautiful, silly. But I am *dying* to do your hair."

We enter the first-floor bathroom, and immediately, Mariabella instructs me to straddle the toilet.

"Hair first," she says, plugging my curling iron in and grabbing my brush. She begins to slowly, leisurely, brush through my white hair, and my eyes squeeze shut with how good it feels. I'm one of those people who loves it when someone plays with their hair.

Mariabella curls the long strands before French braiding the front and connecting it in an intricate loop at the back of my scalp, joining the long tresses cascading past my shoulders.

"Damn," Mariabella drawls out as I stare at my reflection in the mirror. "I did good." She pats the bathroom counter as she unzips my makeup bag, pulling items out at random. "Now sit." Her face scrunches together when she pulls out a pallet of blush that has seen better days. It's clumpy in some places but as loose as sand in others. "When was the last time you wore this makeup?"

"Um…" I shrug helplessly. I rarely, if ever, put on makeup. Maybe some mascara and blush here and there, but never anything overly fancy.

She clicks her tongue as she pulls out my eyeliner, moving to stand between my legs.

"Now close your eyes," she instructs, her eyes flicking to my lips before moving to my lipstick collection. She makes another face at my limited shades, releasing a heavy sigh. "We don't have a lot to work with here."

When Mariabella finally declares she's done, we both step back to admire me in the mirror. I have to admit she did a great job of accentuating my already prominent features. The dark gold, sparkly eyeshadow heightens the amber color of my eyes. She contoured my cheekbones and applied a light layer of blush, the combination looking surprisingly natural. Light pink lipstick was applied to my lips, completing the look.

"You're a fairy godmother," I breathe, a wide grin splitting my face in two. She makes a nonsensical noise in the back of her throat.

"Bippity, boppity, boo," she singsongs before tossing me a dark green gown with a lacy trim. It's long-sleeved, like everything else I own, and has a sheer top that cinches at the waist before cascading outwards, ending just at my knee. It's sexy and stylish and fun…but it's also perfectly suitable for a party. It'll look great with my white blonde hair.

"I'll go find you some shoes," she says, referring to the ones sitting on a shelf in the entryway that she no doubt noticed when she arrived. "Get changed."

She ducks out before I can even thank her, and I take a moment to run my hand over the soft material. I wore this dress only once before, back at the coven for the Halloween Solstice. I attended with Uriel, and it was one of the best nights of my life. Drinking, dancing, and receiving the powers from the Earth as it coursed through my body like waves of electricity.

The Halloween Solstice represents new beginnings—a time when the Earth's magic replenishes itself. It's only fitting that I wear it now. Maybe, just maybe, this date with Emmett is *my* new beginning.

I strip out of my normal clothes and step into the dress, tugging it up my hips. Before I can finish putting it fully on, the door to the bathroom flies open, and an oblivious Mariabella enters, dangling two pairs of shoes from both hands.

"This one will definitely add a few inches of height, but I'm not sure how comfortable they are. And these are—" She pauses when she catches sight of me, eyes roaming across my body before resting on my bare arms. Her face turns stark white, and the shoes clatter to the floor, forgotten. "Peony!" she gasps as she rushes forward, tenderly grabbing my wrist and straightening my arm.

I'm rooted to the spot. I can't think, can't breathe, can't even see. My heart feels heavy in my chest, like it weighs a million pounds, and my legs shake like they're nothing but noodles. I start to fall forward but quickly catch myself by placing my hand on the granite countertop. Mariabella is speaking, but her words enter one ear and then leave the other. It's almost as if my head is made up of nothing but air, and the words hang suspended there, impossible for me to fully catch.

She saw.

She saw something that no one has ever seen before. Something that I don't *want* anyone to see. It's twisted and fucked up, but it's also mine. My demons and my pain. My internal suffering made flesh.

Slowly, distantly, sounds return to me. It feels as if I'm underwater, hearing muted conversations on the surface but unable to join in. Water rushes through my ears, the sound shattering my eardrums, as I finally orient myself to the here and now.

"What the fuck happened? Peony, I can't... What happened? I just...huh?" Mariabella is saying, her words rushing together in her distress. She's staring intently at my pale arm, at the physical manifestation of my emotional pain. Marring the porcelain skin are deep, jagged scars. Hundreds of them. Some are barely the width of a string, but others are large, as if someone has taken a knife and gorged out the skin. They extend from the inside of my wrist to my elbow, each one telling a different story.

"It's fine." I try to sound dismissive, even happy, but Mariabella's fierce expressions stop me in place.

"It's not fucking fine," she rages, glaring at the offending scars. She swallows heavily. "Did you…did you do this to yourself?"

I want to lie—but what lie could I give her, anyway? She's already seen how broken I truly am.

"Don't worry," I reassure her, removing my arm from her steel grip and pulling the green dress the rest of the way up. I give her my back so she can zip it up, and I'm shocked to feel her fingers trembling. "They're from middle school."

"Peony," she gasps. And when I turn back towards her, tears run down her cheeks. "What happened?"

I can feel myself start to break as well, start to crumble into dust. She's ripping open my meticulous packaging, pulling at the pretty ribbons securing me in one piece, and then watching as I come apart around her, revealing a box full of shattered glass. There's nothing beautiful about something capable of cutting you open. The wrapping serves as an illusion designed to deceive and entice, but the inside? That's where you see how ugly someone truly is.

And I'm the ugliest monster of them all.

A single tear travels down my cheek, followed immediately by a second one. And then, I'm sobbing, gasping for breath, ruining the makeup she painstakingly applied.

"You don't remember me, do you?" I say as she stares at me in disbelief and pain. So much pain. It's almost as if my grief has become a palpable entity that she can feel herself. "You don't remember me from middle school."

"Middle school?" Her nose crinkles as she stares at me, and then I see it. I see the moment when understanding dawns, and what little color remains on her face disappears completely. She staggers back a step as if she's been struck, shaking her head from side to side slowly in disbelief. "No. It can't be…"

"We never really talked," I confess in a choked voice, those damn, wayward tears continuing to leave red, blotchy marks on my face.

Horror has her clutching the towel rack, as if her legs are seconds from giving out. "Karsyn…"

And I can see that she knows. She may not have ever talked to me, but she remembers the poor, broken girl teased and bullied mercilessly by the Devils. By her boyfriend. And I can see the pieces clicking together in her mind as she stares at my arms, now hidden by the dress sleeves.

She races towards the toilet, barely getting it open before she throws up. She's crying in earnest now as her hands clench the bowl.

"I am so, so sorry," she sobs, dry-heaving. "I didn't know. I didn't know it was that bad."

I take a step towards her, and she flinches away.

"I don't blame you or anyone other than them," I whisper, grabbing a towel from the rack and scrubbing at my face. I'm going to have to go sans makeup for my date, but I can't find it within me to care.

"But we were there," she screams. "We saw what they were doing, and we just let it happen." She climbs to her feet jerkily, eyes wide with panic. "I swear to you that if I knew it was that bad, I would've stopped it. I was just a dumb fucking kid who didn't want to get on the popular boys' radar. Besides, I just assumed it was because they had a crush on you. I didn't even think…" She trails off with another choked sob. "I'm so sorry, Peony. For everything."

"I know you are," I whisper. I can see the sincerity emanating from her red-rimmed eyes. Can hear it in every breath she takes. I never blamed Mariabella—any of my other classmates—for the actions and sins of the Devils. I never condemned them to hell the way I did my tormentors. I don't know if I would've done things differently if our situations were reversed. I would like to believe I would've stepped in, but the truth is? I can't say for certain. Maybe my fear would've prohibited me from doing so. Fear is a funny thing, but so is ignorance. I don't know which one makes you more culpable.

"I'll make this right, Peony," Mariabella vows, eyes shining with an unspoken vow.

I take her hands in both of mine and give them a reassuring squeeze. "I know you will." I brush at my face with the back of my hand, clearing away the last few drops of tears. "Now, can you please fix this?" I gesture desperately to my red and blotchy face, and Mariabella releases a slightly hysterical laugh. "I need to look semi-good for my date."

Emmett arrives right at six o'clock, a bouquet of flowers in his hands as he stands on the front porch. I have to admit he looks handsome today with his blond hair slicked back and his dimples on display. I wait for the sparks to buzz through my body. For the grasshoppers to start jumping around in my stomach.

But I feel nothing.

"Wow." Emmett's eyes rove up and down my body appreciatively as he hands me the flowers, which I immediately set in a small vase sitting on the entry table. "You look beautiful."

"And you don't look too bad yourself," I tease, nodding at his simple ensemble of a stretched blue-collared shirt and dark jeans.

"Not too bad!" Emmett brings a hand to chest. "I look sexy as fuck."

I roll my eyes as I step out of the house, shutting the door behind me. Mariabella left only a few minutes ago, claiming cryptically that she had something she needed to do. I didn't press her on it, and I promised to call her as soon as I got home. It's nice to have a female friend I can talk to and discuss things with.

And despite my early trepidation, it's a weight off my chest to have her know the truth about me and the Devils. It makes me feel as if I'm not so alone anymore. As if the world isn't resting on my shoulders, crushing me.

Emmett and I continue our light banter as we pile into his car and he drives us to the restaurant.

He takes us to a quaint Italian restaurant located just off the main highway, one town over. The lights are dim when we enter, and all of the staff are meticulously groomed in black pants, black dress shirts, and clashing white aprons. The aroma of baked bread permeates the air as the hostess leads us to a table near the back of the restaurant, directly beneath a low-hanging chandelier. A single candle rests on the center of the table, casting Emmett's boyish face in shadows.

I feel the familiar tendrils of first date nerves jolt through me as I stare at the handsome man before me.

"You really do look beautiful today," Emmett says softly. "You look…powerful."

A blush rises to my cheeks, and I duck my head to survey the menu options. Deciding on ravioli, I close the menu and wait for Emmett to look up as well.

"So, how do you know Jessica?" I inquire while we wait for someone to take our drink orders.

"The girl who's throwing the party?" Emmett asks for clarification. When I nod, he shrugs his broad shoulders and relaxes back in his seat, steepling his fingers together on his chest. "Don't. I heard about the party from some guys on the football team."

"You mentioned before that you moved here. Where did you—"

"What the fuck?" Emmett exclaims suddenly, cutting me off mid-sentence. It's then I hear a familiar, scathing voice from directly behind me.

"Thank you. The lighting over at this table is significantly better." I watch in abject horror as Lucas slides the hostess a crisp one hundred dollar bill before sitting at the table directly beside ours. Cassian, Elias, and Karsyn join him.

What the fuckity fuck?

Why are they here?

Why are they together?

They're not even friends anymore, dammit! They hate each other. I can practically taste the animosity saturating the air.

Emmett narrows his eyes at the four Devils while I just gape wordlessly.

"What are you guys doing here?" Emmett demands through clenched teeth.

Lucas smiles darkly.

"Can't we enjoy a nice meal before the party tonight?"

"Y-You guys...don't talk!" I manage to stutter out, pointing wildly between the four of them.

"And this is a date restaurant," Emmett adds.

"Are you saying we can't be on a date?" Cassian throws his head back in raucous laughter before tossing an arm around the back of Karsyn's seat. If Cassian is here, if he's laughing, it means that he hasn't heard about what I did. Yet. "Come here, baby, and give me a kiss."

Karsyn makes a face. "I'd rather cut off my balls."

"Or let me suck them. Don't play hard to get," Cassian teases.

Karsyn releases a disgruntled huff. "Oh, all right. As long as you don't use your teeth."

Lucas shakes his head at their antics, his expression utterly impassive, before turning to spear me in place with a single look.

"Peony, I didn't know I'd find you here."

"You did," I say firmly, once I finally overcome my initial shock. "You heard Emmett ask me, and then you heard us finalize our plans."

"Did I?" His expression doesn't change once. Not even a minuscule twitch of his lips.

My hands tremble beneath the table as I glance from face to face. What exactly are they up to? What are they planning to do to me?

"If you'll excuse me…"

Ignoring Emmett's protests, I stomp away from the table and exit the restaurant. And then I don't stop walking until I'm hidden in a connected alleyway, my back resting against the cold brick wall. I take deep, stuttered breaths as anger rampages through me.

How dare they?

How *fucking* dare they?

"I told the guys I needed to take a piss," a familiar voice says nonchalantly, a moment before he leans against the wall beside me. "I don't think they believe me, but they were too busy glaring daggers at each other to stop me."

"Elias," I say coolly.

"Peony," he replies back, but unlike me, there's the slightest hint of amusement in his tone. He reaches into his leather jacket pocket and procures a box of cigarettes and then a lighter. He places one between his lips and then uses both hands to light it.

"Isn't that super stereotypical of you?" I deadpan as I stare at his face illuminated by the crackling orange fire. "The leather-jacket wearing, bad boy biker smoking?"

He releases a rough guffaw.

"And isn't this stereotypical of you? Pretty girl hiding from her date because she knows she doesn't belong to him."

"Fuck you, Elias," I hiss. "You're such an asshole."

"Maybe." He shrugs, seemingly unconcerned. "I'm a lot of things. A nightmare, for one. A monster. I never said I was the good guy, and I don't think I ever will."

"So you're okay with walking through life acting like a massive dick?" I snap, folding my arms over my chest as a sudden gust of wind causes goosebumps to pebble on my legs.

"I *have* a massive dick," Elias teases as he unzips his leather jacket. Before I can protest, he drapes it over my shoulders, and I'm assaulted by his distinct scent of leather and grease, combined with something sweet from his cologne.

"Why are you here?" I demand, trying to ignore the desperate urge I have to bury my nose into his jacket and inhale deeply. "And I know it's not for the breadsticks."

"The breadsticks *are* good, but no. That's not why we're here." His eyes bore into mine, but he doesn't bother to answer my question. Fucking prick.

"I see that the old gang is back together again," I say curtly, and he simply nods his head once.

"We are."

Silence descends as we stare at one another, the frigid wind battering against our cheeks.

"*Why* are you guys back together again?" I hiss when it becomes too much. Then again, everything about these Devils is too fucking much.

"The same reason we got together in the first place. The same reason we broke up."

My heart hammers in my chest, but I can't figure out why. His eyes captivate me, making me incapable of speech.

"I hope that reason isn't me, Elias Briggs," I say slowly, carefully, watching every shift in his expression. "Because I despise you and the rest of your so-called friends. You're monsters, every last one of you."

He doesn't even bother to deny it. "Maybe." He holds his cigarette casually between two fingers. "But maybe that's why we're so fucking obsessed with you."

I don't bother dignifying that with a response. Instead, I shove his jacket off of my shoulders, push past his muscular body, and storm back into the restaurant. It doesn't appear as if the other four men have even blinked since I left, all engaged in a fierce stare off.

Well, all of them except for Cassian, who has cut a hole into a breadstick and is using a second one to fuck the first. When he sees me looking, he smirks dangerously and brings the bread to his mouth, running his tongue over the top before swallowing it whole.

I quickly look away, focusing instead on my date for the evening.

"How about we skip dinner and head straight for the party?" I suggest, keeping my back to the Devils.

"And maybe get dessert after?" Emmett questions with a glint in his eyes that speaks louder than words. There's no missing the sexual innuendo.

Instead of answering him, I merely take his hand in mine—allowing my fingers to trail over his before grasping firmly—and pull him out of the restaurant, leaving behind the infuriated Devils.

CHAPTER 26

Jessica Simmon's house is nearly as large as Mariabella's, a huge, faux-Italian villa with a circular driveway displaying a marble fountain, wrought iron gates, multiple balconies, and potted plants dotting the walkway.

We're forced to park on the street in front of the house, Emmett's tiny car barely able to squeeze between two trucks.

As we begin to climb up the steep driveway, the lawns on either side already crowded with cars and drunk teenagers, Emmett reaches coyly towards me and interlocks his fingers with mine.

I turn to him in surprise, cheeks flaming, but allow him to take my hand and pull me the rest of the way to the house.

My mind keeps circling back to the Devils. Why did they show up? What did they *want*? Obviously, this is part of their grand plan or whatever, but I have no fucking idea what that plan is. I'm going to drive myself crazy in my quest for answers, I just fucking know it.

Still, I try to focus only on Emmett's hand in mine as we enter Jessica's house.

If I thought the exterior was massive, the inside puts it to shame. Flood lights hang from the ceiling, each one with a different colored piece of paper taped overhead. The combination is a rainbow of light illuminating the makeshift dance floor, which is nothing more than a bunch of couches pushed to the edges of the room.

The kitchen is to the right of the entrance, and it's there Emmett leads me first, his hand leaving mine and drifting to the small of my back. He leans closer until his hot breath wafts across my earlobe.

"Can I get you a drink?" he asks, raising his voice to be heard over the roar of the music. At my nod, he gives my hip a squeeze before detangling himself and moving towards the keg manned by one of his football teammates.

I take the moment to lean against the far wall, in direct view of both the kitchen and dance floor, and survey the party in extensive detail.

Have you ever seen a party on television? Where twenty-something-year-old actors pretend to be high schoolers, and they dance and drink and get wasted? Well, this party is a much tamer version of that. People are drinking and dancing, all right, but there are no couples having sex in the corner of the rooms. No illicit affairs in direct view of their classmates. Honestly, I believe a lot of script writers are perverted fifty-year-old men who have no idea what being a teenager is really like.

"A drink for the pretty lady." Emmett returns only a few minutes later, offering me an unopened beer that must've been sitting beside the keg. I take it gratefully as he unscrews the lid on his own and takes a long swallow, his throat bobbing.

"Thanks, Em." The condensation makes my hands sticky as I absently move the bottle from hand to hand, almost as if I'm playing my own version of solo hot potato.

"Do you wanna maybe dance?" He inclines his head towards the dance floor where dozens of teenagers are plastered together, swaying to the beat blaring from the television's speakers. "I mean, if you dance as well as you cheer..." His gaze drags over me suggestively, and he waggles his blond eyebrows.

"Let's dance, you horny freak," I tease, taking his muscular bicep in the hand not currently holding the beer bottle and pulling him into the middle of the dance floor.

I'm not usually one for dancing, but there's something immensely enticing about letting all of your inhibitions fade away. I weave my fingers through my hair as the music rushes through me like sparklers being set off beneath my skin. Emmett continues to eye me as if he's imagining unwrapping me like a present...with his teeth. His hips gyrate against me, sending a thrill straight to my throbbing heat. I don't necessarily know how I feel about Emmett, but I do know without a doubt that he's attractive. Funny. Sweet.

And if the boner pressing against my stomach is any indication, hung.

For a brief moment, I consider asking him to leave with me. I haven't gotten laid since a random hookup after my breakup with Uriel, and I'm desperate for it. Needy. I want to feel loved and wanted, to have someone worship my body with all the reverence of a priest of old times offering sacrifices to the vindictive, beautiful goddess.

Before the words can formulate, Emmett's entire body stiffens—and not just his dick. He glares at something over my shoulder with an expression I'm beginning to recognize. Despite already knowing what I'm going to see, I turn around, just as the Devils enter through the front door.

Immediately, whispers begin to rise up at the sight of all four of them together. The students act as if they're seeing an ethereal unicorn standing beneath a rainbow while a leprechaun feeds it gold coins from his chamber pot. It's a little nauseating.

Karsyn splits off from the other three, his broad shoulders disappearing from view as he enters the kitchen. The other Devils survey the party with varying expressions on their faces. Elias's could best be described as disgusted, his eyes narrowed into thin slits as if he's worried one of us filthy peasants will get too close and ruin his "tough guy" aura. Cassian is smirking like the flirtatious deviant he is, and when a girl passes, tittering obnoxiously, he winks at her. For some reason, that bothers me. It quite literally feels as if he lifted a bow, nocked an arrow, and allowed it to fly straight into my chest.

And then there's Lucas.

His eyes are devoid of any feeling, any emotion, as he surveys the room. When two girls scramble up to him, blushing fiercely and twirling their hair around their fingers, he merely stares at them until they scamper away. He's like an icicle hanging precariously from a low roof. Any second now, it'll dislodge and pierce you.

"What the fuck are they doing here?" Emmett seethes, and I place a hand on his arm, drawing his attention back to me.

"It's a party. They're the most popular guys in school." I roll my eyes. "Of course they'd be here."

Karsyn returns from the kitchen at that exact moment, a nearly empty beer dangling from his fingers. This close, I can see the flush to his cheeks and the glossy sheen covering his eyes. When he moves, he sways, almost as if gravity itself is fighting against him.

He's fucking wasted. Already.

How long has it been since the restaurant? An hour? Two?

Did he literally rob a fucking convenience store, but instead of stealing money, he stole alcohol?

Cassian eyes Karsyn with concern as he begins to wobble out the back door, never sparing me a glance. Lucas says something to Elias, the music masking his words, before clapping his hand on Cassian's shoulder. The two of them follow an inebriated Karsyn, leaving Elias alone.

And I feel another stab of…something. Something I can't name. Something I don't *want* to know. It's selfish and crazy, but a tiny piece of me is upset that they didn't come to this party for me. And yes, I realize how horrible it sounds. I can feel it in my black heart as well. Only a monster as depraved as me would want the attention of demons as cruel and as tortured as them.

I want to prove to myself that what I feel for them is only a fleeting attraction. Stockholm syndrome, as some would say.

In a move that surprises both of us, I push onto my tiptoes and plant my lips onto Emmett's. He freezes almost immediately, shock making him immobile, but it only takes him a second to overcome his surprise and kiss me back. His hands tangle in my hair, destroying the intricate curls Mariabella made, and angle my head to the side, deepening the kiss. I press my tongue to his lips, and he opens to me instantly. My hands travel over his broad shoulders as his own leave my hair, gripping my ass.

I quickly bring my hands to his wrists, dragging them back to my waist.

But he lowers them to my ass again.

For a second time, I grip his hands in a bruising grip and all but shove them off of me, attempting to pull my lips from his. Instead of relenting, he only digs his fingers in my hair once more, plundering my mouth with his tongue.

Emmett is ripped away from me with a growl that I'm not entirely sure is human. If I didn't know that creatures like were-wolves don't exist, I would totally believe that Elias is part wolf right now. He radiates raw, primitive fury as he throws a punch at Emmett's face. The other man staggers in surprise, blood dripping from his lips, before his eyes harden. He lunges at Elias like a fierce bull, headbutting him and propelling both men to the floor.

"Stop it," I deadpan. "Oh no. Stop."

They continue pummeling each other's faces.

"Please stop," I continue dryly.

No response.

I turn towards the girl gaping beside me and shrug my shoulders once. "I tried."

As a crowd gathers around the fighting boys—and that's what they are, little boys—I weave my way through the crowd, feeling dirty and slimy.

What the hell was Emmett doing? I know I instigated the kiss, but did he really have to keep groping my ass when I tried to get him to stop? I tell myself he was no doubt in the heat of the moment, his body taking on a mind of its own, but it doesn't negate the icky feeling unfurling in my stomach.

And Elias…

I don't need a fucking knight in shining armor. And if I did, that role definitely wouldn't fall to him. He's the dragon keeping me locked in a tower, unable to escape. I can never free myself from him.

Wrapping my arms around my waist, I debate texting Nana to pick me up early. Or hell, even Mariabella. There's a lot I need to discuss with my friend.

My decision solidifying, I step into the backyard, leave the outdoor pool through a door in the fence, and begin to walk around the side of the house, currently devoid of any students. I take my phone out of my pocket and shoot a text to Mariabella. Her response is instantaneous.

Mariabella: Sorry. Can't. Sick.

Sick? She looked fine when she left my house.

Me: No problem. Feel better!

I text Nana next, and she replies saying Christian will be at the address in a half hour.

I've just reached the corner of the house when I notice a hulking shadow sitting on the ground, his back against the house and his body slumped forward. My steps slow as I squint my eyes.

"Karsyn?"

His blond hair, still buzzed from my little prank, has what looks like a piece of candy stuck in it. Before I can stop myself, I reach forward and pluck it from the short strands.

He lifts his head and blinks at me drowsily, almost as if he's having difficulty recognizing me. Instead of the usual hatred I expect to see from his piercing hazel eyes, I see nothing but sadness. It's so pronounced and suffocating that I stagger back a step.

"What the hell is up with you?" I ask before I can remind myself that I don't care. I *shouldn't* care. I should rejoice in his pain the way he did mine, the way he no doubt still does.

"Mariabella broke up with me," Karsyn says dispassionately. He averts his attention to the beer bottle between his fingers. Five others litter the grass around him.

I swallow uneasily, knowing damn well that I'm the cause of their breakup.

"I'm sorry."

I don't know for sure if my words are sincere or not.

Karsyn laughs hollowly, smashing his head against the brick siding of the house.

"Don't be. Don't ever feel sorry for me, Peony Simone," he slurs as he takes another chug of his beer. "Monsters deserve this…and more."

I know I should leave, but I can't help but inch a step closer to him, my curiosity getting the better of me.

"Is that what you think you are?" I ask carefully, gauging his reaction. "A monster?"

Another deranged laugh leaves his lips, and the distinct scent of alcohol barrages my senses.

"I know I am, princess. The worst kind. The kind that makes all other demons terrified."

"I don't know about that," I say lightly, unable to comprehend why the fuck I'm comforting him. "I'm pretty sure if the devil ever rose from the ground, he would cower before the likes of Lucas Scott, not you."

Karsyn roars in laughter, slapping his knee and causing the beer to douse his jeans.

"You're really drunk, aren't you?" I murmur, and a twisted part of me wants to use that to my advantage. It wants to learn all of his secrets, humiliate him, make him pay.

But I made rules for myself when I indulged on this revenge scheme, and there are certain lines I refuse to cross.

"I don't even know why!" He whacks his head once more against the wall, and I can't quite hide my wince at the noise. He's going to bruise his fucking head if he keeps this up, and that thought bothers me more than I care to admit.

"It's because you're sad," I say softly. "Mariabella broke up with you."

"But our relationship was never like *that*," Karsyn responds cryptically, confusing the ever-loving shit out of me. His long, curled lashes flutter shut before they reopen, spearing me in place. "Peony, I'm sorry."

"You're...what?" All I can do is gape at him, sure I heard him wrong. "For what? For talking to me now?"

"I'm so, so sorry for all of the horrible things I've done to you. I'm sorry for taking your homework and pissing on it. I'm sorry for picking on you in gym class. I'm sorry for cutting off your hair..."

The more he speaks, the angrier I become. It's like he's repeatedly picking at old wounds that barely had a chance to scab over. The things he did...

It sounds even worse coming out of his deliciously cruel mouth.

"Do you remember in seventh grade?" I interrupt his rambling, kneeling down before him. He blinks rapidly up at me, as if my face is too blurry and distorted for him to focus on. "In Mrs. Lysol's English class?"

"I was always so fucking jealous of you," he slurs. "You were always so much smarter than me."

My lips twitch, but I continue on as if I haven't heard him. "She used to force us to write short stories every day, remember? Based on whatever prompt she gave us?"

His brows furrow together as he attempts to figure out where I'm going with this story.

"Yeah…?"

"You sat directly in front of me." I lick my chapped lips, moving my gaze away from his eyes to rest them instead on his forehead. It's easier to speak when I'm not looking directly at him. Though, with the way his body is tilting and his eyes are blinking, I have the distinct feeling that he's not truly seeing me. Maybe that's what gives me the courage to continue speaking—the fact that he won't remember this story in the morning.

"We were always graded on a ten-point scale, do you remember? Ten was the highest you could get, and zero was the lowest."

"I don't understand," he murmurs, squinting up at me.

"I always got a zero on that assignment," I admit. "Because I never turned in an actual story. Instead, I just doodled pretty pictures on the sheet of paper before turning it in." I remember that the teacher had been infuriated with me, calling my mom after the tenth turned in assignment. Mom, of course, didn't care enough to attend the parent-teacher conference. So instead, Mrs. Lysol gave me a warning—actually write a short story, or she'd continue giving me zeros on the assignment. And if I got zeros on all of them, the highest my grade in the class could be was a C+.

"I don't get it," Karsyn says, jutting his lower lip out petulantly.

"I never wrote a story, Karsyn, because I was too busy reading yours."

"Huh?" He cocks his head in confusion.

"It felt like the one weapon I had in my war against the Devils," I say, unwittingly saying their nickname out loud. I wait to see if he'll respond to that, but he's too out of it to do more than blink wearily up at me. "I thought that I would be able to pick you apart and destroy you if I could read all of your hidden thoughts."

His brows scrunch even further together, until there's a noticeable crease directly in the center of his forehead.

"I suck at writing," he murmurs. "I don't think I got above a five on any of those assignments." He scratches at the stubble coating his jawline. "Words are hard."

"You're right." I nod firmly. "The stories sucked. The one about the camel taking a rocket ship to Mars and then finding the gold toilet? Classic." I rub my hands together before placing them both on my knees. My muscles are cramping from holding myself in a crouched position for so long, but the grass is too damp for me to sit down on. "But I figured something else out about you, Karsyn. Something I don't think you wanted me to know."

"What?" He frowns, those glazed eyes of his seeming to stare into my soul.

"That you're lonely. At least, that you *were* lonely. Each of your stories were about one little boy, taking on the world by himself. No friends to help him. No parents. Why is that, Karsyn? And then it got me thinking...the reason you tortured me. The reason you humiliated me. It's because you hated yourself, didn't you? And you couldn't damn well take that hatred out on yourself, so you instead put it onto me and made me the villain of your story."

He releases a bark of dry laughter. "So you think you know me because of some stupid shit I wrote when I was, like, thirteen?" I shake my head mutely, but that only seems to exacerbate his anger. "Then what the fuck are you going on about?" he rages, but as quickly as his anger rises, it deflates, almost like air leaving an over-filled balloon with a loud hiss. He sags against the wall once more, his head lolling to stare at me sleepily. "I hated Elias, Lucas, and Cassian when I first met them, back in elementary school."

I bite my lip, thinking back to that time. Before I became public enemy number one. Before my life was a living hell. Before they targeted me.

And I remember...

Four cute boys, their bond closer than that of most blood relatives.

And me, the tiny girl who followed them around with wide eyes. I thought they would be my protectors, my slayers against this cruel world and the beasts living inside of it, but instead, they proved themselves to be the monsters.

"I thought Cassian was an annoying prick who talked too much. I thought Elias was always trying too hard to be a cool little shit and didn't care about anyone but himself. And don't even get me started on Lucas. Did you know that he once destroyed all of my shit in my locker and then blamed it on Tony Farter?"

I can't quite reconcile his words with the image of the four of them in my head. It's almost as if he's talking about a different quad entirely.

"Why would he do that?"

"Isn't it obvious?" Karsyn laughs, the sound darker than the night currently pressing in on us. When he doesn't continue, his huge body slumping forward, I release a heavy sigh before reaching forward and giving both his cheeks a gentle slap. His eyes flutter as they fix on me, and I roll my own heavenward.

"Come on. Get up, you ugly fucker," I murmur, rising to my feet and extending a hand. He eyes it as if he doesn't quite know what he's supposed to do with it, before locking his fingers with mine and allowing me to pull him to his feet. His big body sways, but I quickly wrap my arm around his waist. He practically dwarfs me, and I doubt my tiny frame will be much help if he tumbles, but he seems alert enough to walk with my assistance.

I dig my phone out and quickly scroll through the web until I find the nearest cab company. Then I dial the number, rattle off the address, and hang up.

"What are you doing?" Karsyn murmurs, his body at an unnatural angle so he can rest his head on my shoulder.

"Calling you a cab, jackass. You're drunk and it's late and I don't know where the rest of your evil friends are."

"Probably partaking in a sacrificial blood ritual," Karsyn murmurs dryly, and I snort.

"You can't even begin to understand the irony behind that statement," I say, too soft for him to hear.

We move to the front of the house, and I spot Christian's car idling near the end of the driveway. Fortunately, he's ducked over his phone, the screen light illuminating his face, and paying no attention to anything around him.

It only takes two minutes for the cab to show up, and I all but shove Karsyn's big ass into the backseat. I wait until the driver rolls down the passenger side window before handing him all of the money in my purse, easily twice as much as the cab fare.

"Just in case he throws up," I explain, and the man wrinkles his nose in disgust.

"Address?" he queries, and I recite Karsyn's address from memory.

"How do you know that, princess?" the man in question asks from the back. His cheek is smooshed against the leather seat as his large body hangs half off and half on. It's so fucking adorable that I want to take a picture.

"Because I stalk you," I deadpan. "I tie cameras to the claws of ravens and then send them out of my window with the offering of fresh hearts when they return."

Silence reigns as the driver stares at me in abject horror. Karsyn just snorts in amusement.

"You're fucked up. My pretty, fucked up, black-hearted princess," he murmurs sleepily. "I think that's why I loved you."

His words cause my entire body to freeze as if ice has been injected directly into my veins and is wreaking havoc on my system. I tell myself that it's just the ramblings of a drunk man. That he doesn't know what the fuck he's saying. That he's delirious and so fucking out of it, I could be wearing a penis suit and he wouldn't notice.

But my traitorous heart jumpstarts in my chest, before dropping through my stomach and landing in a discarded heap at my feet.

"Goodbye, Karsyn," I whisper, backing away from the cab as it begins to pull out of the driveway. The passenger window is still rolled down, so I'm able to hear Karsyn's voice, clear as day.

"Goodbye, my princess."

My princess???

What the fuck just happened?

CHAPTER 27

I wake up with the hangover from hell…though it shouldn't be at all surprising, considering that the second I got home, I raided Nana's fridge and stole every last bottle of beer. I needed to drink the confusion away. The chaos. The stormy clouds hovering at the edges of my mind, just waiting to roll forward and release heavy torrents.

Regretting all of my life choices, I throw off my covers—my stomach turning queasy, as if dozens of tiny hands are twisting up my insides—and squint at the sunlight shining through the small, triangular window. Usually, I love the feel of the sun's rays warming my skin, but today, I wish I invested in a curtain or something. The sunlight brutalizes my too sensitive eyes.

I fell asleep wearing the pretty green dress, so I quickly strip it off and change into a pair of sweats and a ratty T-shirt. I don't bother with my hair, allowing the snarled, tangled strands to hang limply down my back. I'll shower as soon as I get food in my system.

My head throbs as I descend the ladder, my footsteps threatening to burst my eardrum. When did I become so fucking loud? Where's the silence when you need it? Feeling disgruntled, I waddle to the kitchen, continually wincing at the blinding lights and every loud noise.

Surprisingly, Nana, Christian, and Polo are already seated at the dining room table, deep in conversation. For a brief moment, I worry they're going to reprimand me, or hell, even punish me for getting wasted. An apology is on the tip of my tongue when Nana whips her head in my direction, her eyes glossy with unshed tears.

Like a cold bucket of water being dumped over my head, the drowsiness abates, leaving me alert and cautious.

"What's going on?" I ask tersely, moving forward until I'm directly behind Christian's chair at the table. "Is it Gabriel?"

Nana shakes her head silently, tiny tracks of tears continuing to rain down her red cheeks. I can't quite understand the expression on her face. Her lips purse as she nods towards the seat opposite her, and I don't hesitate before sitting down.

"What's going on?" I repeat. "Is it Mom? The coven?"

The silence is so fucking pronounced, it seems to cover all four of us like thick syrup. I can feel it sticking to my arms and legs, to every bare inch of skin exposed, and try as I might, I can't rid the substance from my body.

"There was another murder," Nana admits in a choked voice. She focuses on her hands, currently ripping apart a blank piece of paper. I don't even think she realizes she's doing it; the movement is almost mechanical, as if it's the only thing keeping her tethered to the here and now. Overwhelming guilt and pain shadow her features as she drops her gaze back to the tabletop.

"Is it someone I know?" I can barely speak above a whisper, pain bombarding me from all sides. Is it Yoselin? Uriel? Someone else? Death is such a funny thing. In our culture, we often celebrate it, considering the death of a witch a renewal of sorts. They give their energy back to the coven, and we lap it up like hungry, desperate carnivores. But when the life is snuffed out before it's time, when the witch is brutally murdered like with the case of the Bloods, it's mourned. There's nothing natural or serene about the way these witches are dying now. Their energy isn't simply recycled back into the population, their spirits living on. It's destroyed completely, consumed by men and women with a god complex.

"It's no one you know," Nana rushes to reassure me, but she still won't meet my eyes. Her hands continue to rip, rip, rip at that small paper, watching as the pieces flutter onto the table like snow.

"There's something we need to tell you," Christian blurts, and Polo shoots him a look, as if annoyed with his less than tactful approach.

The last bit of fogginess in my brain dissipates like a fan in a smoky room. I sit up straighter in my chair, allowing my gaze to travel over the three adults present. Nana, with her violet hair and eyes laden with worry. Christian, his normally jovial smile nowhere to be found. And Polo, looking uncharacteristically distressed as he reaches forward and places his hand on top of Nana's.

"There's a reason why the witch's council asked Gabriel to investigate the recent string of Blood murders," Polo begins softly. When Nana pales even further, her bloodshot eyes standing out starkly in her face, I feel my heartbeat ratchet up a dozen notches. I can barely hear over the pounding of it.

"And why is that?"

And I know, right then and there, that I'm not going to like their answer. It's going to change everything I ever thought, everything I ever knew. It's going to so effectively rattle the very foundations of my being, I'm going to be left as nothing but a shattered shell, smaller than even the ripped paper raining down on the table like confetti.

When Polo doesn't immediately respond, eyes dropping to his thumb stroking Nana's knuckles, Christian takes over. "Because my brothers and I were once Bloods."

His words send a cold, electric shock racing through my system, skittering down my spine, before settling in the pit of my stomach like a watermelon-sized lump. All I can do is stare at the man who I considered a friend, family. I always thought Bloods would be noticeable at first glance. That I could distinguish them with one speculative look.

What did I honestly expect? For them to have the word BLOOD tattooed across their foreheads? For their eyes to be crimson in color, the evil they hold reflected in their gazes?

But Christian, Gabriel, and Polo look normal. Healthy. Hot, even.

"W-What?" I manage to stutter out, and the urge to run away as fast and as far as I can hits me.

"It was a long time ago," Polo rushes to say, but I can barely hear him over the sudden roaring in my ears.

Because if what they told me is true, they're murderers. They killed humans and witches alike, consuming their blood like filthy, fictional vampires, all in the name of power and immortality.

"How long ago?" I whisper, white-knuckling the edge of the table.

Silence descends as the two men exchange wary looks. Nana continues to rip apart the paper even further, until each piece is the size of her nail. I can't help but stare at her in betrayal. In pain. How could she not tell me?

"Nineteen-forty," Christian confesses at last, his words a low sigh.

"Nineteen—" I release a dry laugh, one that quickly transforms into something borderline hysterical. Nana appears even more distraught with every passing second, wincing as if my laughter is a physical punch to her lying, traitorous gut. "So you really are old men?"

Polo purses his lips. "We met your grandmother when she was eighteen, and we fell in love with her."

I turn my accusing stare towards the woman in question, the woman studiously avoiding my probing gaze. I know from the wrinkles on her face and the gray streaks in her hair that she, unlike the others, isn't a Blood as well. But she knew. There's no doubt about that. She knew this entire fucking time and allowed me to sit and talk cordially with a bunch of murdering assholes.

"So, what?" I glare between the three of them. "You guys fell in love, she decided to keep your dirty, little secret, and you ran off into the sunset to be together?"

"No," Christian says, voice devoid of inflection. He almost sounds like Lucas. "When she discovered the truth about us, she turned us into the witch's council."

"By then, we'd already stopped," Polo adds, as if that makes me feel any better about the atrocious acts they must've partaken in. "And don't look at me like that, Peony," he states firmly, only pissing me off further. What right does he have to snap at me? "We never killed anyone."

"We took the blood from willing witches," Christian explains tiredly, running a hand through his shaggy dark hair.

"So witches you fucked?" I guess bluntly, enjoying the way Nana jerks, pain splintering her features. Polo's hand tightens over hers, as if he's afraid she's going to try and pull away.

"We never killed anyone," Polo emphasizes.

"But when Cardinal discovered the truth about us, that we partook in dark, blood magic and were now immortal, she was horrified. We were locked up the very next day." Christian turns to gaze at Nana, and there's no hiding the love that emanates from his gaze. The need. Even after she got them fucking arrested, they both look at her like the world starts and ends in her eyes. It's incredibly nauseating.

"During that time, we were…interrogated by the witch's council for our crimes." Polo's face darkens significantly, and I have no doubt that "interrogated" is just a fancy word for "tortured."

"And Cardinal met your grandpa," Christian cuts in. And just like when Polo's face darkened at the mention of the torture they endured, Christian's eyes cloud over at the thought of Nana with another man. His hand clenches around his coffee mug.

I don't know how to even begin processing their words. The triplets are Bloods, for fuck's sake. And I've always been taught that Bloods are the epitome of all evil. They don't care who they hurt, all in the pursuit of power. And to hear that they're actually older than Nana, trapped forever in young bodies? My head spins from the torrent of revelations sprung on me. Pain splinters in the center of my chest as my heart quite literally shatters into thousands of irreparable pieces.

"So then what? You guys made some sort of deal..." I trail off, because I know that's *exactly* what happened.

Christian tries to smile, a mere twitch of his lips, but it doesn't quite meet his eyes. "And behold! We can become the resident Blood experts."

I ignore him, focusing instead on my nana. "And you just took them back? After everything they did?"

Finally—*finally*—she meets my gaze, tears continuing to run down her puffy cheeks.

"They never killed anyone, Peony," she begins in a hoarse whisper, but I release a dry, humorless laugh. "Even now, they only drink blood because they have to, and the donor is *always* a willing participant. Just look into their eyes. They're not red, see? They haven't been using dark magic."

"But they hurt people, didn't they? I mean, I think it would be pretty fucking painful to be set out on a stone altar and have my blood forcibly removed from my body." All three of them wince at my tone, but I'm not done. Not even fucking close. "And you didn't bother to tell me. I'm your fucking family, and you didn't bother to tell me the truth."

I want to run and rage and fight. But instead of doing any of that, I push myself out of the chair, squeezing the wooden table so tightly, I'm afraid I'll break my knuckles.

"Peony, please, I can explain."

But I don't want to hear her excuse. Maybe, in time, I'll be able to look her in the eye, but that time isn't now. My anger is an almost physical entity, pulsating in my body as steady as a heartbeat.

"Is this about your father?" she demands, but her question only exacerbates my rage.

"It has nothing to do with him!"

"I know that it's ha—"

I interrupt her. "Don't you dare. Don't you fucking dare say that you know it's hard."

"Not all Bloods are evil," Polo interjects softly, and I spin towards him, vitriol spewing from my eyes.

"No," I agree with a glare. "But it was still a Blood who killed my father."

Without giving Nana or the others a chance to stop me, I shove my feet into a pair of shoes, sans socks, and storm out of the house.

CHAPTER 28

I don't know where to go.

Hell, I don't even know where I *want* to go. My body feels like an orchestra, but every musician is brutalizing their instruments with their bows. There's no harmonious music. It's simply…chaos. Pure and absolute and dissonant chaos. The instruments don't play music; they scream their souls to anyone who will listen. Every note is brutal and fierce and unrelenting.

I feel irrevocably altered, and I can't tell up from down. Left from right. My entire world is shaking on its axis, and I'm helpless to keep my feet planted. I quake and tremble, but it's like an earthquake is rippling just beneath the ground, threatening to throw me off-balance.

Christian, Gabriel, and Polo…

I know that they claimed they never killed anyone, that all of their victims were willing, but a niggle of doubt echoes in my mind that doesn't just whisper at me…it screams. And I can't help but think that the scream sounds an awful lot like a young girl being sacrificed on an altar.

Fuck.

I begin to walk aimlessly down the driveway, the wind whipping at my bare arms. It rained last night, and numerous puddles line the sidewalk, which I stealthily attempt to avoid. There's a spell I can perform that can warm my frigid body up, but I don't have the energy or mental capacity to do it. I just feel...tired. So incredibly tired, the exhaustion permeating my mind and body, weighing me down.

My phone in my sweatpants threatens to burn a hole in my pocket. I try to resist, I honestly do, but I can't stop myself from taking the phone out and dialing Mom's number. Did she know? I would imagine that she did, considering that Nana is her mother. Why didn't she tell me? I know that history is naturally horrid, dripping with secrets and lies and deceit, but I never expected this.

When Mom's voicemails pops up, I all but growl, ending the call and shoving my cracked phone back into my pocket much harder than necessary. Emotions rampage through me, battling and warring, but I have no idea which one will win. I just want to...want to what? I don't even know anymore.

Escape?

Run?

Cry?

Do I want my mommy to comfort me and tell me everything is going to be all right?

I could scoff with how ridiculous I'm acting. It's not like it was *them* who murdered my father, just their species. And honestly, it's not like I even know the man. He's just someone who got my mother pregnant...and then died, leaving me alone with a woman who despises me. But fuck, hearing the triplets confess to being Bloods opened up old wounds, and suddenly, I'm grieving a dad I never met all over again.

Quickening my pace, I realize I've gone in the opposite direction of the school and am coming up to the downtown area. Only then do I slow my pace, perusing the various storefronts nestled on a cobblestone street lined with artificial trees and benches. There's everything from a toy shop to an antique store to a cozy restaurant. For the first time since I heard the news about the triplets, my lips twitch in the beginnings of a smile as a memory assaults me. But unlike all of the others, this one doesn't leave a sour taste in my mouth or suck the air from my lungs.

"Come out, come out, wherever you are!" Lucas's cold voice wafted to me, chasing away whatever remaining warmth I felt. I tugged my arms tighter around my chest as I peeked over the top of the garbage can I was hiding behind. I could hear Cassian's jovial laugh followed by Karsyn's holler, and Elias's slow, almost lazy chuckle. But despite hearing them, I couldn't see them, and that only amplified my fear.

"Why are you hiding?" I jumped ten feet in the air, straightening from my crouch to see a tall, handsome man standing behind me. He appeared to be maybe ten years older than me in his early twenties, with honey-blond hair, vibrant green eyes, and a crooked grin. "Are you okay?" The smile slipped from his face as he took in my disheveled appearance. I'd been running from the Devils for the last two hours, and my body bore the evidence. My white hair was tangled, hanging in limp snarls down the front of my face, and dirt was streaked across both of my cheekbones.

"Just some rude bullies," I huffed, flushing with embarrassment at being caught in such a disarrayed state by this beautiful man. I lowered my head and attempted to tuck a strand of my sweaty hair behind my ear.

As if on cue, Cassian's voice rang from the inky darkness. "Where ya at, Pee-ony? Come play with us."

"Unless you're scared," Karsyn taunted, and all four of them broke into laughter once more.

"Peony?" The new guy quirked a brow. "As in, Peony Simone?"

"Yes?" I stared up at him in wide-eyed wonderment, shocked that he knew my name. But then that shock quickly transformed into terror as thoughts of stalkers and creepy men flitted through my mind.

No doubt seeing the hesitation splayed across my face, the man chuckled warmly and extended a hand, palm up. Immediately, a tiny flame danced across his skin, the perimeter a deep orange while the center was a sky-blue.

I inhaled sharply as I stared, mesmerized by the flame flickering in his hand and lighting up his chiseled face.

"You're a warlock," I whispered, awed.

"I am." He chuckled deliciously, the sound vibrating through my bloodstream. "I'm actually interning with my coven's leader, so I have meetings with your mom often."

"Greengate?" I queried, referencing the coven located just to the north of us. His smile broadened, two dimples appearing in his cheeks, as he nodded once.

"Now, tell me about these bullies of yours," he demanded, and with only a small amount of trepidation, I did.

His grassy green eyes hardened the further into the story I got, until they somehow appeared darker. In all honesty, they might've been. Some witches' appearances were tied to their emotions. For example, I knew a girl named Libby Young whose eyes turned bright blue when she was excited, brown when she was pissed, and a gorgeous green when she got upset.

"They don't just sound like bullies. They sound like sociopathic assholes," he seethed, indignant on my behalf, and I'm not gonna lie, I totally developed a crush on him right then and there. It was nice to feel cared for, if only for a moment and by a complete stranger.

"Princess!" Karsyn roared from somewhere nearby, and I automatically blanched, taking a step behind the newcomer's hulking frame.

"They're coming," I whispered tersely, already preparing myself to crouch back down and wait until they left. But the warlock surprised me by holding up a single finger, indicating for me to wait. He then smirked deviously as he peered around the corner of the building, watching as the four Devils sauntered their way forward as if they had absolutely zero shits to give. My heart hammered in my chest, the uneven rhythm threatening to send me into cardiac arrest, as I stared at the warlock in wide-eyed horror.

What exactly did he plan to do?

I watched as he lifted his hand and pointed a single finger at first one Devil, then the next, then the next, and then finally ending on Lucas.

And then all four of their pants fell down around their ankles.

I covered my mouth with my hands to contain the giggle that wanted to escape as I watched the four of them gasp in disbelief.

"What the fuck?" Cassian exclaimed as he stared at his green-colored boxers.

Karsyn was as bright as a tomato as he quickly pulled up his own, covering his tighty-whities.

Only Elias and Lucas seemed unperturbed. Elias was more amused than anything as he slowly pulled his jeans up, covering his pitch-black boxer briefs, but Lucas's expression could almost be described as calculating. Maybe even a little impressed.

"Come on," the warlock whispered, grabbing my arm and forcing me out of my hiding place. This time, my heart wasn't just pounding erratically. It was practically in my throat, making it difficult to swallow. Still, the warlock didn't slow down as he meandered towards the Devils, still holding my hand to drag my unwilling feet forward.

"Boys, that's inappropriate," he lectured, garnering their attention. All four of their heads snapped up, but instead of focusing on him, they turned towards me. Their eyes darkened twenty shades when they noticed his hand in mine, and Cassian's jaw clenched. "Peony, let's get you home."

Elias stepped in front of me before I could leave, expression intense. There was no sign of his usual teasing as his violet-tinted eyes roamed over me.

"Peony, do you know this man?" he asked urgently.

Karsyn moved to stand at Elias's side, scowling severely. "You shouldn't go alone with him if you don't know him."

"So she should stay here with you?" The warlock released a loud snort. "Fuck no. Her mom would have my ass."

"Stay out of this, shit brains," Lucas snapped...though I don't know if I could even call it snapping, considering his inflection didn't change. He

used his middle finger to push up his dark glasses. "I'll kill you before you can even scream for help and then dispose of your body in Lake Michigan."

Fucking damn.

"Damn," the man drawled, echoing my thoughts. "You're crazy, kid. How old are you? Ten?"

If it was even possible, Lucas's expression turned even colder, hewn from ice.

"Thirteen," he sniped. "But that doesn't mean I don't know how to properly dispose of a body so it won't be found by the cops. Don't underestimate me."

"That's a level of psycho I don't think I'll ever achieve," Cassian murmured to Karsyn. "But I like it."

"And on that fucking creepy ass note..." The warlock pulled me the rest of the way forward until we had breached the wall of Devils. When we were far enough away that they couldn't overhear, he whispered, "Have you talked to your mother about them? That redheaded one...there's something not quite right about him."

I just barely reined in the heaving sigh that wanted to escape. How could I tell him that I tried to...multiple times? That she never listened, and when she did listen, she never cared?

Simones were supposed to take care of themselves. If there was a threat, it was our sacred duty to eliminate it, with or without magic. At least, that was what Mom always told me whenever I came home crying.

"I'll talk to her," I rushed to assure him when the silence dragged on. "But I think you humiliated them enough so they won't go after me."

I didn't believe that, not truly, but I could tell it made him feel better when he physically straightened, puffing out his chest.

"Good. They shouldn't be allowed to treat you that way." His crooked smile returned at full force, and I practically swooned. "It was nice meeting you, Peony!"

It was only when he walked away, hands in the pockets of his faded blue jeans, did I realize that I never got my savior's name.

I smile at the memory as I plant myself on an empty bench,

reveling in the way the wind blows my tresses around my face. Sometimes, I wonder what happened to that guy, my first crush. I picture him married with kids right about now, and the thought makes me smile. He was a good man.

"Peony?" I glance at the sound of my name, unable to cover up my irritation when I see Elias Briggs stalking towards me like a man on a mission. And that mission is, apparently, to make my life hell. Why can't he just leave me alone?

Whatever he sees on my face stops him abruptly, hurt flashing across his face before he can contain it. He releases a sigh I can feel all the way to my bones before moving to sit beside me on the plastic bench.

Silence descends as we focus on the sidewalk in front of us. There's a family strolling down the narrow pathway—two parents and a kid. Her smile is brilliant, devoid of any shadows, as she points to the window of the toy store which displays a lovely doll. I wonder what it would be like to be that innocent. To not have your past laden with pain and fear and anger. I imagine it would be freeing.

When the silence becomes too pungent, contaminating the air like a sickly poison, I say, "I never said you could sit."

"You seemed upset," Elias replies, glancing at me out of the corner of his eye. "I wanted to make sure you were okay."

"Why do you care?" I don't mean for the words to sound bitter, but alas, I can't seem to control myself today. Karsyn's drunken confession the night before combined with the triplets' sober one this morning all spin around in my head, a rough and brutal merry-go-round with no end in sight. Instead of slowing down, it merely speeds up until I cling to the golden pole in desperation and pray I don't go flying to my death.

"Believe it or not, I care about you," Elias confesses softly, and I can't help but release a dry, humorless laugh.

"I find that hard to believe." Because the Devils are inherently selfish, and they only care about two things—themselves and humiliating me.

"You don't have to believe me for it to be true," Elias states firmly. And for some reason, those words serve as my breaking point. Something inside of me snaps, something I can't even name, and suddenly, I'm a sniffling, blubbering mess. Fat, hideous tears cascade down my cheeks as I attempt to regain control of my tenuous emotions, but they repeatedly slip through my fingers like fine and delicate grains of sand. The next thing I know, I'm buried alive. Suffocating.

"Oh, Peony." I'm dimly aware of Elias pulling me into his arms, and at any other time, I would shove him away. Scream at him. Punch him in his stupid face.

But I don't have control of myself as I fall apart at the seams. I feel like a fucking Jenga tower after someone pulled the wrong block. One second, I'm whole, and the next, I'm toppling forward, praying that I'm not irreparably damaged.

"I wish you didn't have to feel all of this pain," he whispers. "I wish I wasn't the *cause* of all of this pain."

I tilt my face up to stare at him, feeling incredibly weak and vulnerable.

The bright sunlight bathes him in a faint glow, and eyes that normally make me think of stormy nights, when the sky is a canvas of metallic violet interwoven with dark streaks, now appear golden in the sun. I can't help but note the bruises on his cheek and the cut on his lower lip. But somehow, those blemishes demote him from terrifying to comforting. His gaze moves to capture mine, and time seems to stand still. I can feel his heart beating beneath my palm, which somehow reached for him without my explicit consent.

And for a brief moment, a connection flares to life between us. Something beautiful and ethereal. Something pure and delicate. I can hardly breathe. All I'm aware of is him and his too-perfect face.

"Peony..." Elias looks away first, and it's like a rubber band snapping as I come to my senses. Still, when he releases me and helps me sit up straight, I'm left with a feeling of stark isolation so intense, it's like a physical blow. "I don't know what's going on, but if you ever need to talk—"

"I don't," I snap, my familiar ire returning. "Especially not with you."

His tongue licks his plush upper lip as he leans forward on the bench, resting his muscular, leather-clad arms on his knees.

"You hate me. I know you do."

Something about his self-deprecating tone grates on my nerves. I ball my hands into fists as I stare stubbornly ahead, refusing to allow myself to be pulled back into his magnetic orbit.

"How could I not, Elias? After what you did to me…"

"The things I did when I was younger were awful. Horrendous." He leans back, reaching into his jacket pocket to grab a cigarette and a lighter. Silence ensues as he lights one up. "I fucking hate myself for the things I did to you, and I don't blame you one bit for hating me as well."

"Then why do you keep doing this?" I gasp as tears prick my eyes. I'm so fucking sick of crying, of falling apart in front of the four men I vowed would never again witness my tears.

"What do you mean?" Elias asks, genuine confusion lacing his voice.

I gesture back and forth between the two of us desperately.

"This!" I stress. "Why can't you just leave me the fuck alone?"

I don't know where this plea is coming from. Shouldn't I want their attention? Heaven knows I'm giving them all of mine in the name of revenge.

But for some reason, this is different. It would've been less painful for Elias to stick the nub of his cigarette into my arm.

"I don't know," he whispers. "I know I should, I know that I'm only hurting you further, but I can't fucking stay away. I'd let you go if I was a better man, but I'm not. I'm selfish and dirty. Maybe I just need to know that you forgive me—"

"I don't."

"—or maybe it's because it's *you*. I don't know how many more times I can say I'm sorry—"

"But that's the thing," I cut him off again. "You haven't yet. Just now was the first day you actually apologized for the things you've done." He opens his mouth, closes it, and then immediately opens it a second time, eerily resembling a fish out of the ocean, gasping for water and flopping about. "You might've been thinking about it, but you've never actually apologized to me before."

His shock quickly transforms into something I can only describe as determination. Immediately, he slides off the bench and drops to his knees before me, taking my hands in both of his. I twist my arms inwards so he won't see my scars. Not that he's even looking at them; his eyes are fixed on my own.

A jogger passing nearby begins to ooh and aww at what she no doubt thinks is a marriage proposal.

"Elias!" I hiss, flames heating my cheeks.

"Peony," he says seriously, his lips compressed in a grim, unrelenting line, "I'm so fucking sorry for everything I did to you. I know you don't forgive me—I know you *can't* forgive me—but the apology is sincere. If I could go back in time and undo all of it, I would."

"Then why did you do it?" I question, feeling bereft and broken. Empty. It's like his soft hands turned into talons and shredded my heart.

"Because I'm an asshole?" The words come out more as a question than a statement, as if he isn't quite sure of the answer himself. "Because I'm a monster?"

"Elias…"

"I was born in the dead of night, Peony. And I think that's why I targeted you." He purses his lips, seemingly lost in thought. Almost absently, his thumb traces my knuckles, causing goosebumps to ripple across my skin. "You were this beautiful, happy, smiling girl who represented everything I wasn't. I think a part of me felt the need to blow out your flame for fear that I'd get burned."

"I don't understand," I whisper.

"I don't understand it either," he admits. "There's no logical explanation for any of it, except for the fact that I'm a fucked-up creature who does fucked-up things to the people he actually gives a fuck about. I'm rotten straight to the core. All of us are...even now." His grip tightens almost imperceptibly around my hands, squeezing to the point of pain. "Nothing I say will ever excuse what I did, and I don't want it to. I own who I am, every fucked-up facet, but I can only pray that you'll forgive me."

And...

And I believe him.

Staring into his violet-tinted eyes, I know innately that he's telling the truth. I can hear the sincerity in every word he says, see it in his eyes. They say that eyes are a window into a person's soul, and I'm beginning to believe they're right. Because in Elias's, intermixed with regret and guilt, is something dark and tainted. Something that resembles beasts prowling through the forest late at night, searching for their next prey.

"I believe you're telling the truth," I confess at last, my voice no louder than a hushed murmur. "But I also don't know if I can forgive you...if I can ever forgive you. The scars you gave me weren't physical, Elias, but they destroyed something inside of me. When I see you, I see the person who made my life hell for many, many years. I see the man who taunted and terrorized and laughed at me. Who kissed me and then broke my fucking heart, all in the name of a vicious prank."

"I meant every word I said that night," he protests adamantly, no doubt thinking back to the middle school dance we attended together. When he told me he had feelings for me and wanted to start a relationship. When he kissed my lips so tenderly that errant fireworks exploded in my belly.

And when he led me to the stage, humiliating me in front of all of my classmates.

"I see the darkness inside of you, Elias," I confess, pulling my hands free of his and moving to my feet. With him still kneeling, his head comes to just below my breasts, and I have the irrational urge to run my fingers through his purple-streaked hair. "Even if you are truly sorry, I can never trust you again."

"Then I'll have to prove myself to you," Elias vows resolutely. "I'll have to prove to you that I can be worthy of your forgiveness. That even if I haven't changed, I'll never hurt you again. I might be a monster, but I can be yours…if you want me to."

His words are the equivalent of a proverbial whip slicing open my chest.

Instead of gracing him with a response, I stumble past him, my stomach churning like maggots are feasting on my insides.

I can't help but glance behind me just before I turn the corner at the next block over.

Elias is still kneeling where I left him, his head lowered. He remains on his knees, even when I turn the corner and he becomes nothing but a distant memory.

CHAPTER 29

I almost forgot about the Saturday football game until Mariabella shows up on my front steps, hips canted to the side and honey-blonde hair styled to perfection.

"Why the hell aren't you dressed?" she demands, eyeballing my ratty shirt, stained sweats, and slightly wavy hair from the night before.

When I arrived back at the house after my confrontation with Elias, Nana and the triplets graciously made themselves scarce. I don't know how I would've reacted if I had to look at them right then. Maybe with time, I'll be able to look them in the eyes without recoiling in disgust.

"Why do we have this random Saturday game again?" I gripe as Mariabella glares at me.

"Because JV had to play Friday and they needed the field. Varsity got moved to Saturday. Now go change!"

As I climb into the passenger seat of her silver Mustang an hour later, I shake myself out of my depressive fog long enough to notice the dark, burgundy shadows underneath both of her eyes. She looks as gorgeous as always, but there's something almost haunting in her gaze.

"How are you doing?" I ask tentatively as she backs out of my driveway. I swear I see the drapes in the living room twitch as Nana peeks out.

Mariabella's lips purse. "You heard?"

"Yeah." I swallow heavily, unsure how to comfort my friend. "I heard. And I'm sorry. I know you broke up with Karsyn because of me—"

"It's fine," she cuts me off, hands tightening around the steering wheel. "I don't want to talk about Karsyn or my breakup or anything. We talked. I confronted him. We're over."

My heart is suddenly racing, racing, racing—thumping and dancing to a tune only it can hear. Perspiration beads on my forehead as I turn towards her desperately, wildly, like a caged bull set free for the first time.

"Mariabella, I'm so sorry. I never asked for you to do this, and I don't want you to resent me." Because if I lose her, my only female friend, I will fucking die.

She reaches across the center console and places her hand over mine, giving it a reassuring squeeze.

"It's okay, Peony. Really. I promise you I'm not mad." She releases me to focus on driving once more, expression unreadable. "It was a long time coming."

Awkward silence ensues, and I hate it. Fucking *loathe* it. She has quickly become one of my closest friends, and I hate the tension I can feel thrumming between us like an E1 of the bass.

"So..." I say, attempting to defuse whatever *this* is.

Mariabella taps her fingers against the rubber of the steering wheel as if she, too, is thinking of something to say.

"So you heard how important this game is, right?" she queries, finally breaking the silence that has grown so uncomfortable, I'm starting to feel nauseous. I take the olive branch she extends and grasp it firmly.

"How so?"

"College scouts." She turns the car into the school parking lot but doesn't immediately exit the vehicle. "Karsyn hasn't been able to shut up about it. Apparently, State is going to be there."

"State?" I make a face. "Is that his dream school or something?" I already know the answer to that question. Last month alone, he was on their website over one hundred times. To say he's obsessed is an understatement.

"He literally has a shrine to it in his bedroom," Mariabella says with a snort, and my heart jumps at the thought of Mariabella...alone...in Karsyn's bedroom. "His dad went there. It's literally his dream."

"Oh it *literally* is, is it?" I tease her, and she rolls her eyes, elbowing my stomach, but she can't quite hide the grin on her face. I call that a win.

"Come on." She reaches behind us and grabs her cheerleading backpack. I grab mine as well, and together, the two of us begin the trek towards the stadium.

But I'm not thinking about the movements for the cheers or if I'll actually be allowed to perform with the team this time.

I'm planning Karsyn's downfall, once and for all.

LIKE THE LAST GAME, FANS ALREADY LINE THE BLEACHERS, DESPITE OUR early arrival. We go through the warmups with Helen, right up until the buzzer sounds, indicating the start of the game.

"Are you sure you can cheer today?" Helen asks nervously, eyeing me as if she expects me to topple over at any moment. I flash her a saccharine sweet grin, one that gives me a toothache, and her body relaxes incrementally as she nods sharply. "All right, if you're sure."

As the game begins and Mariabella leads us through cheer after cheer, I scan the crowd for any of the Devils. Lucas is once more in the stands, but this time, an entourage of girls doesn't hang from his arms, listening to every word he says like he's some ungodly king. I don't see Elias, and for reasons I don't wish to look into, that sends red-hot pain straight to my heart, as if someone doused my veins with gasoline and then lit a match.

I continue my search, only my eyes moving as the rest of me performs the choreographed cheer to perfection, but I don't spot Cassian either. I wonder if it's because he finally figured out what I did. I'm beginning to believe that I don't even know the first thing about Cassian's hatred. Because when he comes for me, and I have no doubt that he will, his revenge will be swift and brutal, a sword piercing flesh. He's not like Lucas in that regard, able to meticulously plan out every fucking detail of someone's demise.

His cruelty stems from his own insecurities. When he lashes out, he does so in a manner that makes me think that he secretly wishes *he* was the victim. He's passionate, hotter than fire, but that only makes him more dangerous.

And then finally, my eyes latch on to a group of older, distinguished men sitting near the top of the bleachers, jotting notes into spiral-bound notebooks. My lips twitch when I see the peppered-hair man wearing a State sweatshirt.

The first half of the game runs smoothly, and by the time halftime rolls around, we're ahead by ten points. It's only then that I drop my red and black pompoms and hurry towards where Helen sits with her back against the railing.

"Yes?" She narrows her eyes suspiciously. "Are you feeling okay, Peony? Did you overexert yourself? I knew I shouldn't have let you cheer after the accident last game."

"Actually, I was hoping I could use the bathroom," I confess, adopting a petulant expression. "I'm not feeling the greatest, if you know what I mean."

"Oh, of course." She gestures towards the bathrooms, just outside the gate that separates the public from the field. I nod once and then break into a run, stopping once to swoop up my backpack.

At Mariabella's confused—and slightly worried—look, I mouth "period," and she nods with understanding.

I move briskly down the track running adjacent to the field, opening up the gate and slipping out. The bathrooms are located directly beside the concession stand, with a dark sliver of space between them. It's there I go, glancing in both directions to ensure that no one sees me.

Fortunately, the crowd is too captivated by the game to pay me any mind.

And I'm too much of a nobody to ever capture anyone's attention.

I drop my backpack to the ground and fall to my knees, digging through my clothing and shoes until I grab the voodoo doll with a blond strand of hair wrapped around its throat like a noose.

And this time, I'm going to see Karsyn fucking hanged for what he did to me.

As I creep to the opening, I can't help but note how badly my hand trembles. I mentally curse myself and run through a list of all the horrible things Karsyn and his friends did to me. It's hard to think that I'm in the wrong after what I endured at their hands.

But at the same time...

How does this make me any better?

I shake those thoughts away, brutally sweeping them beneath the metaphorical rug in my mind, and focus on the game. From this angle, I can see the field, but the shadows make it so no one can see me.

Perfect.

I murmur a soft incantation, activating the doll, and then hold it at the ready.

On the field, Karsyn claps his hands together, breaking from the huddle with his other teammates. I can't help but admire his muscular build, clearly defined in the football uniform. Even with his head covered by the helmet, I'd recognize him anywhere. Heat prickles my spine, shooting scorching flames to my core.

I suddenly have a very, *very* vivid image of him wearing that uniform while I wear my cheerleading one…

His cock sliding through my slick folds as he pulls my skirt up over my ass, his hands cupping my breasts as he bends me over a locker room bench…

Dammit, Peony! What has gotten into you?

In my agitation, my grip on the doll tightens, and I watch in both horror and fascination as on the field, Karsyn jerks slightly.

"This is just the beginning, Alder," I whisper darkly as the center snaps the ball to him. Karsyn watches the field intently, backing up a few steps, and pulls back his arm to throw…

Only to spike the ball into the ground instead.

I release a giggle as the ref blows his whistle, declaring intentional grounding and giving the guys a penalty.

The next time, Karsyn tries to run with the ball, but I make it so his feet can't move. That they're cemented to the ground. He stands there looking like an imbecile until the other team tackles him.

"Ouch!" I wince in faux sympathy. "That's gotta hurt."

For the next half hour, I make him throw the ball to the other team, run in the wrong direction, and trip over his own two feet more times than I can count. I don't want him to get physically hurt though, so I make sure that he moves out of bounds before he can be tackled.

Eventually, the coach pulls Karsyn from the game and replaces him with Emmett, of all people, and I watch as the Devil wrenches his helmet off and throws it, muscles bunching with anger.

Realizing I've been gone long enough to cause concern, I quickly drop to my knees and shove the doll back into my backpack. I've only just begun to zip it up when I hear slow clapping from directly behind me.

My body tenses like it's been struck by lightning, and I lift only my head slightly, the barest tilt of my chin, to meet the icy blue gaze I can feel drilling a hole in the side of my head.

Lucas smiles sharply, a smile that looks more like a shark thirsting for blood than that of a human.

"Well, well, well. What do we have here, little witch?"

CHAPTER 30

"I don't know what you mean," I respond tersely, shrugging my backpack over my shoulder and attempting to shove past him. But since he blocks the only entrance in and out and he's stacked with muscle, all I do is bounce off his chest.

Scowling, I back away and cross my arms.

The shadows cause Lucas to look like death personified, coming to reap my soul and condemn me to eternal damnation. Just enough light graces this area to enable me to see his icy eyes travel from my toes up to my forehead, lingering briefly on my chest. Then, they travel to the backpack on my shoulder and narrow almost imperceptibly.

"I saw what you did." His words freeze my insides. My stomach clenches, threatening to expel the meager contents of my lunch, and I instinctively stagger back a step.

"I don't know what you mean."

Instead of answering, he merely reaches into his pocket, and I brace myself for...for what? For him to pull out a gun? A knife? When he pulls out his phone, I practically sag against the brick wall in relief before quickly regaining my senses.

Is he going to call the police?

And tell them what? That I was performing witchcraft at a foot-ball game? I actually want to smile at the thought. *I* wouldn't be the one carted away and locked in a cell.

Lucas turns the phone in my direction, just as a video starts to play on the screen.

"Are we watching your porn collection?" I snap, attempting to cover up my jitteriness with sarcasm. Lucas doesn't bother to dignify my quip with a response. He merely hands me the phone, presses play, and backs away, expression grim.

The video is of…me. From only a few minutes ago. I watch in horror as I jerk the doll's arm, and on the field, Karsyn's arm jerks as well. My heart is thumping erratically in my chest, seconds from breaking out of my rib cage like the monster from *Alien*. I know, logically, that there's not a whole lot Lucas can do with this video. No one will believe him. They'll merely think it's a prank we pulled or the video was doctored. But if a Blood or a witch hunter stumbled upon this…

Hands shaking, I press the garbage can in the upper corner of the screen. And then, to ensure that the video is gone completely, I go to albums and click on recently deleted, getting rid of it once more.

"That won't help." Lucas's voice fills me with a sort of insidious fear that slithers through my mind and grasps my heart. It conjures up images of acid eroding rock. Of frosted swords and glinting scythes. "I emailed myself the video."

"What the fuck do you want, Lucas?" I ask as he steps forward and removes his phone from my frozen fingers. Warmth migrates from where our hands touch, settling in my chest and lighting it on fire.

"A conversation," he answers lightly, just as the crowd breaks into raucous cheering. On the field, Emmett is chest-bumped by some of his classmates for a play he just performed. Karsyn's scowling from the sidelines, standing slightly apart from the rest of his teammates.

"When and where?" My voice trembles slightly, and his eyes sharpen at the sound.

"Erica's Diner. Right after the game." He leans closer until his presence overwhelms me, until I'm aware of nothing and no one but him, until he shrivels my lungs, making it so what little air they held, fled. Lucas fucking Scott.

He squeezes his eyes shut and runs his nose up the side of my cheek, inhaling deeply. I tense automatically, while simultaneously, butterflies take flight in my stomach. I make sure to spray poison on those incessant fuckers until they die.

"I'll be waiting," he purrs.

And then, like a sentient being of the night coming to steal my soul, he's gone.

I can't focus the rest of the game.

Not Mariabella's inquisitive look at my extended absence. Not Helen's worried hovering. Not even Emmett's wide grin as he races over to me at the end of the game.

I have a feeling I'm walking to my execution, but I've run out of options. And for some reason, I think death by Lucas's hand is the best way to go.

Mariabella doesn't question me when I ask her to drop me off at Erica's Diner, explaining that I have plans to meet Nana. Instead, she waves cheerfully, her earlier depressive fog nowhere to be seen, and promises to call me tomorrow.

My heart thrashes as I step inside the diner, checking the booths until I see Lucas's sleek red hair.

"This isn't the type of place I thought you would like," I say in lieu of greeting as I slide in opposite him. Surprisingly, he has a burger and fries already in front of him, along with a chocolate shake. It's not something I would've ever pictured the great Lucas

Scott eating. He always seems so...refined, as if finger foods are beneath him.

"Do you still like chicken fingers and strawberry shakes?" he questions as soon as I'm fully seated. I raise my eyebrows at him inquiringly.

"Yes?" It comes out as a question. "How did you know?" I can't keep the incredulity out of my voice.

Like before, he doesn't immediately answer. He simply leans forward and places his wickedly luscious lips around the straw of his shake. My eyes are drawn to his throat as he swallows before I force myself to look away.

He pulls back, his slashing eyebrows drawn low over his sea-blue eyes. "I love this place," he confesses, surprising me with the sheer randomness of his statement. "It's a hidden gem. Not enough people eat here."

I glance around at the ragtag diner. All of the booths are a hideous shade of bright red, while the floor is a checkered pattern of black and white tiles. There's a long counter near the kitchen with over a dozen red stools, only a few of them currently occupied. The waitresses themselves wear ugly blue dresses and white aprons.

"But I take it you didn't bring me here just to try their shakes," I muse, but before Lucas can respond, a waitress arrives at our table carrying a plate of chicken tenders with French fries and a strawberry shake. It's exactly what I would've ordered if I had done it myself.

And I hate it.

Hate *him*.

"I think this is the first time Luke over there ever brought a girl with him!" the waitress gushes. "You must be special."

A petty part of me wants to complain and send the food back, but it's not the staff's fault that Lucas is a prick. A prick who happens to know my fucking food order.

Smiling cordially, I put a French fry in my mouth and bite down.

"Oh, I'm special all right," I say, swallowing. "And Lucas is only just beginning to realize how much."

The waitress titters before walking away to check on one of her other tables. And then it's just Lucas and me.

His long, elegant fingers pick at his fries as he brings them to his mouth, one after the other.

"You wanted to talk, so talk," I huff, leaning back in the vinyl booth and crossing my ankles. Lucas eyes my plate, red brows furrowing.

"Aren't you going to eat?"

"Lucas…" I warn, but he doesn't respond right away as he grabs his burger and takes a huge bite. Juices drizzle down his chin, and it's such a shock on the normally immaculate Lucas that I can't help but stare. The twisted, kinky bitch inside of me imagines leaning across the table and licking his chin and lips, but I shut that shit down real fast.

"I know what I saw," he says at last, setting his burger down as if it's suddenly unappetizing. "And don't even bother trying to deny it, Peony Simone. I'm not an idiot." He sniffs, sitting up straighter in his seat.

And that's the exact problem.

He's *not* an idiot—he never has been. His warped mind sees and understands more than the average person. Maybe that's how he rose to power in this school—blatant manipulation. He sees what the heart desires and either offers it to them for a price or he keeps it for himself, all the while cackling gleefully.

That's what makes him the most dangerous of all the Devils.

"I can see it in your eyes," he begins, chuckling ruefully. "You're going to deny it, aren't you?"

I glare defiantly. "No, I'm not going to." I have the immense pleasure of seeing disbelief splay across his features before he reins in his shock. "Give me your phone."

He quirks a brow but doesn't ask questions as he slides it across the table. I quickly turn it off and shove it in my pocket. The last thing I need is him recording this conversation.

Then again, it's not like anyone will believe him.

Only the worst of the worst will—the devils to my Devils.

"What are you?" Lucas asks abruptly, and I jerk my head back as if I've been slapped.

"A female. Thank you for noticing," I quip as I shove a chicken tender into my mouth, chewing quickly.

"What you did with that doll…" He scratches absently at his chin. "It almost looked like…"

"Voodoo," I supply at last, searching his face for any outward reaction. Instead of terrified or angry or even disbelieving, Lucas almost looks…curious.

And I can't decide if that bodes good or bad things for me.

"Voodoo," he repeats slowly as he takes another long sip of his shake. "Are you a…voodoo priestess?"

I can't help it. Immediately, I break into obnoxious laughter, throwing my head back until my hair brushes the top of the booth.

"No," I say when I finally wrangle my laughter back under control. "No, I'm not that."

"Then what are you?" He places his elbows on the table and leans forward eagerly, eyes alight with the prospect of discovering new knowledge. Of something unexplainable. He's always been a curious boy, desperate to uncover anything and everything this world has to offer. It's unnerving to be the sole focus of his gaze. It feels as if he has placed me on a petri dish and is now studying me beneath a microscope. No matter what I do, I can't hide from him.

"I'm a witch," I admit candidly, spreading my arms wide. "A full-blooded, satanic-worshiping witch. We sacrifice pigeons and everything."

His eyes practically bug out of his head, and he begins to choke on his shake. To see Lucas do something as mundane and normal as *choke* reminds me that despite his apathetic exterior, he's still human. He's not truly the robot I was beginning to believe he was.

"Really?" he gasps, and I laugh lightly.

"No. I mean, yes, I'm a witch, but we're a variety of religions. And we don't partake in blood sacrifices." The latter statement is said almost coldly, as the picture of that missing—presumed to be dead—girl comes to the forefront of my mind. And then I picture Christian, Polo, and Gabriel surrounding her, black hoods pulled over their faces as they chanted in harsh Latin, their voices clipped and their words deadly.

"You're a..." Lucas stares at me for a long moment without blinking before nodding once, as if this is something he has always suspected. He daintily chews on a French fry, those damn eyes of his never leaving my face.

"Did you know that red hair and blue eyes are the rarest combination in the world?" I blurt like a lunatic when he *doesn't stop fucking staring.* Finally, he blinks at me, and my breath leaves my body in a swooshing exhale.

"Are they now?" He taps his fingers on the table, only his neck craning to the side to sip his shake. I don't think he lifted it once since I sat down. Not Lucas. It's *beneath* him to hold his own drink.

"It is." I nod empathetically, but I'm mercifully saved from talking more when the waitress returns.

"How's everything tasting?" she queries, cocking her hip to the side. She glances at my full shake and then Lucas's nearly empty one. "Another shake, hon?"

"Yes, please," Lucas answers, and the smile he throws her is capable of moving the clouds in the sky. I swear the heavens open up right then and there, all in an attempt to feast their eyes upon this stunning man. He looks so incredibly sure of himself and powerful, that another flare of heat explodes inside of me. I doubt Lucas would even bow to Satan if he rose at this exact moment, attempting to take control of the world. Instead, I believe Satan would cower in front of *him*. In front of this gorgeous man with the elegant, aristo-cratic face and a smile capable of making angels weep.

It takes me a long moment to realize I'm staring blankly at Lucas. And it takes me a minute more to realize he's staring back just as intently.

Those damn eyes of his crawl over my skin, and while they normally feel like thousands of fire ants, today they remind me of a lover's finger lightly caressing my bare flesh.

"So you're a witch," Lucas clarifies.

"Yes." I finally take a sip of my strawberry shake, nearly groaning at the explosion of flavors. "But I think you already knew that."

"Suspected," he says, voice completely monotone.

"How?" I didn't have my magic in middle school, so there's no way in hell that I gave myself away. And I can't remember a time when I talked about my powers with anyone outside of my coven.

"Do you remember when we played hide and seek?" He folds his hands primly on the table, nudging his now empty plate to the side.

"Do you mean when you and your asshole friends would chase after and terrorize me?" I ask, and his eye twitches.

"In a manner of speaking…"

"Which time are you referring to?" I cut in.

"That college fraternity member." A bitter sort of darkness slides across Lucas's face as his eyes harden. "The one who held your hand."

"When he made your pants fall down?" I can't help but chuckle darkly at the memory. "It's kind of funny. Most boys would try to think logically. They would assume that their pants were loose or something…not automatically think that magic was involved."

Lucas appears genuinely affronted. "So all four of our pants were loose at the exact same time? No, I suspected something was different about you right then and there. I imagine your Prince Charming was behind that incident?" He spits out the nickname as if it's vile-tasting, coating his tongue in a sickly poison.

"He was," I agree with a nod. And then, "I really did plan to thank him with sex when I turned eighteen. Oh well. Maybe next week."

A vein in Lucas's forehead bulges.

"I always knew there was something different about you, Peony," he says softly. "Something…special."

"So you only suspected I was a witch then and there?" I ask for clarification, and when he nods, I continue, "Then why did you guys always call me little witch?"

Obviously, I didn't think they knew my secret, but I could never figure out the nickname. Was it meant to be demeaning? Hurtful? Annoying?

"Because, my little witch, you enchanted all of us," he confesses in that same impassive voice.

"Okay, fine. Don't tell me the truth," I say around my chuckle.

Lucas blinks.

"Sometimes the truth is directly in front of you, but you choose not to look at it. And when you look at it, you don't acknowledge it," Lucas supplies cryptically.

I can't help but snort. "That's deep. Did you get that from a fortune cookie?"

"Snapple cap," he deadpans. The joke is so unexpected coming from him, that I can't help the bark of laughter that escapes. "But seriously, what can you do? Is this apparent 'magic' inside of you? Do you feast off of the energy of others?"

He reminds me of a third grader attempting to learn everything he can. I half expect him to begin waving his hand in the air as he asks questions.

"We have a natural magical reserve inside all of us," I confess, and it occurs to me that this is the first time I've ever told a norm about my abilities. I always thought that if I told someone, it would be a lover. *Not* a fucking Devil. Even a week ago, I would've laughed my ass off at the concept. But now here I am. Isn't life funny like that? "The natural reserve is what allows us to do this."

I glance in both directions, ensuring no one is paying us any mind, before reaching forward and pretending to grab Lucas's hand like some romantic, sappy couple. Instead, I use his palm as cover to hide the fact that my hand is now in flames. As quickly as they appear, I extinguish them, allowing the power to flow back into my stomach.

The only indication that Lucas is shocked by my display is the nearly imperceptible widening of his eyes. Other than that, he remains as cool as always, his poker face firmly intact.

"So you can use fire," he breathes.

"All of the elements, actually. When your pants fell down, he was using air." I move to take another sip of my shake. "We can do this type of magic naturally with training. But other magic? Harder spells? They require ingredients and spell chanting."

"Like in the books," Lucas replies, and I purse my lips to keep from smiling.

"Most people would compare me to the witches in the movies," I point out. "Like the three sister witches from that one Halloween mov—"

"I don't waste my time with trivial things such as television and movies," he says with a sneer, and this time, I can't hold my laughter in. It escapes completely unbidden, and his eyes narrow at the sound.

"One day, Lucas Scott, I will force you to watch *Hocus Pocus* with me, you mark my words." It's only when the words leave my mouth do I realize how they sound, how they could be construed. It almost sounds as if I'm—gag—*flirting* with Lucas. Asking him on a goddamn date.

I would rather stab my own eye out than ever willingly be alone with him.

The corner of his lips curls upwards a millimeter, but he doesn't comment, choosing instead to resume his relentless questioning.

"Does your magic replenish naturally? Or do you need to do something to fill the reserves?" he fires off.

"Enough about me," I huff. "Why can't we talk about you?"

"Me?" His red brows furrow ever so slightly. "What do you want to know?"

"Everything," I blurt automatically, my cheeks heating at my confession. He doesn't need to know how fucking obsessed I am with him and his ex-best friends. His frosty eyes search my face, but I don't have the faintest idea of what he's looking for. After a moment, he nods his head and removes a quarter from his pocket.

"How about a wager?" he queries seriously. "Tails, I get to ask you a question. Heads, you can ask me one."

I bite my lip, wondering if he has something up his sleeve that I don't know about, but I can't see what he has to gain by lying to me. If it's a wager he wants, it's a wager he'll get.

"Fine. Deal." I cross my arms over my chest as he flips the coin, both of us watching it sail through the air until it lands on the back of his hand, his other palm covering it. He flips it over for me to see the back end. A slow, beguiling smirk dances on his lips.

"Now, I would like to go back to my original question," he says. "Your magic. How do you refill your magical reserves, or does it replenish automatically?"

"My coven does rituals on certain holidays," I confess. "On Halloween, we plan to do another one. We take the magic that all of our deceased ancestors have put into the earth and distribute it between us all." Normally, it's a big event with grand parties, weddings, and parades. A part of me wishes I could be with my coven during the celebration, but I shove those thoughts aside.

"Coven…" Lucas tilts his head to the side, and I can't help but notice that not a single hair falls out of place on his head. "What is that exactly?"

"Nope," I draw out. "Coin." His lips twitch, but he complies without complaint. Primal satisfaction oozes in my stomach when it lands on heads this time. "My turn," I singsong, tapping my lip with a fry. "How did you discover this place? No offense, Lucas, but this doesn't seem like your usual five-star restaurant."

He drops his gaze to his empty shake, absently plucking at the straw. "As you might have guessed, my parents were not often involved in my day-to-day affairs as a child." A pensive expression crosses his features before he contains it, swiftly sweeping it beneath the proverbial rug. I don't know why that bothers me as much as it does. I can't fathom why I would ever want Lucas to be open and honest with me emotionally. Wouldn't it just make my revenge scheme that much harder? "They often sent me away to a nanny."

"You had a nanny?" I don't know why I'm even surprised. Isn't that something all rich people have? Nannies? Or is that only in the movies?

"I did," he admits with a soft smile. "Martha."

"Martha," I snort. "What a stereotypical nanny name."

His grin widens, but otherwise, he ignores my comment. "A lot of times, we would go to her house. She had two kids of her own, both of which already graduated high school, but she kept all of their toys from when they were younger. It's actually a few blocks away from here." He stares out the window, almost as if he can see past the brick buildings and dirty windows to his old nanny's house. "She would take me to eat here once a week. I still remember the first time she brought me. I tried to cut my hamburger with a fork and knife, but she clicked her tongue and instructed me to use my hands like a real boy, not a stuck-up, pompous prick."

"She sounds fun," I observe, watching as his face lights up at the mention of her. It's apparent that he treasures this woman immensely, and my heart flutters dangerously. I *like* seeing him happy...and that realization scares the shit out of me. "What happened to her?"

Lucas wags his finger in front of my face disapprovingly. "Nope.

The coin." He once more throws it into the air, smirking when it lands on tails.

"Now, what is a coven?" he questions eagerly.

"It's like…" I bite on my lip, thinking of the best way to describe it. "It's like a magical family. A community. Some are smaller, maybe about one hundred members, but others, like the one I left behind in California, encompass an entire town."

"Did you switch covens when you moved from Michigan to California five years ago?" he questions, always quick on the uptake.

"I did." I stare down at one of my golden fries. "Mom got offered the position as leader at the California one."

"So she just left? What about coven loyalty?" Lucas asks, sounding aghast, and I can't help but smile.

"I thought the same thing," I admit with a shrug. But the last thing I'm going to do is talk to Lucas about my *mommy* issues. "You know…I'm surprised you're taking this so well. I mean, I half expect you to break into laughter and say that you always knew I was insane. Maybe there are even doctors standing nearby."

There aren't. I checked.

"Now, I just answered three questions," I point out with forced lightness. "It's only fair if you answer one of mine."

"Very well." He dabs daintily at his lips with his napkin before setting it back in his lap. I can tell he's nervous by his fidgeting hands, though his face remains expressionless. "You want to know about my nanny, correct?" He doesn't wait for me to respond, forging on ahead like a semi-truck approaching a brick wall at one hundred miles per hour. "Nothing tragic happened, if that's what you're thinking. She didn't die or anything. It's quite simple. One night, I got scared of the dark and cried for Martha to protect me. Mother got jealous and fired my nanny immediately, instructing her to never contact me again or risk criminal charges. I knew Martha cared for me, but I was also well aware that I wasn't her biological son. She had two other children to think about, and Mom offered to write them glowing recommendations to the college of their choice. Obviously, most colleges would be thrilled to have students recommended by Heidi Scott, queen of the perfume industry." His tone turns bitter, scathing, and my heart breaks for him before I remember to harden it.

"Thank you for telling me." I take another sip of my shake to give my mouth something to do. "I know it couldn't be easy."

He laughs, the sound low and chilling. "You told me you were a goddamn witch. The least I could do was share a little bit about my pathetic excuse for a childhood."

Lucas once more taps his fingers against the table. It's something I never noticed before, but is now blatantly obvious—it's his tell, the only indication that he's worried or anxious or fearful or anything besides an emotionless robot. Someone must've updated his programming while I was away.

"To be completely honest, I'm surprised you're telling me any of this," he continues slowly. Only his eyes twitch to survey my expression, but I take a page out of his playbook and keep my features neutral. I swear I see his lips begin to form into the beginnings of a smile, but it must be a trick of the light. I'm ninety-nine percent sure that he doesn't know how to use his facial muscles. Except for that one smile… "There's a lot I can do with this information."

I laugh bitterly. "What are you going to do? Tell someone? No one will believe you."

This time, I'm definitely not mistaken. There's a very clear upwards tilt to his lips. "Maybe I plan to hunt you down for myself."

His words make my body grow cold, as if I was plunged headfirst in the Arctic Ocean. My hands shake, dropping the French fry my fingers were brutalizing. Immediately, that minuscule smile on his face fades, replaced by an intensity that threatens to steal my breath and stop my heart like a lethal injection.

"Don't joke." I search his gaze somewhat desperately, only relaxing marginally when a myriad of emotions flit across his face faster than the wings on a hummingbird. Confusion. Shock. And then anger.

"There are people who hunt witches, aren't there?" he questions.

I nod once. "There are normal witch hunters—humans who see us as monsters. They seem to think that the monsters you see in movies...I mean, read in literature are real. But they aren't. Not really. They're all variations of witches. Some witches are extremely powerful and can take the form of animals, hence the superstition of werewolves and shapeshifters. Some witches are even gifted familiars, though I don't know anyone who's had one in centuries. And finally, there are Bloods."

"Bloods?"

I swallow. "They're witches who have been tainted by blood magic. *Dark* magic. It usually involves the sacrifice of humans...and in most recent cases, witches. It gives the witches performing the ritual immortality, but in return..."

"They have to live off blood," Lucas finishes. "Like vampires."

I tremble slightly as terror unfurls in my stomach. "No one will believe you if you tell them the truth, but—"

"The people who might hurt you *will* believe me," Lucas finishes with a contemplative expression.

"Lucas, I'm being serious."

"As am I." His face is graver than I ever remember it being. Even more so than when I threw fruit punch on his shirt in seventh grade. "No harm will come to you, Peony Simone." This time, there's no mistaking the malevolent grin that contorts his features. It's all sharp teeth and deadly intent—the smile of an apex predator. "I'll kill anyone who even tries."

CHAPTER 31

Cassian stops me before first hour. I can see him storming down the hall, his intent clear in every hard, taut muscle of his body. Pure, unrestrained anger emanates back at me from his dark gaze as he slams his hand against the locker over my head.

"We need to talk," he murmurs harshly. Mariabella, standing beside me, flashes me a worried look, but I smile to reassure her, as if I'm *not* going to be murdered today and have my body hidden in the bushes outside of school.

Probably not.

"I'll be right back," I assure my friend softly before following Cassian down the numerous hallways until we reach an empty classroom. The light is off when we enter, and that somehow makes everything seem even more eerie. At this early hour, the sun still has yet to rise, painting everything in shades of black and dark gray. A skeleton sits in the corner of the room with eggshell-colored bones and a creepy grin that causes goosebumps to skitter up my spine and both my arms.

Cassian doesn't bother to turn on the light as he begins to pace in front of the teacher's desk.

A sort of quietness fills the room that has every hair on my body standing on end. It's that inevitable moment during a hunt, where the predator is stalking its prey through the forest's underbrush. A knife in a killer's hand, seconds before it plunges downwards and pierces your heart. It embodies nightmares and monsters and the things that go bump in the night.

And this time, that "thing" is Cassian, and my terror is so quick and sudden that I feel ill.

The silence implodes like a bomb detonating when the large man whirls on me, acid spewing from his eyes.

"I know it was you!" he all but growls, his tone acerbic, almost bitter. "I know you turned in that fucking video!"

I want to cower in submission, demand his forgiveness, but I lock those thoughts in a steel box and throw away the fucking key. I think a part of me will always be terrified of the Devils, always fear their retaliation and retribution. I know that they grew up, as have I, but the little girl inside of me keeps expecting them to cut off my hair or laugh at me or chase me through the streets at night. That fear lives in the pit of my stomach, mildly uncomfortable but no longer agonizingly painful.

And at the same time, I want to hug him. Comfort him. Soothe away his fears as he leans on me for support. I want to kiss his soft lips and run my fingers over top of his buzzed black hair.

I don't have time to look at the plethora of emotions waging a way inside of me, not when Cassian looks seconds away from either ripping my head off…or kissing me senseless.

"I don't know what you're talking about," I whisper, but that's not the right thing to say. If there's something Cassian hates more than anything, it's liars.

As his eyes narrow into unforgiving slits, I feel myself drift away into another memory.

"Not until you submit." Lucas took a menacing step forward. "Not until you know that we don't accept freaks in our town."

Cassian and Karsyn broke into laughter, while Elias merely looked annoyed. He rolled his violet-tinted eyes as he nodded towards the exit.

"Can we go? I don't want to stay in her presence longer than necessary."

His words felt like a dagger being embedded into my heart. I always knew that they hated me, but hearing their complete disdain spoken out loud was an entirely different matter.

"You just want to finish your goddamn Die Hard movie," Lucas responded dryly, and Elias flashed him a tight-lipped smile.

"You know me too well, brother."

They continued bickering as they exited the locker room, but their words weren't able to penetrate my brain. I could hear them, but I couldn't understand what they were saying.

How long were they going to keep me in here?

I knew that Mom wouldn't notice if I didn't come home. She never did. I could be gone for weeks, and so long as it didn't disrupt her routine, she wouldn't bat an eye. Would I be here for hours? Days? Weeks?

"Please," I whimpered, bringing my knees to my chest and wrapping my arms around them. "Please don't leave me alone."

A muffled voice reached my ears, and I perked up, listening. "I forgot something. I'll be right back."

The door to the locker room opened, and Cassian stepped inside, lips straightened into a grim line. He glanced around the congested, pungent-smelling space before shouting, "Found it!" I watched in rapt fascination as he stalked back outside...only this time, he didn't shut the door behind him.

Was it intentional? A mistake? Why did he tell the others he left something when he truly didn't? Was it a trap? Did he plan to lie in wait with the others until I made my escape? Why did he leave the door open?

Not one to look a gifted horse in the mouth, I waited until I heard their van pull away before scrambling to my feet and running outside. The cool, bitter wind whipped at my hair as I ran and ran and ran, desperate to escape my demons, both literally and figuratively.

The next day, the Devils gave Cassian hell for not locking the door behind him. Called him a fucktard and an idiot.

But as they passed me in the hall, I could've sworn that he made eye contact with me and gave me a subtle nod, almost as if he had done it on purpose.

Almost as if he was my guardian angel.

I'm pulled out of my memories when Cassian takes a step closer, hands balled into fists and chest heaving with every ragged breath he takes.

"You fucked up my life!" he bellows, before he seems to remember that we're still at school and could be interrupted at any fucking moment. He glances at the closed classroom door, takes a deep breath, and says in a quieter voice, "She got fired."

"Good," I huff, crossing my arms over my chest. "She was a pervert and a fucking rapist. She deserved it."

"That may be, but I *needed* that A," he snaps. "Without it, my GPA isn't high enough to get into Juilliard. I'm just fucking lucky that I was still a minor during the majority of our interactions, so the DA is leaving my name out of it. She's fucking going to jail, Peony."

"And do you care?" I inquire seriously, arching a white brow. At his flabbergasted expression, I continue on, "Do you care what happens to her? Do you have feelings for her?"

Maybe I read the situation all wrong. Maybe he was a willing participant...though that doesn't change the fact that he's a student and she's his teacher. That he was only seventeen when they first began hooking up, maybe even sixteen. That she was bribing him with better grades to get him on his knees before her. It's all kinds of fucked up, and I don't feel an ounce of guilt for bringing this injustice to light. I always knew I was vindictive, but I never suspected that my need for revenge would expand to include people other than myself.

Cassian stares at me for a long, tense moment. He crosses his tree trunk arms over his chest, the muscles rippling with every breath he takes.

"No," he bites out at last. "I don't have fucking feelings for that crazy bitch. I told you that already. I first had her as my teacher my junior year. When I started failing the class, she offered me a deal."

I don't need to be a brain surgeon to know what, exactly, that deal entailed.

"And you just took it?" I ask, struggling to hide my shock and horror.

The look Cassian throws me is capable of freezing lava in a volcano. It's a look I normally would have expected to see from Lucas, not Cassian. Not my fiery, passionate king.

"Of course not. But then I realized that I needed that fucking A. Besides, it wasn't like it was a horrible hardship. Mrs. Town was hot and had big tits," he snaps scathingly. I can tell how hard he's trying to act like it's not a big deal, like he truly wanted it, but he flinches slightly. And I can just picture it now—a slightly younger Cassian desperate to get into his dream school and willing to do anything to make it happen. Including having sex with his older, married teacher.

"I want to say I'm sorry, but I'm not," I confess slowly, trailing my fingers over the top of the wooden desk. "But I understand what you're going through."

"You don't have any fucking idea!" he hisses through clenched teeth. "No fucking idea."

"Some people abuse their power," I continue on, ignoring his outburst. "They make you feel small and young and fucking weak." Tears burn my retinas as my eyes follow the trail my fingers take. I lazily doodle circles into the tabletop to distract myself as the ghosts of my past finally catch up with me. "Sometimes, they offer to change your grades. And other times, they offer you protection from middle school bullies."

I turn towards him pointedly, and he staggers back a step as if my gaze is a gun and he's just been shot. Horror blossoms on his face as he stares at me with dawning realization.

"No," he breathes.

I shrug noncommittally, trying to act like I'm not flaying myself open, my guts dripping down my body and landing in a puddle at my feet.

"Yes." I shake my head vehemently. "I mean, no. I didn't accept his offer." Though that didn't mean he didn't try to force me to. "You remember Mr. Gurrel, right? The science teacher?"

Every muscle in his face freezes as his hands clench even *further*. I can see the whites of his knuckles as his breaths saw in and out, the noise nearly deafening in the suddenly silent room.

"I went to him for help," I confess, my voice still a hushed whisper. "And he wanted something in return for it. Cassian, I fucking despise you, but I understand what you're going through. I understand that you feel powerless and that you're trying to justify it any and every way you can. I understand."

Like too much pressure being applied to a flimsy layer of ice, Cassian *explodes*. Cracks. Fucking shatters.

He releases an agonized scream capable of being heard by God himself. He throws his head back, unclenches his fists, and roars. My stomach tightens and goosebumps race across my skin in response to the pained sound. I can hear his agony and anger, his fear and denial. All of it is as clear as it would've been if he had put words to his dissonant music.

I ache to comfort him—not because I suddenly like him or anything, but because my pain recognizes his. My soul calls to his, a cacophony of noise disrupting the tranquility of this room. It's almost as if we're connected, as if our shared traumas have brought us together in a way nothing else can.

But maybe that's just my own delusions, my own wistful dreams of peaceful harmony, because in the next second, Cassian shoves me out of the way and storms from the room.

It's like a string snapping on my violin, stalling the music once and for all. Silence reigns as I stare after his broad back.

Maybe in time, he'll realize that telling the principal the truth about him and Mrs. Town was the one selfless thing I've done since I arrived at this godforsaken town. I don't necessarily want him to forgive me—it would make obtaining my revenge that much harder —but I can't stand this animosity saturating the air.

And maybe it makes me all kinds of fucked up, but I can now mark Cassian's name off of my list, alongside Karsyn's.

His dreams are crushed, his chances of getting into Julliard slim to none. His reputation hasn't been tarnished, but that's okay. I think he's self-destructive enough to do the work for me.

The great and mighty Cassian has fallen. And though it's much quieter than I would've wanted it to be, it still feels pretty damn good.

At least, it *should* feel pretty damn good, but I don't feel the satisfaction I thought I would. I rub a hand over my heart, as if that could somehow fill the gaping hole present. But I don't think anything I do will abate the lingering pain that remains.

You got your revenge, Peony. This is what you wanted. This is what you needed.

My resolves begin to harden as my hands ball into fists by my sides.

Hell has a new ruler. Better watch out.

I'm coming for you all.

CHAPTER 32

The entire confrontation with Cassian makes me feel icky and gross. It leaves a sour taste in my mouth, one that no amount of water can completely eradicate.

He seemed so fucking angry. Was that anger still directed at me and what I did? Or was it for what I told him about Mr. Gurrel?

And more than that, he seemed hurt, as if I betrayed his trust by going to the principal.

But I also swear I saw *relief* in his brown gaze, though those other emotions masked it.

My heart races in tandem to my thoughts as I hurry to my first hour, arriving a few minutes after the bell rings. When I enter, all eyes in the room flicker towards me, and I blush under their scrutiny. Emmett waves at me cheekily, while Mariabella looks on in concern. And there, looking like a regal king on his throne, sits Lucas. Today, he wears a soft, cashmere gray sweater with a white collared shirt underneath it. His blue jeans have been ironed, not a wrinkle in sight, and conform to his muscular legs in a way that should be illegal.

Like, *hello? Your legs are distracting me, dammit. You should change your clothes.*

It's the equivalent of bra straps for girls.

"You're late, Peony," Ms. Auperlee reprimands, reaching into her drawer and grabbing a detention slip.

"She's fine," Lucas cuts in. "She had to help me with something before class." His eyes dare Ms. Auperlee to contradict him, to punish me, and her cheeks turn scarlet as she drops the slip of paper back into the top drawer of her desk and shuts it.

"Oh, um, yes. Please take a seat."

It never fails to astound me the amount of power these boys possess in the school. Even the teachers will look the other way if the Devils so decree it. I wonder if the people here actually believe that they're supernatural creatures that have risen from hell's bowels, claws extended and teeth serrated.

"I didn't need your help," I murmur harshly to Lucas as I slide into my seat behind him.

Lucas doesn't bother with a response. Instead, he sits up straighter in his seat and begins to take diligent notes as Ms. Auperlee begins her lesson.

"Hey," Emmett mock-whispers from the left of me. I feel something soft whack me across the cheek, and I spin towards the football player in alarm.

"What?" I ask, and he nods towards the wadded up piece of paper he just threw at my face.

Ignoring Mariabella's inquisitive stare and the way Lucas's muscles tighten, I slowly unwrap the paper and smooth it out over my desk.

I like you. I think you like me. Second date?

Beneath the scrawled words he drew two boxes, one marked yes and the other marked no.

I bite down on my lower lip anxiously. The thing is, I *do* like Emmett. He's funny and sweet and sexy as hell. But then I remember how he persistently grabbed my ass when we were kissing, forcing his tongue between my lips, and my good thoughts evaporate like rainwater when the sun is high and blistering in the sky.

Instead of answering, I merely slide the note into my backpack and focus once more on the lesson. When Ms. Auperlee gives us the remainder of the class period to work on our homework assignment for tonight, I know I'm in trouble.

"Hey, did you read my message?" Emmett persists, tapping his foot against my own.

"I did," I confess.

"And?" He leans sideways across his desk until he's practically sprawled on mine. "I know our date got cut short because of some assholes." He glares at the back of Lucas's head. I can tell that the red-haired Devil is listening keenly, despite his attempts not to. His shoulders touch his ears as he rips a hole in his homework with the tip of his pencil. "But I think we could really have something. And that kiss…" He groans low in his throat. "The thing you did with your tongue…"

Lucas spins in his chair so abruptly that the air shifts, propelling his papers off his desk.

"Maybe we should talk about our own date instead?" Lucas asks with an evil grin. His eyes slide to Emmett before locking on my own. "The one we went to on Friday after the football game? That cute little restaurant I brought you to? You looked radiant in your cheerleading uniform. I kept imagining ripping it off of you…with my teeth."

Have mercy.

The thought of Lucas on his knees before me, his teeth grazing my inner thigh before clamping down on the hem of my skirt, has lust pooling in my belly.

Nope. Not going there, Peony. Head out of gutter.

I know exactly what he's doing, and I refuse to be a part of their pissing match a second longer. If they want to measure their dicks, then so be it. I'll even be willing to grab the measuring tape and do it for them. But this? Putting me in between them like I'm some sort of toy to be fought over? Fuck no.

"Fuck you, Scott," Emmett seethes, baring his teeth. Lucas smiles, every inch the feral mutt.

"That's what Peony said on our date," he quips.

Mercifully, the bell puts an end to the conversation. I glare at both of them, mustering all of my anger into that one loaded look, before picking up my backpack and turning towards Mariabella.

Only to see that she has already left the classroom, golden hair trailing behind her.

"Mari!" Forgetting about the stupid boys, I hurry after my best friend, watching as she gets swallowed by the crowd. "Mariabella!" I break into a jog, practically shoving students out of the way, before I reach her near the stairwell. I tug on her arm to get her to stop, and she whirls on me.

I'm momentarily taken aback by the anger in her gaze. It somehow distorts her angelic features into something unrecogniz-able. Something, dare I say, demonic?

"What do you want, Peony?" she asks haughtily, and I take a step back at the venom spewing from her lips. I've heard her mad before, but never like this. *Never.*

"What the hell is up with you?" I demand.

"Why do you care?" She cocks out her hip. "Maybe you should just talk to Lucas, since you seem to care *so* much about his feelings."

"What?" She's not making a lick of sense. I half wonder if she hit her head or something at cheerleading practice. Maybe she has a fever...?

"I just don't understand you!" She throws her hands up in the air as she begins to pace. In the hallway, a few curious underclassmen stop to watch our exchange, but I narrow my eyes at them until they scurry along. I have no doubt that rumors of our fight will reach the rest of the school by the time second period begins.

"What don't you understand?" I try to keep the bite out of my voice, but it's fucking hard. I don't like being yelled at, especially when I don't know the reasoning behind it. Did I do something to piss her off?

"Those guys!" She jabs a finger into my chest, red splotches erupting on her cheeks with each word she says. "Karsyn, Cassian, Lucas, and Elias. They bullied you, Peony. They made you want to fucking die! How can you just sit there and chat with them like best friends? How can you go on a date with one of them? How can you fucking *forgive them*?!"

The fight drains out of me instantly, the anger easing. I feel hollow and exhausted, and somehow, that's even worse. She didn't just reach into my chest and grab my heart. She grabbed *all* of my organs, leaving me as nothing but an empty shell.

Mariabella sags too. Now that she's said all that she wanted to say, her shoulders deflate like a balloon full of helium being popped. She squeezes her eyelids shut tightly, wrinkles forming on her face.

"I didn't mean it..."

"You did," I whisper. "You did...and I understand." There's a lump in my throat, one that I desperately try to swallow around. Still, it feels as if it's clogging my airways, making something as simple as breathing impossible. "I know what it looks like—"

"It looks like you ditched me for Cassian this morning and then went on a date with Lucas after the football game. A date that you lied about, by the way," she snaps, some of her original ire returning. "I broke up with Karsyn for you! Because in my mind, what he did to you was unforgivable. I just don't understand how you can forgive them!"

"I don't," I say firmly, grabbing her hand and squeezing it in both of mine. "I want them to pay for the things they did to me. I'm so fucking furious, and not just at them, but at myself. I feel weak, Mariabella. Every time I smile at them. Every time I laugh at their shitty jokes. Every time a sliver of me forgives them. Because I know

I shouldn't. I know the things that they put me through are inexcusable. These guys are twisted, but a part of me thinks that the answer to my pain is more darkness. More of them. It's fucked up, I know. But let me make one thing clear—I'll never forgive them for what they did to me. I hate them."

But do you? Do you really? an annoyingly chipper voice contradicts in my head. I can just picture mental me smiling smugly. *Is that really hate you feel for them? You can see that they changed and maybe even care for you now. How many apologies do you need, you selfish bitch?*

An angel and a demon sit on my shoulders, but both of them tell me the exact same thing—enact revenge on the Devils and then get the fuck out of there.

"I shouldn't have to be pissed on your behalf." Mariabella's voice is nearly inaudible, the barest breath of sound. "But I am, and it makes me furious that you forgave them so easily."

"I haven't forgiven them!" I snap back. "And I didn't ask for you to do anything on my behalf! They bullied *me*, not you. Get off your high horse, Mari. If you don't like the way I handle things, then stay the fuck away."

I regret the words as soon as I say them. I wish I could scoop them back in my mouth and swallow them down, never letting them see the light of day again. That feeling only intensifies when Mariabella blanches, features twisting with hurt.

"If that's what you want," she replies stiffly.

"No, Mariabella—"

But she's already turned on her heel and stormed away. My blood simmers in my veins as I stare at her retreating back, guilt and agony tangoing in my stomach. I think...

I think I may have lost my only friend in this fucked-up place.

And I *know* that it's my fault.

CHAPTER 33

I still haven't mended things with Mariabella by the times lunch rolls around. I search our usual table eagerly, only to see it empty. Normally, Mariabella would've already been sitting and waiting for me, a wide, beatific smile on her elfin face. I scan the room with a heavy heart—a heart that feels to be growing in a rapidly shrinking vise—only to find her sitting across the cafeteria with the rest of her cheerleading friends. A thousand teeth are ripping me apart from the inside out, and I bite down on my lip to quell the urge to cry.

Not now. Not today.

With my chin held high, I move to my seat and remove my lunch bag from my backpack. This morning, Polo left out a sandwich, apple, and cup of pudding with my name on it, but I stubbornly threw the items away and grabbed cold pizza from the fridge instead. I'm being stubborn just for the sake of being stubborn, but I don't care. He and his brothers hurt me. A lot. Maybe it's petty, maybe I should get over it, but I'm too damn angry to care. They may not have killed anyone, but how many did they hurt? How many lives did they destroy? None? A few? A dozen?

How many fathers did they take from little girls?

Rationally, I *know* that the answer is zero. I *know* that they never killed anyone. I know that, I do, but try using logic when your heart is in shreds.

I will myself not to cry as I pick at the pepperonis on my pizza, feeling more lonely than I can ever remember feeling. That loneliness leaves a distinct taste on my tongue. Bitter, almost, leaving me hollow.

You'll talk to Mariabella after school. She can't stay mad at you forever. All you need to do is apologize.

The erratic beating of my heart gradually slows from a gallop to a trot. I force my fingers to uncurl as I take a deep breath.

You can do this.

A large body sliding into the seat opposite me interrupts my internal tangent. I glance up from my pizza, expecting Emmett, only to see Karsyn sitting across from me in his usual spot. He doesn't look up as he digs into the food on his tray—a gray sludge-like clump of meat, a browning banana, and a carton of chocolate milk. I haven't spoken to him since the night at that party, when he drunkenly confessed that he used to be in love with me. And since he hasn't brought it up, I take it to mean that he either doesn't care about our encounter...or he doesn't remember it. Still, my heart skips a beat all the same, shooting phantom fireworks through my bloodstream at the memory.

"Mariabella isn't here," I say tersely, burning holes into his forehead.

"I know," he replies as he takes a huge bite of the gray meat. His face shifts and contorts, a scowl marring his features at the repulsive taste.

Silence descends, but I don't bother with the pretense of eating.

"I was at the game," I begin conversationally, and when his eyes shadow, pain twisting his features, I don't feel the satisfaction I thought I would. My conversation with Mariabella plays on a continuous loop in my head. It feels as if I'm standing in a barren field with the wind whipping at me from both directions, and I know that any second now, one particularly strong gust will blow me away.

"Yeah," he murmurs gruffly as he unpeels his banana and shoves it in his mouth. He immediately makes a face and spits it into his napkin. "Don't think I'm going to be playing for State next year."

I should be happy about that, right? My plans have finally come to fruition, after months and months of planning and scheming.

But instead of satisfaction, I feel hollow.

"I'm sorry," I whisper, and I'm surprised when those words are actually sincere.

Karsyn shrugs his broad shoulders in an "it is what it is" type of motion. "I don't think my grades would've been good enough anyway."

"I'm sure that's not true."

Instead of answering with words, Karsyn opens up his backpack, grabs a stapled packet, and places it on the table so I can see. On the very top of the front page is a glaringly large red F. My curiosity piqued, I read through the questions and see that it's for U.S. History. Since I'm taking AP U.S. History, I don't have this class with him, but I can already see the topics he struggles the most with. He nailed all of the multiple-choice questions, but the second the test demanded short answers and essays, he bombed. Spectacularly.

"Martin Luther King Jr. *is* bomb AF, but is that really appropriate for the essay?" I question, and he blows out a raspberry.

"Words are hard," he murmurs.

I want to bring up a theory I've had for a while, since middle school, but I don't dare overstep. I've caused enough discord for one day, thank you very much. But if I'm correct, it would explain why he struggles so much in his English classes, as well as all of his written exams.

"You talking about my cock again?" Cassian slides into the empty seat beside Karsyn, flashing him a belligerent smile before turning towards me. "Naughty, naughty, baby. You know I don't like getting frisky at school."

"Which one is your baby here?" I gesture between myself and Karsyn.

"We all know the answer to that." Cassian leans forward with a conspiratorial grin. "Karsyn prefers the name honey cock."

"I'm going to stab you and end your miserable existence," Karsyn murmurs as he pulls out a textbook from his backpack and leans over it, attempting to finish up an assignment for the health portion of our gym class. Cassian grabs a grape and tosses it into his mouth as if everything is okay.

Are they…?

Are they planning something?

Isn't Cassian furious with me?

I glance between the two men warily, feeling scared and cornered. And honestly? Confused. The last time I talked with Cassian, he screamed at the top of his lungs and stalked away like he couldn't stand to be in my presence for more than two seconds. And Karsyn doesn't even *remember* our last encounter.

So why are they sitting across from me at the table, looking buddy-buddy? And why do I actually *want* them here with me? Why do I want them to eradicate all of the loneliness plaguing my very soul?

It feels as if my chest is caving in under an intense avalanche of pressure. My head repeatedly volleys between the two men, as if any second, one of them will lunge forward and embed a knife in my throat.

That thought makes a wry grin twist up my lips. There's nothing nice or even sincere about my smile. It's cruel and cunning and coated in darkness.

Five years ago, I quite literally held a knife up to my throat with every intention of slashing my neck. The pain had grown to an unbearable level, and I just wanted it to end. Some might say I was a coward; others would argue that I was actually strong. I don't know the answer to that moral dilemma.

All I know is that I wanted—no, *needed*—a way for my emotional pain to end. I wanted to feel the cool cut of the blade on my skin and watch as blood drizzled into the collar of my shirt. There was something so seductive and enticing about death. It lured me in, the call a siren's sultry song, and I was the helpless sailor succumbing to it, despite knowing it would end me.

At least if I was no longer alive, the pain would stop.

"Baby girl." Cassian's low, rumbly voice, almost like thunder, shakes me out of my depressive thoughts, but it doesn't diminish the rising anger percolating in my stomach like molten lava in a volcano. "Did you hear me?"

"Fuck you, Cassian!" I snap, rising from my seat. I grab my backpack and pizza, and without another word, storm from the cafeteria.

I don't even know where exactly my anger is coming from right now. Mariabella? The triplets? The Devils themselves? It's all suddenly too much, and the tension squeezing my ribs has me wincing in pain.

One of my rules for revenge was to *not* let my emotions get the better of me. I was supposed to be cold and detached, handing out vengeance like a college RA hands out condoms.

Now, pure emotion drives all of my interactions with the Devils. I'm no longer in the driver's seat of my own mind. Instead, I'm forced into the trunk, where I'm kicking and crying and demanding release. My lungs burn with the scream I refuse to unleash.

Out of the corner of my eye, I spot Lucas rising from his table—surrounded by the rest of his preppy, popular friends—and hurrying towards me. Karsyn and Cassian are still behind me, talking in urgent tones too low for me to hear.

I don't see Elias, and I only figure out why a moment later when I run smack dab into his hard chest.

"Peony." He places his hands on my shoulders to steady me, but I flinch away. My fear sours each breath I take, until it feels like I'm inhaling poison. "What's wrong?"

"What's wrong?" I slap his hands away and turn towards an empty hall, walking aimlessly with no explicit destination in mind. Of course, all four of them follow me, their footsteps pounding on the stark white tiles.

In direct juxtaposition to my earlier thoughts of wanting them near me, I now want them as far away as possible.

"What the fuck did you asshats do?" Elias whispers harshly from behind me.

"I just asked her if we could talk after school," Cassian defends.

"Why would you do that?" Lucas demands, his voice reminding me eerily of a dog's growl in the dead of night.

"Enough!" I spin on my heel, the tenuous control I have on my emotions snapping, the rubber band pulled too tight. "Just fucking stop! All of you!"

I'm panting, my chest heaving, as I stare at each of their almost wickedly beautiful faces.

"I can't do this anymore," I whisper, feeling smaller than I can ever remember being reduced to. Smaller than I felt even back in middle school. "You guys need to stay away from me. I'm done. Fucking done. I'm going to go back to California."

All four of them stare at me in growing horror. Even Lucas, who I'm pretty sure is a mannequin with how expressive he normally is.

"What the fuck are you talking about?" Cassian demands. He turns towards the others, his scowl firmly in place. "Am I the only one hearing this crazy?"

"How can you guys look at me and act like nothing's wrong? Like the past didn't happen?" I demand, and dammit all, I can feel tears dripping down my cheeks. I feel like I've suffered for centuries in a never-ending pit of loneliness and despair. All I can see is darkness. That's all I've ever seen, after all—darkness, the kind that seeps into your heart and soul, mangling them until they're unrecognizable. Until *you're* unrecognizable.

"Peony." Elias takes a step closer, hands held up placatingly, but I step back until I'm flush against a locker.

"Why did you guys do it?" I sob. "Why me?"

They exchange unreadable looks before Karsyn sighs heavily, his eyes glossy with tears he won't let fall.

"Because we're assholes," he states, as if that's fucking enough. As if that explains years and years of torment and hatred. Being an asshole isn't a justifiable excuse for being a bully.

Though I don't think "bully" is a strong enough word.

Tormentors…

Abusers…

Assholes…

"Not fucking good enough." I move to walk away, and I know this time, it'll be for good. I'm not going to come back once I leave.

Lucas reaches forward, movement so quick his hand is almost a blur, and grasps my wrist.

"You're right," he confesses. "It's not good enough. I'm sure we all have our own individual reasons."

"Not. Good. Enough," I hiss, yanking my hand free. The movement causes my sleeve to slide up marginally, giving Lucas his first ever view of my scars. I try to slide my sleeve back down inconspicuously, but I'm not fast enough.

With a gentleness belying the madness swirling in his blue eyes, he rolls up my sleeve, baring me to these men. I would've preferred standing before them naked to this. Anything but this.

It's one of those moments when time stops. When all you can hear is your own erratic breathing and the pounding of your heart. When darkness encroaches the edge of your vision, and you don't know if you want to pass out or throw up.

"Please. Please stop," I whisper, but I don't pull away. I know that if I truly wanted to, he would release me, but for some reason, I stay. My heart pounds furiously as the guys gather closer.

"We did this to you," Karsyn whispers, the barest breath of sound. The tip of his pointer finger very softly brushes one of the largest raised scars—the one meant to end my life.

"How can you guys think that your actions don't have consequences?" My voice trembles as more tears slide down my cheeks, landing on the corner of my lips.

"We didn't know," Cassian gasps, his entire body shaking. "We didn't fucking know."

"You didn't know?! You guys relentlessly picked on a girl who was already beaten down by the world. What did you think would happen? I wanted to *die*. Don't you see it? Don't you understand? I wanted to fucking die! And I tried. I really did. If I would've just placed the knife a little more to the right…"

"Don't say that!" Lucas snaps harshly, and unlike the others, tears don't line his eyes. Not him. Instead, those blue orbs, oceans of unfathomable depths, are wide and manic, as if he's half considering throwing me over his shoulder and never letting me leave his sight. He looks every inch the psychopath I always suspected him to be.

"It's the truth!" I pull my hand free of his grip and allow my sleeve to slide back down, covering my marred skin from view. "You guys might not have been my only reasons for wanting to die—hell, you might not have even been my biggest—but it doesn't change the fact that whenever I look at you, I see the boys who tormented me for years. That'll never change."

"Sorry is just a fucking word, and I know that in this case, it's entirely inadequate," Cassian whispers, his head dipped. Delicate tremors course through his body. "But we mean it. *I* mean it. How the fuck can we prove it to you?"

My emotions are going haywire. It's impossible for me to

untangle one from the next, to understand exactly what I'm feeling at this moment.

So instead of giving voice to any of the tumultuous thoughts warring in my head, I murmur, "You can't."

But I don't know entirely if that's true or not.

CHAPTER 34

I feel as if I've been flayed raw. I'm bloody and bruised and seconds from falling apart completely.

The next hour passes in a blur. Since I have AP Lit immediately after lunch, I choose to skip it and instead hide away in the locker room. I don't know who they chose to replace Mrs. Town, and I don't care. I don't care about anything anymore.

Caring only gets you hurt.

I squeeze myself into a tight ball as I sit in one of the changing rooms and cry. I don't know what exactly I'm crying about. Or whom I'm crying for. All I know is that my body feels like one of those Capri Sun juice pouches that have been blown full of air and then stepped on. I sag, depleted and spent, as the remainder of my tears dry on my cheeks. I don't like this…this…*pain*. Not one bit.

My body feels inside out, my organs on display for everyone to see.

When the girls enter the locker room a few minutes before gym class begins, I finally have myself under control. At least, I'm eighty percent sure I won't break into tears the second I set eyes upon the Devils.

I already texted Uriel my change in plans, and his response was instantaneous.

Uriel: R u sure?

Of course I'm not sure—I'm not sure about anything anymore— but I know that the longer I remain here with the Devils, the more potent my pain becomes. Thoughts of the Devils threaten to send me slinking into oblivion, but I know I need to remain coherent if I have any chance of escaping.

And that's what I'm doing—escaping. I'm finally freeing myself of the shackles Lucas Scott, Cassian Jereome, Karsyn Alder, and Elias Briggs put around me, chaining me to them. I don't know how long it'll take my brain to completely eradicate the memories, but I'm praying it's soon. I don't know how much longer I can last.

I wait until the locker room is silent before creeping out of the stall. I'm going to be late to class, but fortunately, Mr. Builder doesn't give enough shits to notice. I'll sneak in through the back door of the gym just long enough to be present for attendance, and then I'll retreat to the locker room once more to lick my wounds in private.

Or that *was* my plan.

The second I enter the main portion of the locker room, I see Mariabella sitting on the lone wooden bench in front of our lockers. She nervously twiddles her fingers together as her gaze darts to the entrance of the locker room and then back to her lap. She's wearing a pair of spandex leggings and a neon green sports bra. It's completely inappropriate to wear to class, but then again, Mr. Builder gives zero fucks what we do.

"Mari," I say softly, and she jumps five feet in the air, her blonde hair whipping around her face.

"Peony," she breathes, slowly rising to her feet. "I thought you left. I've been waiting here for you."

"I was…" I gesture towards the changing stalls, releasing a self-deprecating chuckle. What was the word for having a pity party alone in a changing room?

"I'm—" she begins, twisting the front of her shirt.

"—so sorry," we both blurt at the same time. We stare at each other for a long moment, before breaking into giggles.

"No, I'm sorry." Mariabella huffs ruefully. "I shouldn't have said what I said. I'm just so *furious* on your behalf, you know?"

"And I'm sorry, too." I reach forward to take her dainty hands in mine, and this time, the tears that cascade down my cheeks are happy ones. "Please don't ever fuck off. And please ignore me when I tell you to. Or better yet, slap me silly. You're a really good friend, Mari."

She blows out a breath. "Those guys are complete assholes."

"I know." There's no point in denying that, because despite my confusing feelings for all four of them, it's the truth. They *are* assholes.

They're devils.

"But," she continues on, "I trust your judgement. If you want to be friends with Satan's little helpers, then go for it."

"Mariabella, you're a fucking rock star," I say sincerely, giving her hands a squeeze. She blushes instantly, attempting to duck her head, but I place a finger under her chin to hold her attention. "I'm being fucking serious. You're an amazing friend, and I'm so happy to have you in my life."

Mariabella smiles coyly at me through her fringe of lashes, but before I can comment on that strange look, she pushes herself onto her tiptoes and kisses me. For a moment, I'm struck speechless, standing there like an imbecile as her soft lips move over mine. She grabs my hands and places them underneath her sports bra until I'm touching the bare flesh of her pert boobs. I can feel her nipples grazing my palms.

For a moment, I consider kissing her back. I've never kissed a girl before, and I have to admit that her lips are softer than a male's. And I've never touched any breasts before that weren't my own. And fuck, I wish I could love her, truly love her in that way. I wish my damn, traitorous heart wasn't pulling me in four different directions, towards guys I know will irrevocably hurt me.

"Mari," I say gently, dropping my hands and stepping away. Her eyes are half-mast, glazed with lust, but at my rejection, they snap open and pain blossoms in their dark depths. "I'm so sorry."

"I thought you were—" She begins to tremble slightly, her bra still bunched at the top of her breasts so I can see her beaded, rosy pink nipples. Feeling slightly awkward, I lean forward and rearrange her bra so everything's covered. She lets me do it with a dumbfounded expression. "I thought you, maybe, liked me."

"I fucking love you, Mari," I admit. "But…"

"But not like that." She sounds tired, defeated, and her entire body slumps as she drops onto the bench once more. "I just thought…" Another weary sigh escapes her again. "You looked at my boobs."

"They're really nice boobs," I point out lightly, attempting to make her smile. When she continues staring despondently at her hands as if she's never seen them before, I clear my throat. "Look, Mari, I had no idea you even felt this way. Especially after your recent breakup with Karsyn."

"It's not like we were actually dating," Mariabella sniffs, and her words send a jolt of awareness through my system.

"What do you mean?" I whisper, stunned. I feel like I'm throwing a dart in the dark and praying it doesn't kill anyone.

Mariabella snuffles again and brushes at her eyes with the back of her hand. I hate that I'm the one who caused her this pain. Fucking hate it.

But I can't change my feelings.

"Karsyn has been one of my best friends since freshman year. He knew about my crush on Rebecca Dawson after I drunkenly confessed it to him. But he also knew about my parents."

"Your parents?" I only met her mom that one time, but she seemed really cool.

"They're super strict and…" She trails off somewhat helplessly, but I can hear what isn't explicitly stated.

"They wouldn't approve." I place a hand on her shoulder before quickly dropping it, unsure if she even wants my touch right now.

"They would fucking disown me," Mariabella confides. "Especially my dad." She releases a choked, hollow laugh, finally glancing up from her hands to stare at the ceiling. "Karsyn and I decided to fake date last year. It was easy enough, considering the fact that we already hung out a lot. My parents didn't ask any questions, and Karsyn wasn't constantly hounded by girls. It was a win-win. That's actually what you heard us fighting about. He wanted me to come clean, but I was scared, so he agreed to continue dating me. Well, *fake* dating me."

"Until you broke up with him," I muse softly, feeling a stabbing guilt in the pit of my stomach. But instead of the blade being sharp, it's blunt and covered in rust. I'm more likely to die of infection than blood loss, but that only makes the pain more intense. My wounds reopen and ache with the fiery inferno of hell itself.

"I didn't want to even fake date a guy like that. Especially someone who hurt you." There's something near pleading in her cognac brown gaze as she stares at me through her fringe of dark lashes. I know what she wants me to do, wants me to say. But I can't just kiss her and declare my undying love. Trust me, I wish I could. Everything would be so much easier for me if I could just make myself love someone as simple and kind as Mariabella.

But my stubborn heart conjures up images of four very different men instead.

Mariabella must see the denial in my eyes, for once more, her body deflates like a punctured tire.

"I'm so sorry, Mari," I whisper, wishing desperately I could change how I felt and whom I was attracted to.

"It's not your fault." Her voice is a soft murmur. "You can't choose who you're attracted to or who you love. Fuck!" The harsh explicative takes me by surprise, but she's not looking at me. "I just made things fucking awkward, didn't I? You know what they say—once you touch boobies, there's no going back to dick."

Her words cause me to break into peals of laughter. It feels good to laugh like this. If there's one thing being here has taught me, it's that life's hourglass never stops trickling. You have to cherish these little moments when you can. You have to hold on tightly to the people you care about and never let them go. "There's not? Well, damn. What the hell am I supposed to do now?"

We giggle softly, and it feels like the Titanic-sized pressure on my chest finally eases.

"Peony," Mari says suddenly, and I know that the joking mood is over. She pierces me with a stare, the sharp intelligence tempered by her unrelenting kindness. "I'm sorry if I made you feel uncomfortable—"

"You didn't," I cut in adamantly. "Not at all. And I'm sorry that I don't—"

"No reason to apologize." This time, it's Mariabella who cuts me off, waving her hand in the air as if she can dismiss my words physically. "But I need to know... Are we good?"

I throw myself on the bench next to her and place my head on her shoulder.

"Super good. I really do love you, you know that, right?" I ask softly. "You're my best friend."

"I better be!" she jokes, before instantly turning somber. "And I promise to get over this stupid crush I have on you. Your friendship is too important to me to lose. But..." Her body tenses. "I still hate those asshole pricks, and I'm going to remind them of that every day. And they can't even do anything to stop me, because *hello*. Best friend perks."

Tears well in my eyes, but I twist my face to hide them from her. "I don't think you have to worry about them anymore."

All I can do is pray that I'm strong enough to stay away.

CHAPTER 35

After practice, I feel significantly lighter. Not necessarily happier, but freer, as if the shackles which have held me captive for far too long have finally cracked enough for me to pull my hands free.

But that doesn't change the fact that I still have my legs tethered to the ground, making every step forward immensely more difficult.

As I begin the familiar trek towards my house, I can't help but feel a pang in my chest when I don't spot either Elias's Jeep or his motorcycle. The pressure only amplifies the farther away from school I get.

Why do I care if he follows me home? I'm leaving. Nothing he says will get me to stay, though…

Thought after thought collides in my head like a twenty-car pile-up. I bring my fingers to my temples and massage the sensitive skin, attempting to alleviate the pressure forming. I'm going to have a massive headache tonight if I don't get a handle on my emotions. But trying to do that is like trying to wrangle over fifty wild bulls. They refuse to cooperate with me.

As I turn another corner, I can't help but wonder what Elias is currently thinking. Does he regret what happened? I know he apologized, and I truly believe he was being sincere, but does he even begin to understand what his torment did to me? Or *their* torment? I need to dispel all four of them from my life if I ever want a chance at being happy.

So why does that thought make my insides tighten like a nest of angry snakes? Why does it feel as if pure ice is coasting through my veins?

You need to stop thinking about him and the rest of the Devils, Peony. You need to—

"What is a pretty thing like you doing all alone?" an austere voice sneers from behind me. Immediately, it conjures up images of cracked teeth, broken watches, and sinking ships. Stuff that might've been normal in any other circumstances but currently makes my muscles tense up as I prepare to fight.

I spin on my heel, hands raised, to see a man sauntering towards me. Black hair grazes his jawline as he tilts his head to the side. His skin appears so white, it's almost translucent. A pair of sunglasses hide his eyes from view as he steps in front of me.

Immediately, I take a step back, only to stumble into a second man.

I whirl madly, chest heaving, to see two more men cage me in on the remaining two sides. Four in total.

You can handle this, Peony.

"Come with us quietly," the original speaker says darkly, and any hope that I have a chance to escape these fuckers dissipates when he raises his hand, ice forming on his palm.

Warlocks.

With a casualness belying the intensity of his voice, he takes another step towards me, removing his sunglasses. "Don't put up a fight. We don't want anyone to get...hurt." The last word is said with noticeable amusement.

For the first time since I've been cornered, I finally get a good look at their eyes.

To a human, the change might not have been evident, but for a witch trained in the art of protection, I can tell right away that they're something *other*. A rim of bright red surrounds their irises, the color screaming at me to run. Run fast and run far and never look back. It's the color associated with one subset of witches and warlocks, one group parents warn their kids to steer clear of.

Bloods.

A practicing one, if their eyes are any indication. Only witches and warlocks who actively use dark blood magic have red eyes. That explains why the triplets have hazel eyes while these men have red ones. All Bloods, regardless of whether they use their powers or not, are required to drink blood to survive. If they don't, they'll wither away and turn to dust and bone.

Immediately, I break into a run, pushing through two of the men. One of them reaches for my blonde hair and tugs sharply, sending pinpricks of pain racing through my scalp. I release a startled cry, tears forming in my eyes, as he yanks my head back. He grabs at my backpack for purchase, and I hear the telltale sign of a rip.

"Where do you think you're going?" he asks, showcasing a row of yellowing teeth.

I begin to fight with wild abandon, kicking and jabbing and punching at any bare skin I can reach. I relish in every grunt of pain, every hissed curse word, every degrading word hurled my way. I know I'm not winning—I'm not even fucking close—but I'll be damned if I go down without fighting tooth and nail.

I shoot a fireball at the dark-haired man, and he jumps to the side, just narrowly avoiding the blazing inferno. With newfound confidence, I allow flames to heat my hand and direct it at a second Blood's face. He screams in agony, releasing my arm, and falls to the ground with his hands over his eyes.

"You'll pay for that," a blond-haired Blood bellows as he lunges towards me. In his hand, water begins to harden and transform into a sharp, deadly icicle. I know that if he spears me with that, there'll be no walking away. No more fighting. I doubt I'll even survive long enough for them to perform a blood ritual on me.

I try to run, but one of the other men holds me in place, stilling my erratic, jerky movements. I scream at the top of my lungs as the blond man gets nearer…

Suddenly, a blur of movement darts in front of me and tackles my attacker to the side, the icicle sliding from his hand. I take advantage of the Bloods' moment of confusion to rear my head back into the face of the man holding me, smiling in satisfaction when I hear the subsequent crunch of his nose. He releases me, and I don't waste any time spinning around and kneeing him in the dick.

Two down.

Before I can even focus on my savior, the third Blood races towards me, wind whipping around his body and stirring his garnet hair. Instead of fire or even water, I use earth—the hardest element to control. I focus on the tree hanging above our heads, its branches long and spindly, and slowly uncoil them. Just before the man can reach me, I sweep my hand out and one of the branches lowers, then rears back and smacks him, sending him tumbling down. When he staggers back to his feet, I use two more branches to ensnare his wrists and yank him into the trunk of the tree, the force knocking him unconscious.

"We need to go!" Elias screams, reaching for my hand. Crimson blood paints his knuckles, and when I turn to the side, I see the fourth and final Blood lying unconscious on the asphalt, his face a mottled and gruesome display of bruises. "Peony!"

I don't have to be told twice. I swing my leg over his motorcycle and wrap my arms around his waist, squeezing as tight as I can. Behind me, I can hear one of the Bloods staggering to his feet, shouting insults and threats, but his words soon become lost over the roar of the engine and the air whipping around my face. Elias takes off like a shooting star in the night, and I allow myself to sag against him, resting my cheek against the leather covering of his back, as all of the hurt and tension drains from my body like water coming out of a faucet.

We don't talk until we pull in front of a rickety, dilapidated building I've never noticed before. The roof curves downwards ever so slightly, in a way that leads me to believe is not intentional but perhaps a product of weather or vandalism. Only two windows line either side of the door, a fine layer of grit and dirt covering both. Maybe some residual ash as well.

"Where are we?" I question as I swing my leg over the bike and attempt to regain my balance. The grass, surprisingly, is a luscious green that glimmers in the sunlight. Despite all other appearances, I can tell someone tends to the yard frequently.

"My house," Elias answers curtly, stomping up a small stone staircase and removing a key from his back pocket. No other houses appear in the general vicinity, the property a solitary fixture, much like the Devil in front of me. Only trees and a swampy-looking river rest nearby.

As I follow Elias, my arms wrapped around my stomach both to ward off the chill and as a physical comfort, I can't help but note the random, rusty car parts filling his garage. The only working vehicle besides his motorcycle is his Jeep.

"My parents aren't home," he states as he pushes open the door and allows me entry into his home.

We step into his kitchen, the dark color of the countertops a startling contrast to the otherwise dull room. The floors and ceiling are a strange eggshell color, while the rest of the appliances gleam so white, they appear to shine. A splash of color somewhere might've made the room seem softer, almost feminine, but the harsh color scheme doesn't allow for that.

Elias moves to the counter and tosses down his backpack and keys before placing his hands on the counter and leaning forward.

With his head bent, he takes deep, shuddering breaths, muscles taut. Following his lead, I shrug my backpack off as well and place it beside his.

I wait for him to gather his thoughts, choosing instead to glance around the rest of the house. At least, the part of the house I can see.

The exterior revealed it to be two levels, and from where I stand, I can see a staircase climbing upstairs towards a slightly extended hallway guarded by a wooden rail.

Nothing about this house makes sense to me. Why is the inside nice and clean, while the outside looks as if it's been hit by a tornado? Why does Elias have two expensive vehicles when they can't afford to fix up the front of the house? Unless they don't want to, of course, but that's a question in itself.

And where are his parents?

While my thoughts run rampant, it seems Elias's do as well. He finds the ability to articulate his questions before I am, however, and I watch as his arm muscles flex as he pushes himself off the table.

"Who were those guys?" he demands at last, and a familiar tendril of fear skates down my spine. To think about how close I came to being taken…

I search Elias's face, wondering how much he saw, before settling on a half-truth. "I think they were going to kidnap me."

Horror darkens his face before it shifts into anger. "We need to call the cops." He reaches for his phone, but I lunge forward, gripping his wrist before he can make that call.

"No!" I plead, somewhat desperately. The human police can't help me with this. "I mean, let me talk to my…errr…friends first." The term "step-grandpas" makes me want to vomit in my mouth, but I can't figure out how else to describe them. "They work for the FBI."

"Those guys Karsyn told us about?" Elias questions, and I can hear the curiosity burning in his voice. He wants to ask who those guys are, what their relationship is to me, why they were at my house with their shirts off, but fortunately, he remains silent.

"Trust me," I plead, imploring him with my eyes. His own flicker back and forth between mine before he swallows heavily, his Adam's apple bobbing.

"I do," he promises. "With my life."

His confession sends a cold thrill racing through me, a juxtaposition to my overheated cheeks. I feel like a crayon in a box, jumping up and down and screaming for him to "pick me, pick me, pick me!" Even just a few hours ago, I would've shied away from these thoughts, but being almost taken—and consequently him saving me—changed something inside of me. Something microscopic. Something I can't put into words.

"I'll talk to them in a little bit," I say, wrenching my gaze away from his. "So…" I run my fingers over the top of the countertop. "Where are your parents?"

"Gone," he answers stiffly.

"Gone?" I repeat. Something in his tone…

"How are you feeling?" he asks, and I should be startled by his abrupt change in topic, but I'm not. Something tells me that the last thing he wants to talk about are his parents. Tenderly, he cups my jaw, his thumb soothing across the bottom of my cheek. "Did they hurt you?"

"No." I attempt to shake my head but find it difficult with his hand holding me still. "You got there in time."

I stare into his face, his features so striking, he's a statuesque, marble relic. I ache to reach up and run my fingers through the violet highlights in his brown hair. Would they feel as soft and smooth as I imagine them to be?

"Do you want me to take you home?" His brows pinch as he lowers his gaze to my lips for half a second before quickly snapping his eyes back up. But I saw it.

"Elias," I whisper as his thumb continues to move across my smooth skin, reaching the edge of my lips. "Where are your parents?"

We're so close that every breath he takes causes his chest to rub against mine. My nipples sharpen into fine points with the menial connection.

"Gone," he replies hoarsely.

And then...I understand.

"They left you, didn't they?"

His eyes turn melancholic as his thumb grazes my lower lip and then my upper.

"Before middle school." He nods sharply, but his gaze does not waver from where it's fixed intently on my lips. He's given up on all pretenses, staring at me with hungry, *scorching* eyes. A trail of heat lingers everywhere he looks. "One day...they just didn't show up after work. I called them, and they assured me they were fine, but they told me they weren't coming home. They sent money weekly—up until I turned eighteen—so I could buy groceries. And they always came up with an excuse for the school officials who asked why they couldn't attend parent-teacher conferences or whatever. No one knew I was living alone, so the social workers were never called. It was just...me. A big house and no way to take care of it. Two vehicles I had to learn to drive by myself."

"Elias..." My heart breaks in my chest, almost as if someone took a hammer to the organ and whacked at it repeatedly. How can I go from hating Elias with everything inside of me to pitying him? *Caring* about him? "How old were you?"

"I don't remember. Ten? Eleven? Twelve?" He removes his fingers from my face, and my body instantly cries at the loss of connection.

"That was when you started bullying me, wasn't it?"

Shame contorts his face as he squeezes his eyes shut, as if trying to quell those horrible memories before they can erupt. But he can't escape them anymore than I can. Our pasts and the decisions we made haunt both of us. You can't possibly exorcise all of your demons or atone for all of your sins.

"As I said before, there's no excuse." He leans down until his forehead rests against mine, until there's barely any space between us. "When I first saw you a few weeks back, I thought I was getting a second chance. Instead of your tormentor, I'd be your protector. Instead of someone you feared, I'd become someone you trusted. I didn't expect…"

"Didn't expect what?" I question when it becomes apparent that he doesn't plan to continue.

"To still be in love with you."

The remaining ice around my heart melts as I stare into his strong and arresting face. Those beautiful, violet-brown eyes peel back layer after layer until he sees *me*. The real me.

"I know you don't believe me," he whispers, his nose brushing mine. "I wouldn't believe it myself. I think, at first, I was being an ass to you just for the sake of being an ass. But then things changed, and I saw the fire in you. And that light…it was so fucking brilliant, Peony. It burned away all of my hatred and loneliness until all that existed was you. And for a little boy who'd been abandoned by his parents, that was terrifying. That last week before the dance, I meant every word I said. We were young and stupid and foolish, but fuck, I meant it all. I never wanted to hurt you that night—"

"Then why did you?" If we were to get any closer, we would be kissing. The thought causes my internal temperature to become hotter than the depths of hell itself.

"Because I was a coward and a bully. Because I was weak. That's no excuse for any of it, I know it, and I've hated myself every day since," he confesses. "I can't stand to look at myself in the mirror. I thought, maybe, that you returning here would be my chance at redemption, but I was wrong."

"Oh?"

"You, Peony Simone, are going to ruin me."

His lips slant over mine at the same time I reach for him, finally able to tangle my fingers through his wavy hair. He groans low in his throat, angling our heads to deepen the kiss. I slide my hands from his hair to his shoulders, kneading softly at the skin, before raising them back up to cup his jaw. The scruff on his chin pricks my hands as we break apart, the world around us freezing.

For a moment, we just stare at each other. It's a heart stopping, hands sweating, lips tingling type of stare, one that sends fireworks shooting through my veins.

Elias reaches for me at the same time I reach for him, and then we're kissing again. His hands reach for my ass, before lifting me into the air. I wrap my legs around his waist as he pivots us, setting me down on the countertop.

My hands clumsily slide his leather jacket over his shoulders, and he pulls away only once to remove his shirt as well.

"You're beautiful," I breathe as I stare at his broad, defined chest. It's tan, like the rest of his body, with a visible six-pack that causes my lust to ratchet up a billion notches. When I see the piercings through both of his nipples, I almost spontaneously combust, unable to hold back my audible groan.

"Peony…" He whispers my name reverently, almost as if he's in a chapel. His hands tighten on my waist as I lean forward and lick one of the shiny bars and then the other. He hisses through his teeth, his hip bucking so his cock brushes my thighs through his denim, before tugging my lips back to his. "I want to worship you."

"What is this, Elias?" I whisper as he pulls at my legs, dragging me forward until I'm once more wrapped around him like a spider monkey.

"This is fate."

Something inside of me clicks together, almost as if my soul is finally reconnecting after centuries in diminutive pieces. Tenderness I never expected to feel towards any of the Devils bombards me as I stare into his handsome, masculine face. I want to trace his lips with my tongue, feel his hair in my hands, worship his body the way he is mine.

I *want* to love him, and the sheer intensity of that emotion sends my head in a tailspin and my heart in overdrive.

He begins to move down the halls, his arms firmly beneath my ass to provide a makeshift chair, and into the master bedroom. I only have a moment to glimpse a king-sized bed, open closet, and a desk cluttered with science books, before he drops me onto the bed. I bounce slightly as he stands above me, every inch the infuriatingly perfect Devil.

I sit up and cup his cheek, begging him with my eyes to kiss me. Something changed between us, something irresistible and irreversible. I can feel it in the depths of my very soul. This discovery is both terrifying and exhilarating. I don't know a lot, but I know that I'm tied to him now. That maybe I always have been.

Like an apex predator in the jungle, he begins to crawl towards me on the bed, moving forward until I'm forced to lie on my back and stare up at him. Violet-brown eyes peer back at me, emanating so much love and warmth and guilt that my breath catches.

"I'm going to spend the rest of my days proving to you how sorry I am. For everything," he vows as he presses a tender kiss to the corner of my lips. "For the laughs." Another kiss, this one to the hollow of my throat. "For the cruel words." This one to my nipple through my shirt and bra. He slowly slides down my body until he reaches my belly, pulling my shirt up slightly so he can kiss bare skin. "For everything."

He creates a blazing pathway up my body, pulling my shirt up with each stroke of his tongue on my abs. I help him take it completely off, and he pulls himself onto his elbows to stare down at me.

"Fuck, you're more beautiful than I imagined," he whispers as he kisses the top of my breasts, directly at the edge of my lacy white bra.

"You imagine this often?" I tease breathlessly.

His voice is serious when he responds. "Every damn day since you came back. And more times than I can count before that."

I arch my back slightly to reach behind me and unclasp my bra, allowing it to fall down my arms before I toss it to the ground.

Elias's breath hitches as he sees me, sees *all* of me, for the first time. The tip of his finger traces one nipple, watching as it hardens.

"A part of me still thinks this is some horrible prank." My throat closes up, and I fucking hate that my emotions are quite literally choking me. "That you'll just laugh in my face tomorrow."

"I fucking hate myself for putting those doubts in your head." Elias pulls away from my breasts to kiss underneath first one eye and then the next. It takes me a long moment to realize he's kissing away my tears. "I'm so sorry, Peony. I'll tell you that every day for the rest of my life, but I am. I'm sorry."

He glides his hand up my body to tweak one of my nipples as his other hand moves to the waistband of my jeans. His finger, feather soft, brushes the top of my panty line as I writhe and moan, demanding more.

"You want to prove to me that you're sorry?" I pant, and he freezes, tilting his head so it lies in the valley between my tits.

"Of course." His eyes burn with dark promises and wicked intent.

"Then make me come."

He doesn't wait to be told twice. He stands from the bed and pulls down his pants and boxer briefs, his cock springing free. It's thick and long, with pre-cum already glistening on the tip. And is that...? Is that a cock piercing? Two of the Devils have fucking piercings?!? Did they all get them at the same goddamn time in an attempt to torture me? Fuck, that's hot.

His dick bobs as he walks forward, and I suddenly wonder if this is how the three little piggies felt when faced with the big, bad wolf, knowing you're about to become prey to a beast far more domineering and dominant than you could ever imagine.

He wastes no time, yanking down my jeans and panties until I'm bare before him. Instinctively, I move to squeeze my legs together, but he tsks, giving me a saucy, devious look.

"Naughty girl. I can't make you come if I can't see you. And you want to come, don't you, baby girl? Don't you want to be filled with this massive cock?"

I nearly cry out as I spread my legs for him. Normally, I'm not a fan of dirty talk. I tried it once with Uriel, and we both agreed that it wasn't our kink. But with Elias, I could happily listen to him speaking to me like that every day for the rest of my damn life. I might just come from his voice alone.

He kneels at the foot of the bed, grabs my ankles, and drags me forward, his eyes intent on my bouncing breasts. He swings one leg over each of his shoulders and then lowers his mouth to my throbbing core.

My hips jerk when he languidly licks a line up my wet slit.

"You taste fucking divine. You're so wet for me, baby girl. So fucking wet."

"Better than you imagined?" I whisper as he begins to lazily circle my clit with the tip of his finger. It's utter fucking madness, and I swear I'm about to lose my mind.

"Nothing could compare to this." He licks another pathway before pressing a kiss to one inner thigh and then the other. "Touch your pretty tits while I eat you out, okay, my love?"

I don't know what it is, his dirty words or the fact that he called me his love, but I swear I come right then and there.

Gasping his name, I place my hands on my breasts and begin to knead them, running my thumbs across my painfully hard nipples.

Elias watches the show, eyes half-mast, before he dives between my legs and begins to devour me. His tongue laps at my pussy like it's the nectar of the gods.

"Elias!" I gasp when he begins to suckle on my clit. I pinch down on my nipple, just as he inserts a finger into my aching cunt.

Combined with his assault on my clit, I'm a goner, and I come with a scream capable of being heard from miles away.

Elias doesn't relent as he tongue-fucks me through my orgasm, a low moan emitting from his huge body.

"Fucking hell," he murmurs as he pulls himself away. He reaches around me, towards his night stand, and grabs a condom, sliding it over his throbbing length. "Fuck, Peony."

"That's the idea." I tug at his hair until he crawls up my body and thrusts his tongue into my mouth. I can taste myself on him, taste how badly I want him.

The tip of his cock lines up with my entrance as we break our kiss.

"Is this okay?" he asks, sounding hesitant for the first time in his life. At my nod, he slowly inches himself inside of me, giving me time to adjust. I gasp as his piercing brushes my inner walls, my pussy automatically clenching around his girth. "Fuck, baby girl, I need to move."

As he slides in and out of me, our eyes remain connected as if we're the only two people in the world. I forget about the Bloods attacking me on the street. The other Devils and Mariabella. My decision to go home to California. I forget everything except for this man before me—a man shrouded in darkness and anger but somehow clawing his way into the light.

What we're doing can't be described as just fucking.

It's making love.

His hands move to my back as we tumble on the bed, switching positions, his cock still inside of me. I place my hands on his chest to balance myself as I begin to ride him. This new position allows his piercing to rub against me with every upwards thrust of his hips.

"Yes, Peony, yes," he moans as I bounce on his cock, my breasts dangling enticingly over his face. He arches his neck to take one in his mouth, dragging his teeth over my sensitive peak and releasing it as I gasp.

"I'm so close."

"Not yet," he grits out as his fingers move to rub at my clit. "Milk my cock, baby girl. Fuck, just like that."

He begins to suckle on my nipple again as he applies more friction to my clit. I can feel myself unraveling, nearing the finish line…

"Come," he demands, and I do.

I fucking detonate.

My pussy clamps down on his cock like a vise.

"Fuck, fuck, fuck!" he curses as his cock swells and explodes inside of me. I take a moment to appreciate his orgasm face—flushed cheeks, closed eyes, parted lips with his tongue slightly out. Elias is so fucking hot that I feel myself getting wet again. "Fucking hell. I love you, woman," he says as I collapse on top of him, his cock still inside of me.

I love you.

He said those words to me. Did he mean them? Were they just a product of a mind-blowing orgasm?

Did I want to say them back?

What does this mean for me and the other Devils?

And why am I even thinking about them now?

I can feel his cock growing hard inside of me again, and I can't help but laugh.

"Already?" I joke, pushing on his chest to stare down at him. He bites at my breast with a teasing grin.

"What can I say? You make me insatiable." He rolls us over until I'm on the bottom, the hard planes of his body flush against mine. "Round two? And three? And four? And five? I did promise you that I'll get you to come."

"But we never gave that a specific number," I jest breathily as he begins to move inside of me. His smirk is pure sin.

"Who says orgasms need a number?"

The answer—they don't. They really, really don't.

CHAPTER 36

After a few more rounds with Elias, I finally wear him out enough to sneak into the bathroom and dial Nana.

"Peony!" she exclaims as soon as she answers. "Thank God. I've been so—"

"I'm still pissed at you," I warn her, pressing my back against the bathroom door and staring up at the ceiling. Water stains are beginning to discolor the white paint, and the fan is in desperate need of a dusting. "But there's something I need to tell you."

Quickly, I recap what transpired on my way home from school. I describe each of the Bloods in detail before assuring her I'm alive and well. Still, that doesn't stop her from panicking, her voice becoming more and more frazzled with each new snippet of information.

"You need to come home," she declares adamantly, her breathing shallow. "Peony—"

"I'm fine," I assure her for what feels like the millionth time. I twist my body, so my forehead now presses against the wooden door. It's almost as if I can see Elias on the other side, see his naked body still sprawled across the bed. The thought sends a smile to my face before I can curb it. "I'm with a...friend."

Nana promises me that she'll talk to the triplets before reluctantly hanging up. Do I like being mad at the one relative who has always been there for me? Not at all. But she lied to me. Maybe the triplets aren't psycho murderers or evil, blood-crazed warlocks, but they're still Bloods. They still drank the blood of defenseless witches on an altar, whether said witches were willing or not.

Shoving those thoughts aside, I tiptoe back into the room and crawl into Elias's monster bed. His arm comes up to wrap around me, pulling me snuggly against his chest. I'm not even sure he's awake. It seems to be pure instinct driving him, even when he nuzzles my hair and plants a tender kiss to the back of my neck.

For the first time in forever, I allow myself to smile and relax.

I allow myself to believe that everything will be okay.

I should've known that my happy ending would turn out like this. Fairy tales have it wrong. There aren't magical wands you can wave to make all of your problems dissipate like paper in a fire. No handsome princes wait around, waiting to save you on large, white horses.

There are only demons and more demons. Darkness and more darkness. Pain and more pain.

When I wake up the next morning, I feel sated and content. I stretch my taut muscles, feeling very much like a lazy house cat, and reach for Elias beside me. My hand touches nothing but sheets, still warm, and I drowsily pull my eyelids open.

"El?" I query, the nickname falling from my tongue before I can think better of it. And...it sounds right. Natural. As if I was always meant to call him that. "Elias?"

"What is this?" Elias's voice is clipped, darker than I ever remember hearing it. I twist my head to see him standing at the end of my bed, still naked from our tryst between the sheets. His hair is tousled, giving him that just fucked look I find so irresistible in men, but his purple-brown eyes are hard and jaded. I don't even have the time to trail my eyes over his naked body appreciatively.

My focus is reserved for the items in his hands.

"Where did you get those?" I ask, sitting upright in bed and pulling the sheets up to my neck. It doesn't feel right to have this conversation while I'm naked and vulnerable.

"What is this?" he repeats as he holds up one of the voodoo dolls, a strand of his hair wrapped around its throat. "And this?" In his other hand, he waves around one of my old spell books, the binding practically nonexistent as a few yellowing pages flutter to the ground.

"Were you going through my backpack?" I demand, aghast.

"I wasn't going through your fucking backpack! I went downstairs to grab it for you," he snaps, nodding towards something on the ground. I crawl forward on the bed, still using the blanket for covering, and see my bag lying on its side, a massive hole near the bottom. It must've been ripped during the fight yesterday, and when Elias grabbed it this morning, it broke open even further.

Numerous photos of the guys surround my bag. The other three voodoo dolls. A few loose spells. My journal.

Everything.

"What the fuck is this, Peony?" He almost vibrates in place, his eyes flicking wildly between me and the strange, unexplainable items. "Are you in a cult or something? Are you, like, a Satan worshipper?"

Normally, his conclusions would've brought a timid smile to my lips.

But there's nothing remotely funny about today.

"No," I confess. I scour his face to see how close he is to running, to leaving me. And I decide, right then and there, to tell him the truth, even if he thinks I'm insane. Lucas didn't, but then again, I believe that boy has a few screws loose. My hands shake with adrenaline, my stomach a tumultuous mixture of dread and nerves. What will Elias think? Will he run? Will he even believe me? "I'm a witch."

"A witch?" He releases a dry, humorless laugh, one laced with disbelief. "Peony, don't joke with me right now."

"I'm not joking!" I scramble to my feet, quickly tucking the sheet in at my breasts so it stays up. It cascades around my feet, nearly tripping me, but I hurry towards Elias regardless. "Elias, listen to me. There are things that you don't know—"

"So you're, what? Trying to fucking spell me?" He holds up the voodoo doll once more, betrayal and pain emanating from his eyes. "Kill me?"

"Elias, no!"

"Or maybe you're just fucking crazy. Or maybe *I'm* crazy for believing you." He scrubs a hand through his hair. "Fuck!"

"Elias—"

"What am I supposed to say, Peony? What the fuck am I supposed to say to all this? How am I supposed to believe any of this?"

Trembling from head to toe, I slowly lift my hand, allowing a blistering ball of flames to appear in the center of my palm. He jerks back as if I physically slapped him, throwing up his hands to protect himself, as if I'm going to chuck the fire ball into his face like some sort of video game heroine. He shakes his head from side to side in denial.

"No…"

"Elias, please—"

"What is this? Were you just using me? Was any of this real? Do you even have feelings for me?" He all but shoves the doll into my chest, his voice nearing a scream. His tone is acerbic, almost bitter. "If it was all true, then what the fuck is this? I said I *loved* you. I know…I know I deserve everything you planned to do to me, especially after what I did to you. But…I mean…I thought…" He stares intently at the doll once more, a broken expression marring his handsome face. "What is this?"

"It's a mistake," I whisper, and I see that now. My need for revenge...

It makes me no better than them.

I don't know if I can be forgiven.

It's a bitter pill to swallow. I feel like one of those delicate, hand-sewn sweaters that is being eaten at by a moth. The hole gradually becomes larger and larger before it unravels completely, leaving nothing but frayed yarn.

"I think..." Another dry spurt of laughter escapes him. "I think you should leave."

"Elias!" I cry, reaching for him, but he stealthily sidesteps my hand and storms into the bathroom. The door rattles as he slams it shut, and I hear the distinct sound of a lock clicking. A moment later, the shower turns on.

No. No. No. No.

How could everything turn so wrong so fast? I came to this town with one goal in mind and one goal only—get my revenge on the Devils. But life has a funny way of derailing you completely. I don't know if I'll ever get on track again, nor if I want to.

What I want is Elias. Cassian. Lucas. Karsyn.

It's a kick to the gut to know that Elias is currently washing away the evidence of our lovemaking. Am I really that disgusting to him now? Will he ever forgive me? Does he even believe me?

I feel weak, my legs trembling like mad, but I can't find the strength to leave this room. I want to melt into the floorboards until Elias is forced to acknowledge me. Then, we'll talk this out. I'll explain to him my reasoning, and hopefully, he can learn to forgive me the same way I did for him.

On shaky legs, I drop to my knees and begin to grab my stuff. Only the main pocket of my backpack was destroyed, so I shove my belongings into the smaller ones instead. I can still hear the sound of the shower running, the water pelting against the porcelain tub.

My tears feel like multiple infernos burning my eyes as I duck my head, pity and self-hatred rushing through me. My eyes automatically drift to the scars on my arms, and I wonder, not for the first time since that night, if everyone would be better off if I'd died.

A ragged breath left my lips as I brought the razor blade to my skin once more. At first, the cut was small, merely a trickle of blood, but as I relished in the pain, I found I needed more.

Way more.

I began to sob as I brought the blade to the protruding vein and dug as deep as I could go.

I just wanted the pain to end

I wanted everything to end...

Mom found me in the bathtub only a few minutes later. Enough time to take me to the ER and get me bandaged up.

But the memory of that night remains, along with my scars. It's embedded inside my very soul; I'll never be free of it.

I'm bleeding again, and I don't know how to stop it.

My phone begins to ring, and I reach for it absently, expecting it to be Nana.

"Yeah?" I say, not bothering with pleasantries.

"Peony?" At first, the voice is unfamiliar, but as I claw my way out of the dark abyss I started down, shock replaces the confusion.

"Karsyn?" I ask with heady disbelief. My whole body feels uncharacteristically sluggish and heavy, as if Earth's entire gravity is pushing down on me. "Why are you calling me? How did you get my number?"

"Can we talk?" he questions softly. "Please?"

"I...I don't..."

"Coffee House. On Taylor. Twenty minutes. *Please.*"

I glance at the closed bathroom door, the shower still running, before swallowing.

"All right."

He exhales in audible relief, almost as if he's been holding his breath this entire time.

"I'll see you then," he says, hanging up before I can question him further.

Quickly, I get dressed, taking slightly longer than I need to in case Elias exits the bathroom before I leave.

He doesn't.

I scribble a note on a piece of notebook paper and place it on his pillow. It's two simple words, but I hope he can read the sincerity in them.

I'm sorry.

With one last glance at the bathroom, and in the direction of the man who has stolen my heart, I hurry out of his house.

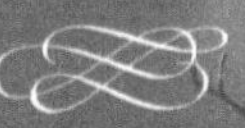

I enter the coffee shop before Karsyn and place an order at the counter—a large white chocolate mocha with a blueberry muffin.

He still hasn't arrived by the time I retrieve my goodies and head towards a table near the far corner.

The coffee shop is actually crowded, nearly every table full. I spot a few business men and women bedecked in sleek suits. A couple college-aged kids. Even some students I recognize from my school.

Worry churns in my stomach as I recall his panicked voice. Did something happen? The sudden, vivid image pops in my head of the Bloods hunting him down as a lesson to me. But surely those sadistic bastards don't know how much he means to—

He means nothing to me. I try to remind myself of that as I peel at the sticker on the side of my Styrofoam cup.

The bell above the door rings just as a frazzled Karsyn enters the building. His eyes scan the crowd before he lands on me, immediately charging forward. I can't help but note how disheveled he appears. His blond hair—still short from my spell, but just as unruly as when I first saw him—is in complete disarray. Strands stick up in all directions as if he stuck his finger in an electrical socket. Today, his hazel eyes look as green as blades of grass, his jawline just as sharp. His shirt is untucked on one side, and there's a large brown stain on the thigh of his jeans.

"You can get a drink if you want," I say when he approaches the table, nodding towards the barista. He ignores my suggestion, choosing instead to sit opposite of me at the table. And then, he just stares. I try not to squirm, but there's something so incredibly intense about Karsyn Alder that I can't help it.

"We need to talk," he settles on at last.

"So talk." I busy my hands by taking another drink of my coffee. My hands tremble so bad that the liquid sloshes over the edge. Cursing, I grab a napkin out of the dispenser and dab at the spill.

Karsyn continues to stare without speaking, his hazel eyes demanding something of me that I can't put into words. When the silence grows unnerving, I stand. I'm not just going to sit here like some circus, side-show freak for him to gawk at.

"Wait." It's one word, but it freezes me in place.

"You called me here to talk, Karsyn. So talk," I say, and he nods, lips straightened in a grim line. When he gestures for me to reclaim my seat, I do so somewhat reluctantly.

Immediately, he begins to pull at his blond hair again, his agitation making his movements jerky.

"I don't even know where to begin," he confesses, voice raspy as if he hasn't used it in a while. He nibbles on his lower lip, seemingly deep in thought. "I'm stupid."

His candid statement leaves me reeling.

"What?"

"I mean, I'm not *stupid*, stupid. But I'm never going to be some fucking straight A student like Lucas," he continues, staring at his hands as if they hold all of the secrets in the universe. There's a tiny golden freckle on the back of his left hand, and a teeny, tiny part of me wants to reach across the table and trace it with my finger. I quell that ridiculous urge by balling my hands into tight fists.

"Where are you going with this, Alder?" I cock a brow at him as he swallows.

"I...I don't know." He scrubs at his jawline in irritation. "No, that's not true. I *do* know. I'm never going to be some damn rocket scientist or anything like that. I'm good at only a few things, apparently. Football and being a complete jackass."

"I still don't know where you're going with this," I say lightly, running the pad of my thumb across the top of my coffee cup. Karsyn doesn't answer, his head lowered as he glares daggers into the white tabletop. I take advantage of the moment of silence to look around the room for the first time since I entered.

Not a lot has changed. It still has a makeshift assortment of archaic furniture, distressed wooden tables painted white, and long, floral couches against each wall. A tiny bookshelf sits in the far corner with a healthy collection of dust on each novel. The only item even moderately new is the register—a touch-screen computer. Even the cappuccino machine is the same as it was five years ago.

"Do you remember," I begin, purposely keeping my voice light and airy, "seventh grade?"

"I remember a fuck ton of things from seventh grade," Karsyn retorts. "You have to be more specific."

"You locked me in that cupboard right over there." I point with my chin towards a closet-sized room behind the counter. I remember the fear I felt being trapped in the dark with no escape. The worry that the cops would come and arrest me for trespassing... despite the fact that I hadn't gone willingly. But these boys, these Devils, had money and power while I had none. Each of them lived in sprawling mansions, or so I believed, while I lived in a modest, two-bedroom apartment with my mother. I was just the town freak.

"Shut up." I whip around to face him, gaping at Karsyn's quiet, yet vehement, reply.

"Excuse me?"

"I said shut up." He finally lifts his head, and I'm shocked to see tears in his eyes. "Just…just stop."

"Stop what?"

I feel as if we're at a turning point, as if we're at a crossroads and each direction beckons us forward. We can choose to remain together, no matter which road we take, or we can separate. Time stands still as my amber eyes lock with his. This close, I can see golden flecks surrounding his pupils, almost like errant fireworks have been set off.

"I thought about you a lot since you've been away," he confesses, voice a hushed murmur. He pauses and nervously licks his lips, before continuing. "And I replay what we did to you over and over again in my mind. I try to think things through, try to understand why we did the things we did. And you want to know what I come up with?" I stay silent, awaiting his answer with bated breath. "Jack fucking shit."

"I don't—"

"I remember the first time I saw you, back in elementary school. Do you remember?" he continues. I try to think back to that time, when I saw him as a classmate and even a friend, but all of his wicked sins taint my memory. I slowly shake my head no. "Well, I do. You were seven, maybe eight. Hell, maybe you were younger. What I do remember is you were this little scrap of a thing. Tiny. Petite. Cute." He shrugs his broad shoulders, and I can't help but feel butterflies in my stomach at the fact that he thought I was cute. It's actually kind of laughable how pathetic I am.

"What happened?" I ask quietly as he continues to stare off into space, lost in a memory only he can see.

"These kids were making fun of me because I still had trouble reading." His face creases together as he absently reaches across the table, picks apart some of my muffin, and shoves it in his mouth. I tentatively shove the rest of the treat towards him—a peace offering. "I remember they were calling me stupid and pushing me around a bit. Keep in mind, I was a scrawny fucker back then." He chuckles ruefully. "And there you came, this slip of a girl with gorgeous white-blonde hair and the strangest eyes I've ever seen. Do you know what you said?"

Once more, I shake my head. I don't remember any of this.

"You said, 'Don't be a bully! Bullies are mean and nasty!'" He chuckles once more, and this time, I can't help but join in. Oh, the irony of that statement.

"Younger me really needed to work on her retorts," I jest.

"You were the only person who stood up for me that day," he continues. "There were other kids who watched them pick on me, but only you actually stepped forward and put a stop to it. And I vowed to myself, right then and there on the playground, that I would marry you one day." He scratches at the inside of his arm as he continues to stare off into the distance. I half wonder if it's because he doesn't want to meet my eyes. "But less than a few years later, I..." He trails off, but we both know what he was going to say. A few years later, he became my bully. My tormentor. My living nightmare.

"So why did you do it?" I whisper.

I feel worn out, the emotional whiplash these boys put me through taking a toll on my body. Sooner or later, the events of the last few days are going to catch up to me like a twenty-thousand-pound ship running into an iceberg. I'm going to crash and drown, and there's nothing anyone can do to save me.

"Honestly?" Karsyn touches the corner of his lips with his pointer finger. "Because I had a crush on you...but so did the others. We decided that none of us could have you, and that made me..."

"Mad enough to hurt me?" I surmise, feeling sick to my stomach. It's funny, in a way, that the people we hurt the most are often the people we care about more than anything. Why do we always hurt the people we love? When will this sick, twisted cycle end? First my mom, then Nana, and now…

"No." Karsyn shakes his head from side to side, body radiating a sort of desperate, primal energy. It reminds me distinctly of a caged lion you would see at a zoo. You're aware that it's one of the most powerful predators on the planet and that the only thing containing it is a few flimsy bars. What if it breaks free? Beasts like that aren't made for captivity. "It wasn't like that," he continues.

"Then explain it to me," I hedge, my nerves frayed like I'm a live wire about to whip around and spark at anyone who comes too close. "I know you have this need to assuage your guilt—"

"Guilt?" He laughs harshly. "You think I *just* feel guilt? You have no fucking idea, Simone."

"Then what the hell are we doing here, Alder? I'm just trying to understand!" The muscles in my shoulders are so tense, they spasm. "If you don't feel guilt, then why am I even here?" Pain rushes through me, but my rage quickly tempers it. What did I expect from him? An apology like Elias gave me? An acknowledgement that he wronged me? "If you're not sorry—"

"I never said I'm not sorry," he interrupts, tone caustic and acidic. "And I never said I don't feel guilty. I just said that guilt isn't the only emotion I feel. I have a plethora of emotions inside of me right now." He distractedly scratches at the nape of his neck, avoiding eye contact once more as the fight drains from him. "I feel a lot of fucking things. And…and I know sorry isn't good enough."

I wait him out, crossing my arms over my chest and leaning back in the uncomfortable plastic chair. My coffee sits in front of me, forgotten.

"I feel anger at myself. Hurt. *Guilt.* I feel so fucking much that I'm going insane." Abruptly, he leans across the table, his desperation growing from an ember to a blazing inferno. "Simone, I'm so fucking sorry. And I hate the fact that it took me five years to say those words. I hate the fact that I didn't reach out to you after everything that happened. And I'm so fucking sorry that I'm one of the causes for..." He allows his words to drift off, lowering his gaze to stare at my arms. With my long-sleeved shirt on, my scars can't be seen, but I know he's envisioning them nonetheless. Heaven only knows that I do daily as well.

"What do you want from me, Alder?" I rip my eyes away from his and focus on my coffee. I take a tentative sip, allowing the lukewarm liquid to chase away the chill.

"I want to start over. Maybe as...friends?" He speaks the last word with hesitance, hope flaring to life in his striking eyes.

And...

I want that.

Just like I wanted a relationship with Elias.

But how can I? The knowledge of what I did to him consumes and overwhelms me like a twenty-foot wave. I *destroyed* his chance of playing college football. I've already heard the murmurings that State rescinded their offer after the game. I'm not saying that the Devils don't need to atone for their sins, because they most definitely do. But maybe, just maybe, I need to atone for mine as well.

And I can't be Karsyn's friend while I still hold on to so much anger and hurt. So much guilt and pain. There are so many emotions associated with these men, and not all of them are good. When I see his face, I feel anger at the memory of what he and the others did to me. But I also feel hurt. And, more recently, guilt. How can I look him in the eye knowing what I did? Knowing what *he* did?

I'm so fucking lost and confused, I'm afraid my head will explode, the blast taking it clean off my shoulders.

"No." I can barely speak, barely breathe. All I can hear is the unsteady thump of my heart in my rib cage.

"No?" Disbelief laces his tone as he stares at me in shock.

"We can't start over, Alder. Not now. Not ever."

Before he can mount another protest, before he can convince me otherwise, I grab my backpack off the ground and hurry out of the coffee shop.

Why does everything have to hurt so damn much?

CHAPTER 38

It's raining when I exit the coffee shop. How did I not hear the heavy patter of rain on the vaulted roof? The answer is simple—I was distracted.

Karsyn Alder consumed every bit of my attention. The only words I was capable of hearing were his. The only thing I could see was his face. His chiseled jawline. The slow, seductive tilt of his lips. His hazel eyes, a melt of autumn tones. It's those eyes I focus on now, like some lovestruck tween writing in her diary. When he was jovial or even passionate, they sparkled with mirth. But when he was sad or desperate, they grew dim, the brown capturing and eradicating any traces of green from his irises.

It feels as if my heart's been through the shredder, but despite that, I'm still standing. Still breathing. Still walking, one step after another. I'll fall apart tonight, in the safety of my own bed.

I'll envision Elias's face, rife with betrayal and frustration, and the hurt in Karsyn's eyes when I refused his offer of peace.

I'll see Nana's tear-stained face, and Gabriel's snarling one.

Mariabella's shuttered expression when I rejected her.

Lucas's cold, tight-lipped smile that makes him look more demonic than human.

The anger in Cassian's gaze when he confronted me about my involvement in Mrs. Town's firing.

The disappointment and annoyance in my mom's expression every time we talked.

Pain and grief have a way of chipping at your soul, one tiny sliver at a time. In small doses, you won't even notice anything's amiss. But if it comes at you all at once, you'll lose yourself completely. Lose the fundamental thing that makes you *you*.

Cold, biting rainwater plasters my hair to my head as I step onto the sidewalk. I don't immediately begin walking. Instead, I tilt my head upwards, allowing the rain to pelt my face like a thousand icy kisses. Bloated, gray storm clouds shroud the sky above me, the sun nowhere to be seen. It's fitting, I suppose, to have such a dark and dreary day for a time like this, a time when my world is in shambles, falling apart around me, and I'm helpless to do anything but watch.

"Peony!" Karsyn's raspy voice reaches me, and I blink water out of my eyes as I stare at him. His dark shirt clings to his chest, accentuating his muscular frame, as he bounds towards me in three quick steps. He places his hands on my waist, and this close, I can see raindrops suspended on his lashes like tears. "You don't get to leave me. Not like that."

And then he kisses me.

Or I kiss him.

It's quick and sudden, but I swear lava sloshes in my stomach, a once dormant volcano springing to life. His lips move against mine fiercely, and I surrender to him, to the feelings he evokes inside of me. Maybe I should be cautious after everything that's happened. Maybe I should be cynical or even feel guilty. After all, I had sex with Elias not even a few hours ago.

But this…

His lips against mine…

His tongue caressing my own...

It feels right. I can sense it in the very center of my soul, throbbing in tandem with my pounding heart. All that exists is him and me, locked in an embrace capable of sizzling the water pelting us from up above.

But my life is like the rain clouds in the sky, opening up and releasing torrents on the unsuspecting population. As quickly as the kiss begins, I end it, all but shoving Karsyn away from me. Tears fill my eyes, blending with the rainwater, as I stare up at one of the men I hate and love most in the world.

Isn't this what most girls dream about? A fairy tale kiss in the rain? That inevitable collision of stars in the galaxy?

"We can't do this," I whisper, and I wonder if he can even hear me over the flurry of rainfall.

"Simone, don't say that..."

"Because you were right." I throw my hands up in the air and tilt my head skywards once more, laughing maniacally. "I'm a freak."

"*No one* talks bad about my girl," Karsyn all but growls, taking half a step closer to me. "Least of all my girl herself."

"I'm not your girl, Alder," I protest around a weak laugh. Inside, it feels as if my heart is shredding into thousands of intricate pieces. Too many for me to ever hope to stitch back together again. They just sit in my chest, a mildly uncomfortable presence I yearn to yank out and stomp on. "I can't be."

"Peony, I care about you. I always have. And I'm sorry—"

"It's not even about that anymore!" A gust of wind blows my white hair around my face, and a few of the wet strands stick to my cheeks. Karsyn stares at one intently, almost as if he wishes he could reach out and brush it behind my ear. His hands ball into fists.

"Then what is it?" he demands.

"I'm a freak! I'm that weirdo you always accused me of being." I don't want to feel this...this...this *hurt* anymore. I don't want to feel anything, if I'm being honest.

Love and hate are like a swinging pendulum. Once it goes in one direction, the laws of physics dictate that it has to swing in the other at some point in time. Back and forth, back and forth, never ending. A continuous and toxic loop of blood-curdling hatred combined with toe-curling love and lust.

I don't think I love the Devils. At least, not yet. But I can see myself irrevocably and irreversibly falling for them if I remain around them. They're the suns that I desperately orbit around, chasing them despite the risk of getting burnt.

"Peony…don't think like that," Karsyn whispers as he tugs on my hands. I didn't even realize that I was digging my nails into my palms, reverting to some of my nastier habits from five years ago. "Don't listen to things a little shit like me said in middle school. I never meant any of it. What do you need me to do? How can I make you forgive me?"

"Karsyn, you're not listening to me," I huff, attempting to wrench my hands free. His grip remains firm. "You were *right*. You were always right. I'm not normal, and I don't think I'll ever be. A darkness resides inside of me. Don't you see? So this…" With my hand still in his, I attempt to gesture between the two of us. "Can't be a thing. Though I don't even know what kind of 'thing' we would be."

"Whatever we fucking want to be," Karsyn replies adamantly, lips pursed.

He doesn't understand, and short of me screaming that I'm a witch, I don't know how else to drill it into his stubborn head.

"I wanted to hurt you," I blurt out. "I mean, I *want* to hurt you. I came to this town for one reason—revenge. I wanted you and the others to pay for what you did to me." My words rush together, a strange combination of past and present tenses, but honestly? I don't know which one is true. Revenge is the last thing on my mind at the moment. Do I still hate him? Hate *them*? Do I still want to destroy their lives the way they did mine? The way I *thought* they did mine? Are they as cruel and capricious as I thought them to be?

He blinks at me, seemingly unable to comprehend my words. Those gorgeous, curled lashes of his appear even darker and thicker in the rain. His hands drop from mine as if I burned him, as if some sticky, toxic substance coats my skin instead of rain water.

It's better this way. It's better if he hates me.

Because that means I'm still allowed to hate him.

"I sabotaged you at the football game," I confess, watching as his eyebrows draw together in confusion.

"That's not possib—"

"I'm not a good girl, and you're not a good guy." My pain refuses to relent, like a splinter embedded beneath my fingernail. "So now you see." All I can hear is the pounding of my heart, each heartbeat threatening to be my last.

Almost mechanically, he repeats, "Now I see."

"You just need to let me go," I continue, staring at the broken man who stole my heart and then crushed it in his fist. And I think that's another problem. It's not just *him* who has a piece of my heart.

"I just need to let you go," he parrots dumbly.

This time when I walk away, he doesn't follow me.

CHAPTER 39

I don't make it far before I fall apart. My knees hit the sidewalk as I collapse just a few blocks away from my house. The rain slows, now nothing more than light sprinkles that caress my face, and the sun begins to crest the gray, pregnant storm clouds.

It's almost as if the universe itself wants to remind me that this isn't the end. That this isn't over. That the sun always comes out…

Okay. Even I know that's complete and utter shit.

My phone rings in my back pocket, and I awkwardly reach for it. Fortunately, I'm in an area of town most people don't travel to, where nothing but country houses, acres of trees, and the occasional corn field ornamented with silos reside. I imagine they would grow quite concerned at the sight of a crying, disheveled girl kneeling in a puddle of mucky rain water.

"Yeah?" I answer hoarsely.

"Peony?" It's Nana, her tone even more frazzled than it had been the first time I called her about the Bloods. "Are you okay? Why aren't you home?"

"I told you." I bite my nails into my palms, reveling in the slight bite of pain. "I was with a friend."

"It's not safe," she snaps. And then, in a softer voice, she adds, "Polo and Christian are putting a protection spell on the house right now. Come home. *Please.*"

I rub at my face, collecting a disgusting mixture of snot and tears on my palm, evidence of my literal unravelling. There's no other word that can even begin to encapsulate what I'm feeling. I can't tell up from down, right from wrong, love from hate. The emotions tangle together inside of me, growing tighter and tighter, until it feels as if they're suffocating my heart.

"I don't know if I can come home. Not yet."

"I know you're mad—"

"I'm fucking furious!" I scream, hating that I'm forced to have this conversation with her here. On the phone. In the rain. "You *lied* to me. My entire life, everyone has lied to me. I thought you, of all people, would be the one person who wouldn't." Silence reigns, and I pull the phone away to make sure she hasn't hung up. "Okay, look…" I scrub a hand down my face, moving my matted, wet hair off of my cheeks. "I'm not saying I'm never coming back. That I don't forgive you. I just need a little more time to wrap my head around this."

"It's not safe." Her voice wobbles ever so slightly, and I know she's right. Being out by myself, especially after the most recent attack, is stupid. Obviously, the Bloods are in this area, and they now know that I'm a witch. At the same time, I can't imagine they would be stupid enough to remain here after I saw their faces and got away. "We called the council, and they said they'll send Gabriel back home to track the Bloods, but it's not safe, and I don't—"

"Hold on." I balance the phone between my shoulder and my ear as I dig through my backpack. My searching fingers find an old necklace Uriel got me for one of our anniversaries. I lay it carefully out on the ground before grabbing my spell book. "I have a necklace here. I can place a protection spell on it."

It won't protect me from all harm, only the magical kind. If a Blood decides to throw a fireball at me or shoot me with ice, the necklace will vacuum it up. But if he punches me instead? Kicks me? Grabs me? I'm on my own, the spell ineffective against physical attacks. Another problem with these types of charms is that they will only last for a few days, at most, and the power you need to expend in order to perform the spell takes a toll on your body.

"Do you have the ingredients?" she demands as I continue pulling items out of my backpack.

I flip open the book and trace my finger over the faded text until I find the spell I need.

"Bone of a sparrow," I read aloud. "I have that."

It's always good to have sparrow bone on hand. The majority of spells require it.

"A ten-year-old leaf," I continue, turning my attention towards my ragtag collection of ingredients I always keep with me. If asked about them, I can lie and say they are for a science experiment or an arts and crafts project. I bite my lip as I push aside some loose papers, a couple jars of decaying beetles, and a bag of preserved rabbit feet, before smirking in satisfaction at the sight of the brittle brown leaf in a Ziplock bag. "Have it."

"And you need—"

I grab a sleek, black feather. "Have that as well."

"Okay, good. And do you have the incantation?" Nana presses, and I nod, before remembering she can't see me.

"I'll do the spell now." I glance nervously in both directions, ensuring that the streets are still empty and that the nearest form of life is only a tall oak. Placing my phone down, I position the bone, feather, and leaf in a triangle around the necklace. I use the book for reference as I begin to chant slowly, magic coursing through my veins as if it's a ten-foot worm crawling just beneath my skin, attempting to slither its way out. Blue light emits from the necklace as one by one, the three ingredients burst into brilliant, bright red flames. The flames begin to curve inwards, almost in the shape of a pyramid, as the color transitions from red to a deep, unnatural purple.

I close my eyes as an invisible wind catches my white-blonde hair, causing the wet strands to fly around my face. My shirt billows in the breeze as well. I know that to any outside observer, my eyes will appear an eerie combination of blue and purple as raw power emanates from my very pores. My voice reaches a crescendo until I'm practically screaming, my throat feeling raw and brittle, like someone has just rubbed it down with sandpaper.

The power dissipates with the final word of the spell, leaving behind three piles of ash and one normal-looking necklace.

My hands shake as I reach for the silver chain and clasp it around my neck. It feels warm to the touch, stealing the remaining cold of the rainwater from my body.

"It's done," I tell Nana, and she breathes out a sigh of relief.

Silence once more engulfs us for a few, tense minutes.

"Where are you going?" Nana interjects at last.

"I don't know," I whisper, and I'm not just talking about now. Do I stay here? Do I go back to California?

I've been letting the tides carry me away, but now I want to swim and resist the current. To adhere to a greater purpose beyond revenge.

"Stay safe, Peony," Nana whispers.

"You, too."

As I end the call, I allow my mind to wander to that *night*. There's always that one moment in someone's life when everything changes. It's a tiny, barely decipherable dot on the blueprint of your life, standing out starkly like black ink on a white sheet of paper. For me, that moment was the night of my eighth grade dance. The night where my very world crumbled around me like after a tornado wreaks havoc.

I stood in the center of the stage, the spotlight blistering hot where it glared down on me. Sweat beaded on my forehead as my eyes drifted first to

Lucas, looking every inch the unattainable prince with his slicked back red hair, and then to Cassian beside him, his smile malicious. On the opposite side of the stage, Elias stood with Karsyn, both of them exchanging wary, and weary, *glances, before the latter replaces his frown with a shit-eating grin.*

Lucas smiled widely and stepped back up to the microphone. I couldn't help but think how dashing he looked in his three-piece gray suit.

"Good evening, ladies and gentlemen," he began, his butterscotch voice making my blood sizzle. Cassian began to snicker, and even Karsyn joined in, using his fist to hide his laughter. And that was when I knew. *The revelation was swift and brutal, a blade on a guillotine cutting off my head. All I could do was stand there frozen as my eyes slid to Elias.*

He couldn't, or wouldn't, meet my eyes.

Trap! *my mind screamed at me, begging me to run. But for some reason, my feet remained cemented to the ground, watching this horror show unveil before me. I couldn't breathe through the sudden, agonizing tightness in my throat. I felt light-headed, like I was thousands of meters below the ocean's surface, struggling to resist the currents. But they continually pulled at me, dragging me deeper and deeper into an abyss of endless darkness.*

"We decided that we're going to start a new tradition," Lucas continued. "The crowning of High Groves Middle School's queen!" The crowd broke into raucous cheering, a few of them already giggling like they knew what was about to happen.

My eyes latched on to the teachers standing around the perimeter of the gym. How could they let this happen? Why weren't they stopping it? A few of them met my eyes before quickly looking away. But more than one of them refused to even make eye contact, staring very purposefully at the ground. And I realized...they had no intentions of stopping this, of putting an end to the Devils reign of terror. Their parents paid their paychecks, and that was all that mattered to them in this small community, where wealth and power spoke louder than words.

I wished the secretary, Patricia Brooks, was there. She would've stopped this.

Mr. Gurrel was the only teacher who met my gaze and held it, winking slyly. I felt sick to my stomach when he lowered his hands down his toned stomach and cupped himself through his pants. Before any of the other teachers could see, he quickly dropped both of his arms to his sides and adopted a nonchalant pose.

I was alone.

Truly alone.

The thought should've terrified me. It should've made icy, insidious fear skate down my spine. It should've made my hands sweat and my heart pound and my eyes water.

Instead, I felt empty.

I couldn't muster up a single emotion besides loneliness.

Elias used me. I had no friends. My mother hated me.

I was alone.

"...and that's why we chose Peony Simone as our new queen!" Lucas waited for the cheers to die down before turning towards me. "As most of you know, she overcomes adversity each and every day. Some of you may not know this, but Peony is a hermaphrodite." A group of girls standing closest to the stage began to giggle, while the rest of the room went completely silent. I could feel every eye on me as Lucas spun his story like a spider spinning a web. He was enjoying this, I realized. He lived for being in the spotlight, for having every eye fixated on him with undivided attention.

All of the Devils did.

They did most of their evil acts in the shadows, but when they stepped into the light...

You just knew it was going to be bad.

"I saw for myself that Peony has a cock dangling between her legs. Isn't that right, boys?" He turned towards the other Devils. Cassian and Karsyn nodded with glowing smiles on their faces. Elias's jaw was clenched tightly, but he nodded as well.

And that did it. Those nods were what finally broke me. I was a sinking ship, finally submerging completely beneath the persistent waves battering against my sides. Pain exploded inside of me like one of those basement-made bombs. It wasn't pretty or precise. It was just...boom.

"But, boys," this time, Lucas addressed the crowd, "don't be afraid. Peony still gives great blowjobs."

The laughter was louder, almost encouraging. This entire situation reminded me of Tinkerbell. She needed attention to survive, just like the Devils did. How much power would they have if no one gave them the time of day? If no one laughed at their stupid jokes and taunts? None. My classmates handed the power to them on silver fucking platters, allowing them to feast like kings.

More and more laughter broke through the throng of students like rippling waves.

The eyes weren't on me, though, but on something behind me. Unwittingly, I twisted my head to see a hastily created photoshop blown up on the screen. It featured me on my knees with my mouth open and the four Devils huddled around me, their cocks out. They had enough decency to blur their genitals, but they hadn't extended the same courtesy to me. Instead, a pair of saggy breasts, covered in moles and warts, were placed on my body. Above the picture was the caption, "Witches be crazy."

"All right, that's enough!" Principal Maynard stormed through the crowd just as the slideshow changed to a new picture. It was still one of me with the hideous, saggy breasts, but instead of the Devils, I was on my knees before Principal Maynard.

The laughter amped up, but I could barely hear it. It sounded muffled, as if I was hearing it through a tunnel.

All I knew for certain was that I wanted to die.

I pull myself out of the memory with a jerk. It feels as if I've been trapped in there for hours, but I know it has only been a few seconds.

Hands trembling, I begin to pick up my ingredients and shove them back into my backpack. I don't know where I'm going to go yet, but I know it's not home. Not yet. I'll get a hotel if I have to and spend the night there.

I straighten to my feet, my pants soaked from the muddy puddle I'd been kneeling in, before twisting to walk back into town.

Only for my feet to falter.

Karsyn Alder stands behind me, rainwater running down his face and his blond hair drenched. He stares at me for a moment, not blinking and mouth slightly agape, before those hazel eyes of his lower to my necklace.

I'm frozen as well, my heart hammering in my ribcage loud enough for me to hear.

And then, his voice barely above a breath, he says, "What-what the fuck was that?"

CHAPTER 40

A tightness grips my lungs. I suddenly find it impossible for me to inhale air. Am I dying? Is that what this feeling is? My nails dig into my palms hard enough to draw blood, but I don't focus on that. It's a distant thought, like seeing an airplane flying across the sky while you're outside in your lawn. You hear it, maybe even see a trail of white, but you don't think anything of it.

"W-What…what do you mean?" I manage to stutter out, preparing to walk around him.

"The flames…" He nods towards the ash piles, his movements jerky. "I saw—"

"Are you okay?" I cut in. "Did you hit your head?"

My heart gallops in my chest, sort of like one of those animated cartoons where you see the heart extend and inflate from the character's body.

Fuck. Fuck. Fuck! First Lucas, then Elias, and now Karsyn. How many more people will learn my secret? Will he become furious like Elias or only show curiosity as Lucas did? Will he want to hurt me? I don't believe that last thought for even a second, but I can't help but feel cautious, especially after Elias's explosive reaction.

"Peony." Karsyn takes a step towards me, thinks better of it, and then steps *back*. I scared him—*scare* him. I can see that clear as day on his face. He bites down on his plush bottom lip before pulling it through his teeth. Then his tongue snakes out to lick at his top one. He repeats this a few more times as he stares at me. Just stares. I wait for him to begin yelling, to begin screaming, to threaten to call the police on me, but all he does is pierce me in place with that pene-trating gaze of his. I think out of all the Devils, his eyes are my favorite, even more than Elias's strange color. The soft reflective browns, spreading to hills of grassy meadows, with the outer edge rimmed in russet-hued gold. They complement his shorn blond hair and the days old stubble on his chin.

When the silence becomes too much, I begin to ramble. "I don't know what you think you saw, but I can assure you that—"

"Don't!" He lifts a hand into the air, and I notice it shaking. He swallows, finally peeling his gaze away from me as if it hurts to look at me. "Don't fucking act like I'm dumb. I already told you I'm not."

"You're not dumb." I slowly remove my nails from my palms and grip the strap of my backpack. "Karsyn, you're *not*."

"But you're acting like I am," he growls, and this time, he *does* stalk to me, his intent clear in every hard line of his face. He pauses when he's directly in front of me and places his hands on my shoul-ders. It's not tight enough to hurt, but firm enough for me to know he won't let me leave without some sort of explanation. "Tell me the truth. I know what I saw." His eyes watch mine intently, fluttering between my amber orbs. "Are you a...witch?" He says that word hesitantly, almost fearfully, as if he expects me to laugh at him for such an outlandish claim. But honestly? If the situation was reversed, I would jump to the same conclusion. A girl chanting in Latin while magical fire burned around her? A girl with pure power seeming to ooze from her very being?

Instead of answering, I simply stare at him. Just stare. Turning the tables back on him.

"What would you do if I said yes?" I query at last. Would he be like Elias and run? Would he be curious and yearn to study me like Lucas?

Karsyn doesn't even blink. "I believe in the supernatural," he confesses bluntly. "I always thought…" Once more, that pink tongue of his traces his upper lip, and I can't help but imagine that tongue in more…intimate places. I shake those thoughts off before they can solidify.

"You suspected I was different," I whisper, and the nickname "little witch" suddenly takes on a new meaning. After all, it wasn't Lucas who gave me that nickname. It was Karsyn.

"No." He swallows. "But what I just saw…you can't explain that away." His grip tightens almost imperceptibly, but I don't wince. I don't allow him to see any outwards signs of my discomfort. "So please. Don't act like I'm an idiot. Tell me the fucking truth."

"Why?" I tilt my chin up stubbornly, despite feeling small and weak and vulnerable. Young. I feel young. First Lucas, then Elias, and now Karsyn. Why is it that three of the men capable of hurting me the most are the ones who know my deepest, darkest secret? The universe must be laughing at me right about now, giving me the biggest middle finger known to mankind.

"I won't…" He trails off with a harried, broken laugh. "I won't tell anybody."

"How can I trust you?" He smells vaguely like the rainwater soaking us both and something I would almost describe as cloves. I wonder if it's his natural scent or that of his cologne. Either way, I find that I want to inhale deeply. "Because if you want the truth, the whole truth, I'll give it to you. But you're going to hate me after." The last sentence is said on a breath of air, nothing more than a whisper.

But I'm so tired. Tired of my revenge scheme. Tired of hiding. Tired of feeling so fucking scared all the damn time. It's like my body is full of metallic pipes and slowly, almost painstakingly so, someone is taking a wrench to each and every one, allowing the pipes to burst, filling me with disgusting brown water. I don't want to feel like this anymore. I *refuse* to.

"Tell me." His eyes flutter shut, and I swear his chest stops moving as he holds his breath.

"You're right." The words hurt coming out of my throat. "I'm a witch."

He doesn't reopen his eyes when he speaks next. "And at the football game...was that you?" When I don't respond, he pleads, "Don't. Lie. To. Me."

"Yes."

Romance novels lie. You don't get the sweaty hands, rapidly beating heart, and weak knees when you're around the boy you love. You get those when you're in the midst of breaking said boy's heart. When you're about to break your own.

Karsyn exhales noisily, finally stepping back so he can brush at his wet hair. It proves ineffective, the blond strands flopping messily back across his forehead. I brace myself, preparing for his ire, but it never comes. His shoulders droop as he dips his head, staring intently at his dirty tennis shoes.

"I always knew you hated me," he whispers. "But enough to do *that* to me?"

I shake wildly, hands clenching and then unclenching by my sides. "You deserve way worse than just a shitty football game, and you know it."

He opens his mouth as if to protest, likely to remind me that all of his dreams were riding on that game, when he snaps it closed, twisting his head to stare off into the distance. When he finally speaks, it's not the words I expected. "You're right."

"Excuse me?"

"I said, you're right. I deserved that and much, much worse for what I did to you. The things I said. The fucking dance." He laughs, but the sound holds no mirth. "That fucking dance. I still think about it, you know. That night." He pulls his gaze away from the horizon to focus on his hands. They may not be stained with blood, but that doesn't make them clean. "I planned to apologize the next day, you know? I knew that you probably wouldn't believe me, but I couldn't live with this…"

"Guilt?" I supply, but he shakes his head.

"Pain," he corrects. "I couldn't live with this pain. I hurt someone I cared about, all in the name of popularity. Looking back, I can barely recognize myself. Like, who was that little fucker? Why did I do what I did? I don't have an answer to any of those questions, Peony, and that's what scares me the most. Shouldn't I have a reason? Don't most evil people do evil things for evil purposes? Not me. I do evil things just because I fucking want to. Or not even really that. Because I fucking can. And I *hate* myself. If I would've known…"

"I tried to kill myself that night," I confess, and he blanches, his face turning stark white. "It wasn't just because of you four, though. It was everything."

"And then you moved to California?" he surmises, and this time, I'm the one who shakes their head no.

"And then I was placed in a psychiatric facility just north of here." I snort at the memories. "We talked about *emotions* and *how did that make you feel?* No one accepted my answers. They asked those questions, but when I said that I wanted to die, they told me I was wrong."

"You were," Karsyn blurts, looking fearful. "Wrong, I mean. This world would be a much shittier place without you in it, Simone." Up ahead, thunder cackles and lightning sparks across the dreary, gray sky. Karsyn extends a hand towards me as the clouds open up, once more drenching us in a downpour of icy rain. "My house is close by."

I hesitate, staring at his proffered hand as if I expect it to leave his wrist and crawl across the ground like something out of a horror movie. Karsyn remains standing there, patient despite the incoming storm.

After a tense moment, I place my slippery hand into his and allow him to pull me down the street.

I may regret this decision in the future. He may want to hurt me because of what he knows, because of what I did to him.

But I can't find it within me to care.

KARSYN DRIVES ME TO A CUTE, SUBURBAN, THREE-STORY FARMHOUSE. I only have enough time to see fresh yellow paint, a perfectly mani-cured lawn, and a bike near the front entrance before Karsyn pulls me inside. I shake wildly, the frigid air causing goosebumps to erupt on my skin and numb my fingers.

"Mom! Dad! I'm home!" Karsyn bellows. He kicks off his shoes and rips off his wet jacket. He then reaches for me and helps me remove mine as well. I take my shoes off much more gingerly than he did, hating that my sodden clothes leave a puddle in their foyer.

Before his parents can respond, a small dog comes barreling around the corner, yipping like crazy. Her fur is a colorful combina-tion of red, brown, black, and white. A single pink bow rests on her head, and she wears a bedazzled collar.

"Yorkie?" I question as the playful dog runs through Karsyn's legs.

"Honey Pot," he tells me before bending down and scratching behind her ears.

"Kar? Is that Mari?" A woman comes from around the corner, wiping her hands on a yellow rag. She pauses when she catches sight of me, her green-brown eyes, almost an exact replica of Karsyn's, widening. "Oh. Who is this?" A wide smile blossoms on her face as she hurries forward, hand extended.

"Peony," I introduce, staring at the woman with stunning golden hair, a dimpled grin, and rosy red cheeks. I can see the resemblance between the two of them immediately. "You must be Mrs. Alder."

"Please. Call me Charlotte." Still gripping my hand, she turns her head to call out, "Michael! Come here!"

An older gentleman with a protruding stomach, sandy-blond hair peppered with white, and a smiling face exits the kitchen a moment later. He, too, pauses when he sees me before a mischievous smile splits open his face. My eyes drift down to the faded State sweatshirt he wears, and an awkward, uncomfortable pang shoots through me. I don't know if it's guilt, regret, satisfaction, or a combination of all three. Hell, I can't even tell if my desires still center around my revenge, or if I'm ready to move on with my life.

I'll look into all of that at a later date.

"Well, well, well. What do we have here? Is this the 'Peony' you always talked about?" His wife releases me as he steps forward, tenderly taking my hand in both of his and giving it a shake. "I'm Michael." The sly dog then turns towards Karsyn and winks. "She's pretty."

"I know," Karsyn grumbles, color rising to his cheeks as he stares at the ground.

"Can I get you two anything to eat? A hot chocolate? You must be freezing," his mother croons, flitting between the two of us. I bite my lip to keep from smirking when Karsyn's blush deepens.

"I'm actually going to take Peony upstairs to shower," he tells them, and I watch as Charlotte and Michael exchange conspiratorial looks.

"Shower. Is that what the kids are calling it these days?" Michael whispers to her in an overly dramatic, horrified stage-whisper. "Dad!" Karsyn huffs, and Honey Pot begins to bark.

"Ignore him," Charlotte tells me with an eye roll. "We all do." To her husband, she says, "Let's leave the kids alone. I want a rematch."

"A rematch?" Karsyn questions, amusement lacing his tone.

This time, Michael's the one to roll his eyes as he scoops down to pick up Honey Pot. It's almost comical to see such a large man hold such a delicate, feminine dog. "She's pissed because I beat her ass at Mario Kart five times in a row."

"And your record ends now," Charlotte deadpans. "Because the only ass getting beat is yours. With a flogger."

"Oh my god." Karsyn looks as if he wishes the ground will open up and swallow him whole. "I'll never be able to show my face again."

"Nah. If what you told me is true, then this one is a keeper." Michael nudges his son with a shit-eating smirk. "By the way, she's even prettier in person."

"Actually…" Charlotte grins up at her husband. "How about we take a long, *long* walk and leave the two of them alone?"

"Yes, let's leave them alone for their 'shower,'" Michael agrees, making air quotes with his fingers.

"Just go." Karsyn all but shoves his giggling parents out of the room until it's just me and him. Once we're alone, I turn towards him with a quirked brow.

"So…you've been talking about me?" I don't know why that thought sets a flurry of butterflies loose inside my stomach. My heart quite literally gains a set of wings and begins to fly.

"And you're apparently a witch, so there's a lot we don't know about each other yet," Karsyn retorts with a teasing grin. His words make my own smile fade.

"How can you be so…blasé about all of this? Most people would be in shock. Or wouldn't believe me. Or would want to justify it however they could. How can you just—"

"I told you," Karsyn cuts in. "I saw what I saw. I heard what I heard. To me, there's nothing else that needs to be said or done. Unless you're pulling some massive prank on me—"

"I'm not."

"—then you really do possess magical powers. And yes, I am fucking curious. So curious that I might just die if I don't get answers. But I also know that you're dripping wet, shivering, and you still don't trust me yet." He shrugs, and I don't even bother to protest. He's right. Trust is a fickle thing, a double-edged sword. You both must be willing to impale yourselves on it in order for it to work. "Now let's warm ourselves up and then we can talk, okay?"

Conversation tapers off as Karsyn leads me to a shower on the second floor. He grabs a fluffy towel, a pair of clean boxer briefs, and the smallest T-shirt he can find.

"You can just leave your wet clothes in here. I'll grab them after you're done and put them in the dryer. Let me grab your backpack and put it in my room." He gently takes it from me, shrugging it over his own shoulder, before nodding back towards the shower. "Here's the shampoo and conditioner. And body wash." Karsyn points to each item before ducking out of the room. I wait until he's gone before locking the door, stripping out of my soaking wet clothes, and stepping beneath the blistering hot water. I make sure to turn it as high as it can go as I throw my head back, reveling in the way the water pelts my naked flesh.

What am I going to do now?

Karsyn now knows the truth, as does Elias and Lucas. And with the Bloods sniffing around, that's immensely dangerous.

I finger the necklace I still have on, feeling the power vibrating through it.

Karsyn will want answers, but how much do I give him? The last thing I want is to inadvertently put him into harm's way because he knows too much. The witch's council has very strict rules about who can know our secrets. Only spouses are guaranteed protection. Or blood bonds, similar to the connection between a familiar and a witch.

As long as the three of them remain quiet, we shouldn't have any issues.

At the same time, they're teenage boys. What if they blurt the truth out when they're drunk at some girl's party? What if they get pissed at me again? What if they decide once more to target me? This time around, they'll have actual ammo in their arsenal capable of inflicting maximum damage. I'm putting all of my trust into the words, "I've changed." But have they? Have they really? Or deep down, are they the same cruel boys I knew from five years ago?

I don't know how long I stand under the spray. Hours? Minutes? When my fingers begin to prune, I shut off the water. Quickly, I towel off and slip into Karsyn's clean clothes, finding myself only slightly disappointed when they don't smell like him. I leave my wet clothes in the sink, knowing that he'll grab them later, and pad on bare feet down the hallway.

The only open door is at the very end of the hall, so I slip into that room, shutting and locking the door behind me.

Karsyn's bedroom.

In the connecting bathroom, I can hear his shower running, so I take a moment to survey his room uninterrupted.

It's homier than I expected, laden with trophies and mementos. An entire shelf dedicated to autographed footballs sits just above his bed. Clothes litter the room, hanging off the side of his laundry basket. His duffle bag, full of his football equipment, lies open in the center of his rug.

Before I can continue my search, the door to the bathroom opens and Karsyn steps out, one towel wrapped around his waist while he uses another one to dry his short hair. His feet falter when he sees me.

"Peony, I didn't expect—"

"I'm sorry," I say, spinning around. "The door was open, and I finished my shower, so I—"

He chuckles, and I hear the sound of a drawer opening and closing. "You're okay. I just didn't expect you to be in here."

"You have...um...good water pressure," I blurt like an idiot, and his laughter only increases.

"I'll make sure to let my parents know that you're a fan of our water company."

I can't take it anymore.

I spin towards him so fast, I actually get whiplash. My power fizzles and sparks under my skin, almost like an errant firework accidentally being set off, as I stare up into his handsome face.

"What the fuck are we doing, Alder?" I demand, and he pauses in the midst of putting a shirt on. I'm grateful to see his pants are already in place. Because Karsyn's cock? I'm not sure even the strongest willed people could resist that.

"What do you mean?" His smile drops, expression turning perplexed at my abrupt question.

"I don't know if I'm supposed to still hate you or what," I blurt, mentally berating my stupid mouth for getting away from me.

Instead of answering with words, Karsyn drops his black shirt to the ground and stalks forward on silent feet.

CHAPTER 41

"What are you doing?" I ask breathlessly, but I don't step away. I'm not even sure I could if I wanted to. Which, oddly enough, I don't think I do.

"Kissing you," he answers softly. My eyelids flutter shut as I wait for the warm press of his lips against mine.

But instead of my lips, Karsyn gently lifts one of my hands and presses a tender kiss to the underside of my wrist. Directly over one of my scars.

My heart picks up speed as he stares at me through his fringe of sooty lashes.

"Karsyn…" I don't know if I'm warning him to stay away or begging him to come closer. All I know is that I can feel each brush of his lips like they have a direct line of communication to my core.

"I hate these," Karsyn murmurs as he kisses another one. "I hate what they represent."

"I love them." My voice is breathy, even for me, as he presses his lips to a third scar. "They're a reminder of what I survived. I'd much rather have scars than have no skin at all, buried six feet beneath the ground." He pauses his ministrations at my words, tilting only his chin up to meet my eyes.

"In that case, they're the most beautiful things I've ever seen." He stops his teasing kisses when he reaches my inner elbow, his tongue sneaking out to lick at the sensitive skin there. My lips part with an audible moan as his other hand begins to caress my waist, where my shirt has risen up.

"Kar, you don't have to do this—"

He pulls away from me abruptly, lips thinning. "I want to. Fuck, Peony, don't you get it? I've always wanted to. But you still don't trust me." It's not a question, but a statement of fact. Still, I can tell how much it pains him to say it, if his melancholic expression is any indication. "I'll stop if you want me to."

The words tumble out of me like ragweed in a Wild West movie. "Don't stop."

"You hold the reins, princess. I'll do whatever you tell me to." He steps forward, but I don't get the sense of being over-crowded. He stares at me as if *I'm* the one who's capable of breaking him, not the other way around.

"Get on the bed," I whisper hoarsely, stepping to the side so he can pass me. He complies easily, perching on the very edge like some sort of descendant of Hercules. With his bronzed chest on display and dark golden hair, he's an exquisite work of art.

Slowly, feeling hesitant and unsure, I move to straddle him, and his hands come up to cup my ass. My hands tremble as I attempt to pull my shirt over my head, becoming stuck. I can feel rather than see Karsyn's body shake with laughter.

"A little help?" he teases, the serious mood from only a few seconds ago dissipating.

"Please," I say through a giggle as he helps me remove the shirt the rest of the way. I hadn't put on a bra after my shower, so my breasts spring free, nipples already beaded. The mirth drains from his face, heat instantly replacing it as his eyes turn hooded and smolder with need.

Fear and excitement war for dominance in the pit of my stomach, but my own need and lust for this man keeps them both adequately subdued.

He doesn't make a move to touch me as I lean forward and bite down on his bottom lip, pulling it through my teeth. I take my time nibbling on his lips, familiarizing myself with the taste of him, before pulling back just slightly to analyze his face.

The heat I find there nearly sends me spiraling over that invisible edge.

"Is that all you got, Simone?" he questions cockily, but the lust in his eyes betrays his true feelings.

"Just watch me, Alder." I narrow my eyes, never one to back down from a challenge. Maintaining eye contact, I remove myself from his lap and back towards the center of the room, making sure there's an extra bounce to my step in order to make my breasts jiggle. His hand moves to his sweats as he cups himself through the gray material, eyes never leaving my own.

It occurs to me then that he could have some video cameras hidden in his room. That this could be a setup designed to humiliate me even more.

But I don't believe that. At all.

I know in my heart that the need and lust I see reflected back at me from Karsyn's eyes are real. I can't tell you how I know, only that I do. Witch's intuition, perhaps?

Keeping my eyes trained on his, I slowly bring my hands to my breasts and begin to fondle them, pulling and twisting at my already sensitive nipples. The moan that escapes my mouth isn't faked in the slightest. I picture his hands and lips replacing my own, driving me fucking mad with pleasure.

Karsyn slides his hand inside his sweatpants and begins to tug on himself, his eyes never leaving mine.

"No," I say, still playing with my tits. "Let me see."

Movements jerky with his desperation, he awkwardly slides down his sweats, nearly falling off the bed in the process. Once he manages to remove the fabric, he grips his rock-hard cock in a tight fist.

"That was graceful," I tease as I move my hands from my breasts to the waistband of the borrowed boxer briefs. "And you're supposed to be a football player? I don't see a lot of athleticism, Alder."

"Come here, and I'll show you how athletic I can actually be," he demands huskily, stroking himself from base to tip. His other hand moves to fondle his balls.

"Nah. I'm just getting started."

I twist, giving him my back, before hooking my thumbs into the top of the shorts and slowly pulling them down. I bend, giving him an unrestricted view of my ass and pussy lips as the fabric pools around my feet.

"Fuck. Fuck. Fuck," Karsyn hisses as I turn, finding his desk chair. I wheel it directly in front of the bed before sitting down and spreading my legs as far as they can go.

"*This* is athleticism," I jest as I bring one of my fingers to my slit and begin to coat the digit in my juices. My other hand travels back to my tit and begins to kneed it, loving the feel of its heavy weight.

Karsyn's breathing turns shallow as his eyes drop from my boob to my pussy then pop back up, almost as if he can't decide where to look.

"If you don't come over here now, princess, I'm gonna place you over my shoulder and spank that gorgeous ass of yours," he threatens, and I can't help but laugh.

"Oh, are you now?" I tease, and he shocks the shit out of me by jumping to his feet and racing towards me. I squeal, practically falling face first off the chair, but he catches me with ease and slings me over his shoulder. Apparently, his "you're in charge" rules no longer apply.

And I love it more than I care to admit.

His palm slaps down on my ass, and I squeak, swatting at his broad shoulder.

"Fucker!" I seethe playfully. He tosses me onto the bed and all but collapses on top of me, nuzzling his face against the side of my neck. My laughter turns into moans as his lips create a searing trail from the hollow of my throat to my lips. It suddenly occurs to me that this is the second time I'm kissing Karsyn Alder. I imagined this exact moment more times than I care to admit, even when he was my bully, even when I hated him, even when he hated me. I always wanted him. And now I've kissed him twice in one day.

As if he's mine.

As if he's always been mine.

He doesn't simply dip his toe in; he jumps off the edge and straight into the deep end. It's not a kiss, but an explosion. His tongue enters my mouth without remorse, taking, taking, and taking. And I give every last bit back to him.

His taste explodes in my mouth as he begins to rock against me, his cock leaving a damp trail across my stomach.

"Princess, I want you," he whispers against my lips as I twist my head, granting him access to my neck. "Is this…?"

I grab his cock, rubbing my thumb over the pre-cum leaking from his tip, and then line it up with my entrance. I don't know for sure what this means, what any of this means, but I do know that I want to feel him. I want the rigid planes of his muscular chest pressed against mine. I want to feel him inside of me, our bodies joined in the closest way two people can be.

I dig my heels into his ass as he inches inside of me, allowing me a few seconds to adjust to his size.

"Is this okay?" he whispers again, planting a tender kiss to the corner of my lips and then my nose.

"Perfect," I assure him, arching my hips off the bed. He begins to rock inside of me, each thrust of his hips sending sparks shooting through my bloodstream.

"I want you, princess. All of you. The perfect arch of your back as you spasm around my cock. Your cries of passion. That silly, half smile you give when you're around people you trust. The glimmer in your eye when you're up to no good. Your love," he whispers hoarsely as he pounds into me, slowing his hips to wait for my answer. But I don't know what to say to him, how to respond, so instead, I lean forward and lick the corner of his mouth.

"I want you to make me come," I whisper. Glazed eyes stare back at me, his wet hair tousled and framing an expressive face. He's so handsome that it physically hurts me.

Mine, a possessive voice bellows in my head. It's a word on my lips, on my soul, tattooed over my heart.

My plea appears to be his undoing. He grips my wet hair, wrapping it around his fist, and tilts my head slightly to the side to reveal the juncture between my neck and shoulder. His teeth graze the sensitive skin there, biting down just hard enough to mark me.

His cock continues to thrust in and out of me as his teeth nibble on my skin. His large, rough hands, products of years on the football field, cup my breasts, his thumbs flicking my sensitive nipples.

I dig my heels even further into his chiseled ass as I climb higher and higher. I can only manage to grip his shoulders and hang on for dear life. When his fingers begin to pluck at my clit, I fucking shatter, my eyes unable to remain open as I fall head over heels for this man.

His cock jerks inside of my pussy as he ruthlessly pounds me into the bed. And when he comes, it's with my name on his lips, roared like a song. A prayer. A plea.

One thought percolates in my head, churning faster than the rapids of the Grand River.

What did I just do?

I fall asleep in Karsyn's arms, feeling happy and sated. His clove scent surrounds me, providing me a strange sense of comfort and security. I feel safe in his arms, as if the world can't hurt me when I'm with him.

I don't know how long I sleep, but when I come to, it's to see a pair of hazel eyes—more gold than green in the waning sunlight—staring down at me tenderly.

"Good morning, sleepy head," he whispers as he brushes a strand of my white-blonde hair behind my ear. I'm sure it's tangled to high heavens, considering the fact I didn't brush it after my shower. "Do you know that you snore?"

"I do not, Alder!" I protest, shoving at his chest to push away, but his arms only tighten around me. And to be completely honest, I'm not sure I want to break free.

"Do too. I think thou doth protest too much."

"Suck it." I stick my tongue out at him, but he captures it between his teeth, tugging on it gently.

"Is that an offer?" he asks with a wicked smirk, bringing his lips to the valley between my breasts and giving me a raspberry.

"You're such a fucking dork." I attempt to pull his head back up, but he begins planting teasing kisses along the arch of first one breast and then the next. His finger idly traces around my nipple.

"Did anyone ever tell you that you have the most perfect tits?" His breath whispers against my skin, and I shiver, my nipples pebbling even further. He chastely kisses the beaded tip of my right breast, before freezing. "Actually, don't answer that. I don't want anyone seeing or talking about your tits but me." There's a surge of possessiveness in his voice, and it causes my blood to sizzle. But his words quell the flames inside of my core, the smile disappearing from my face. Karsyn freezes, his lips on my areola, but allows me to gather my thoughts.

"Karsyn, there's something I need to tell you."

He sits up completely, hovering over me with worry etched onto his face.

"Was this a mistake?" he asks, voice aghast.

"No!" I rush to reassure him. "I mean, I don't know." I rub both of my hands down my cheeks. "I…I had sex with Elias." There. Better to rip the bandage off than force them both to suffer. "Last night."

The sheer reality of what I just did drowns me under a twenty-foot wave. How can I have sex with two different men in a span of a day? Both of them my tormentors? Does this make me a slut? All of their words from five years ago come rushing back to me, and I feel sick to my stomach.

"Hey." Karsyn throws his body over mine, holding himself on his elbows so he can peer down at me. I can feel the tears in my eyes and on my cheeks, but I don't lift a hand to brush them away. "I can see where your mind is going, and I'm gonna need you to fucking stop."

"Karsyn…"

"Shut the fuck up, Simone, and listen." He kisses me savagely on the lips before pulling back and capturing both of my wrists. "It's okay. I'm not mad that you had sex with Elias." He grimaces slightly, as if saying those words leaves a sour taste in his mouth, but he continues on doggedly. "It's what we deserve, after all. What *I* deserve."

"I don't understand…"

"I want you all to myself." He lowers his face to my neck and begins to nuzzle against the skin there. "I want you more than I ever wanted or needed anything in my life. But I know I need to pay for my sins, and maybe this is the way. Maybe I can't be selfish with you."

I tug on his hair until he's forced to look at me, searching his expressive hazel eyes for the truth I can hear in his words. "You're giving me up?" Why does that thought gut me? Why does it leave me feeling hollow and empty, like I'm made of nothing but skin and bones?

"Fuck no! And if you would let me talk..." He quirks a brow, waiting to see if I'll comply, and I squeeze my lips shut and nod for him to continue. He offers me a strained smile, but sadness pollutes it, along with an acceptance that steals the last drop of warmth from my body. "I don't want to give you up. But I also know I don't deserve to keep you. If that means I have to share you with one of my oldest friends..."

This time, his words send a surge of anger through me, and I shove at his chest.

"So what? I'll just be a whore for you and your friends to pass around? Just like you used to imply when we were younger?" I demand, my anger growing from a mere spark to an entire forest fire. "Fuck you."

"That's not what I meant, and you know it," Karsyn hisses, continuing to kiss the nape of my neck. "This isn't just about sex."

"Then what is it about?" Despite the anger in my voice, my body betrays me and begins to grow wet.

"It's about you and our feelings for you. There's no denying that I want you, and now we know that Elias does too. You know what polyamorous relationships are, don't you?"

"Open relationships?" I ask, trying to picture Karsyn with other girls while in a relationship with me. The thought makes me see red, though I try to quell my internal reaction before it can externalize itself.

Karsyn smirks, and I have the irresistible urge to either punch it off of him or kiss it. "Poly relationships can be a lot of different things, but what I mean is a committed relationship between the three of us."

"A..."

"Of course, I need to talk to Elias about it. And we need to decide if it's something we all want. And we need to—"

I cut off his ramblings by giving in to my yearning to kiss him. He responds immediately, his lips going soft and pliant under my careful ministrations.

"I've never felt this way about anyone before," he breathes. "I know it's too soon for love, but I…" He punctuates his words with a kiss to the corner of my lips. "With Mariabella, it…" Once more, he trails off, a guilty expression shadowing his features.

"Hey, you don't have to say anymore. She told me." I cup his cheeks in both of my palms, loving the way his whiskered face tickles my skin.

"She told you?" Karsyn questions in wide-eyed disbelief. And then, his eyes narrow, expression contorting from guilty to suspicious. "That sly bitch." He smiles slightly. "Do I have to worry about her stealing you from me as well?"

I giggle as he runs his fingers down my bare ribcage, tickling me. Karsyn lowers his eyes to my bouncing breasts, before taking one into his mouth. He releases it with a dramatic pop before rolling onto his side next to me. I twist as well, so we're sharing a pillow, staring into each other's eyes.

"I think she's my best friend," I confess as he lovingly kisses my nose.

"She's mine, too," he says. "And in all seriousness, I'm happy that she has another person to confide in. I know she's been lonely and afraid, and having you as a friend has definitely helped her flourish."

Light explodes in my chest at his praise, and I have to bite my lip to contain my goofy smile. I feel drunk off of the sensations he evokes within me. Drunk off of him.

His own smile is glorious. He leans closer…

Just as my phone begins to ring from my backpack.

"Ignore it," he pleads, kissing my bare shoulder, but I shake my head and slide out of bed.

"It could be important," I tell him, padding on bare feet to where he placed my backpack when we arrived at his house. I dig through the pockets until I reach my phone, Nana's name flashing on the screen. Instantly, the lust shifts into fear as I press the green button to answer the call.

"What's wrong?" I ask without preamble. Karsyn moves silently from the bed to stand behind me, wrapping his arms around my waist and pulling me against his hard chest. I allow myself to relax for just a second, for one brief moment of weakness, before stepping out of his embrace.

"You need to come home, Peony. Now," Nana instructs. Her dogmatic tone sends a cold chill coursing through me.

"What's wrong?" I repeat, fearing what she's going to say.

"It's your mother… She's here."

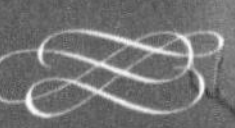

CHAPTER 42

"What do you want?" The words fly from my mouth before I even enter the house.

Karsyn dropped me off only a few minutes earlier, demanding reassurances from me that I will explain everything later. He still doesn't understand what it means to be a witch, what it means for *us*, and I never told him about the Bloods either. They're the biggest threat our community faces, even more so than witch hunters, and if he's serious about this, about me, then he needs to know every facet, the good and the bad.

"Peony." Mom rises gracefully from the chair she's sitting on, allowing me to see her for the first time since I left California. She's a vision of beauty, a portrait that is better fit on a church's wall than in the flesh. I sometimes wonder if she uses magic to make her skin so clear of blemishes, but I don't dare ask. Her black hair, the color of a raven's feathers, glides down her back in perfect curls, framing an angelic face of slitted green eyes and Cupid's bow lips.

"Where have you been?" she asks curtly, gliding forward. She wears a white pantsuit that accentuates her slender, hourglass figure.

The jacket is unbuttoned, revealing the gray, frilly blouse under-neath. She moves with an elegance that I can only attempt to repli-cate. It's an ethereal type of grace and beauty that makes others pale in comparison.

"Why are you here?" The last time I saw Mom, she was, quite literally, shoving me out the door. No passing go. No collecting two hundred dollars. She wanted me out of her life once and for all, if only to secure her position as head of the coven. My power has the potential of surpassing hers, and I truly believe that terrifies her. Terrifies her enough to rid herself of her one and only daughter.

"We need to talk," she states primly, and over her shoulder, on the second sofa, I see Nana sitting ramrod straight. Her hands ball into fists on her lap as she glares at a second figure, one who I hadn't noticed initially.

"Ryan, come here." Mom snaps her fingers like an owner summoning a dog, and a moment later, my ex-boyfriend's brother comes shuffling forward, looking demure and positively fearful. I don't know Ryan well, having only interacted with him a few times, but I do know that he's a powerful warlock. I suppose that power makes up for his less than impressive looks. Mousy brown hair tumbling across his forehead, in desperate need of a cut. Shrewd, narrowed eyes, an unassuming shade of brown. Teeth that are slightly too large in his small mouth. Large, prominent nose that crooks at the end from the time he broke it.

This is the man my mom wants me to marry.

"What the fuck is this? Why is he here?" I demand as I look back and forth between the two of them suspiciously. Mom simply puckers her lips, almost like she's sucking on a lemon, but Ryan gives me a predatory leer when my mom isn't looking, one that makes me feel dirty. When I catch his gaze, he drops his head to the floor with a submissive whimper.

"We need you to return to the coven," Mom announces, sashaying forward to tenderly brush at my tangled white hair. Her lips protrude out even further when she takes note of my faded jeans and sweater. Fortunately, Karsyn remembered to put my wet clothes in the dryer before we fell asleep after sex, so I wasn't forced to wear his T-shirt and boxers home. That would raise a whole multitude of questions I wouldn't know how to answer. Still, I don't like my mother this close to me. Something about her sets off every one of my instincts, warring voices inside of me telling me to scream, to run, to fight, to hide. My necklace warms on my skin, and I wrench my hair free of her grip in abject horror.

"Did you just try to use magic on me?" I ask, horrified. Using magic on other witches, especially those in your coven, is as taboo as they come. It's not a punishable offense, but everyone knows the unspoken rule. And to use it on your own family?

"What is this?" Nana demands, stalking forward until she can wrap a protective arm around my waist. She all but drags me a step behind her, blocking me from view.

Once more, Mom purses her ruby-red lips.

"It was a simple persuasion spell," Mom dismisses, as if we're being ridiculous and over-dramatic. But doesn't she know how intrusive a persuasion spell can be? Is she really that desperate for power that she'd attempt to take away my free will? My stomach turns somersaults as I stare at my mother with new eyes.

"Why do you want her home?" Nana interjects, sounding furious on my behalf. She glares down at her daughter, eyes almost incandescent in anger.

"The reasons are between me and my daughter," Mom hisses, refusing to be intimidated by the more powerful witch. Her nose wrinkles as if she smells something particularly pungent before she steps away, closer to me. "Peony, please come home. Your coven needs you."

"What is he doing here?" I point with my chin at Ryan, who

lowers his gaze to his shoes. I can't help but grimace at the squirming man. Ryan and Uriel could not possibly be more different from each other. It's like a night and day comparison, the moon versus the sun.

Mom appears annoyed by my incessant questioning. She stomps her foot, eyes spewing vitriol, before she gestures for Ryan to step even closer.

"As you know, Ryan is one of the most powerful warlocks of our generation. He's slated to join the witch's council once he's older. The two of you together…"

"You have got to be fucking kidding me!" I gripe, throwing my head back in laughter. I know it's not a joke, that she's completely serious, but I prefer to take it as one. It's the only thing that will keep my sanity intact, especially when I want to lunge forward and wrap my hands around her bird-like throat. "You're still trying to sell me off, aren't you? To *him*?"

"Your marriage will do great things for the community!" Mom implores. "Think of your offspring—"

"I'm just going to stop you there," I interrupt, holding up a hand as if that can prevent her ramblings. "For starters, I will never, not in a million years, marry Ryan. Never. Do you understand that? And don't even act like this will save the entire witch race." Some of my original ire bleeds into my voice, turning each word curt and succinct. "You're doing this to gain more power for yourself. Don't bother to fucking lie to me. You know that Ryan's family is important in the community, and you think that an alliance between our families will further secure your spot as leader of the coven."

I wait for her to deny it, to plead with me, but instead, her expression turns glacial. Any warmth I thought I saw in her eyes fizzles and dies a painful death. She straightens, smoothing out her jacket sleeves, before sighing heavily.

"You don't have to make things difficult," she snaps. "After all I've done for you—"

"Fuck you! You've never done anything for *me*." I level my glare first at her, and then at the pathetic excuse of a man who thought he could claim me. Own me. I'm not a piece of meat for sale that he can weigh and bag. That's not the way life fucking works. To my mom, I seethe, "Helping you is the last thing I'd ever do."

She doesn't slap me. Hell, she doesn't even raise her voice. That's never been my mother's style. Her manner of abuse is much more meticulous than that, more calculating. She takes the time to analyze every pathway before deciding on the one that inflicts the most damage in the shortest amount of time. It's why she never helped me with the Devils. It's why she broke my violin in one of her hissy fits. It's why she confronted me about sleeping with Uriel, calling me a slut and a filthy whore. She pushes down on wounds that haven't begun to scab yet, making sure each press of her dainty finger draws blood.

"All right," she sniffs, refusing to even glance in my direction. "If that's what you want…"

"It is." I don't know what game she's playing at, but I refuse to be just another pawn. Not anymore. Not when I've finally started to get some of my confidence back.

"Then you'll be disowned." Her gaze finally leaves her sleeves to meet my horror-filled eyes. It feels like someone is tying my stomach into dozens and dozens of intricate knots. "You'll be banished from the coven as well."

Disowned…

Banished…

That's the worst thing to happen to a witch. Without a coven, we're considered prey to the witch hunters and Bloods who stalk our kind. If I leave the coven, I'll have no protection. I won't even be able to contact my friends who are currently members, like Yoselin and Uriel.

And if I'm disowned…

All I have ever wanted was to get out from under my mother's oppressive and abusive thumb. But not like this. Witches covet family more than anything else in the world. It's why we celebrate our ancestors monthly and why they gift us their magic from the grave. If she does this...

I'd be cut off from my magic.

"Mom," I plead, my voice a whisper.

"Darlene!" Nana snaps. "You can't be serious."

"Oh, I am serious. Deadly serious." Mom—though I'm not sure if I should even call her that anymore—reaches behind her and grips Ryan's upper arm, dragging him with her towards the front door.

"You can't force her to marry a guy she doesn't love!" Nana snaps, easily keeping pace with the two of them.

"And what are you going to do about it?" Mom whirls on her heel, jabbing a finger at Nana's chest. "This is between me and my daughter—"

"As you said." Nana swats her finger away as if it's nothing but an annoying, pesky fly. "But this is between me, my daughter, and *my* granddaughter. Let me make something clear, Darlene Simone. If you disown Peony, I will not hesitate to do the same to you as well." Her words are sharper than glass, and I can tell that they embed themselves inside Mom just the same. She staggers back a step, jaw slack with disbelief, before the shock quickly transforms into a fiery anger. Her gaze travels past Nana and to me, lips curling away from her teeth in a snarl.

"I'll be back, Peony, and I hope that you'll rethink your decision before then."

"I wouldn't hold my breath if I were you," I murmur dryly. "Actually, go ahead. Hold your breath. See if I care."

Her nostrils flare, oddly resembling a bull preparing to charge, but instead of dignifying me with a response, she storms out of the house, moving towards the town car where Charles waits.

"They'll be back," Nana says softly, placing a reassuring hand on my shoulder. I shrug her off of me.

"I know."

But I don't know what else I can do to hold my mother off. This might just be one battle that I can't win, one war that isn't worth the fight.

CHAPTER 43

"Why are you sucking?"

I turn towards the belligerent voice, not at all surprised to see Felicia blinking at me rapidly through her thick-framed glasses.

"Hi, Felicia. Nice to see you, too," I deadpan as I reach for my water bottle in my backpack's side pocket. I'm still in desperate need of a new bag, but until I can find a job, this broken one will have to do. I suppose my dreams of getting my own violin just went down the toilet with the rest of the shit.

The cool water tickles my throat as I recap it and place it on the edge of my music stand. For the first time in forever, the notes don't make a lick of sense to me. They're just sharp lines and curved points. Some are filled in; some are white. Usually, music comes easily to me. It's a story, a song, another language that I'm intimately familiar with.

But now, it's just…gibberish.

"You haven't played one note right," she sniffs haughtily, using her index finger to push her glasses farther up her nose. She glances towards Mr. Tucker, who is working individually with the cellists before turning back to me. "My cat can play better than you. And my cat's dead." She nods towards my violin resting on my thighs, the bow grasped loosely in my other hand. "Do you even know what that thing is? It's not a weapon of mass destruction."

"You're just a big ball of sunshine, aren't you?" I quip, resisting the urge to slug her with said bow. I swear my muscles are wound up tighter than the strings on it.

"I just want us to sound good this year," she huffs, irritated. "And as Mr. Tucker's star pupil," she practically rolls her eyes into the back of her head, "I expected better from you."

"Well, that's your own fault." I begin to sift through the sheet music, no longer able to meet her probing, keen gaze. It's like she's looking into my soul, and the thought makes me uncomfortable, like a mosquito that's sitting on my arm but not biting. A mildly irritating occurrence, but not something I can't handle. "For expecting better from me."

"Guy issues?" she guesses, cocking a dark brow. When I don't respond right away, her face puckers and she tilts her head to the side curiously. "Those four popular guys?"

"Don't act like you don't know their names," I snort. Everybody knows their names. They rule this school and every person in it with an iron grip. People either bow to their will...or they perish.

And I just happen to fall into the latter category.

She begins to tick them off on her fingers. "Karsyn Alder. Cassian Jereome. Elias Briggs. Lucas Scott." Once again, I don't give her the satisfaction of a response. "Or is it none of them? Maybe it's your pretty friend, Mariabella?" I bite down on my lip to keep from snapping at her. I have the desperate, irresistible urge to tell her to mind her own damn business, but I truly believe that would only fuel the fire. She's a bloodhound that finally found her prey's trail, and now she's on the hunt. "Or is it a family thing...?"

She waits, gauging my reaction, and I try to keep my expression impassive. But I can tell I gave something away when a bright smile twists her features, making her actually appear pretty instead of devious.

"Family issues, then." She nods once, as if she expected that answer. "Dad? Mom?" I don't know what tell I have, whether it's an almost imperceptible tightening of my mouth, a clenching of my jaw, or a twitching of my eye. Either way, her smile widens. "You have mommy issues."

"Fuck off, Felicia." Am I hissing? That definitely sounded like a hiss. I feel sort of like a feral cat when a pesky human attempts to lure it home with promises of food and shelter. I'll come to you if I want to be pet, but for the most part, I want everyone to stay the fuck away from me.

"I understand, you know," she states, smoothing her hands down her pencil-straight skirt. It stops just below the knees, revealing a hint of bronze skin. "My parents are major dick bags, too."

"Oh?" I turn back towards the music, staring intently at the squiggly lines and begging them to turn into a language I recognize. One I understand. Why is this happening to me? Music has always been my escape, my chance at freedom. I'll be furious if the Devils took that from me with their confusing kisses and sweet words that leave me feeling disoriented and frustrated. I haven't seen any of them since yesterday morning, when Karsyn dropped me off. Elias didn't follow me to school, as he usually does.

Should I look for them?

Are they looking for me?

Is Elias still pissed? Will he tell somebody?

Will Karsyn?

Will Lucas?

I don't like all of these unknown variables. It makes the equation impossible to compute.

"...join the family business," Felicia is saying now, and I feel a stab of guilt that I haven't been paying any attention to her. Is she trying to have a heart to heart moment with me? After she just insulted me?

I don't know whether to be amused or annoyed or a combination of the two. If there's one thing I learned from this class, it's that Felicia is volatile and crass.

But she's a damn good musician.

"They don't understand that I have no intentions of that," she continues. "I don't want to join the damn family business."

"Sucks," I agree, and she nods, her chin looking even sharper in the golden sunlight drifting through the opened blinds.

"Peony!" We both turn towards Mr. Tucker at the same time, and Felicia's cordial smile freezes on her face before disappearing completely, replaced by a scowl.

"Teacher's pet," she hisses, stomping back towards her seat. I roll my eyes at her dramatics before walking towards the front of the classroom.

"Yes?" I ask him when I'm closer. Instead of answering, he simply beckons me to join him in his office—nothing but a hole in the wall behind the conductor's stand. I wait hesitantly in the doorway as he grabs something from the highest shelf. Easily recognizing the sleek black case, I hold my breath as he pries it open. Nestled in red velvet is the most gorgeous violin I have ever seen. I can't tell what type of wood it's constructed out of, but it appears more red than brown in the artificial light. It's polished so meticulously, I can see my reflection in it. It's obviously new and very, very expensive.

"The new violin you ordered just came in," Mr. Tucker explains, closing the case once more and handing it to me. I hold it reverently, almost fearfully, in my hands, as if the slightest breeze will take it away from me.

But then I come back to my senses with the force of a fifty-car train barreling into me.

"I didn't order a violin," I protest vehemently, attempting to hand it back. He holds up both hands in a placating manner and takes a step away.

"It's not mine or the school's, darling. It arrived this morning.

The delivery man said it has already been paid for and that it belongs to a Peony Simone. And since you're the only Peony Simone in this school…" He trails off with a grin, patting me good-naturedly on the shoulder. "It seems as if you have a guardian angel."

Or a stalker.

The rest of class passes in a daze. It's even harder to focus on the music than it was before. I don't dare touch the new instrument. Who bought it for me? And why? Is it a bribe? An "I owe you" type of deal?

When I step out of class a few minutes later, reluctantly carting around my gorgeous violin, I see a familiar figure leaning against the far lockers, watching me. A girl stands at his side, attempting to garner his attention, but he doesn't spare her a glance as he stalks towards me, every inch of him the sexy, primal hunter.

"I should've known you had something to do with this," I say as Cassian pauses directly in front of me. Today, he's wearing a light blue shirt that makes his onyx skin pop and a pair of dark skinny jeans. His black hair is buzzed once more, accentuating his arresting and chiseled facial features.

He looks fucking good, and he knows it.

"I don't know what you're talking about," he says bluntly, but I see his eyes flicker to the violin case.

"I don't need your charity," I chide.

At this, his smile slowly expands into an infuriating, teasing wave.

"Is that what this is, baby?"

I make a face. "Don't call me that."

Cassian continues to smirk unrepentantly as he remains beside me, his muscular arm brushing against mine with every step we take. He stares at me out of the corner of his eye and offers me a salacious smile. It's sometimes easy to forget that despite his charms, he's cruel and capricious. Wicked. The shadows are his best friends, and the night is his domain.

As if he can't handle the silence anymore, he blurts, "Is it just 'baby' that bothers you? Or is it the fact that I gave you a nickname to begin with?"

"Both," I deadpan as I hurry to my third hour class.

"But what if I want you to be my baby?" he asks nonchalantly, but then winces when he realizes how that sounds. "Oh. That sounded bad."

"Tell me, Cassian," I begin. "How many girls have you called 'baby' in the last…let's say…month?"

"The last month?" He throws his head back in laughter. "Only you, baby."

"Fine." I clear my throat, dislodging the wrecking ball that wants to take up space there. "In the last…five months?"

His laughter fades, and he offers me his most contrite look. "A few?" It turns into a question.

I whirl towards him, offering him a smile that isn't all that pleasant. "Being your 'baby' isn't exactly special then, is it?" Before he can think up a reply, I hurry away from him, using my heavy violin case as a physical shield between me and the outside world. Cassian breaks into a jog in order to catch up with me.

"How about sugar tits?" he questions seriously, and I give him a look capable of melting the skin off of most people. "Ptero*dick*tyl," he suggests.

"That's bad."

"Boomer?" He scratches at his chin in consideration. "Yeah. I like that. Baby boomer."

"Just stop." I drag a hand down my face, trying my hardest to hide my smile. Why does he have to amuse me so much when I'm still mad at him?

"You can pretend to hate me all you want, baby, but I know you're charmed." He places his head on my shoulder, causing my feet to stumble mid-step. His smirk only grows, a mischievous, wicked type of smirk that promises pain and darkness.

"Goodbye, Cassian." We finally reach my third hour, his head still resting snuggly on my shoulder. I can smell his shampoo, a combination of pine and citrus, as well as the scent of oil.

"I'll see you later, baby," he purrs, straightening and snaking an arm around my waist. He pulls me flush against his hard body, smirking down at me.

"Don't. Call. Me. That," I snark through gritted teeth. "I'm not your baby."

"But you are my something," he croons, not the least bit cowed.

"I'm not your anything." We're so close I can see golden flecks dancing in his eyes, almost like the stars taking up residence in an inky black sky. My eyes drift automatically to his pillowy lips, before I quickly come to my senses, lean forward, and bite him on his nose.

"Ow!" He steps away from me, holding his face in horror. "Did you just bite me?"

"Yup. Haven't you heard?" I lower my gaze to his crotch, where I can see a visible erection tenting his pants. "I bite back this time."

"Fucking hell, baby. Will you just marry me already?" he begs.

Ignoring him, I hurry through the doorway and move to my usual seat near the middle of the room. Normally, I sit between Elias and Emmett in this class, but today, both of their seats remain empty. I bite my lip, glancing at the clock to make sure I have time before class begins, before pulling out my phone. My finger hovers over Elias's number that I've had in my phone since I saved it when he texted me after the football game. I actually have all of the Devils' numbers, like some sort of creepy, evil stalker.

Well, I sort of am...

Shaking my head vehemently, I move to the number directly below Elias's. Emmett's.

Me: u here?

His response is instantaneous.

Emmett: Why? You miss me?

I lick my upper lip, contemplating how I want to respond. In a way, I *do* miss the teasing, flirtatious boy with the mossy green eyes. But then I think about his hands on my ass. I know it was probably a spur of the moment thing, but I didn't like it. At all. He should've stopped when I wanted him to, when I was pulling at him. Maybe he misunderstood? Maybe he thought I was pulling him closer instead of away?

Instead of responding, I slide my phone into my pocket. I told Mariabella about Emmett, and she was livid. She asked me, and I quote, if I wanted her to "kick his ass to heaven and then back down to hell."

She's downright scary when she wants to be.

Mr. Milk arrives a few minutes after the bell rings, looking frazzled and unkempt. His dark hair, speckled with gray, is hanging limply in front of his dull brown eyes.

"What's up, Mr. M?" one of the football players from the front row inquires.

Mr. Milk places his briefcase on the desk and takes a deep, fortifying breath. When he glances up at the classroom, I'm surprised to see unshed tears in his eyes.

"I'm not supposed to tell you guys this yet…" Immediately, every student gives him their undivided attention, myself included. If we're not supposed to know something…

That means it's all the more sweeter when we do.

"But there was an attack on a teacher earlier this morning." He forks his fingers through his disheveled hair. "His…um…manhood," he glances down at his crotch, flames entering his cheeks, "was removed."

"No fucking way!" someone exclaims. "A teacher had his dick cut off?"

"I don't know why anyone would do that," Mr. Milk continues. "I didn't know him well, but the few times we met up at events, he seemed like such a good man." He shakes his head sadly. "He's in the hospital now."

"Who was it?" a girl asks excitedly…though I find it kind of demented for her to get excited about a cockless teacher. But to each his or her own, I suppose.

Milk's next words have me freezing in place, stealing the remaining warmth from my body. "He doesn't teach in the high school, but the middle school. Science. Maybe you guys remember him? Mr. Gurrel. But again," he levels us all with a penetrating glare, "you didn't hear this from me."

Mr. Gurrel.

Mr. Gurrel.

Mr. Gurrel.

His name plays on repeat in my brain as I stare blankly at my desk.

My middle school pervert teacher just had his dick cut off.

It could be just a random coincidence…

But when has life ever been that simple?

CHAPTER 44

When I arrive at the cafeteria, none of the Devils are there. I scan their usual tables and then the one I sit at with Emmett, Karsyn, and Mariabella.

But no Devils.

I don't even know what I plan to do when I find them. Confront them about Mr. Gurrel? I know they're behind this. Cassian no doubt told the others what I told him. Ask them if things have changed between us? Punch Lucas in the face? The last one sounds the most appealing, to be completely honest. While my anger towards Elias and Karsyn has ebbed somewhat after our nights together, I still can't figure out how I feel about the two remaining creatures of hell.

I bite my lip, feeling uncharacteristically anxious as I approach the empty table, but a soft hand on my arm stops me.

"Pee!" Mariabella begins to drag me towards the table she sometimes sits at with the other cheerleaders. "You're sitting with us today."

"Don't call me that," I whine, scrunching my nose up and sticking out my tongue. "It's worse than baby."

"Baby?" She cocks a blonde brow as she slides into a seat next to Brittany, a senior cheerleader. I've always liked the quiet redhead with the pretty, heart-shaped freckled face and glimmering green eyes. "Are you getting kinky on me?"

"It's a long story that involves one of those people who shall not be named," I say with a pointed look at the other girls. I know all of them, but I haven't ever engaged them in conversation. I think the one to my right is Laura? Maybe Laurel? And despite our budding friendships, I'm not quite ready to reveal all of my deepest, darkest secrets to them.

Especially the ones involving the Devils.

"So which one do you prefer? Pee or baby?" Mariabella teases, and I can't help but note the jealous glare Brittany throws my way. Interesting.

"Neither, you weirdo."

Mari simply sticks out her tongue at me.

"Practice is going to be brutal today," a cheerleader named Cat gripes as she shoves a grape into her mouth. She brushes a dirty blonde lock behind her ear as her other hand plucks at a thread on her oversized hoodie. I swear that girl has an entire collection of those things, since she wears a new one every day. "Coach is making us start practice for competitive instead of just sideline."

"I heard that we're going to spend two hours just on tumbling," Gabriella adds.

"It shouldn't be too bad," Brittany muses. She reaches across the table to steal a fry from Cat's plate, her arm purposely brushing against Mariabella's breasts. I am *so* going to ask Mari for all of the juicy details tonight. Because subtle boob touches?

Girl, what are you hiding?

"You would say that," Gabriella huffs. "You're the best tumbler on the team. Well, besides Peony."

It feels good to talk and laugh with other girls. I love Mariabella, don't get me wrong, but this...hanging out with a group of girls...

feels nice. I've never experienced the comradery of female friendship before. The gossip. The inside jokes. For the first time in forever, I feel like I belong somewhere.

But a pit opens up in my stomach and swallows me whole at the reminder that I used a spell to get where I am. I wouldn't be on the team without the flexibility potion.

"What the fuck?" Gabriella breathes, snapping me out of my pensive thoughts. Across the table, Mariabella's eyes widen into saucers as her mouth drops open. I follow the direction of her gaze to see four familiar figures stalk into the cafeteria.

They move with an imperiousness and grace that make everyone stop what they're doing and stare. The sheer confidence they exude takes my breath away. They seem to innately command the respect and attention of everyone in the immediate vicinity.

"What do they have in their hands?" one of the girls whispers, but I don't look away from the Devils to see who spoke.

One by one, the four men move to stand on the table in the center of the cafeteria, scowls marring their handsome faces. In their hands, they hold bowls of a foul-smelling, clumpy-looking liquid. Is that...? I lean forward to get a better look, my eyebrows practically disappearing into my hairline.

Is that chili?

I remember back in middle school, when they cornered me in the cafeteria and dumped cold chili over my head. They began to laugh obnoxiously, while angry and humiliated tears pricked my eyes. I remember thinking about how much I hated them, how I wished they would pay for their sins.

If the Grim Reaper had a physical form, she would look like Peony Simone.

Smoke wafts from each of their bowls now, indicating that it's still hot, as their cold, expressionless eyes survey the crowd.

Before locking on me.

I wilt underneath their combined stares, even as the rest of the cheerleaders begin to whisper amongst themselves, wondering what the fuck is happening. Only Mariabella remains quiet, reaching across the table to take my hand in hers.

And then in complete unison, almost like they rehearsed this beforehand, the Devils dump the bowls over their own heads.

Silence descends as every student gapes at them in stunned disbelief.

And then the laughter starts. It's not instantaneous, more like a rippling wave. One person breaks into loud laughter near the back of the room, followed immediately by another. And then two more. And then ten more. It isn't long until the entire room breaks out into giggles and points at the disheveled kings.

"What the fuck?" Gabriella screeches, tears of laughter running down her cheeks as she stares at the Devils. The reddish-brown clumps stick to their heads and drip down their faces, staining their clothes.

Mariabella glances at me with an eyebrow raised, and I nod once, easily able to read the question in her eyes. Her face darkens when she realizes that the Devils once did the same thing to me, five years ago, and I wonder if she remembers that moment. If she remembers me standing in front of all of my classmates, shaking and terrified. How can she not? I doubt there've been a lot of instances in her life where she witnessed a girl being shamed in front of the entire school at the hands of chili.

Behaving as if nothing unusual has happened, the four Devils step down from the table and move to their usual seats, seemingly oblivious to the chili covering their bodies and faces. Lucas sits beside his student council friends, while Cassian joins members of the marching band. Elias simply sits in an empty table near the corner of the room, his eyes never leaving mine as he kicks up his boots and places them on the table.

And Karsyn...

Instead of joining his football friends, he moves to the empty table he's been sitting at with me, Mariabella, and Emmett.

"Fucking hell…" I murmur, pushing back my seat. To Mariabella, I whisper, "I'll be right back," and she nods in understanding.

I move through the throng of giggling students, all of whom point at the Devils as if they're caged animals at a zoo. I stop when I'm in front of Karsyn, my hands on my hips.

"We need to talk," I say sternly as my eyes latch on to the glop of blood-red meat in his blond hair and dripping down the front of his white shirt.

Like before, the other three get up as well and follow when we move into the empty hallway. This close, I can smell the chili wafting from their bodies. Since the incident five years ago, I've had an aversion towards it. I refuse to even be in the same room whenever we have chili dogs. Of course, that didn't stop my mom from having them as often as she could. I'm pretty sure they're her favorite food by now.

"What the hell was that?" I ask when I'm positive we're alone, whirling on them.

"A grand gesture," Cassian says with a smirk. "What did you think, baby?"

I pinch the bridge of my nose, trying to remember how to breathe properly.

Don't get arrested for murder, Peony. Don't get arrested for murder.

"I don't understand. Why the fuck would you do that?" I snap, feeling as if I'm standing on a tightrope located hundreds of feet above the earth and someone has placed a match near the end of the rope. I'm forced to watch it smoke and burn, helpless to save myself.

"Because we once did it to you," Lucas responds. Those icy orbs of his caress my face as he takes a step closer. "You wanted your revenge, didn't you?"

"Revenge doesn't fucking work when you do it to yourself!" I huff…though, I'm not sure if my words even make sense.

"So, would you prefer to pour chili on us yourself?" Karsyn queries, genuinely confused.

"What? No!" I shake my head from side to side, struggling to articulate my thoughts. "Look, I know what you're trying to do—"

"We're trying to apologize for the shitty things we did once upon a time." Cassian shrugs his broad shoulders. "You said you wanted us to pay, so we're helping. We made a list of everything we ever did to you. By the end of this week, all of that will be done to us. It's called karma, baby. But in this case, we're bringing karma down on ourselves."

Are they completely insane?

I glance from face to face, searching for a voice of reason, but the other three all nod seriously. Even Elias, though when my eyes meet his, he quickly looks away.

I can't help but note how tired he seems. How disheveled. His brown and purple hair doesn't look brushed, hanging in loose waves around his neck. Dark shadows mar the skin beneath both of his eyes. I hate the cloying darkness I can see in his face, emanating from his very pores.

And...

"Oh my god. You idiots." I reach towards Elias, ignoring the way he winces, and brush at a particularly large dollop of chili that is resting on his neck. Beneath the meat, his skin is red. "Why did you guys use hot chili? You fucking burned yourselves!"

Lucas gives me a droll look, almost as if I'm an imbecile. I would take offense to that if it wasn't Lucas's natural expression.

"I told you. We did it to you five or so years ago. Now, we're doing it to ourselves...but we're making it ten times worse," he supplies, voice impassive.

"Next week, we're heading to the paintball arena," Karsyn continues, resembling an eager, besotted puppy. He reaches forward to take my hands in both of his. "We paid a bunch of freshmen to shoot at us. We'll have to run and hide without any guns for two hours."

The smile fades from his face as he lowers his forehead to my own. "I was sincere before when I apologized. I—*we*—want to make it up to you."

"But I don't want *this*," I hiss. "This is…"

"Revenge," Lucas states simply. "Our revenge on ourselves."

"You're all fucking crazy." I shake my head vehemently, almost as if I can unhear all that was said. Do they even hear themselves? Surely they're not deluded enough to think that physically harming themselves will assuage everything they did to me once upon a time.

"Crazy for you, baby," Cassian teases with a wink, and I roll my eyes. I honestly can't tell if he's serious or full of shit. Half of the time, I think he actually has feelings for me, but then the other half…

"We were talking," Elias whispers, staring at the ground. "About you."

The air seems to spark with an electrical charge as all four of the men glare at one another. It's Lucas who decides to speak first, unsurprisingly.

"We all have feelings for you," he confesses, but like every other word he has said so far, his voice remains devoid of any emotion. He could've been telling me that he stole my homework instead of something like *that*.

"And we know about the whole…" Cassian makes one of his hands into a circle and slides a finger on his other hand in and out of it. "Dirty, dirty, bang, bang."

"And you want me to…what? Choose one of you?" When they don't immediately answer, staring at me with an unnerving type of intensity, I laugh humorlessly. "*Date you all?* Is that really what you guys want?"

"It might not go anywhere." Cassian shrugs again, attempting to appear cool and nonchalant, but I can see a hint of vulnerability spark in his dark eyes. "But we all want to see if this…" He gestures between the five of us. "…is something."

"It's *nothing*," I protest immediately, but a little, tinny voice in my head begins to scream at me to accept their offer, to forgive them. "Who said I even wanted to date any of you?"

Hurt flashes in both Karsyn's and Elias's face at my words, and I instantly feel like shit. The moments we had together were special, I admit that, but Lucas and Cassian? Why in the world would I ever even consider dating them?

But then I remember the way Lucas sat across from me in the diner, listening to my story without judgement. The fierce glimmer in his eyes when he promised to protect me.

I recall Cassian's face when he saw the new violin case in my hand only a couple hours earlier. He tried to hide it, I can tell he did, but for a brief moment, his face was unguarded and full of hope. And later, when we were talking and he smiled down at me, it wasn't tainted by pain or anger. It was just...a smile. A heart-thumping, toe-curling smile.

Oddly enough, it hurts more to heal than it does to be broken in the first place.

"Mr. Gurrel," I blurt as another thing occurs to me. All four of them freeze, only their eyes moving to track my every move. I begin to pace in front of them, feeling an awful lot like a caged tiger. "Did you guys...?"

Lucas smiles, slow and predatory. A shark sniffing blood. "And if we did?"

I gape at him—at them—in unsuppressed horror.

"You cut off a man's cock?" I try to sound outraged, but amusement laces my tone before I can contain it. There's no denying that a darkness exists inside of me, a beast that demands freedom. And maybe that's what always connected me to the four of them. They saw the roiling sea of darkness in me from the very beginning, and instead of running from it, they embraced it with their own form of...affection? No, that's the wrong word. What happened five years ago was in no way affectionate or loving.

But was it torture?

Maybe for some, it was designed to be, but not for all. As I allow my eyes to drift from face to face, I find them landing on Lucas more often than not. The way he stares at me now…

It's the same way he stared at me years ago.

It's fucked up and so incredibly twisted, but I have to wonder…

Was that his way of showing affection?

Lucas's smile curls upwards, though the shadows remain haunting his eyes.

"We made the little piggy squeal for what he did to you," he says without preamble. Without even fucking remorse. "He didn't see our faces, though."

Lucas Scott is quite literally a monster. A psychopath, I think they're called. Or maybe it's a sociopath. I can never remember the difference between the two, even with the AP Psychology class I took last year.

I also have the feeling that, if I let him, he'll become *my* psycho.

"I…I can't deal with this right now." They're the only words that spring to mind. I can't even begin to unravel my own emotions, so how the hell am I supposed to deal with theirs? I wonder if this is how it feels to jump off of a plane. To feel your stomach tighten as the ground rushes towards you like a dart approaching a bullseye. And then, there's the stomach-dropping feeling you get when you pull open your parachute, allowing the currents to drag you aimlessly through the sky.

Even a month ago, I wouldn't have believed this possible. That Elias, Cassian, Karsyn, and Lucas would stand in front of me, wanting to be…in a relationship? With me? It sounds stupid even to my own ears, and I half wonder if there's a cameraman hiding behind the corner, ready to jump out and scream, "Gotcha!" That thought stings worse than if I walked straight into a hornet's nest.

"Peony…" Karsyn takes a step towards me, expression verging on desperation, but I easily sidestep his hands.

"I'm going to go, um, practice," I mumble.

I'm feeling too much, too soon, too hard. This shouldn't be allowed. I don't *want* my own emotions to smother me. But trying to grapple them back into submission proves to be impossible. I bite my lip to hold my tears back as I shove Karsyn and Lucas aside, easily stepping between their muscular bodies.

How can they want to date me? They barely even know me.

Maybe they're deluded, stuck in a fantasy where the charming, handsome guys get the poor girl. A Cinderella-type story where they're the lead characters.

Because in reality? I'm not a catch. I'm not the girl they'll all orbit around like planets with the sun. I'm just a crazy bitch with a voodoo doll and a slight obsession with the four of them.

Maybe they just want me because of what I am, what I represent.

Maybe they have gotten a taste of my darkness and now want more.

But they'll come to find out that my darkness is encased in barbed-wire and pointed blades. The moment you touch it, you get stabbed.

There's no escape.

CHAPTER 45

I stare intently at the closed violin case, willing it to…do something. Anything besides sit there and taunt me. My fingers itch with the need to touch it, caress it, pluck its strings.

But doing so will feel like surrender, and I'm not quite sure I'm ready for that yet.

Biting down on my lower lip, I turn back to the sheet music and bring the school's violin back underneath my chin. As I begin to work through a song I wrote for my music composition class, I allow my mind to wander.

The Devils' words tug at something inside of me. At the desperate little girl yearning for a family of her own and people who love her. Why do they have to do this to me now? When I'm finally beginning to heal? Sooner or later, they're going to pull the rug right out from underneath my feet.

They want a relationship…

With me?

That concept is comical, and for the hundredth time, I wonder if this is some elaborate prank. Is this a way for them to abate their guilt? Develop a relationship with the freaky witch and then voila! All of your sins will be washed away. Or is it possible that they actually *do* have feelings for me?

I don't even realize I've stopped playing until the bow clatters against the cold tiles of the practice room. Surprisingly enough, the air outside is warm, though the air conditioning blowing through the vents combats the humidity.

Lunch has long since ended, but I remain hidden in the practice room at the end of the hall. No one ever travels this far, so I doubt I'll get caught. And if the school calls Nana about my attendance, she'll cover for me. She owes me that much, at the very least.

The last thing I want to see are any of the Devils and the sub who replaced Mrs. Town for Lit.

Unbidden, my eyes flicker to the brand new violin case again before I chance a glance at the closed practice room door. I even go as far as to poke my head out, ensuring that the hall is empty, before tiptoeing on silent feet to Cassian's present.

I can barely hear anything over the pounding in my heart. For some reason, it feels as if accepting this gift will mean that the war is over and I lost. It means that I've laid down my weapons and am now awaiting my punishment with bated breath. It's utterly ridiculous, I know, but it's how I feel as I unclasp the case and pull it open.

I don't want to be in anyone's debt, least of all Cassian Jereome.

Tentatively, I run my hand over the smooth, reddish-brown wood. It's cold to the touch, but unlike the violin the school gave me, not a speck of dust or dirt adorns the instrument. I pluck first one string and then another, squeezing my eyelids shut as the notes reverberate through the room.

At the top of the case is a bow, made out of the same wood as the violin itself. The strings are stark white, not the murky brown of the archaic one still lying on the ground.

I want to play this beautiful instrument so bad that it's a physical ache. I want to feel the music rumble through me like a storm inside of my body. Thunder crashing like cymbals. Lightning splicing the sky apart in golden-white light. Rain battering against the pavement, the noise destroying my eardrums.

Like a woman possessed, I lift the violin and place it beneath my chin. I settle the bow on the taut strings and slowly, almost hesitantly, begin to play.

The song courses through me. A song of hope and joy. Of despair and pain. It's a myriad of emotions and feelings, some of which I don't even understand.

And then I realize.

It's the ending of my song, "Charming Devils." It's the bridge. The final chorus. The grand finale.

I allow the music to guide me, my eyelids fluttering shut as I drift away with the music. A few things still need work, a few notes that weren't hit perfectly, but when I allow my eyes to reopen a few minutes later, I know I have it.

The ending.

Tentative clapping breaks me out of my reverie, but I don't turn around.

"How long have you been there?" I question tiredly, crouching down to place the bow and violin back into the case.

"Long enough to hear you kick ass," Cassian replies from somewhere behind me. I hear his footsteps against the tiles as he comes closer—close enough for his breath to waft across my neck, stirring my white-blonde hair. "That was…"

"Why are you here?" I finally turn towards him, straightening from my crouched position. He stands directly before me, his muscular arms crossed over his broad chest as he stares down at me. I notice that he cleaned off most of the chili, though a few stains remain on his shirt. Those brown eyes of his, flecked with gold, seem to reap my very soul from my body. I just don't know if he intends to bring it to heaven or hell.

"I wanted to talk to you," he replies, and for once, I don't see even a hint of his customary teasing grin. His face is uncharacteristically solemn.

"About what you guys said? About how you guys all want to date me?" I ask, allowing my disbelief to bleed into my tone. He winces slightly before nodding.

"I know it sounds crazy—"

"It sounds absolutely fucking insane. You know that, right?" I demand. When he continues to stare at me, pleading for me to hear him out, I shake my head slowly. "You don't even like me."

"That's not true," he protests adamantly, a fire burning in those dark orbs of his. He starts to take a step closer but then thinks better of it, and clenches his hands into fists. "The reasons why I did what I did…it was *never* because I didn't fucking like you. I think that was my problem."

"You liking a girl?" I ask, voice laced with disbelief.

"Yes." Unlike me, he's being completely serious, almost confusingly so. "There are a lot of reasons why I did the things I did, baby," he presses on, his lips quirking slightly when I growl at the nickname. "My dad left my mom and me before middle school began, but I think we both know that wasn't the real reason. Or at least, it wasn't the only one."

"You're making no fucking sense, Cassian." I scrub a hand through my hair, loosening the ponytail I haphazardly threw it into when I arrived here.

"And you swear too much, baby," he teases with a wink. "How come I didn't know about this filthy mouth of yours back in middle school?"

"There's a lot I can do with this filthy mouth of mine," I purr, sashaying forward until I'm directly in front of him. I press onto my tiptoes and stare him in the eyes. "But you're never going to find out what."

"Damn, woman." He pantomimes fanning himself before

lowering his hand and repeating the process with his crotch. "You're making me hot."

"At least it's 'woman' and not 'baby' now," I retort, attempting to pass him, but before I can take more than a step, he grabs my wrist, forcing me to a halt.

"Joking aside, Peony, I would very much like to explain."

I twist my head so his striking face fills my vision. Currently, his brows are pinched, but that doesn't make his features any less statuesque, like a marble relic. Heat sizzles through my veins as I stare into his muddy eyes, and he offers me a tremulous smile.

"Okay. Talk. I'm listening."

He releases me then, nodding for me to take a seat. He distractedly scratches the back of his neck, avoiding eye contact with me once more.

"You're probably so fucking sick of hearing this already, but I'm sorry. About everything."

"Actually," I interrupt, "it's pretty damn satisfying to hear those words. But I prefer it when you're on your hands and knees, with your head pressed to the floor in a bow." The words are meant as a joke, as a way to lighten the mood, so you can imagine my surprise when Cassian drops to the floor like he's on fire and fucking *bows* at my feet.

"Is this better?" The tiles muffle his voice from where he's pressed against them, but I can hear the underlying amusement. I can actually feel my body's internal temperature increase by a billion and one degrees as my entire body burns.

"You're such an asshole," I hiss, reaching down to pull at his shoulders. He finally lifts his head, his smile growing when he sees my red face. "Stop laughing."

"You wanted me to bow at your altar," he points out with a wry smirk. "And what my girl wants, my girl gets."

"I'm not your girl," I protest automatically. The words are entirely instinctive now, though I'm not even sure if they're the truth anymore. At least, not the full truth.

His smile fades as he ambles back to his feet, returning to his incessant pacing.

"And that was my biggest problem," he confesses, and I can barely hold in my snort.

"Because I wasn't your girl, you decided to bully me? That really doesn't make me feel better, Cass," I snap, feeling the familiar wisps of anger slither around in my stomach.

"No, that's not what I meant." He once more runs a hand over his buzzed head, his movements jerky with agitation. "Fuck! This is coming out all wrong."

"Well, you're not making any sense," I huff, crossing my arms over my chest. "You're acting as if liking me is what made you bully me. Is that what this is? You pull a girl's hair because you have a crush on her and want her attention?"

"That's Lucas's style, not mine," Cassian says automatically. "And no, that's not what I meant."

"So you were mad that I wasn't dating you?" I'm really not understanding where he's going with this, and every word he says only exacerbates my rage.

"No, I was mad that I liked you," Cassian snaps, but this time, I don't know if his irritation is directed at me or himself.

"That doesn't make any—"

"I was mad that I liked *girls*," he stresses, finally whirling on me. His chest heaves, and for once, he doesn't look as meticulously groomed as he usually does. He has never been as put together as Lucas—though I don't think anyone alive is. But I've never seen him this...*disheveled* before. I don't know how else to describe it. His eyes look wild and unhinged, his dark shirt is untucked and still stained with chili, and there's a hole in his jeans that I swear hadn't been there earlier.

It takes a few moments for those words to click in my brain, and

I can't help but drop my mouth open in shock. I quickly try to hide my completely instinctive reaction by snapping it closed.

"What do you mean?" I manage to ask, and he rubs a huge hand down his face.

"It means exactly what it sounds like, baby."

"You like...guys?" I try to connect what I know about Cassian with what he's telling me. It just doesn't add up. He's the biggest womanizer around school, constantly bragging about a different conquest every day.

"Yes and no." He shakes his head and shrugs his shoulders simultaneously, staring at me helplessly. "At that time, yes. I was mainly attracted to guys. But then you came along, this tiny little girl with beautiful white hair and alluring amber eyes, and I found that I couldn't look away. I didn't even want to. You quickly monopolized my every thought. Not gonna lie...my first masturbation? It was to you." He releases a haggard breath as he stops pacing, facing the far wall. "You have to understand, I was confused as fuck. I thought I liked dudes, and then there's you, this fucking anomaly. I think a part of me resented you for that, for making me so fucking confused." He spins towards me once more. "You want to know what really did me in? What was the final nail in my coffin?"

I shake my head wordlessly. Do I want to know? I timidly lick my upper lip before my head shake turns into a head nod.

"We never broke you," he whispers. I immediately open my mouth to protest, but he shakes his head and continues before I can voice my mounting thoughts. "It's the truth. We didn't. Not completely." A small grin twists up his lips as he scratches at his chin. He must've shaved recently, not an ounce of hair visible on his artfully handsome face. "You always got this stubborn glint in your eyes whenever we...whenever we bullied you." Pure despair clouds his eyes. "I'm not going to pretend like we did anything else. We bullied you, Peony. Plain and simple. But when you stood up to us... it only made my feelings for you grow."

I bite down on my lower lip, struggling with the plethora of emotions crashing through me. No, not through me. *Into* me. Is this what it feels like to be hit by a car? To topple over sideways as glass shatters around you?

Before I can even think to articulate one of the thousands of thoughts clamoring for attention, Cassian continues, voice grave. "When you left, it was like I'd been kicked in the balls. I never experienced such crippling pain before. I searched for you, you know. I even went to your house, but it had already been abandoned. And then I realized…I was in love with you. It was a demented, fucked up sort of love, but it was all I had to offer you. At least then."

"Do you still…?" I don't even know what I'm asking. I place my fist to my mouth and bite down on my knuckles, relishing the sting of pain from my teeth.

"Like guys?" He quirks a brow. "Yeah. Girls, too. I've been with both." He takes a step forward until he's in front of me before dropping to his knees. His large hands land gently on my thighs, squeezing once. "I'm not gonna lie. I'm attracted to both genders. But there's only been one person I've ever had true, genuine feelings for, and that person is you."

I can scarcely breathe. I'm pretty sure that my lungs fail me at this moment. Heaven only knows that my heart does. This proud, arresting man is on his knees for *me*. To confess his feelings for *me*.

And I have no idea how to respond.

Vulnerability emanates from his eyes as his hands tighten on my knees.

"You're the only girl I ever truly had feelings for, baby. There are not enough words in the fucking dictionary to tell you how sorry I am."

For the first time in forever, I'm not pissed or upset by the nickname "baby." If anything, warm sparks ignite in my bloodstream as I stare into his expressive, chocolate eyes.

"All I need is one chance to prove myself to you," he charges on.

"One fucking chance. Maybe we won't work. Maybe we'll realize that we're not compatible when we're not actively trying to destroy each other." His pouty lips twitch slightly, as if he finds our war amusing. "And maybe I'll discover you put pineapple on pizza and then we'll have to break up."

"Fruit doesn't go on pizza," I counter, my brain struggling to process all of his words. "You don't see raspberries or apples on pizzas, do you?"

He flashes his shiny white teeth at me in a smile. "Or maybe I'll discover you think Carol Baskin is innocent."

"Nah. Bitch definitely killed her husband," I breathe as my eyes flicker to his mouth. I want to taste it, taste *him.*

"I want a chance to woo you. Wine and dine the fuck out of your perfect ass. Which is why..." He jumps to his feet and moves towards the door of the practice room. Before I can ask him where he's going, he grabs his backpack from where he must've discarded it in the hallway before he came in.

"What are you doing?" I ask as he unzips his bag and takes out a checkered blanket. Next comes a few electronic candles, a Tupperware container, and a smooshed flower. "What is all this?"

"This is our first date," he says with a cheeky smile. He lays the blanket out and places a candle on each corner. Lifting the lid off the Tupperware, he reveals a sandwich cut in half. Turkey, cheese, lettuce, and tomato. My favorite. Next, he grabs his water bottle, opens the top, and places the wilted flower inside of it, setting it directly in the middle of the blanket. "A romantic picnic."

"While we're skipping class?" I ask dubiously, though my heart begins to do gymnastics in my chest and dozens of birds fly around in my stomach. This feeling is too intense to be mere butterflies.

"Well, I wasn't sure if I would get another opportunity to woo you," he replies unrepentantly, tossing me another one of those megawatt smiles. I'm beginning to realize that this particular smile is different from the ones he usually gives out. It's not as forced, and it actually reaches his glossy, chestnut eyes.

"Did I even say yes to this date?" I ask as I move from the chair to sit opposite him on the blanket. He hands me one half of the sandwich, and the fluttery feeling in my stomach intensifies. Now, instead of just birds, it's fucking airplanes nosediving from the sky. My hands actually begin to shake.

"I just bared my soul to you, baby. This totally counts as a fucking date." He takes a large bite of his sandwich, eyes never leaving my face. It's almost as if he's afraid that if he looks away, I'll disappear. Like a mirage in the desert.

"Am I...?" I clear my throat. "Am I really the only person you ever had feelings for?"

That smolder of his returns as he undresses me with his gaze. "I wouldn't lie about that."

"And I know you said you're attracted to both genders, so I was just..." Once more, I'm unable to finish my thought, so I settle on shoving the sandwich into my face. He smirks at me.

"Are you asking if I'm sexually attracted to anyone else at this moment? Say...one of your other boyfriends?"

I begin to choke on my sandwich bite. "Not. Boyfriends."

"Like, do I imagine licking down their abs? Taking their cocks in my mouth? In my ass?" His grin grows as my blush deepens. "I realized that I like taking, by the way. So if you ever want to try pegging..."

"Oh my god!" I bring both hands to my cheeks in an attempt to hide my embarrassment. But his dirty words did the trick, and I can feel myself turning damp. The thought of him with one of the other Devils...

"But to answer your question, yes, I think they're attractive men. No, I don't have feelings for them, and I doubt I ever will. But sex? Only if you're between us, baby."

"I'm pretty sure my cheeks will stay this color if you don't shut up," I hiss, and he laughs, completely unperturbed.

"I like that color on you. I like everything about you." He pauses, glancing down at the crunched up flower. Is that a...? Is that a peony? His next words effectively break through my lust-filled haze. "I even like that you're a witch."

"What?" I ask, aghast. Did I hear him right? Maybe he said "bitch." Yes, that makes more sense. He thinks I'm a bitch.

"You heard me." That cocky smile never leaves his face, though it does wilt in the corners like the flower before us. His eyes suddenly turn serious. "Peony, I know."

"What...? How...?"

"And I know you put that fucking boner spell on me as well." His lips twist into a grimace. "That was really mean, by the way. Though it was surprisingly easy to break." He leans forward to whisper, "All I had to do was envision you while jerking off."

"Cassian," I beg, "how did you know? I mean...how? What? Why?"

His expression turns contrite even as he shrugs. "I knew for a while. I told you, I went to look for you."

"Yes, but you said that my house was empty."

I'm floundering, sinking beneath wave after icy wave. I struggle to replenish my air supply before I'm pulled back under again and again and again.

"I went to look for you," he repeats, dropping his eyes to the floor. "And my search led me to California. To a certain town way in the middle of nowhere that is apparently run by witches and warlocks."

I'm unable to speak, so instead, I simply stare, mouth agape.

"At the time, you were dating that fucker, Uriel. I saw the two of you together." Darkness momentarily steals the light from his eyes before he contains it. "Nobody told me anything explicitly, but it was easy to put two and two together. You're a witch. You're *all* witches…or warlocks. Whatever the male term is. Wizards? Anyway, I left the town before anyone really noticed me."

I doubt that. Cassian is far too good-looking and charismatic to ever fly under the radar.

"You knew this entire time?" I ask in shock, and he smiles sheepishly, fluttering his lashes at me.

"Don't be mad?" He turns the statement into a question as he moves the water bottle/vase to the side and begins to crawl towards me, forcing me onto my back. "I know that you told the others as well," he whispers as he plants a chaste kiss on my shoulder.

"Did they tell you?" I demand as he continues kissing down my body, stopping when he reaches the waistband of my pants.

"They didn't need to. I could see it in their eyes." He pauses, a frown marring his face. "I'll admit, I was pissed as fuck when I first found out. But then I remembered that you didn't owe me anything. Hell, you hated me, and I sure as fuck gave you no reason to trust me. Gradually, that anger turned to yearning and jealousy. I'm still fucking livid to think about you with that stupid fuck," he seethes, and I can't help but smirk, running the palm of my hand over his buzzed head.

"For someone who says I swear a lot, you have the mouth of a sailor."

"And I have a cock as long as a ship, too," he teases with a wink. "You can tug on my boat anytime you desire, baby."

"You mean a little toy boat?" I pretend to think about it. "I'm pretty sure I had one when I was younger. It was about this big." I bring my thumb and index finger together. "But at least it was nice to look at."

"I'll show you nice to look at," he mutters under his breath, planting a kiss to the top of my thigh. Suddenly, a devious expression appears on his face as he glances up at me through his thick fringe of lashes. "How about a game?"

"A game?"

"Did you know I used to watch your performances back in middle school?" he asks almost conversationally, and his abrupt change in topic gives me whiplash.

"What does this have to do with a game?" I demand, still lying on my back with Cassian between my legs. I have the irresistible urge to squirm, to rub my thighs together and alleviate the ache between them.

"I want you to play with me again someday," he continues, ducking his head to place another kiss on the juncture where my thigh meets my hip. "Me on the guitar. You on the violin. I want you to play that one song you wrote. When we played together before… You felt that, didn't you? The magic?"

"Still don't understand the game," I breathe, and I swear I can feel him smiling against my pants.

"That wasn't the game, baby. That was just a distraction. We're going to have a spelling test."

I sit up abruptly to stare down at him. "A what now?"

He places one hand on my chest to guide me back to the floor while his other hand moves to my leggings and panties and slowly glides them down my legs. He pauses when they're bunched around my thighs, turning towards me for permission, and I nod despite myself.

"Cassian…" I whisper in warning. We're at school, for fuck's sake, in a room that doesn't lock. Anyone could walk in here at any moment and catch us.

Why does that thought only amplify my desire? Why does it make me so fucking wet, I can feel it dripping down my now bare thighs?

"You like this, don't you?" he asks in wonderment. "The thought of getting caught." He rubs a finger up and down my slit, groaning softly.

"So this game…" I breathe, voice raspy.

"You have to guess three words," he says simply. "I'll write it for you with my tongue."

"What do I get if I win?" Fuck, what am I doing? What are *we* doing? Am I actually considering this, getting into a relationship with all of the guys? Or at the very least, trying it out? I don't know for certain, but I do know that my traitorous body refuses to pull away. My brain gives me thousands of reasons why this is a bad idea, but my heart contradicts each and every one.

"How about the two of us at the same time?" a heated voice declares from the doorway, and Cassian smiles in his friend's direction.

A moment later, Elias shifts until my head is in his lap.

"How does that sound, baby?" Cassian questions as one of his fingers begins to circle my clit. "Do you want Elias to stay? Do you want the two of us at the same time? We're already yours, baby. It's just a matter of whether or not you want to be ours."

"Fucking hell. Fuck, yes. Both of you," I groan loudly as Elias helps me pull my shirt over my head and then my bra. I'm naked... with two of the Devils...at school...ditching class.

I'm so going to hell.

"Let the spelling test begin, boys," I breathe.

CHAPTER 46

The first swipe of Cassian's tongue against my center has me bucking my hips, desperate for more. I pant his name as he grips my thighs, attempting to hold me steady.

"She's so fucking wet, man," Cassian groans to Elias as the other man begins to pluck at my nipples, playing them as expertly as I do my violin.

"Cassian…" I don't know if it's a warning or a plea, but either way, he understands my unspoken message.

"Word number one," he says, bringing his tongue back to my aching pussy. He creates long strokes, zigzagging a few times, before he pulls away with a question in his eyes.

I was too lost in the sensations he evoked to even pay attention.

"Do it again," I demand as Elias's fingers trail up and down my breasts, flicking my nub with every rotation.

"So greedy." But Cassian complies, bringing his mouth back to my wet heat and writing out a word with his tongue. I gasp when he touches my clit, fire racing through my veins, but all too soon, he pulls away.

"Witch," I say with certainty, and he grins at me.

"Very good. You ready for word number two?" At that exact moment, Elias slaps one of my tits, watching it sway as I cry out in pain and pleasure. I swear I can feel the sting of it reverberate all the way down my body before landing in my core.

"Go." I dig my nails into Elias's thighs, wishing that he was naked as well. I want there to be no layers between the three of us.

Cassian languidly licks another word into my pussy, my thighs squeezing his head like a vise. He chuckles darkly, a noise I can feel racing through my veins as I writhe and buck against him.

"Sexy?" I guess tentatively, and his smile expands.

"Word three?"

"No," I say immediately, and before he can question me, I shift in Elias's embrace until I'm on my hands and knees, my ass facing Cassian. Elias immediately begins to tug at my swinging breasts, his thick erection straining against his jeans impossible to miss. "I thought you were mad at me," I whisper, too quietly for Cassian to hear. This is just between me and Elias. I need to know he forgives me, that he understands, before we can move forward. I was coming from a place of hurt, and though that pain remains, still prevalent, it no longer overwhelms me.

Maybe we *can* move forward. Maybe we can allow our past hurt and pain to wash away, returning back to the ocean where it'll remain.

"I shouldn't have run away," he confesses, voice just as soft. "And I can promise you, I never will again."

"This is all very touching and all," Cassian drawls lazily as he kisses one of my ass cheeks. "But we didn't finish my game."

"New game," I rasp as I unzip Elias's jeans and free his rock-hard cock. I love to see the effect I have on these men, to be sure in the knowledge that they want me just as badly and desperately as I want them. "I'm gonna suck Elias off while you fuck me from behind."

Cassian pauses behind me before he ducks his head, lapping at my pussy with gusto.

"I like the way you think, baby," he purrs as his tongue circles my clit. Elias's eyes shutter shut as I jerk him twice, before darting down and offering him a small lick across the slit at the crown of his cock.

"Fucking hell, baby girl," he murmurs, and Cassian once more pulls away from my entrance.

"Hey! That's my nickname for her, fucker. Get your own."

"Fuck off." Elias lazily gives him the middle finger as I begin to lick down his length like it's my own personal lollipop. A vein runs down the left side of his girth, and I begin to plant teasing kisses up and down. Down and up.

Behind me, Cassian continues to devour my pussy like a man possessed. Like he's starving and I'm a tasty, decadent feast.

"Do you know how gorgeous you look right now, my little witch?" Elias pants as I wrap my mouth around the head of his cock and take him deep into my mouth. I hollow my throat, watching through hooded eyes as he throws his head back. Behind me, I can hear the shuffling of clothes and the crinkling of a condom wrapper before the head of Cassian's cock lines up with my wet entrance. He begins to rub the tip of his dick back and forth across my slit, collecting my juices.

Elias reaches for my hair, still in a disheveled ponytail, and tugs at it until the white-blonde locks cascade free. His other hand slides to my dangling breast and squeezes.

Seeing his unencumbered joy, the lust in his eyes...

It's nearly my undoing, and Cassian hasn't even entered me yet.

My heart inflates to the point it might burst.

Cassian winds both hands in my hair, lifting my head from Elias's cock and turning me slightly so I can meet his lips in a searing kiss that heats my blood and liquifies my limbs. From this angle, I have my first view of Cassian's sculpted body—all of those rigid muscles on display under beautifully dark skin. He's the largest of the Devils, every inch of him hewn from stone.

When he pulls his lips away from mine, I'm a panting, shaking mess.

"Get your fucking clothes off, man," Cassian snaps at Elias, reaching down to tug on the other man's cock. My mouth waters at the sight, my heart rate increasing. Elias wastes no time stripping out of his jacket, shirt, and jeans, before kicking off his shoes and socks.

Now, I'm naked between two sinfully handsome men.

Elias places his hands on Cassian's shoulders as they cage me in between them. And though their horny gazes fixate firmly on me, it's obvious that they're not afraid of each other's bodies either.

"Someone could see us," I whisper. This is wrong. So, so wrong. Anyone could walk down this hallway and look in through the window. A teacher, the principal, a student.

But the thought of getting caught, the thought of someone watching, only makes my nipples harden into taut peaks and liquid heat coil low in my belly.

As one, the guys touch me, igniting a frenzy in their wake. Elias claims my lips for his own as Cassian pulls and twists at my breasts, leaving a myriad of kisses across my neck and shoulder.

Elias rocks his hips into mine as his tongue invades my mouth.

I feel Cassian line up at my entrance as his hand lowers down the front of my body. It brushes against Elias's cock, but neither guy pulls away as Cassian brings his wandering fingers to my clit.

"Is this okay, baby?" Cassian murmurs into my ear, and at my nod of consent, he grips my hips tightly and thrusts inside of me in one fluid stroke. Automatically, my hands fly to Elias's shoulders as I break our scorching kiss.

"Fuck," I breathe, dropping my head to the juncture between Elias's neck and shoulder and kissing desperately at the skin there. My hands seem to have a life of their own as they travel down his broad shoulders, over his pert nipples, and then across his rock-hard abs. Each one is clearly defined and visible, and one day, I'm going to take the time to memorize them with my tongue.

But not now. We're too frenzied and desperate for something that chaste.

Cassian rams his cock in and out of my pussy, while one of his hands plays with my clit and the other cups my breast.

"Fuck, you feel better than I imagined. You're so fucking tight," he praises as I grip Elias's shaft firmly. Our gazes lock, my amber eyes meeting his violet-tinted ones, and the world around us stills. This entire moment is surreal, but I know without a shadow of doubt that I forgive Elias. Karsyn. Even Cassian.

The most overwhelming surge of emotion consumes me, stealing my breath as I pull Elias into another heated kiss. I've never felt anything like this in my entire existence.

I tangle one of my hands in his gorgeous brown and purple hair, loving the feel of the silky strands beneath my fingers. My other hand continues to jerk him off in tandem to Cassian's hard and unrelenting thrusts.

"I love you," Elias whispers.

Before I can formulate a response, Cassian tweaks my nipples and slams his cock so hard into my pussy, I see stars. White spots dance in my vision, pleasure cascading through me. I swear my vagina takes a picture to commemorate this moment.

I begin to stroke Elias faster and faster, feeling myself plunge headfirst—or as the case may be, pussy first—towards that pool of orgasmic bliss, drowning in wave after fucking wave of it. I come with a scream, my walls tightening around Cassian's cock as his hips stutter. He then begins to pound into me with renewed vigor, placing a hand on my shoulders to push me towards the ground. This new angle allows me to put my lips back around Elias's dick, which I do, loving the taste of his salty pre-cum. I begin to fondle his balls with both of my hands. The only thing keeping me upright at this moment is Cassian's grip on my hair.

Cassian comes first, his cock jerking inside of my pussy as he explodes. He screams my name as he continues to rub at my clit, begging me without words to come with him a second time. My walls clamp down as I scream my own release, my thighs shaking with my second mind-numbing orgasm.

Elias follows soon after. He tries to pull away, but I move my hands to his hard ass, holding him in place as I swallow every last drop of his release. I lick the remaining cum off of my lips as he stares at me, eyes wide with lust and wanton need.

"Fucking hell."

"That's my perfect girl," Cassian whispers as he kisses down my naked spine.

Between the two of them, sated and sweaty, I begin to believe that this might actually work. That I can forgive them and we can move on. Together.

CHAPTER 47

I can't stop smiling as I walk to my fifth hour. It's a genuine smile, not one tinged with anger and the desperate desire I have for revenge.

My body feels deliciously sore as I move briskly through the halls towards the gymnasium. I know bruises will dot my thighs from how savagely Cassian gripped and fucked me.

Not that I'm complaining.

I feel more alive than I can ever remember feeling. It's like a flame has been lit inside of my chest, slowly building into an inferno. The fire licks at my nerve endings in the most addictive way possible. Can someone become addicted to sex?

I can't imagine feeling this way with anyone other than the Devils, though. Already, my body begs for theirs. Craves theirs. I want to run my fingers over the hard, massive planes of Cassian's chest. I want to kiss Elias's plush lips as his cock rams in and out of me. I want Karsyn to brush my hair away from my neck and plant light, teasing kisses across the skin there. I want Lucas—

I shut that thought down as I hurry into the locker room.

It's empty, as class began almost five minutes earlier, but I don't intend to actually enter the gymnasium today. Instead, I sit on a bench in front of the lockers and grab my computer from my back-pack. I click on a file labeled Karsyn and begin to sort through some of the videos I acquired of him playing football over the years.

I've been at work for only a few minutes when Mariabella enters, brows pinched.

"Hey! I was wondering where you were hiding," she exclaims airily as she steps forward, sweat clinging to her body from the workout. I quickly slam the laptop closed before she can see what I've been working on. "Whatcha doing?" She eyes me curiously, but she doesn't make a move for the laptop, trusting me to tell her what is necessary for her to know.

"What are *you* doing?" I counter, and she thankfully drops the subject.

"The fucktards asked me to check on you." Her mahogany-colored eyes narrow ever so slightly. "I know that you have this whole mysterious, secretive aura going on, but you have to be straight with me, pun unintended. Is there something going on between the five of you?" She plants a hand on her hip and cocks it to the side. "I won't judge. Those guys are more possessive than fucking dogs, if you get my meaning. Some junior mentioned your name, and I'm pretty sure Lucas dug a hole to bury his dead body in the school yard."

I quirk a brow at my best friend. "I'll tell you mine, if you tell me yours," I taunt.

"What do you mean?" She makes a face at me.

"I saw that little boob touch at lunch," I point out with a wry grin, enjoying the way she squirms.

"I don't know what you mean," Mariabella says quickly. Too quickly.

"Hhmmm," I hum. "So do all of your friends touch your titties or just some of them?"

"You did," she retorts, a pink tint to her cheeks. "And stop saying titties. It's gross."

"You don't like titties?" I flutter my lashes at her innocently. "Big titties? Little titties?"

"I hate you so fucking much right now," she snarks, shoving at my shoulder.

"Orange titties? Pink titties?"

"Oh my god! Stop!" She brings both of her hands to her cheeks and ducks her head. "You're such a bitch."

"A bitch with titties," I say, because I honestly can't help myself.

"Okay, we need to have a girls' night, and soon," Mariabella states decisively. "I'll tell you all about my…err…friend, and you can tell me what the hell is going on with you and those assholes. Do we have a deal?" She holds her pinkie finger towards me, but before I can link it with my own, she pulls away. "And no saying titties ever again," she adds firmly.

"Titties. Titties. Titties. Titties. Titties. I think I got that off my chest," I say with a pointed look down at my boobs. I swear her eyes are going to get stuck in the back of her head with how hard she rolls them.

"You're lucky I love you."

"Luck has nothing to do with it." I wink at her before placing my laptop back into my broken backpack and shoving both inside my gym locker. "It's my natural charm."

MARIABELLA'S RIGHT.

The guys are acting stranger than usual, which is saying something, considering that all four of them are eccentric enigmas.

The second I enter the gym, Cassian and Elias step towards me. The former throws his arm around my shoulders, pulling me against his chest in a possessive move, while the latter links his fingers with my own. I blush at the inquiring stares from the other students, attempting to duck my head and cover my face with my free hand. Some of the guys stare at me with decidedly leery expressions, while others appear wary. And the girls are either confused, angry, or jealous.

Lucas slides in front of me instantly, gently grabbing both of my wrists and pulling my hand away from my flaming cheeks. His glacial blue gaze freezes me in place as he whispers, "Don't hide. Queens should never hide from their subjects."

Before I can comment, he gives me one last unreadable look—a look that I would almost describe as wistful—before storming away.

At one point during dodgeball—the worst game in existence, where I simply hide behind Cassian and Elias, grateful that they're on my team instead of against me—Karsyn walks over, wraps a muscular arm around my waist, and kisses my forehead. Mariabella's eyebrows practically climb up her forehead as the rest of the class whispers amongst themselves. I can already hear their probing questions now.

What is going on?

Why is she touching and flirting with all of the guys?

Is she sleeping with them all?

Slut.

Whore.

Trash.

Witch.

It's funny, because most of them are true.

But I don't care what they think about me. At least, I tell myself that I don't. I'll own my sexuality and everything it entails. If that means sleeping with more than one guy when I feel like it, then so be it. I won't apologize for being who I am ever again. There's nothing wrong with liking sex, and I hate that most women get shamed for it while men are celebrated. The double standards in society never fail to infuriate me.

The only Devil who isn't affectionate with me is Lucas, but I can feel his eyes on me throughout class.

When the bell finally rings, I change quickly into my normal clothes and begin to head towards sixth hour, unsure if I should wait for Cassian and Lucas, the only two Devils in the class with me. Is that something we do now? Walk to class together? Fuck, why am I so confused?

"Peony." I'd recognize Emmett's voice anywhere as he creeps up behind me.

I spin towards the football player as he towers over me, looking unkempt and haggard for the first time since I've known him. Out of my peripheral vision, I see Mariabella linger near her locker, offering me support if I need it.

"Emmett," I say, unsure how to speak with him. We went on one disastrous date and haven't really spoken since. I think a part of me is still mad at him for the way he touched me when we kissed. Though...I have to wonder if I played some part in that. Did I lead him on? Did he think I wanted the kiss to go further? At the time, I was just proving a point to both myself and the Devils. Maybe I'm the one in the wrong because I used him. "Are you okay? You don't look too good."

He shifts from one foot to another uncomfortably, running a hand through his sandy blond hair and messing up his carefully styled fauxhawk. His dimples are nowhere to be found.

"I was hoping we could talk..."

"About?" I question, just as he frantically grabs at a strand of my hair, bringing it to his nose and inhaling. "Emmett, stop." Using both hands, I shove at his chest, attempting to extract myself from his tightening grip.

"Why don't you love me?" he slurs, and the sheer intensity emanating from his eyes has me frowning.

"I don't understand what you mean," I whisper. "We went on one date, it didn't really work out, and we haven't talked a lot since. We're still friends, though. I think."

At my words, his jade green eyes darken significantly until they resemble a jungle during the dead of night. He takes a step closer, crowding me against the wall.

"It didn't really work out because you're a slut who opens her legs for any guy who gives you a few dollars," he hisses, and my head jolts back at the sheer venom in his voice. His words...his words I can handle. They're cruel and demeaning, but they're not anything I haven't heard before. Granted, I didn't expect for *him* to say them, but they're not going to break me.

His tone, on the other hand...

They match the fire burning brightly in his eyes. His entire body radiates anger, so pure and volatile that it's almost palpable. If someone dropped a match right now, I'd half expect the entire hallway to burst into flames.

"What the fuck is your problem, Em?" Mariabella snaps, moving to stand beside me. She reaches forward and shoves Emmett back a few steps. Despite Mariabella being shorter by almost an entire foot, Emmett actually stumbles, almost as if he's drunk.

"You're taking her side? Really, Mari?" Hurt briefly flashes in his gaze before it diminishes in a puff of anger. "You barely know her! We've been friends for fucking years! What the hell?"

"Walk away, Emmett," Mariabella warns darkly. "You won't like what happens if you don't."

"Fuck you," he seethes, baring his teeth. He glances over Mariabella's shoulder, towards me. "And fuck you, too. Dirty fucking slut."

Out of the corner of my eye, I see Cassian and Lucas come around the corner, whispering softly to each other. Lucas spots us first, and his eyes harden instantly. Cassian freezes for a single moment before breaking into a run.

"When a girl says no, you walk away, Emmett," Mariabella

continues, seemingly oblivious or choosing to ignore the fact that Emmett looks ready to rip her head off. For a moment, I worry for my best friend, and I allow tiny flames to dance in my palms behind my back. If Emmett attacks, I'll be ready. "You're drunk. Go home."

"Won't have your pretty little bodyguard around forever," Emmett taunts as he reaches forward and captures one of Mari's perfect ringlets. She jerks her head back, anger swirling in her brown eyes. Emmett levels a penetrating glare onto me, one that makes me ill. "I'll be back for you, my pretty flower."

"Hey! Asshole!" Cassian finally reaches us at the same time Emmett turns on his heel and runs away like the fucking coward he is. Cassian immediately moves to follow him, but Lucas grips his arm, pulling him to a stop.

"Don't," he warns softly. "It's not worth it." A wide smile erupts on his face, chasing the cold from his eyes, as he stares after Emmett's retreating back. "The coward will get what he deserves sooner rather than later." As if coming out of a daze, Lucas shakes his head before turning towards me and extending his arm like an old-fashioned gentleman escorting his girl to a ball. He ignores a fuming Mariabella completely. "Come. We need to get to class."

"Are you okay?" I ask Mari, ignoring Lucas for the time being.

"Yeah." Her jaw clenches. "I don't know what his problem is. I don't think I've ever seen Emmett drunk in his life."

"Some guys are just assholes," Cassian replies as he slings an arm over my shoulder once more. I'm beginning to realize that out of all the guys, Cassian demands the most physical affection. Hugs, casual touches, chaste kisses. I'm sure if I would allow him, he would fuck me in front of the entire school, if only to prove to them that I'm his.

And he's mine.

"You do see the irony of that, don't you?" Mariabella retorts, giving him a narrowed-eyed glare. He scoffs.

"I'm a reformed man now, Mari." He ruffles her hair like a parent would a toddler. "Get with the program."

With one last glare at my…umm…boyfriend? Friend? Acquittance? Enemy? Mariabella turns towards me and offers me a one-armed hug.

"I need to go. See you at practice." She glares at the guys, waves goodbye to me, and then stalks down the hall towards her sixth hour. I swear she's the only person alive who would dare to go toe to toe with the Devils.

And live to talk about it.

Maybe Karsyn will beat their asses if they ever disrespect her, or maybe they know how much she means to me. Either way, Mariabella is immune to their wrath.

I wrench my gaze off of my friend and focus on Lucas, surprised to see his arm still extended the same way it was a minute ago.

"Shall we?" he asks, and after only a moment, I place my hand in the crook of his elbow and allow him to guide me to class.

CHAPTER 48

After cheer practice, I exit the school to see all four guys waiting for me in front of Elias's Jeep. Even Karsyn, whose football practice got canceled when the head coach came down with the flu.

My eyes wander over all four of them, marveling how lucky I am to…

To be dating all four of them.

The thought slips into my head unbidden, and I immediately try to stomp on it, refusing to stop until it's nothing but guts and blood. Because I'm *not* dating all of them. There is one Devil that I refuse to even think about like that—Lucas fucking Scott.

"Hey, baby!" Cassian's eyes glimmer like we're sharing an inside joke. I suppose, in a way, that we are. I bite my lip as I remember how his cock felt sliding in and out of me, how his huge hands felt tangled in my hair and pulling at my breasts, how his lips felt on my skin.

"We thought we could hang out for a little bit," Karsyn confesses as he pulls me against his chest. Is this going to be our thing now?

Casual, intimate touches? Despite years of ingrained hatred towards the Devils, I can't deny how badly I want this. All of this.

"Like a date," interjects Elias as he slides his fingers through his shoulder-length hair. He grabs an elastic off of his wrist and quickly piles the silky strands into a bun at the nape of his neck. I don't know which look I find sexier on him—the unruly, disheveled one that makes me think of bad boys and motorcycles, or this one, where only a few wayward curls frame his strong jawline and chiseled cheekbones.

"A date," I repeat as Lucas wordlessly takes my backpack from me. "With all of you?" My eyes drift to Lucas before I can stop them, and he winces. It's barely perceptible, a slight twitch in his features, but it's enough for me to see that my words unwittingly hurt him. But like always, he covers up his emotions with a droll, almost bored look.

"I can go somewhere else, if you wish," he states expressionlessly.

"*If you wish,*" Cassian mocks with an eye roll. "What century is this, man?"

Lucas stiffens ever so slightly as he smooths a hand down the front of his pressed sweater. I can still see a visible chili stain near his collar, and I wonder if that bothers him. For as long as I've known him, he refuses to look anything less than immaculate. It must be hell for him to walk around school with that hideous red stain.

"There's no need to be a Neanderthal." Lucas steps forward and brushes at Cassian's shoulder, removing a tiny piece of lint. "I simply wanted Peony to be more comfortable."

"Comfortable my ass—"

"No, it's fine," I blurt before an argument can ensue. "You guys can all come with me back to my house."

I slide into the backseat of the Jeep before anyone can protest, hugging my backpack to my chest. Karsyn moves to sit on one side of me and Cassian on the other, caging me between their warm bodies. Lucas gets the passenger seat, no surprise, while Elias drives.

"Your house," Karsyn mumbles as he digs through his backpack, grabbing his history textbook. I'm pretty sure he mentioned that he has another test tomorrow in that class. "Where those shirtless guys walk around?"

All four of them stiffen, even Lucas, who is trying his damn hardest to pretend like he's not eavesdropping.

"You mean my step-grandfathers?" I ask, internally wincing at the term. It's still strange as fuck to think about them like that. I know they are *way* older than they look, but it's hard for me to wrap my head around that when they look like models in their mid-twenties. Besides, I'm still pissed at them for keeping the truth about them being Bloods a secret. I haven't talked to them since their explosive confession, where my entire world tilted on its axis before nose diving to its untimely end.

"You mean your grandma...and them?" Cassian seems to be struggling to wrap his head around it. "They actually have, you know, sex?"

"For the love of... Cassian! Can we *not* talk about my grandma's sex life? Please?" I implore, throwing my hands up in the air.

"Is that normal for witches and warlocks?" Lucas asks from the front seat, effectively ending any suggestive comment Cassian might've made. "Having harems? Or as the case may be, having significantly younger harems?"

"No." I shake my head slowly. "At least, not that I've heard. Most witches and warlocks are monogamous. And to be honest, the triplets actually aren't younger than my grandma."

"What do you mean?" Lucas demands as the other three volley their heads between us. It's easy to forget that I haven't yet shared all of the gory details being a witch entails. "You told me that the only immortal witches are vampires."

"Vampires are real? As in, the sparkly, stalking kind?" Cassian asks, agape.

"You mean Bloods," I correct Lucas. To Cassian, I add, "No. Not in the way that you're thinking. Bloods are witches corrupted by dark magic, requiring them to drink blood in order to survive."

"So you're saying that your grandma's boyfriends...husbands... whatever they are..." Karsyn begins slowly, as if struggling to comprehend a difficult math equation, "are these Bloods. These vampire-like creatures."

I stare from face to face, honestly surprised by the anger I see reflecting back at me.

"Yes," I admit at last, and a flurry of curses accompany my single-word declaration.

"You told me that they're evil," Lucas snaps. "So are you telling me that you have three blood-sucking monsters in your house at this very moment?"

"That doesn't sound safe, Peony," Karsyn adds seriously, his expression grave.

"They wouldn't hurt me," I snap adamantly, shocking myself with the strength of my conviction. And just like that, another piece of my anger tapers off and transforms into dust that catches on the breeze. It's shocking how much anger and hatred I held in my chest, but to finally lose another bit of it is freeing.

Because despite everything, I trust the triplets. I don't believe they'd ever hurt me. From what I'm told, they never killed anyone anyways, just used them. How is that any different from what I'm doing...what I *did*...to the Devils?

"Enough about that," Elias says calmly, winking at me in the rearview mirror. I smile at him gratefully. "I'm hungry. How about we stop for some fast-food?"

"No tacos," Cassian blurts instantly. He makes a face and rubs at his stomach. "Please, for the love of all that is good and holy, no tacos."

"Bad experience?" I question.

I swear his face actually turns a little green. "We don't talk about that day."

We stop at a burger joint, and the guys order about ten burgers to split between the four of them. I choose to get chicken tenders instead, with a side of ranch dressing and some fries. Lucas smirks at me when he hands me back my food in the car, and I can't help but smile back.

He freezes, Adam's apple bobbing, as his eyes drop to my lips. A need so strong that it leaves me breathless pours from his gaze before he quickly looks away, as icy and impassive as ever.

As Elias pulls back onto the road and begins to drive us towards my house, I notice Karsyn once more bent over his textbook, his burger sitting forgotten on his thigh. I nudge his shoulder inconspicuously.

"Hey, you okay?" I ask softly, and he glances up with a tentative smile.

"Yeah. Just stressed as hell about this exam. I need a scholarship to college, especially now that I don't have the football one..." He trails off, cheeks tinting pink, as my own insides tighten into thousands of knots. Guilt stabs my stomach, twisting like a knife until my guts and innards spill onto the ground for the world to see. "Hey, don't look at me like that." He leans forward and plants a tender kiss to my lips. "I told you. It's okay. I deserved everything you did to me, and I'm not even mad."

"You know..." Cassian begins casually from the other side of me. "You still haven't gotten your revenge on Lucas and Elias yet. That's not fair, baby." He pushes out his pouty lip.

"I got beat up," Elias points out, rubbing at his cheek where there's still a slight yellowish mark from his fight with Emmett.

"Would you like to get your revenge on me, Peony?" Lucas questions seriously, swiveling in his seat to face me. "Because you are more than welcome to. I won't even stop you. Might I give you some suggestions? I have a trust-fund that you are more than welcome to. Or we can get rid of it completely. I'm sure my parents would write me out of their will if they discover I'd…let's say…snorted weed."

I choke out a laugh before I can contain it, and on either side of me, Karsyn and Cassian throw their heads back. Even Elias begins to chuckle from the front seat as he turns onto my street.

"What?" Lucas's perfect lips curve into a frown as he glances between the four of us.

"Lucas…you can't snort weed," I say around my giggle, and I swear he actually blushes. Maybe it's a trick of the lighting, though. I doubt Lucas will ever do something as cute as blush.

"Oh."

"And I don't want to get my revenge on you guys," I add, staring down at my pale hand holding a French fry. "Not anymore."

It's mercifully silent the rest of the ride as the Jeep slows to a crawl. Karsyn once more resumes his diligent reading, a tiny crease forming between his eyebrows.

Like before, I nudge his shoulder until he glances up at me.

"Everything okay?" I whisper.

"Yeah." His lips straighten into a taut line. "I mean, no. This shit is hard."

"Karsyn…" I keep my voice low so as to not be overheard by the others. Fortunately, Lucas and Elias are engaged in conversation at the front of the car, and Cassian has his earbuds in, nodding along to his music. "Have you ever…"

"Have I ever what?" He places his book down completely in his lap and offers me his full attention. I squirm slightly. I don't think I'll ever get used to that.

"Have you ever been tested for dyslexia?" The words tumble out of me before I can stop them. I wince, waiting for him to get mad, but instead, his expression turns contemplative.

"You think I…?"

"I noticed it before in middle school," I confess. "When you were writing, you would often forget certain words or they would get swapped around in a sentence. And I also couldn't help but note that you struggle the most with the essays on your exams." I shrug my shoulders helplessly, worried that he'll be pissed at me for overstepping my boundaries.

He scratches at his eyebrow with one of his long, calloused fingers. "I've never thought about that before. Reading and writing have always been harder for me than it was for a lot of the other kids my age."

"I'm not a doctor or anything." I release a dry chuckle. "Just a crazy witch. But…"

"But you think I should talk to my doc about it," Karsyn finishes, that same thoughtful expression on his face.

"It might be a good idea, because even if it's not that, it might be some other learning disability." I wince again, wondering if he'll take offense to the word "disability," but his face remains serene.

We pull into my driveway, and Elias collects all of our garbage in the bag our food came in.

"Don't want my baby getting dirty," he warns with a pointed look at all of us. Even me. I'm pretty sure he even pets the car like some sort of dog when he thinks none of us are watching.

As we exit the vehicle and Elias, Cassian, and Karsyn make an immediate beeline towards the front door, Lucas stops me by caging me against the hood of the Jeep. He leans forward to sniff my neck, eyes rolling into the back of his head.

"I wouldn't be mad," he whispers.

"What?" I blink at him rapidly.

"I won't be mad if you got your revenge," he clarifies. "And we're also going on a date. Tonight."

"We are?" I try to sound casual, like this gorgeous man with slicked-back red hair and icy blue eyes doesn't affect me, but my tummy flutters with thousands of butterflies despite my best efforts.

Lucas smiles sharply before interlocking his fingers with mine and dragging me up the front steps, where the other three wait for us. Elias appears pained as he stares between the two of us, and Karsyn grunts, jealousy flaring to life in his eyes before it quickly abates. Only Cassian, my kinky boy, flashes us a wicked smile and winks at me.

"Naughty, naughty," he mouths, pantomiming giving me a spanking. And suddenly, I have a very vivid image of Lucas bending me over a table and—

"Peony." My mother's nasally voice greets me even before I enter the house completely.

And there goes my spanking fantasy.

"Mom." Every muscle in my body goes taut as she sashays from around the corner, looking as meticulous as ever. Today, she wears a white pencil skirt that stops just below her knees and a matching white blouse, not a speck of color to be seen. I'm not going to lie, it looks fantastic with her onyx curls tumbling freely around her shoulders and painted lips.

All four of the Devils stiffen as she appraises them, though her expression is anything but friendly. I can't really describe it. It's almost like...surprise? Maybe shock? Smugness?

What the fuck?

Instead of asking for their names, Mom dismisses them and focuses on me.

"Have you made your decision?" Mom questions snidely, snapping her fingers. Just like before, Ryan hurries forward, head bowed in a subservient pose.

"Who the fuck is that twit?" Cassian demands, eyeing Ryan with an almost incandescent fury.

Mom stares at him with barely veiled annoyance. "Boys, meet Peony's fiancé, Ryan."

"Fiancé?" Cassian bellows, and Karsyn throws me a hurt look. Elias balls his hands into fists while Lucas just steps forward, every inch the arrogant prince.

"I didn't know that Peony had a fiancé," he says diplomatically. He tilts his head to the side, sizing up the other boy. And while his face remains an impassive mask, a chilling smile prowls just beneath the surface, waiting for a chance to be unleashed and wreak havoc. "Especially one so…"

"Weak," Karsyn murmurs.

"Fucking dumb," Cassian seethes.

"With a death wish," throws in Elias.

"I'll ask you one more time, boy." Lucas takes a step closer, and though he displays no outwards aggression, there's no denying that he could snap Ryan's neck if he so desired, witch or no witch. Lucas is the monster that other monsters fear. "Is it true?"

"Err…"

"No," I cut in. I may not like Ryan, but he's still Uriel's brother. I don't want him dead, just slightly maimed. "It's not." I glare at my mother. "Disown me. Cast me out. Does it look like I give a damn?"

Mom's ruby-red lips twist in disgust. "It looks like you're fraternizing with the boys who tormented you throughout middle school." She turns her keen stare onto each of the men. "Lucas Scott. Karsyn Alder. Cassian Jereome. Elias Briggs. Aren't these the men who bullied you to the point where you wished to take your own life?" Mom taps a manicured finger to her chin in contemplation. "I still remember finding you in that tub, you know. With those scars zigzagging across your body. Your eyes puffy and swollen from crying. Your skin pale as the water turned a sickly shade of pink. There was so much blood."

"Shut the fuck up," Karsyn snaps, his lips pulling away from his teeth. "How can you talk about your own daughter like that?"

Mom is suddenly in his face, eyes flashing with malice. I automatically move to step between them. If a fight breaks out, I'll be damned if Karsyn gets caught in the crossfire.

"Maybe I can talk about her like that because she's no longer my daughter." She says each word slowly, curtly, as if she's trying to hurt me. As if she wants me to feel those words deep in my very soul. All she has to do now is renounce me as her daughter to the coven, and then all of my magic will disappear. But...

But will that be that bad?

My magic whines inside of me, a desperate plea for me to fight for it.

"You're disowning your daughter because she doesn't want to marry some fucking creep?" Elias asks in disbelief, and I know that this must be hitting a sore spot for him, considering his own parents left him. His eyes are wild as he balls his hands into fists, looking point two seconds away from slugging my mother.

"Do you boys think you know Peony?" Mom erupts into laughter. "The true her? You guys can't even begin to understand—"

"We know all about her being a witch," Karsyn interrupts with a scowl, and cold horror winds its way through me, taking me hostage. My first instinct is to lunge forward and place my hand over his mouth, stopping any more damning words from leaving his lips. My second one is to kiss the shit out of him for the way he defends me. For the way he normalizes something that others perceive as weird or different.

Mom's face turns cold, chillier than a Michigan December, and behind her, Ryan gasps.

Lucas is the first to realize that Karsyn said something he shouldn't. I can tell by the way he takes a small step backwards, moving so his body is protectively in front of me, shielding me from the ire in my mother's eyes.

"You told them?" Mom asks me, and I can hear distinct amusement lacing her tone. She laughs haughtily, throwing back her head and holding her stomach. "You know what this means."

I move to step around Lucas, but suddenly, Elias is there, pushing me farther back until there's a solid wall of muscle separating me from my vindictive, malicious mother.

"Don't," I warn softly.

"What does this mean?" Karsyn sounds confused, having not yet grasped the severity of his slip.

"There are only two options," Mother purrs, running a ruby-red nail down Lucas's cheek. He glares at the offending limb as if he's imagining biting it off. "One, and the most common, is a memory spell. It will remove all traces of witches and warlocks and magic from your itty-bitty little brains." She begins to walk her fingers up Lucas's chest, but he grips her wrist tightly before it can touch bare skin.

"And?" Elias crosses his arms over his chest.

"And nothing." Mom shrugs innocently. "Besides the fact that you'll also lose all memories of Peony."

Ryan, the fuckwad, begins to chuckle gleefully, as if the thought of me separated from the Devils means that he actually has a chance with me. In his fucking dreams. Actually, no. I don't want that coward dreaming of me.

"Next option," Cassian seethes through clenched teeth.

"A simple binding spell." Mom lifts her hand to her face, surveying each nail with rapt fascination.

"It's similar to the ones witches use when they gain familiars," I explain, my voice shaking ever so slightly. "It allows the witch to harness their energy if they ever need to, and it sometimes even gives the human in question some of the witch's magic."

"But it also makes them bond for life," Mom throws in helpfully. "The men or women bonded will be dedicated completely to their witch."

We can all hear what she's not saying. If they do this, if they bind themselves to me, they will never be able to fall in love. Never get married. The magic will make them want to be around me at all times. Sometimes, witches and humans do this ceremony because they're desperately in love. If that's the case, the fates that be will declare them as "mates" of sorts. The bond between them is unbreakable and will only grow with time. More often than not, witches will bind humans to them for one thing and one thing only —more power.

So my choices are simple. Either erase the guys' memories of me completely.

Or bind the men I once despised to me until my death.

And if I choose incorrectly, we're all going to pay the price.

CHAPTER 49

"You cannot be serious." I can feel myself starting to bristle as I stare at my mother with narrowed-eye disbelief. "You can't ask them to do any of that."

"I can, and I will," she retorts, flicking a strand of long black hair behind her shoulder. "They're not supposed to know the truth. It's the rule."

"I don't give a damn about that!" My voice raises to a screech as I take a threatening step closer. This new position puts me face to face with her. How have I failed to see how wicked my mother has become? She wasn't always like this. I truly believe that there was a time when she actually loved and wanted the best for me. But her need for power twisted her mind, warped her into someone entirely unrecognizable. Who is this fair-skinned woman staring back at me? What the hell happened to her to make her so bitter and jaded?

"Peony…" Karsyn begins softly, running his fingers down the length of my arm. Goosebumps automatically rise in their wake, even as I shove him off of me.

"I'm so sorry," I whisper tearfully, turning to stare at each of them. Karsyn's hazel eyes, the color of autumn leaves, and his pinched face. Cassian's cocky swagger, even now still firmly in place as he gifts my mother a smile that isn't at all pleasant. Elias's worried gaze as his eyes flit from me to my mother and then back to me again. And then finally, Lucas, who regards the entire scene with a cold disregard. "I never should've brought you into this world."

"Oh, please," Mom scoffs. "They've been in this world far longer than you know."

"Wh-what do you mean?" I stutter, even as the four Devils stare at her in confusion.

Lucas's voice is as cutting as an icicle when he speaks next. Just as cold, too. "I can assure you, Mrs. Simone, that I've never been involved in this...world before." His nose crinkles.

Always so polite, that one, even when faced with my evil, bitchy mom.

"It's *Miss* Simone," Mom corrects automatically, stiffening ever so slightly at the mention of my father. He died when I was two, maybe three, and it destroyed a piece of her. The last shred of decency she possessed. I don't remember her at all from *before*, but people tell me she was kind. Funny. Compassionate. Everything she is no longer. "And you don't need to be aware of witches to be hexed by one."

She smiles chillingly, a smile designed specifically to give the room frostbite, and I feel my heart steadily begin to grow in a rapidly shrinking vise. I gape at her wordlessly, sure I heard her wrong.

"What the fuck do you mean?" I demand when I finally find my voice.

Mom levels a blistering glare in my direction. "Language, Peony. I taught you better than that."

"She asked you a fucking question, you fuckity fucking bitch," Cassian seethes, and I can tell that he's using colorful language just to piss my mother off further.

Mom stares at him, aghast at the way he spoke, before a slow, cunning smile twists up her lips. It's not pretty or even elegant, a direct contrast to her immaculate appearance. This particular smile makes her look...evil.

"It's a simple hex bag," she states snootily, snapping her fingers until Ryan scurries forward, dropping something into her open palm. To me, Mom says, "See? How can you not want a man who will do whatever you say, whenever you say?"

"Because I'm not a manipulative bitch like you," I counter, and I take great satisfaction in seeing red blotches erupt on both of her cheeks. She tries to keep her anger in check, but it seeps out of her before she can contain it. Above us, the hanging light shutters and sparks, before going out completely. The table near the front entrance begins to rattle as well.

Reining in her emotions, Mom opens her hand to reveal a tiny brown bag. It's tied at the top with a piece of my white-blonde hair, and a familiar symbol is painted in red across the side.

The mark of the devil.

"Is that...is that my hair?" I instinctively bring a hand to my head, as if I can assure myself that all of my hair is still firmly in place, thank you very much.

"I've been using these hex bags since forever," Mom confesses, turning it around in her palm. She then glances up and spears the four Devils with an unreadable look. "I put one bag in each of your rooms."

"What the fuck?" Karsyn exclaims, and I mentally echo his statement.

What the fuck, indeed.

"It's a rage spell," she continues, glancing back down at the hex bag in her hand. "Simple, really. A fang of a snake. Blood of a sinner. Blade of grass blessed by a priestess. And then your hair, Peony, sealing it all in."

"A rage spell?" I can feel myself growing numb. Not cold necessarily. Just...detached, like I'm floating feet above my body and watching the scene unfold with a clinical detachment. That girl with the haunted amber eyes isn't me. It can't be. That woman with the pitch-black hair isn't my mother. No. No. No.

"Even at a young age, you were too powerful," she continues, tone almost indolent, like she's having a lazy day around the house. "I knew I needed to contain you, however I could. So, I found four of your classmates you seemed to have a liking for. These hex bags are designed to exacerbate their natural rage and hone it in on you. I used this exact spell for many, many years."

"What?" Lucas's voice isn't cold anymore. It's shocked. Broken. Confused. There's a slight hitch to his breathing as he stares at my mother.

"You fucking bitch." Tears stab my eyes as my hands tremble by my sides. I don't know if it's rage or sadness I feel. Hatred or hurt. She's my mother, and she allowed the four of them to torture me relentlessly, all so I wouldn't grow more powerful.

"I needed to keep you adequately subdued," she continues, oblivious to the tsunami of emotions gathering in my head. "And what better way to do that then give you something besides your magic to focus on?"

"You're crazy," Cassian whispers, voice hoarse.

"Maybe." Mother shrugs her shoulders as if she doesn't give a damn either way. "Or maybe I'm just smart."

"I tried to kill myself!" The words are a scream, a cry into the abyss where I'm just begging for someone to hear me. To listen. The entire fucking house begins to rattle as my power escapes its confinement. Outside, thunder booms and lightning streaks through the sky. Rain pelts against the windows, demanding entrance, as a large crack appears in the floor. "I tried to fucking kill myself."

There's no guilt in her gaze. No pity. It's colder than even Lucas's as she regards me with haughty distaste. "I figured that was a possibility when I created the hex—"

"Get the fuck out of my house." The voice doesn't come from me, though it's exactly what I want to say.

Nana appears in the doorway to the kitchen, her entire body shaking. Her face is red and blotchy as if she has been crying, and her violet hair is frazzled, long strands sticking in every direction.

When Mom—I mean, Darlene—makes no move to leave, Nana rushes forward, shoving at her chest.

"Get out of my house. Now!"

Wind whips my long, stringy hair around my face, and the floor begins to shake as Nana's own power joins mine. More lights begin to shatter in an explosion of glass. I feel strong arms wrap around me protectively, shielding me. The leather visible over my chest allows me to see that it's Elias.

"Ryan, come!" Darlene stomps towards the door, pausing to wait for the wiry warlock to open it for her. She glances back only once, her eyes a burning brand against my forehead. "I'll be back later for your decision."

And then she's gone.

And I've never felt more hollow or alone than I do in that moment.

...

I can't talk to the guys. Fuck, I can't even look at them. All I can do is practically shove them out the door, desperate to be alone with my tumultuous thoughts.

Darlene hexed the guys? She was behind their bullying?

My head begins to throb as confusion and pain war for dominance. I stare at my reflection in the bathroom mirror, unable to recognize myself now that my hands are coated red in the name of my revenge. Because these Devils? They weren't meant to bleed. Not by my hands, at the very least.

How can this be? How can my entire life be flipped on its head in a span of seconds?

I know that the Devils aren't all sunshine and roses. There's a darkness to them, one that I recognize in myself. I have no doubt that they're capable of unspeakable cruelty, but at the same time...

How much of what happened in middle school was a product of my mother's spell? How much was real? Did they truly want to hurt me, or did Darlene's spell make them channel all of their pent-up anger and rage onto me?

At one point, Nana knocks on the bathroom door, asking if we can talk, but I ignore her. I don't want to talk to anyone. I just want to stare blindly at the water-stained wall in front of me and feel my heart shrivel into dust.

Pain.

So much pain.

It's like fire ants are crawling through my veins. I want to cry, but my eyes seem incapable of it. I think I cried too much recently and now my tear ducts are empty.

I slowly slide to the ground and wrap my arms around my knees. Staring. Just staring. I don't even know what, exactly, I'm looking at.

When there's another knock, only a half hour later, I jump to my feet and storm to the door, throwing it open hard enough that it careens against the wall.

"What?" I bellow, expecting to see Nana. Instead I see...no one. I glance in both directions, but the hall is empty. It's only then that I notice the object lying demurely on the ground.

A peony flower made of paper.

My curiosity getting the better of me, I bend down and rub it against my cheek. The amount of work someone did to create something so intricate...

On one of the petals, I notice words written in ink. I have to strain my eyes in order to read them.

Where the green ends.

Where the green ends? What the hell is that supposed to mean? And who sent it?

I narrow my eyes suspiciously at the innocent-looking flower, running the tips of my fingers over the soft edges. The resemblance to a peony is almost uncanny. From the green stem to the pink flower unfurling at the tip. It's beautiful, and unlike real flowers, it'll never die.

Whoever sent this just made me immortal.

Where the green ends...

My feet begin to move before my brain can catch up, bypassing the kitchen and dining room until I'm standing on the back porch.

Where the green ends...

My eyes latch on to the manicured lawn that gives way to a forest of maples interspersed with oaks, all currently leafless.

Where the green ends...

Feeling almost euphoric at my discovery, I race barefoot through the grass, loving the way the soft strands prick my skin, and stop at the edge, where green grass transitions into rough dirt.

I glance in both directions, smiling smugly when a splash of pink captures my attention.

I hurry forward and grasp the green stem of a second paper flower. Like before, there's a note written on the leaf.

Where the sun is a triangle.

Where the sun is a...?

Oh.

Quick as lightning, I run back into the house and climb the ladder leading to my attic space. Directly behind my bed is the tiny, triangular window that looks out into the driveway. And on that ledge is a third flower.

Golden stars.

Golden stars? I scour my memory for anything that has golden stars in it but come up blank. I even type it into my phone, wondering if it's a location I've never heard about before.

Nothing.

Golden stars.

Golden stars.

Golden stars.

I begin to pace, ducking when I come too close to a precariously hanging rafter.

Golden stars.

Golden stars.

Golden stars.

A memory hits me seemingly out of nowhere.

"Can I play?" I asked tentatively as I stared at the four large boys standing before me.

The redheaded one, Lucas, smiled brightly, showing off his missing tooth. I didn't think it was fair. I still had yet to have a loose tooth.

"Sure." He tossed me the basketball, which I caught easily.

"Do you know how to play?" the biggest one queried. He had dark, obsidian skin and brown eyes that twinkled when he smiled. His black hair hung in loose waves down to the nape of his neck.

"Like this?" I awkwardly began to bounce the ball, wincing when it got away from me and rolled into the grass.

Karsyn, the kind one with an easygoing grin and tangled blond hair, hurried to retrieve it.

"Good job," Elias said softly. I knew I was awful, but his praise made a smile rise to my face regardless.

We played for only a few minutes before Cassian groaned, throwing his head back against the basketball pole.

"I need to get going," he announced, dropping the ball. "Mom said I needed to be home for dinner by six. Elias, you still coming?"

"Yeah," the brown-haired boy said, nodding. "Lucas? Karsyn? Peony?"

"I need to be going home," Karsyn cut in, lifting his shirt up to wipe sweat off his face. My eyes caught a glimpse of his slender stomach, and heat instantly rose to my cheeks. I glanced away before he could catch me ogling. Boys were stupid and ugly, but that didn't mean I wasn't curious.

As Cassian and Elias left in one direction and Karsyn in another, I found myself alone with Lucas Scott. Something about that boy always intimidated me. He wasn't the largest in the group—to be completely honest, he was the smallest—but his eyes were archaic, almost as if he had seen too much, too soon.

An old soul, *Nana would tell me.*

He was only eight, and life already chipped away at his innocence. There was something hard in his eyes, like a keen knife that was beginning to rust over.

"You want to come home with me and see my room?" Lucas asked, sounding eager. And all thoughts of him being an old soul vanished. He looked extremely young just then. Innocent.

At my timid nod, he grabbed my hand and pulled me away from the park. Mom's driver had dropped me off an hour or so ago and wouldn't be back to pick me up until later tonight. As long as I was in the park before eight, she'd never know I left.

The thought of pulling one over on her, of doing something naughty, made me grin. I no longer dragged my feet into the ground as Lucas led me towards the largest house on the block.

I only had a second to marvel over the gigantic home with more balconies and windows than I could count, before Lucas dragged me inside. A regal looking man in a tailored black suit and white gloves nodded at us when we entered. Lucas merely waved his hand back in greeting.

The redheaded boy led me up a twisting staircase until we reached the second, maybe third, level of the house.

"You live in a castle," I marveled as we stopped in front of a door at the end of the hall.

"Does that mean you're the princess?" His lips twitched in a teasing grin.

"No, silly. It's your house. You're the princess...or prince."

"And what does that make you?" He pushed open the door, stepping back to let me through first.

"The dragon!" I roared at him, and he threw his head back in laughter. I began laughing too, until it dried in my throat. My mouth popped open in shock. "Lucas..."

"My daddy never takes me camping," Lucas whispered, a hint of vulner-ability creeping into his tone. "But I always wanted to sleep under the stars."

He reached behind him to flip off the light switch, and immediately, the room turned dark. Before I could get scared, the tiny stars plastered on the ceiling began to turn on one by one, engulfing the room in a yellowish-tint.

"Golden stars," I whispered dreamily. I didn't need to see him to know that he would be smiling as well.

"Golden stars," he agreed.

I shake my head, clearing the remnants of the memory from my mind, as I stare at the flower in my hand.

Golden stars.

Lucas.

Quickly, I change into a sweater and blue jeans, throw on a pair of socks and shoes, and race outside.

And there he is, standing in my driveway with a bouquet of paper peonies in his hands.

He looks dashing in his teal sweater and khaki pants, his red hair brushed away from his elegant face. His eyes sweep over me slowly, as if he wishes to devour me, as he extends the hand holding the paper flowers.

"I thought we could go on our date tonight beneath the stars," he says simply.

"Lucas..." My body begins to tremble, both because of his grand gesture and my mother's words. It was never truly him, was it? The bullying, the teasing, the pranks. It was always *her.*

"But then I figured that you needed all of us more than you needed just me, and I refuse to be selfish with you any longer." He takes a step around the side of the house, obscuring himself from view, and I hurry to follow him.

Standing in the backyard are all four of my Devils.

Elias steps forward with his hands raised, a wary and guarded expression on his face

"I think we all need to talk."

CHAPTER 50

I swallow heavily, feeling suddenly very small, as I'm surrounded by the four of them.

"We need to talk about this, sweetheart," Cassian whispers, and the term of endearment makes tears spring to my eyes. Fuck, I'm a hot mess. An emotional, wrecking ball of feelings.

I hate it.

"You want to…" A bark of laughter erupts from my chest. "You want to talk? I…I…" My head starts to shake, even as I begin to step backwards. Retreating. Always retreating. Because despite my bravado, I'm a coward, just like my mother. I run from things when they get hard, and sooner or later, people will stop chasing me. It may not be today. Hell, it may not even be tomorrow. But the time will come when I'm truly and completely and irrevocably alone. I'll have no one to blame but myself.

I break into a run before I can think better of it, retreating back inside of the house.

"Peony!" Elias. I'd recognize his raspy voice anywhere.

I make it to the ladder and begin to climb when I feel a hand caress my ankle. Tilting my head down, I see all four Devils standing directly underneath me, expressions unreadable.

"Please," Lucas pleads softly, and I can't resist. I don't want to. Lucas has never in his life begged for anything, but he's doing it now for me. To just listen. To talk. I can do that, right? I can listen to them.

I've only just nodded when all four of them rush to the ladder at the same time. Cassian releases a growl when Lucas jams an elbow into his chest.

"Ow, you fucker. Be careful."

"This is my date," Lucas says calmly as he begins to climb. He reaches the top of the hole just as I pull myself over the edge, collapsing on the wooden boards.

"You coerced her into it," Cassian argues as his head pops up next, eyes lighting up as he surveys my room. "It doesn't count."

"Yes it does," Lucas mumbles in irritation, brushing nonexistent dust off of his clothes. He eyes the room with a barely concealed grimace, gaze lingering on the collection of dust on the highest rafter. His lips tighten as he stares at my small bed, before a tiny smile appears on his face. I follow the direction of his eyes to see he's looking at the three peonies I collected during the impromptu scavenger hunt. He doesn't make a comment, though, as he moves to gingerly sit on a rocking chair in the corner of the attic.

"I don't think this room was designed for big people," Karsyn huffs, bending forward to avoid hitting his head on one of the numerous wooden rafters. He shuffles forward until he's able to sit on my bed beside a nosy Cassian, who's currently rifling through my nightstand. Only Elias remains standing, his back hunched slightly in order to fit.

"You can't go through her drawers!" Karsyn exclaims, whacking Cassian on the back of his head.

"Do you not keep the dildos in your nightstand?" Cassian asks me, sounding genuinely affronted.

"No," I deadpan. "I use the real thing."

The teasing smile on Cassian's face instantly fades as he releases a low growl.

"You know how we feel about you talking about other cocks, sweetheart," he snaps. "Especially the cock of that dumb fuck."

"Her fiancé's?" Elias raises an eyebrow, even as anger hardens his eyes.

"Worst. Her ex-boyfriend, Uriel." Cassian mock shudders.

"Uriel and Ryan are actually brothers," I point out helpfully as I move to sit crisscross on the plush rug in front of my chest.

"Brothers?" Cassian gasps dramatically. "Well I'll be damned, my little spitfire. Why wasn't I invited to that sandwich?" He pauses, left eye twitching, before a severe frown creases his brow. "On second thought, I don't want to see that dumb fuck touching you, so we'll save the threesomes for later, m'kay?"

"Enough." Lucas doesn't yell, but he doesn't need to. I always thought the guys deferred to him because he was bossy and demanding, and while that's true, it's not the whole story. Power radiates from Lucas, and even I feel an undeniable pull towards him that demands I do as he says. I would almost describe it as...respect. Desire to do as he wishes. If we were considered a wolf pack, there's no doubt in my mind that Lucas would be the alpha. "We need to discuss what happened with Peony's mom."

This is the exact conversation I was dreading. I don't even know how to begin to respond. Do I apologize for everything I did in the name of revenge? Do I beg them for forgiveness? Do I even deserve it? I bring my fists up to my eyes and scrub at them desperately, almost as if I can dispel the last few hours from my mind completely.

"Peony..." Lucas's voice is gentler than I ever remember hearing it. "Do you want to start?"

I shake my head rapidly, feeling my heart crack like fine porcelain. I feel tears wetting my fists, but I refuse to drop my hands. I'm nothing if not stubborn, and I'll go to hell before I let another tear fall.

"Peony, maybe you should—"

I cut Karsyn off, still refusing to lift my head. "I'm so fucking sorry."

Silence descends, almost as if the world itself is holding its breath.

My tongue snakes out to lick my upper lip as I think about what to say, how to articulately express how sorry I truly am.

"We say that to each other a lot, don't we?" I chuckle darkly. "Apologize. It seems as if we can never stop hurting one another."

"It's not your fucking fault—" Cassian begins.

"But it is!" I finally drop my hands and lift my head, clenching and unclenching my fists. Every muscle in my body coils tight, ready to spring at a moment's notice. "I put you guys through hell because of what you did to me, and come to find out, it wasn't even your fault." I release another dry, humorless laugh. Even to my own ears, it doesn't quite sound right. It's too...broken.

Is that what I am? Broken? I always knew I would lose myself in this quest for vengeance, but never like this. It feels as if I'm missing too many pieces for the puzzle to ever be complete.

"I felt like shit for the things I did," I confess, scratching absently at my arm. And then, when licks of pain shoot across my skin, I relish in it, digging my nails in even harder. "And I had more planned. A lot more. I wanted you all to pay for everything you did to me. And now I'm sitting here in front of you, feeling fucking broken and empty, and I don't even know if I want your forgiveness. Well..." Blood begins to well on my arm. "That's a lie. I *do* want your forgiveness, but I don't deserve it."

"We feel the exact same way, princess," Karsyn says gently from somewhere behind me on the bed. "We now understand the reasoning for our...extreme rage towards you." Hatred laces his tone, and I know it's directed at my mother, not me. He's no doubt thinking about everything he put me through, every scar on my skin. For years, I blamed the four men sitting in this room, but now I know where that blame truly lies. It's maddening and confusing and frustrating. My head swirls with thousands of thoughts, but trying to grasp only one is like telling an ocean wave that it can't return to the shore. "Despite everything, we're still the ones who put you through that hell. We're still to blame."

"No." I squeeze my eyelids shut. "It's never been you. I did horrible things to you—"

"And we did the same to you," Cassian cuts in seriously. "Why can't we call a fucking truce and put this behind us?"

"Peony." Lucas is suddenly in front of my face, gently dislodging my fingernails from my arm. Pain dances within those blue depths as he stares at the visible scars on my arm where my sweater has risen up, but he doesn't comment on them. Instead, he takes my cheeks in both of his hands and holds my face steady. "We forgive you. But now we need you to forgive us."

"What?" I whisper, blinking to dispel the copious amount of tears hanging suspended on my lashes.

"Forgive us," Lucas breathes. "And forgive yourself."

"I...I..." A thought occurring to me, I pry Lucas's hands off of my face and crawl towards the chest. Using my magic, I pop the lid open before rifling through the contacts, searching...

"What are you doing, baby?" Cassian asks, leaning over the edge of the bed to peek inside.

My probing fingers finally find what I've been looking for, and I remove the brown doll with a triumphant smile.

"What the hell are you doing?" Karsyn demands as I rip a strand of my hair from my head and tie it around the doll's neck. I begin to chant quietly in Latin, ignoring Lucas's hand shaking my shoulder. Once the spell is completed, I thrust the doll at Cassian, who stares at it as if it's a live scorpion crawling up his arm.

"Hurt me," I demand, and his eyes widen.

"What?" he sputters.

"Hurt me and then we can be even." An immense ball of yarn sits inside of my throat, one that makes swallowing impossible. "It's the only way I can say sorry for what my mom did to you. It's the only way I can say sorry for what *I* did to you. So hurt me."

Cassian drops the doll as if it burnt him, his face contorted into an expression of horror.

"Fuck, no!"

"Karsyn?" I plead with the normally jovial football player. Now though, his lips droop into a deep frown, one that makes him look more like his dad than ever before.

"You know I can't do that to you," he whispers, tears in his eyes.

"Elias?" I turn towards the third Devil, who glances at the doll with heady distaste. He doesn't even need to speak for me to know his answer.

I turn towards the last Devil. The cruelest.

Lucas cocks his head to the side, staring at me as if he wishes to dig into my soul and uncover all of my secrets. Never breaking eye contact, he reaches forward and grabs the doll from the bed. Immediately, the other three begin shouting at him, threatening him, cursing at him, but Lucas doesn't respond as he slowly lifts the doll in the air…

Before setting it gently onto the rocking chair he abandoned.

"No one is going to hurt you, Peony," he says simply, rising gracefully from the floor to his feet. He extends a hand to me, and I mechanically grab for it, allowing him to hoist me up. I stumble, my legs still wobbly and leaden from my meltdown, but Lucas grabs my hips, keeping me steady. "No one." It's a vow. A promise. A prayer.

It happens right then and there. The last tiny piece of anger I held on to, that I carried close to my chest, vanishes, floating away in a strong gust of wind. There's no pain. No sadness. No hatred.

Just need and lust and something I would almost call love.

Lucas stares into my eyes as if he's waited for this moment his entire life. As if he's traveled aimlessly through the desert for years, for centuries, and stumbled upon the first stream of fresh water for miles and miles. He looks at me as if he wishes he could devour me whole.

"Fucking hell. I don't want you to ever talk about hurting yourself again," Cassian gripes, forcing me to break eye contact with Lucas and shattering the moment between us. The large man stands directly behind me, face solemn, and I hate that I'm the one who put that expression on my smiling giant's face.

Before I can second guess myself, before I can truly think about the ramifications of doing this in a room with three other men, I grab the back of Cassian's neck and force his lips down to mine. Shock makes him freeze up before he responds to my kisses with heated, passionate ones of his own. Slowly, the ice surrounding him from our conversation begins to melt, bringing the carefree, joking man back to me once more.

I can feel another body at my back, and at first, I think it's Elias. But when he begins kissing the back of my neck, hands roaming underneath my sweater, I realize that the clover scent belongs to Karsyn.

My breathing stalls as Cassian finally releases my lips, his own swollen from our kisses, and twists my head towards Karsyn. My quarterback wastes no time teasing the edges of my mouth with nibbles and languid licks. I don't even know if we can call what we're doing kissing, but it still sends heat racing through me.

Cassian tugs at the bottom of my sweater, asking without words if he can remove it, and I pull away from Karsyn's lips just long enough to toss it over my head.

Karsyn reclaims my mouth, and when his tongue traces the contours of my lips, I gasp and he takes advantage, plunging his tongue inside.

Cassian grips both of my breasts through the flimsy material of my lace bra and begins to knead them, coaxing my nipples into sharp points.

"Doesn't she have the prettiest tits?" Elias's husky voice comes from somewhere behind Cassian, and it's only then that I remember that all four of the Devils are present.

I break away from Karsyn and take a step to the side, my chest heaving as I survey the room.

Karsyn and Cassian remain where they were, eyes half-mast with lust and need. Their erections strain against their blue jeans.

Elias must've relocated to the bed, for he's leaning against the pillows, stroking his cock that he freed from the confines of his pants.

And then there's Lucas.

He has once more moved to the rocking chair and holds the voodoo doll tenderly between his hands. When he catches me staring, he drags a finger down the doll's stomach. Goosebumps erupt on my flesh as I feel his touch, feel it as if he's actually here, physically caressing me.

"Is this okay?" Lucas whispers as all eyes focus on him.

I can barely breathe as I nod once.

"Please, Lucas," I beg as his teasing finger moves to the doll's chest.

Instantly, my nipples bead even further, and I cry out, my back arching into the phantom touch.

"Fucking hell," Cassian hisses as he whips his shirt off one-handed and wiggles out of his jeans and boxers. He unabashedly stands in the middle of the room, naked as the day he was born. He fists his cock while his eyes drop to my chest. "Though I think this show will be a little better if we can see those pretty tits."

Before I can even blink, Elias has crawled behind me and unhooks the bra, allowing the straps to fall down my arms.

I don't feel any embarrassment or fear as the material flutters to the ground, leaving me half-naked in front of the four of them. How could I, when they're staring at me as if I'm the most beautiful thing they've ever seen?

A banked fire flickers to life in Lucas's eyes as he once more drags his fingers across both of the doll's breasts, directly where my nipples are.

Another gasp leaves me as I fall backwards onto the bed, my head landing on Elias's thigh. I swear my breasts have a direct line of communication to my pussy, and all of them scream at me to come.

Cassian appears at the foot of the bed and grabs the waistband of my pants, dragging them down my legs until I'm left in only a pair of panties.

"Fuck, you're already so wet for us, sweetheart," he breathes as he drops to his knees before me. At the same moment, Lucas lowers his finger between the legs of the doll, and my pussy clenches around an invisible touch.

"I like 'sweetheart' better than 'baby,'" I gasp as I stare down my nose at Cassian. He grins slyly.

"Yeah? I've been working on nicknames for you. Though I do think my favorite is Tooty-toot-toot."

"It's a little bit of a mouthful, wouldn't you say?" I tease.

"Speaking of mouthfuls…" Cassian trails off as Karsyn moves to kneel on the bed beside me, his erect cock bobbing directly over my face. He's naked as well, the glorious planes of his golden abs on display. It never fails to amaze me how stunning these men are, as if they're gods from the old world personified into human men.

I crane my neck back to lick his tip, before trailing my tongue down the side of his cock and to his balls, taking first one and then another into my mouth.

Elias, whose leg my head still rests on, moves his hands to my breasts and begins to play with my nipples.

"You want to play another game?" Cassian asks as he sucks at my pussy through the thin material of my panties. My back bows, and I dig my nails into Elias's thigh.

"No. Games," I manage to grit out.

"Cassian," Lucas drawls from the corner of the room where he rocks back and forth in the chair like some sort of sexy psychopath. The doll rests on the table beside him as he leans forward. "Lick that sweet pussy. Make our girl come. Elias, play with those breasts and suck those pretty nipples. And Karsyn, let her swallow your cock."

It takes less than a second for the guys to move into position. Cassian drags me to the edge of the bed and settles between my knees as Elias gently places my head on a pillow, moving to lay beside me. Karsyn places his cock between my lips, waiting until I open up for him.

From there, everything moves so fast.

Cassian removes my panties and sets to work on eating my pussy like a man starved. There's no denying that he's skilled with that tongue of his, but instead of jealousy, I feel grateful, especially when he begins to make figure eights.

Elias latches on to one of my nipples as he reaches across my body to tweak my neglected breast. He lifts himself up so he's able to dangle over me, seemingly unconcerned or oblivious to the fact that Karsyn's cock is inches from his face. He alternates between both of my breasts, leaving a trail of saliva in his wake.

I hollow my cheeks as I work Karsyn, bringing my hand up to capture the part of his base that my mouth can't quite reach. I allow my teeth to graze the sensitive underside of his cock, taking pleasure in the rumble I extract from him.

When Cassian bites down on my clit, I can't help but moan around Karsyn's cock.

"Fucking hell, princess," he swears, gripping my head so he can fuck himself into my mouth.

I can feel myself nearing that invisible ledge, but before I can plunge over, Cassian removes his lips from my aching core. They glisten when he smiles, and he cheekily licks my juices away.

"I need to fuck you. Is that okay, sweetheart?"

I moan and writhe inarticulately.

"He needs words," Lucas demands from the corner of the room. He grips the armrests of the chair, his knuckles white. I can see the outline of his cock against his khakis, but he doesn't make a move to touch himself.

Or touch me.

"Yes, Cassian. Yes."

Cassian waits until Lucas throws him a condom—does he seriously just carry them around with him at all times?—before lining the head of his massive cock up with my entrance.

Inch by excruciating inch, he pushes himself inside of me, only stopping when he's seated to the hilt. My pussy squeezes around his girth, demanding we move, as Elias continues to nibble at my breasts, no doubt leaving marks.

As one, Karsyn and Elias pull themselves away from me, and I actually cry out at the loss. But before I can think too hard on that, Cassian begins to fuck me in earnest.

He leans forward, his hard, muscular body hovering over mine, as his hands play with my jiggling breasts.

"You're so fucking perfect. So beautiful."

He abruptly grabs my legs, swinging them around his waist so my lower half no longer touches the bed. This new position has me seeing stars as he continues to rut in and out of me.

"I'm close, sweetheart. So fucking close," he growls, and I can feel his cock shudder inside of me. His entire body tenses, dark muscles rippling, as he roars his release. "Fuck! Fuck! Fuck!"

He barely pulls himself out of me before Elias is there, a condom already in place. He flips me so I'm on my hands and knees, my ass to him. Karsyn once more kneels in front of me, his cock at direct level with my mouth.

"Do you know how hot you look right now?" Cassian states from somewhere in the room.

I sheepishly flick my eyes to see him standing on one side of the rocking chair, leaning against the wall. Still naked.

And Lucas...

His pierced cock is in his hand as his eyes flicker from my swinging breasts, to my visible pussy lips, to my heated eyes. And just like before, when he stares at me, the rest of the world fades away. It's just him and me. Us. Energy charges the air around us as he slowly brings his hand to his mouth, licking the length of it, before dropping it back to his hard cock. He rubs his fingers across the slit at the top, collecting pre-cum, before he moves it to his base.

And then all thoughts leave my mind as Elias slams into me from behind, his piercing sliding against my pussy walls. Pleasure quickly overtakes the initial discomfort as I open my mouth wide, allowing Karsyn to drive his monster cock through my lips. I graze my teeth along his dick, and his eyes flash in warning.

"Be nice, princess," he says huskily. Instead of answering with words, I bite down gently on his cock, and he jerks, praises and curse words both falling from his lips.

I quickly find that I don't even need to move my head that much. Each time Elias slams into me, I jerk forward until my lips reach the base of Karsyn's cock. And again. And again. And again.

I see stars when Elias finally takes mercy on me and plays with my clit.

"Jesus, Peony!" Karsyn shouts when his cock reaches the back of my throat.

And when I finally come, it's not a measly little firework. It's an explosion. Thousands of them. Tears prick my eyes as I erupt around Elias's cock. It doesn't take too long for both men to join me, Karsyn shooting ropes of sticky cum down my throat, all of which I swallow like a fucking champ. Elias roars his release as well, fingers tightening on my hip bones, before we collapse in a sweaty, tangled mess on my bed.

Cassian wastes no time in doing a belly flop, landing half on Elias and half on me.

"Dude, I can feel your cock against my thigh," Elias mumbles, but he sounds too tired to do anything about it.

"Don't care," Cassian snipes. "Maybe lick it and it'll go away."

"I thought you lick things to keep them," Karsyn murmurs, voice already laden with sleep.

"In that case..." Cassian twists his head to lick a long trail from the column of my neck to my boob. "My tit."

I swat at him.

"Shut up."

And this...

This is perfection. This is something I never knew I needed until I had it.

It only occurs to me then that something is missing. Or rather *someone*.

I push myself onto my elbows to see Lucas still sitting in the rocking chair in the corner of the room. His cock is tucked back in his pants, almost as if he never had it out in the first place. Not a hair on his pretty red head is out of place. It makes me sad that I didn't get to see him come. The memory of the last time he jerked off in front of me plays on a continuous loop in my brain, causing flames to ignite down below.

Lucas's lips twitch when he meets my gaze, his blue eyes softening ever so slightly.

"Sleep, my beloved," he whispers.

And I do.

CHAPTER 51

I wake up in a body that isn't my own.

Well, obviously, it is my own, there's no doubt about that. Same pasty skin with a hint of gold. Same short nails, the purple polish peeling away. Same white hair cascading around my face. I'm sure that if I were to look into the mirror, I would see amber eyes staring back at me. That I would have a few barely visible freckles on my nose. That a slight flush would color my cheeks from last night's activities.

But I have no control of myself.

I feel my feet touch the ground a full minute before my mind catches up. The last thing I remember is falling asleep between Elias and Karsyn with Cassian draped between my legs, his hand on my stomach. And then, I dreamed the most perfect dream. I can't recall the explicit details, but I know that all four of my Devils made an appearance.

I try to open my mouth and scream, try to demand to know what is happening, but my lips remain shut. All I can do is move forward one painstaking step at a time. Tears burn my eyes as I find myself at the hole to the attic, pulling it open and slowly climbing down the ladder.

What's happening to me?

I'm reduced to nothing but a marionette, and a puppeteer somewhere pulls my strings. These legs are no longer my own.

I'm still naked as I walk barefoot through the halls, the only light from the crescent moon dangling precariously in the inky black sky. That makes this entire experience ten times worse. I feel vulnerable and afraid. Why is this happening?

Once more, I try to open my mouth and scream, but it's like my lips have been sewn shut. I can't do anything more than release a muffled, choked sound.

"Peony?" Lucas. He appears around the corner of the kitchen, holding a steaming mug of coffee in his hand. I'm not even surprised to find him up before the sun is even a speckle in the sky. "You must be freezing." He places his coffee cup down on the hallway table and then removes his sweater one-handed. Instead of giving that to me, though, he takes off his white undershirt and gently slides it over my unresponsive limbs. It reaches the middle of my thighs. "What are you doing up already?"

I try to open my mouth to tell him that it's not my doing, that I don't want this, but the words remain trapped. Tears continue to wordlessly cascade down my cheeks as his blue eyes narrow in suspicion.

He takes a step closer, hands raised as if he means to calm me like one would a frighten horse, but my own hand is already moving before he can make contact.

I can feel my fingers form a fist as I pull my arm back and punch him as hard as I can across the face. Pain reverberates through my hand as a tiny whimper escapes me.

"What the…?"

Before Lucas can finish his surprised question, I lift my knee to his stomach. He curls in on himself, and I watch as the horror in his eyes slowly, gradually, turns into understanding.

"Who's doing this to you?" he demands, and I can't help but note the blood snaking across his plush red lips from my fist.

I try to shake my head, try to tell him that I don't know, but I'm already moving. Moving. Moving.

Lucas lunges forward and wraps both of his arms around my chest, restraining me. My body kicks and buckles, attempting desperately to get away, while my mind screams at me to stop fighting. To remain in his arms.

More and more tears drip down my cheeks, landing on my mouth.

I can feel my head rear back, headbutting Lucas, followed immediately by his bark of pain. I pray that I didn't break his nose.

I spin towards him as he doubles over, holding his face with both hands as more blood drips onto his still bare chest. Before he can make another move for me, I pull my leg back and kick him as hard as I can in the nuts.

"Don't come find her." It's me speaking, but they aren't my words. The cadence is all wrong. Too dark. Too angry. Too malevolent.

Lucas spits out blood as he once more attempts to amble to his feet. "I will find you, and I will fucking kill you. Do you hear me? There is nowhere you can hide."

The person controlling me uses my mouth to break into laughter, the cruel, cold sound grating on my nerves.

"I'd like to see you try, Lucas Scott." Once more, my knee snaps up, knocking Lucas in the face. He falls to the ground, unconscious.

Fuck. Fuck. Fuck.

I'm shaking as my body mechanically turns back towards the doorway, stepping outside and into the bitter cold. With no sunlight to warm the normally tepid air, it's freezing, goosebumps exploding on my arms. A bitter wind blows my hair around my face as my feet move over gravel and pebbles towards a tiny car waiting in my driveway.

I try to see the driver, try to see if I recognize anyone, but the windows are tinted.

The trunk of the car pops open, and it's inside there I go.

Please no, I beg silently in my mind, but I can't get the words past my lips. They're simply trapped inside. Caged and pacing, like a restless prisoner.

I crawl into the trunk, my entire head twisting without my consent so I can't see who comes and closes it.

I send out a plea into the universe, to anyone who could possibly hear me, but I don't expect to receive an answer in return.

Bad girls like me? We never do.

...

I don't know how long we drive, but it's enough time for me to moderately regain control of my flaccid body. The process is slow-going. First, my toes begin to wiggle, followed by my ankles. And then, my fingers flutter like I'm doing jazz hands.

All too soon, I can feel the car pull to a stop, and I'm jerked forward, rolling once before my head hits the backseats of the car.

With my ear pressed against the seats, I can hear soft, murmured voices, but I can't make out if they're male or female. Young or old. They sound almost distorted, as if they're using magic to disguise the sound.

My back faces the opening of the trunk, so I hear rather than see as it's pulled open. I shiver as another gust of frigid air races over me, but that is nothing compared to the tremors that take over my body when I'm pulled against a strong chest.

I will my neck to move, if only so I can see who holds me captive, but my stubborn body remains weak and compliant.

I hear the distinct sound of leaves and twigs crackling beneath heavy boots. A forest, perhaps? That noise transitions into a loud thumping sound. Maybe wooden floorboards? Brick? Asphalt?

After what feels like an eternity, I'm roughly dropped onto a cold, smooth surface. My legs are spread towards each corner, as are my arms, until I'm lying spread-eagle on the table.

No, not a table.

A fucking altar.

It's only then that I regain control of my body. It's fast and sudden, but for the first time since this horror show began, I'm able to thrash wildly, attempting to escape the ropes holding me hostage.

"Let me go!" I scream, my voice raspy from crying.

"No can do," a familiar voice says from somewhere behind me. I twist my head to the side desperately just as he steps from the shadows, like some sort of dark, dangerous god. He holds the voodoo doll I created of myself in his hands.

"Emmett?" I whisper as he moves to stand to the right of the altar, running the backs of his fingers across my cheek and then my neck.

"The one and only." His lips quirk in the beginnings of a smile as he drops the illusion he must've been holding this entire time.

Red eyes, the darkest, bloodiest red eyes I've ever seen in my life, peer back at me.

"You're a…"

"A Blood, yes," he croons as he runs his hand over the top of my sweaty hair. "And you, my dear friend, are a little witch." He leans forward until his peppermint breath wafts across my cheek. Why does his breath have to smell so fucking good? Shouldn't villains have a distinct, rancid smell to them?

His next words send a cold chill racing down my spine.

"And I'm going to drink your blood. After, of course, I have my fun with you."

CHAPTER 52

"Emmett, you don't want to do this," I beg as he straightens his spine, moving away from the stone altar towards a small table. I see a collection of wicked looking knives, a few syringes, and even a saw or two. He picks up each blade individually, holding them up to the flickering hanging bulb overhead, before setting them back on the table, clicking his tongue.

"I'm afraid I do, pretty girl," he says casually as he grabs another sharp blade. This one is decorated with runes and gemstones—it must be the one they use for the sacrifice.

And unlike the triplets, he's not simply going to drink my blood. He's going to kill me.

As he continues to peruse the weapons before him, I allow my eyes to travel around the room. When I escape this table—and there's no doubt in my mind that I will—I need a way to get out.

It appears to be a warehouse of some sort. At least, I'm assuming it is. There are distinct, corrugated iron walls on all four sides of me. The ground is mostly hard-packed dirt; it appears as if the floor has rotted away. Graffiti adorns every empty space available.

Aside from the altar and table, the room is barren. There's not another soul in sight.

If my calculations are correct, we were in the car for about a half hour. So that means that this warehouse isn't too far from town.

And it also means that Nana can track me.

I hold on to that hope, even as the image of a bloodied Lucas lying sprawled across the ground plays on repeat in my mind. A lump forms in my throat, one that I quickly swallow down. He's going to be okay. We all will.

"I didn't know you were a witch at first," Emmett drawls casually as he saunters back to me. A curved blade rests snugly in his hand as he pulls up a stool. "I was such a fucking idiot. How could I not sense all of this power wafting off of you?" He inhales deeply, his tongue snaking out to lick his lips. "It's divine."

Mustering all of my courage, I spit directly in his face. I have the pleasure of seeing shock splay itself across his features before he backhands me. My head whips to the side as blood forms in my mouth, but still, I maintain my smile.

"You crazy fucking bastard. Do you really think you'll get out of this alive?"

"You're talking about your grandmother, correct?" Emmett offers me a boy-next-door type of smile, one that displays his dimples, but instead of the lust I once felt, it makes me sick to the stomach.

His words finally register with me, and I snap my eyes open in horror. "If you hurt her—"

"Don't worry." He waves a hand dismissively. "Grandma is alive and well. I can't say the same about you, however."

"She'll come for me," I reply, feeling the truth of it down to my very bones. "They all will."

"Maybe." He shrugs his shoulders. "But that's assuming Lucas wakes up in time to warn her. That's assuming that she has all of the ingredients for the tracking spell on hand. That's assuming that you're not already dead yet."

"Fuck you," I hiss.

"I wish," he whispers wistfully, running the serrated edge of his blade down my cheek. Only my eyes move to follow it as he rests it on the hollow of my throat. He doesn't apply enough pressure to break skin, but I can feel the threat lingering in the air. "Honestly, Peony, I might've spared you if you've just given in to me. I liked you. Truthfully, I liked you. We could've had something special together." He shakes his head sadly before anger darkens his features once more. "But then you had to go and fuck all of those little bastards. Tell me, Peony. Were they worth it? Were they worth your life?"

I smile cruelly at him as his blade presses even further against my neck, finally nicking the skin.

"Just their cocks alone were worth it," I say breezily, and his face contorts in unbridled rage. Emmett's a bomb ready to explode with only the slightest provocation, but maybe, just maybe, the impending blast will somehow set me free.

It's either that or die tied to an altar.

He drags the knife from my neck to my arm, carving a clean slice directly over my scars. I release a gasp of pain as blood begins to flow freely to the floor. It won't kill me, not yet, but it hurts like a fucking bitch.

"They're little pricks," he whispers desperately, his face inches from mine. "You can do so much better, Peony. You *did* do so much better. With me."

I laugh until tears prick my eyes, even as he begins to growl threateningly. When I finally get myself under control, I hiss, "With you? With a murderous fucking asshole who has me tied up and is cutting me?"

"I only do it to stay alive!" Emmett bellows. "You know that we need blood to survive."

"You don't have to kill anyone," I press. "The triplets don't." They never confirmed it, but I assume they take the blood from Nana. I've never seen scars on her, though, so it makes me think that they use small needles to draw her blood directly from her veins. The only reason their eyes aren't red now is because they're not using dark magic, unlike Emmett. Unlike those other Bloods who attempted to kidnap me.

Emmett's laugh reminds me vaguely of a sword covered in frost. It's as icy and as deadly, the noise immediately instilling fear inside of me.

"There's a lot you don't know," Emmett whispers, leaning forward to lick a pathway up my cheek. I attempt to turn my head away, but his other hand—the one holding the knife—grips my chin tightly. "Don't fucking look away from me."

"Fuck you," I snap.

"I'll admit," Emmett continues, ignoring my outburst. To my immense relief, he releases my chin and steps away from me. "There's something addicting about the power drinking blood gives you. And when you drain a witch completely?" He makes a low groan, eyes rolling into the back of his head. "It's pure bliss."

"You're insane," I whisper, and I realize it's the wrong thing to say when he lurches towards me, once more sitting on that squeaky stool.

"It's an addiction," he protests vehemently. "I thought you, of all people, would understand." He nods pointedly towards the numerous scars on my wrist.

"It's not the fucking same, and you know it."

"Pot meet kettle," he dismisses.

"You need help, Emmett. A lot of fucking help. You need—" My words cut off as he brings the knife back to my body and cuts from my collarbone to my elbow. A scream wrenches from my throat as I throw my head back, agony pulsating through my veins.

"What was that?" Emmett cups his ear with the hand holding the bloody knife. "I couldn't hear you. Insane, you say?"

"Fuck you!" I wheeze through my tears. I can see the violence in his eyes, teetering on the brink of absolute destruction, like an earthquake that destroys entire cities in a span of seconds.

"I'm. Not. Insane!" he roars as he brings his knife back down, this time to the sliver of thigh visible where Lucas's shirt ends.

It suddenly occurs to me all of the things he could do to my body. I'm tied up. Alone. Practically naked.

The fear I felt previously is nothing compared to the fear running rampant inside of me now.

"Look how pretty you bleed for me," Emmett murmurs as he runs his hand through the blood on my thighs. He inches it higher, higher, higher...

"Emmett, enough," a gruff voice commands. Emmett freezes, his hand only a few inches away from my pussy, and releases a low growl.

"You said—"

"I didn't say you could touch the sacrifice," the newcomer snaps. "Step. Away."

Emmett's eyes scream disobedience, but he reluctantly takes a step backwards, bringing the knife to his lips and licking my blood from the blade. His eyes remain on me the entire time, a promise in his gaze.

"We need to do the ceremony before people come looking for her," the obvious leader snaps. Out of my peripheral vision, I can see around six people step around the altar, each wearing a dark robe and hood.

Only one man doesn't have his hood pulled up as he steps directly in front of me, all sharp edges and tawny muscles.

"No," I whisper as I begin to sob. Betrayal like I never felt before embeds itself in my heart. Everything hurts as I stare at the man I trusted, even when I was pissed at him for lying to me. The pain is painted on my heart like a tattoo I can never remove. It's a colorful mural, etched across the surface forever.

Gabriel meets my stare with a bland look of his own before nodding towards one of the other Bloods.

"The dagger," he instructs, holding his hand out. A small cloaked figure, more than likely a female, places the ornamented blade I noted earlier in his hand.

"I'm sorry," Gabriel whispers as I cry. I want to beg him to stop, to spare me. My pain is as thick and as cloying as the shadows currently pressing in on all sides of me.

This is it. My death. It's funny how everything can fall into perspective when you're staring death in the eye. And my Grim Reaper just happens to have a pretty face that belies all of his secrets and cruelty.

I think of my mother just then, and I realize that I can never forgive her for what she did to me. I don't even want to. If I have to give up my magic in order to be free of her, then so be it.

I want to apologize to Nana, to tell her I love her and that she's the only family I have left. I have no idea if Polo and Christian are behind this as well, but if they aren't, if they're truly not aware of their brother's actions, then I'll say sorry to them as well. My actions were those of a petty teenager. They lied to me, sure, but there's no reason for me to hold on to all of this anger and hurt.

I think of Mariabella. How in a span of weeks, she became the best friend a girl could ask for. I hope that once I'm dead, she'll find the courage to be her true self. Because Mariabella? She's perfect just the way she is. The world needs to know her. If her parents can't accept that, then they can fuck off.

And finally, I allow my mind to drift to the Devils. I came into town hating them, but somewhere along the way, that hate became warped and twisted. I can't name precisely when it happened, only that it did. Instead of anger or even fear, I feel nothing but love. I honestly don't know if I'm in love with all four of them, one of them, or none of them. But I want to give a relationship a try. I imagine it'll be unconventional and sinful, but I shouldn't have expected anything else from the four Devils who stole my heart.

I squeeze my eyelids shut, unwilling to see the blade pierce my heart, when I hear a scream. Immediately, my eyes snap open to see Gabriel wrenching the dagger from the chest of the Blood he just killed.

He rushes for my tied wrists at the same time three more Bloods descend on him. He has just enough time to cut away one of the ropes restraining me before he's brought to the ground.

I use my now free hand to quickly untie my other wrist before moving to my ankles. My movements are jerky and frantic, and I keep glancing in both directions to ensure the Bloods are occupied.

Gabriel must've lost the knife in the scuffle, for he's now sitting on one of the men's stomach and pounding into his face. He looks savage and feral, his eyes emanating an almost incandescent rage.

When a second Blood runs at him, Gabriel stealthily spins around and flips him onto his back. The hood falls away, and I'm able to see one of the men who attempted to kidnap me a few days earlier.

I finally free myself from the last restraint and stagger unsteadily, almost drunkenly, to my feet.

A Blood lunges at me, red eyes glimmering in the dim lighting, and I throw my hands out, blasting him with a wave of my power. It's weak, barely an ember after being contained for so long, but it still propels him across the room, where he careens off the wall and lands in a heap on the floor, his body still.

Another Blood advances, this one female, and I can hear her chanting under her breath. I don't recognize the spell, but I can sense the darkness wafting off of her in waves. It shrouds my skin in oil. Before she can finish her spell, I use one hand to call on my fire power and the other to shake the earth under her feet. She stumbles, a pained cry escaping her mouth, as I shove the fireball into her face.

Her skin blisters and cracks as she screams into the night, but I don't relent. Only when she's face down on the ground do I step away from her fallen body. My magic reserves are rapidly depleting, and I know I'm not going to be able to last long without a weapon. Without *something*. Still, even when my power drops to its lowest, it still rivals the potency of the Bloods', despite the fact that they're using dark magic.

Just keep fighting, Peony. Keep fucking fighting.

Gabriel's going hand-to-hand with another Blood as I wobble towards the table, searching desperately for a weapon that can help him. My fingers close over the handle of an axe as I heft it up.

"Peony!" Gabriel screams, and his warning is the only thing that saves my life. The female Blood I noted before had been creeping behind me on silent feet, the dropped sacrificial dagger in her hand. I have just enough time to swing my axe at her, watching in abject horror as she tumbles to the ground, blood pouring from her stomach.

I hear a sharp inhale from behind me, and I turn, prepared to leap into the fray, when I see Gabriel tumble to his knees.

No. No. No.

"Gabriel!" I scream in horror as he stares from me to the knife protruding from his stomach. When he glances back up, something akin to grim acceptance shines in his gaze. And I know without a shadow of doubt, the split second he took to warn me about my attacker was a split second he didn't have.

"I'm sorry," he mouths to me as his emerald green eyes well with tears.

"I always knew we couldn't trust you," Emmett says to Gabriel, whistling softly under his breath.

"Gabriel! Emmett, no!" I run forward with the axe just as Emmett swings his sword in a swooping arc.

And Gabriel's head falls to the ground and rolls, his eyes dim.

Time stops. Everything stops. All I can see is the man who risked his life for mine. My family. One of the very few people in this world

I can claim to care about. And that's what family is, after all. Forming indestructible bonds that simply cannot be severed, because we don't allow them to. Because we don't want them to. Because we fight tooth and nail to keep them whole and strong.

"No!" I begin to sob desperately as I stare, just stare, at his lifeless figure. Gabriel sacrificed himself for me. To save *me*. I can live for centuries, and I'll never find a way to repay him. How can a person live with that knowledge? How can I go about my day knowing that a man's dead because of me? "Why did you do it, you stupid old man?" I scream, my heart splintering in two. Searing agony grips both halves of the organ and refuses to let go. "Why?"

"Because he loved you," Emmett interjects, rolling his eyes as if the idea is absurd. "Because you were his family."

"I'm going to fucking kill you!" I scream, lifting the axe and racing forward.

But like before, my feet abruptly still and my hands drop uselessly to my side. My fingers slowly unclench from where it was holding the axe in a death-grip. The weapon clatters harmlessly against the floor.

"I don't think so, my sweet girl," Emmett whispers. He holds up the voodoo doll with a sinister smile. "Aren't you forgetting something?"

CHAPTER 53

"Emmett, please, I am begging you. Please don't do this," I plead, refusing to allow my eyes to flicker down to where Gabriel's headless body now lies. I know that the second I see it, the second I see *him*, I'll fall apart. And at the moment, that will do me no good.

I have no idea if Gabriel really reverted back to his old ways and decided to spare my life, or if he was simply undercover this entire time for the witch council. That doesn't matter. He saved my life, knowing that it would be the end of his long one.

Fuck! Stop thinking about him, Peony! I mentally berate myself.

"Emmett, please—" I try again, but before I can get another word out, my lips tighten into a straight line. I look to see Emmett has his hand over the doll's mouth, eyes wild and frantic as he stares at me.

"No talking," he hushes, mouth twisted in a rictus grin. He glances around at the bodies of his fallen comrades. Gabriel managed to eliminate all of the ones I hadn't before he fell, and dead bodies now litter the ground around us. Blood pools at my feet, staining my bare soles, and I know this moment will haunt me until the end of time. I'll close my eyes, and I'll see this exact, horrendous moment. Everything from Emmett's cocky smile, to Gabriel's decapitated head, to the bodies of the two women and one man I just killed, are seared into my brain.

"Now…" Emmett begins as he slowly unzips his pants and pulls out his erect cock. He begins to stroke it lazily, almost lackadaisically, his eyes never leaving mine. "I can still do the ceremony without all of these…" His lips twitch in disgust as he decides on a word for his fellow Bloods. "Failures," he says at last. "More for me, I suppose. But…" He moves until he's directly in front of me and slowly runs his finger down the doll's side.

Unlike with Lucas, I feel nothing but revulsion at his intrusive, slimy touch.

I try to scream at him, yell all of the profanities I can come up with, but his other hand remains over my mouth.

He brings a blade, the same blood-soaked knife that stabbed Gabriel, to the front of the doll and slowly lowers it to the middle of its thighs. My shirt splits right down the middle, baring my breasts to him.

Anger like I never felt before thrums through me like a fiery inferno, consuming everything in its path. I squeeze my eyelids shut as he leans forward and kneads first one breast and then the other.

"I imagined this for so long," he breathes as his hand drifts lower until it once more reaches the blood on my thigh. "You have no idea what you do to me."

"Hey! Get the fuck away from her!" a furious voice bellows, and a second later, Emmett is blasted away from me. The doll drops from his fingers, landing in a puddle of Gabriel's blood, as I spin towards the newcomers.

Elias, Lucas, Cassian, and Karsyn stand in the entryway of the warehouse, radiating a raw and primal fury. Behind them are Christian, Polo, and Nana.

It was Karsyn who spoke, I believe, and that spell was definitely one of Nana's. I would recognize her magical signature anywhere.

Before I can run towards them, Emmett clamors unsteadily to his feet, blood dripping from a wound on his head, and picks up the fallen voodoo doll.

"Not so fucking fast. Unless you want your little witch to kill herself." Unbidden, my hand reaches for an unused knife resting on the table and holds it to my throat. I shake desperately as my tear-stained eyes flicker from face to face.

The four Devils hold baseball bats, kitchen knives, and any other makeshift weapon they could probably find around the house. I imagine Nana tried to get them to stay behind, but I know for a fact that their stubbornness knows no bounds. If she didn't bring them, then they would've found their own way to come.

Nana fans out with Christian and Polo on either side of her, hands raised and bright light emitting from their palms. Their faces are set in fierce determination, eyes as hard as granite. I don't think they've seen Gabriel's dead body yet, and for that, I'm glad. I want to spare them the pain, at least for now.

"You're outnumbered, boy," Christian informs, his usually chipper voice solemn.

"Maybe." Emmett smiles darkly, one that shows the blood splatter on his white teeth. "But do you really think you can get to me faster than I can cut Peony's pretty, little throat?" He brings the doll's hand closer to its throat. I yelp as blood wells once more, joining the already steady stream from when he previously cut me.

"Let her go, you fucking asshole!" Cassian roars, his bat raised.

"What are you going to do about it, you magicless swine?" With a flick of his wrist, Emmett sends Cassian flying in one direction. My large, smiling giant careens against the warehouse wall before collapsing on the floor with a pained groan.

At the same moment, Polo takes a step forward, his lips moving too quietly for me to hear as he chants a spell.

"Naughty, naughty," Emmett tsks, turning towards Polo. With a malicious sneer, Emmett twists the doll's arm, and my own arm jerks wildly to the side, the bone audibly snapping in half. Pain explodes inside of me like someone lit up dozens of fireworks. I scream in agony, my entire body sagging slightly to the side. I can feel myself growing dizzy from pain and blood loss, but the magic of the voodoo doll prohibits me from doing anything but standing here.

"I'm going to kill you," Elias thunders, but Emmett merely laughs.

"Look how well that turned out for the last guy." He nods his shaggy blond hair towards Gabriel's dead body. And I can see the exact moment Nana recognizes his dark hair. The exact moment when Gabriel's brothers realize that this sadistic prick killed their triplet.

It's the slightest change, and if I didn't know Nana as well as I do, I would've missed it. Her eyes seem to shutter, almost like a lunar eclipse. All of the color drains from her face as she stares at the man she once desperately loved. The man she *still* desperately loves. But I also see the moment she hardens herself, becoming nothing but a bereft shell with only one goal on her mind—saving me.

Polo releases an agonized scream, running towards Emmett, but the blond-haired Blood merely flicks him away with a wave of his wrist. He's so much more powerful than us, the blood of dozens of witches currently coursing through his veins. I think of the missing witches and humans. At least, the ones that have been reported. How many did he actually kill? How many dead bodies is he actually responsible for? A few? A dozen? More?

His entire body seems to crackle with pure, malevolent energy. It's almost palpable. I swear I can see the waves spouting from his skin.

We can't defeat him.

"You killed my brother," Christian whispers, sounding so broken and despondent that I can feel myself begin to shatter for him.

"He tried to kill me first," Emmett dismisses insouciantly. "Tit for tat, as the kids these days say."

"You fucking murdered him!" Before Christian can charge at him, Nana grips his arm, dragging him to a stop. She shakes her head quickly with a pointed look in my direction. The tension doesn't leave Christian's taut body, but he does stop his pursuit, anger and pain cloying his eyes.

"Can we just accept the fact that I'm more powerful than you?" Emmett asks cockily, turning to face Nana and Christian. "I have the blood of hundreds of witches flowing through me…and that's just from this month alone." He throws his head back in raucous laughter. "It's a shame—"

A loud popping noise echoes through the air.

Emmett's diatribe cuts off abruptly as he staggers backwards, eyes widening in shock. Only his head tilts downwards to stare at the bullet hole directly through his heart.

"You may be more powerful than some witches," Lucas says coldly, staring down the barrel of his handgun. His expression is as cool and collected as always. There's no remorse. No guilt. Just violence. "But even you can't outrun my fucking gun."

The doll once more falls to the ground, and Elias lunges forward to scoop it up, cradling it protectively against his chest. With nothing holding me up, I collapse as well. I would've face-planted straight into Gabriel's pool of blood if Karsyn wasn't suddenly there, desperately brushing at my hair as his face fills my vision.

"You'll be okay, princess. You're going to be okay. Fuck, you're okay. I love you, so you need to be okay. Okay?"

"You're saying okay a lot," I murmur, attempting to lighten the dark mood. Something wet drips from my mouth and down my chin. Blood, I realize distantly. Pain tumbles around in my brain and rattles my skull

"Fucking hell! We need help!" Karsyn screams.

Dark spots dance at the edge of my vision as I teeter to the side. I have just a second to see Emmett's glossy, blank eyes staring back at me and hear Nana's agonized scream as she wails for her fallen lover.

But I can't focus on that. I can't focus on any of that as pain, so much fucking pain, runs rampant inside of me. I throw my head back and scream as the walls begin to shake and the hanging lights explode, one by one. The floor moves underneath me as my power cascades through my veins, alive and breathing and desperate for release. Someone curses, and I feel more than see a hand touch my shoulder.

And then darkness is quick to consume me.

CHAPTER 54

"Can you fix her?" The voice is distorted, muffled almost, as if I'm hearing it while buried beneath layers of sand. My throat feels unbearably dry, almost like it's filled with hundreds of cotton balls. I try to open my mouth, try to speak, but I'm unable to work my muscles.

What's happening?

Where am I?

"I can," a tired, forlorn voice replies. Nana. But why does she sound so…dead inside?

I try to grasp at the missing memories, but they continually trickle through my fingers like the sand I'm buried in. Time seems to stand still for a brief moment. Is that where I am? In life's hourglass? Is that where all the sand came from?

"How?" a cold, forbidding voice demands.

"I can stitch up her doll," Nana says calmly. "And then, I'm going to remove the spell tying her to it and destroy it…as well as the four other dolls my granddaughter created."

There's a pause, and I feel rather than see a hand brush at my hair. Another body leans over mine and plants a chaste kiss to my forehead.

"Will she be okay?" That anxious voice...Karsyn.

"This is going to hurt like a bitch," Nana admits, utterly impassive. "Hold her down."

"I'm sorry, sweetheart," Cassian rumbles, and I feel his large hands grab both of my wrists, keeping me restrained. Another set grasps both of my legs. Somebody sticks a foreign object in my mouth. A belt.

And then, the pain begins.

Agony is alive inside of me. I don't know how it's even possible. It's a tangible entity, roaming just underneath my skin and overtaking everything it comes into contact with. I scream around the belt in my mouth, my back arching off the bed, as a soothing voice whispers reassurances in my ears. I wordlessly plead with them to end this torment and suffering, but like when Emmett had control of my doll, I can't say one word.

Are they trying to kill me?

Do they hate me?

The pain travels to my arm, and I hear a bone snap. Or maybe it doesn't snap. Maybe it's melding back together again. I honestly can't tell; the pain is too overwhelming.

Bright spots dance across my vision as I jerk and shake and cry.

And then, nothing.

...

This time when I wake up, there's no pain. My body instead feels numb, as if it's been doped up with painkillers. I move my neck from side to side, before bringing my fingers to the freshly dressed wound I expect to find there.

But instead of a bandage, I feel nothing but a slightly raised and jagged line.

"Your grandmother healed you," someone announces softly.

I sit upright in bed, head spinning at the suddenness of my movement, to see that I'm on a mattress someone pulled into the living room. Karsyn and Cassian sleep on either side of me, both of their arms sprawled lazily over my stomach, one on top of the other. When I tilt my head back, I see Elias on the sofa, his legs draped over the arm.

But it wasn't any of them who spoke.

Lucas sits in the lone armchair, watching me as intensely as I watch him. His red hair is tousled, almost as if he has run his hand through it a dozen times in the last who knows how long, and he's shirtless, the pale planes of his chest on display. He isn't as muscular as the other three, but his stomach is toned and reveals a hint of abs.

"What…" I clear my throat to dislodge the sudden ball of yarn present there. "What happened?"

"You don't remember?" His expression doesn't change as he raises a dark red brow. With his face cast in shadows, he looks like some sort of demon sent to drag my soul straight to hell.

"I remember…"

Emmett. The altar. The knife piercing my skin.

And then Gabriel's head rolling through the blood, landing directly in front of my feet.

Nana, Polo, Christian, and the Devils arriving.

The fight.

The gunshot.

Emmett's fallen body.

The pain.

Oh, the pain.

I begin to cry wordlessly, and Lucas moves from his armchair to stand directly in front of me. At first, I'm confused about what he's doing, but then he reaches down and plucks me from my spot between Cassian and Karsyn. He moves us both back to the armchair, placing me on his lap and wrapping his arms around me. He leans forward to rub his nose up and down my neck.

"I'm sorry," he whispers, his hands tightening around my waist.

I don't know what, exactly, he's apologizing for. Me getting kidnapped. Me getting almost murdered. What Emmett did to me. Gabriel's death. Or the old scars still marring the skin on both of my wrists. Maybe it's all of the above. Maybe he doesn't quite know what he's apologizing for, either.

"I didn't really know Gabriel that well. I cared about him and considered him family, but I didn't know him," I confess in a whisper. My eyes flicker to the other three Devils, taking comfort in the steady rise and fall of their chests. They look exhausted. I swear a nuclear blast could go off in this room, and they'd sleep right through it. "I mean, I knew him, of course, but we weren't close. He was kind of an asshole." My lips twitch in a small smile when I think about the surly triplet. But that smile fades when I think about his unseeing eyes...

"Hey." Lucas gently shakes me. "Don't allow your mind to wander like that."

"He sacrificed himself for me." I twist my face so I can cry into his neck. "How can I live with that?"

"You can't," Lucas answers bluntly. When I jerk my head back in shock, he sighs, brushing at my cheeks with the pad of his thumbs. He stares at me with an expression I've never seen on his face before. Tenderness. Wonder. Love. "Some days, it's going to suck. Some days, you're going to want to fall apart. But you want to know what?"

"What?" I whisper.

"I'm not going to fucking let you," he growls fiercely. "I didn't know Gabriel at all, but he's now one of my favorite people in this entire goddamn world. You want to know why?" He tenderly brushes at my hair, placing the sweaty strands behind my ears. "Because he brought you back to me."

A myriad of emotions settles in my heart as I stare at this stunning man with the soulful blue eyes. How did I ever think them to be cold before? They're hotter than an inferno, melting at the remaining ice surrounding my heart and setting me free.

I bring both of my hands up to cup his face as he's doing to mine.

"How long was I out?" I whisper as he pulls me even closer to him.

His eyes harden, but not with anger. With pain. "A few days," he whispers dejectedly. "Your grandma and her boyfriends healed the majority of your injuries by sewing up the doll. At least, the ones you got from that fucker, Emmett."

"But not the ones I did to myself," I muse, dropping my hands to my lap to stare at the savage, ugly scars on both of my arms. They'll remain with me until the day I die, of that I'm certain.

Lucas doesn't answer with words. Instead, he brings my left wrist up to his mouth and plants a tender, albeit chaste, kiss on the thickest one. The one that I intended to end my life.

"No. Not these scars," he whispers, and his blue eyes ensnare my own, holding me hostage. The air around us seems to crackle with electricity. And I know without a shadow of a doubt, that everything has changed between us. I've always been unsure about Lucas, even when I began to fall for the other three Devils, but right here, in his arms, I feel a sense of contentment and safety. Of belonging. The emotions crash into me like a wrecking ball, stealing my breath away.

It's Lucas who breaks the moment, though, turning away from me to stare at the strains of moonlight entering through the window.

"You should talk to your grandma," he states abruptly, patting my thigh gently and indicating for me to get down. His rejection feels like a slap to the face, but I work to quickly mask my emotions. "She's outside."

Any hurt feelings I might've had diminish at his words. "Outside? Now?"

It can't be later than one, maybe two, in the morning.

As I begin to move towards the front door, Lucas's voice stops me cold. "This conversation isn't over, Peony." It's a warning and a vow. A promise for the future.

And despite the lingering pain, despite my grief, I smile softly.

"I wouldn't expect anything less from you, Lucas Scott."

...

I find my nana sitting on the porch swing, still dressed in the skirt and billowy blouse she wore to rescue me in. Her hair tumbles around her shoulders as she stares blankly out into the distance. I don't know what she's seeing, what she's thinking about, but I can take an educated guess.

If I lost any of the Devils…

I can't even imagine loving a man for years and then seeing him dead. I feel nauseous just thinking about it, as if someone has stuck their hand into my stomach and is now swirling around the contents.

"Nana?" I prod gently when she doesn't seem to notice my presence.

No response.

I take a step closer and pause, before gingerly perching on the swinging bench beside her. She still doesn't glance over, but I know she's aware of me when her hand reaches across the seat and grasps mine tightly.

"I'm glad to see you're doing better," she whispers hoarsely. Her voice sounds raw and raspy from crying. I can't see her features well in the cover of night, but I imagine her eyes will be red and blotchy as well.

"Thanks to you." I give her hand a squeeze and follow her gaze towards the cluster of trees in the front yard.

"You're my granddaughter, and I love you," she says softly. "We all love you."

Silence once more reigns as I allow her to gather her thoughts. I can tell she has something she wants to say to me, something sitting on the edge of her tongue, but I know she needs a moment to process everything.

After ten minutes, she releases a choked sob, and my heart breaks into thousands of pieces all over again.

"He wasn't truly a part of them," she gasps at last. "You have to know that. He was undercover for the witch's council. He had no idea the witch they captured was you until he got there. He called me as soon—" She breaks off with another rasping gasp, leaning forward and clutching at her stomach as if the pain is too much for her to handle. As if it's spilling out of her and only her hand will keep it inside. "He loved you so much, Peony. He considered you family, even if he didn't show it."

"I know." I wrap my arm around her frail shoulders and pull her to my chest. She begins to weep in earnest, crying for the man she loved and lost. I stroke her hair and whisper words that I know won't help, but I'm at a loss of what to do.

At some point, Christian and Polo exit the house, both of their faces haggard and puffy, and slowly take Nana from me, holding her between them.

I don't know what to say to them, how to express how sorry I truly am, so instead, I walk away.

I don't have a destination in mind as I wander aimlessly through the halls. At least, I don't think I do, until I find myself in front of the bathroom.

Feeling hesitant and unsure, I push the door open and step inside, glancing at myself in the mirror for the first time since I returned.

Dried blood coats my hair, the white color almost appearing pink. A slight, yellowish bruise sits beneath my right eye, and to be quite honest, I can't even remember where I got it from. The two cuts on my neck are now silver, the skin slightly raised. I move my once-broken arm around in a circle, immensely grateful when I don't feel any lingering pain or discomfort.

Because despite my nana's grief, she still took care of me. She still fixed my stupid mistakes. If I recall the whispered conversation correctly, she destroyed all of the voodoo dolls.

Maybe, just maybe, this is finally over.

And I was right—I *did* lose some pieces of myself. I can't tell you for sure how many or if they're reparable, but I'm no longer whole.

My pieces now rest in the hands of four charming devils. Four demons from hell.

Someone must've thrown a ratty T-shirt over my head, and I waste no time tugging it off. My naked flesh is a map of scars. You can try to connect them all, try to understand where I came from, but it would prove impossible. These stories are my own, and I'm very selective about who I share them with.

I set the water's temperature as high as it will allow before stepping beneath the blistering spray. My legs wobble slightly, threatening to collapse, and I give in to the need to sit down, wrapping my arms around myself in a futile attempt to hold all of those broken pieces together.

I don't know how long I stay there. Long enough for my skin to turn pink from the heat, at the very least.

But then I hear the distinct sound of the bathroom door opening and closing. The sound of clothes being shrugged off. The rustling of the shower curtain being pulled open and then closed once more.

A naked Lucas very gently helps me to my feet and then turns me around, until my back faces him. Without a word, he grabs my shampoo from the shelf and squirts it into his palm before rubbing his hands together. Slowly, giving me the chance to tell him no or pull away, he begins to scrub at my crusty hair. He pays particular attention to my scalp, massaging it gently with his skilled fingers, before he washes the shampoo away with the shower head. He repeats this process three times until no more blood resides in my hair. Until the water no longer looks like the scene of a crime movie.

With a gentleness belying the hard glint in his eyes, he grabs my washcloth and pours a generous amount of body soap onto it. He starts at my arms, wiping away all of the dried and crusted blood from the wounds Emmett inflicted. I can see his lips tighten as he stares at the silver scars, but he remains silent.

He moves the rag down my back, over the curve of my butt, before spinning me around. His movements are just as clinical when he washes my breasts, stomach, and thighs. At the moment, there's nothing sexual about what he's doing.

I think for the first time in his life, he's taking care of someone other than himself.

The enormity of my emotions for this strong yet broken man consumes me. I find myself reaching for him desperately, running my fingers through his red hair, made even darker from the water.

"Lucas…"

He swallows heavily, his blue eyes searching my own with raw need.

"Not like this," he whispers. "Not when you're hurting."

"It's not because of that," I promise, standing on my tiptoes to press a kiss to the corner of his mouth. He trembles in my arms, even as his cock hardens, pressing against my stomach. "It's because I realized something." I pause, pulling back slightly to stare into his eyes. "You're taking care of me."

"Of course I am." His hands glide down my sides, resting just over the curve of my ass. "I'll always take care of you."

"Why is that, Lucas?" I plant another kiss to his smooth-shaven jaw. "Tell me."

"Because I…" He trails off, swallowing yet again.

"It's for the same reason I want to take care of you," I continue. "Because I think I'm in love with you."

He inhales sharply, and every pore in my body is instinctively tuned in to his. I can feel his heart beating under my palm as if it were my own. And when his eyes connect with mine, I know he feels it too. This pull. This connection.

It's always been there, lying dormant between two souls who thought they hated each other. But maybe it wasn't hate that we felt. Maybe it never was.

"I love you so much that I can't even breathe," Lucas says doggedly. Almost helplessly, he presses his lips to mine. The kiss is soft and slow, the exact opposite of what I expected from my ice prince. Licks of fire dance through my veins as he pulls me tight against his chest, his mouth never leaving mine.

We're still exchanging soft, reverent kisses when Lucas turns off the water, wraps me in his arms, and carries me out of the shower.

But we don't get far.

We fall to the ground on the bathroom rug in a heap of tangled limbs as he reaches for the condom in his jeans pocket.

And when he finally enters me, it's like two souls converging after centuries apart. It's like soulmates wandering the earth, waiting for this exact moment when they find each other, and the heavens rejoice. It's like stars colliding in the night sky, becoming one.

He's not rough like Elias. Not fast or teasing like Cassian and Karsyn.

He makes love to me with his whole body. Each thrust of his hips tells a story, just like the scars on my wrist do.

His hands travel over the curves of my hips as if he wants to worship me. He tugs on each breast, tweaking my sensitive nipples. Through it all, his lips never leave me. Even when I have to pull away, gasping for air, he just moves them down to my neck, suckling at the skin there.

I come faster and harder than I ever have in my life, and despite

Lucas's frosty exterior, I've never felt so warm. His cock judders inside of me before he comes as well, collapsing his sweaty body on top of mine before rolling over.

We don't speak as he takes me into his arms and holds me close. And no words leave us when he wraps a towel around me and then himself and carries us to the ladder leading to my bedroom. Forgoing the bed, he reclines back in the rocking chair, me still in his lap. He wraps a blanket around the both of us, and the sound of his rhythmic breathing lulls me into sleep.

CHAPTER 55

I'm woken up by the sound of shrill shouting.

Jumping upright, I watch in dismay as the blanket and towel both slide from my body, leaving me naked. I feel a moment of panic before remembering that I'm in my bedroom with Lucas.

My dark prince groggily opens up first one eye and then the other, looking unbelievably cute and rumpled first thing in the morning. I'm unused to seeing him look anything other than perfect, so this is a nice change.

He smiles softly at me, eyes warming, and the familiar tendrils of lust percolate in my stomach.

"Peony!" that high-pitched voice from before shrieks. Mother. I mean, Darlene.

The warmth diminishes from Lucas's eyes as if it was never there to begin with.

I grab a hanging dress and throw it over my head, not bothering with panties or a bra. I know if I keep my mother waiting, her fury will only intensify.

Lucas frowns in dismay when he realizes he left his own clothes in the bathroom. Quickly, I open up my top dresser drawer and throw him a baggy sweatshirt and a pair of clean basketball shorts. They were Uriel's once upon a time, but I stole them for myself at some point during our relationship and never gave them back. What can I say? Men's clothes are comfy.

Lucas's eyes could be hewn from glaciers as he stares at the obviously men's clothing. His lips pull away from his teeth in the beginnings of a snarl, and I just know that if Uriel was here, he would be dead in a span of seconds.

Not bothering to see if he'll get dressed, I climb down the ladder, painfully aware that I'm not wearing underwear and anyone could look up and see me, before hustling towards the kitchen.

Karsyn, Cassian, and Elias stand together on one side of the room, matching scowls on their faces and arms crossed over their chests. I take a brief moment to survey them uninterrupted. Despite their differences in appearances, they look so much like each other at this moment. The same mannerisms. The same fierce expressions. The same hard, unrelenting eyes.

Mom and Ryan sit at the table, the former drinking a cup of coffee as if nothing is wrong. As if her mother hadn't just lost one of her great loves. As if her daughter hadn't been kidnapped and nearly sacrificed.

And then, in the foyer with Nana, Christian, and Polo, I see *them*.

The witch's council.

Twelve men and women of varying ages and ethnicities. The oldest appears to be in his eighties, if not his nineties, his face so wrinkled, it has more lines than the roads on a map. His shrewd eyes assess my nana silently, his lips pressed in a straight line.

Four women huddle together near the sofa, whispering too softly for me to hear. All four of them are gorgeous with willowy frames and soft, dewy features. I imagine they are middle-aged, maybe older, though it's hard to tell with our kind. Unlike the old man, I hazard a guess that they use spells as preventives to keep their true ages from showing.

Two more women stand on either side of my grandma, both placing hands on her shoulders as they offer her condolences. Their black hair has streaks of gray in them, and I imagine they might be twins. At the very least, sisters.

As my eyes scan the other occupants of the room, they stop on the youngest council member. If I had to guess, I'd say he was in his late twenties. Honey-blond hair. Green eyes that seem to glow as if there's a candle lit behind his irises. Crooked grin.

"You," I whisper in shock, the word tumbling from my lips before I can contain it.

Conversation ceases as the young man turns towards me, his grin widening.

"You," he says in wonder, cocking his head to the side.

"Peony," Nana prods warily. She takes a step away from the two sisters until she's standing between Christian and Polo, both of whom take one of her hands in theirs for comfort. "How do you know Councilman Joshua?"

"He...he..." How can I tell her that I met him five years ago? When he saved me? When he confronted the bullies for me when I was too scared to? How can I say that he was the first man I ever truly had a crush on?

"Peony and I are old friends," the man—Joshua, apparently—says with a conspiratorial smile and wink.

I'm suddenly pressed against a hard body as arms encircle my waist and someone rests his chin on my shoulder. Cassian.

Elias and Karsyn move to stand on either side of me, muscles flexing, and I hear rather than see Lucas shift so he's behind me. I half want to look over my shoulder to see if he's in Uriel's clothes, but I refrain myself.

"What is the meaning of dragging us out here?" the older councilman barks angrily.

"We've come to pay our respects to a fallen witch," one of the black-haired sisters snaps. Her twin nods once.

"A fallen *Blood*," the old man sneers, giving Christian and Polo the side-eyed. I bristle, ready to defend them, when Joshua holds up his hands placatingly.

"It was you who called us, Darlene," he says, addressing my mother. I stiffen automatically. She would only call them…

"Yes." Darlene gracefully rises to her feet and stalks around the table, flashing a sultry smile in Joshua's direction. The handsome councilman continues to smile at her indulgently. "As you guys already know, these four humans were made aware of the existence of witches and warlocks." She scoffs the word human as if it leaves a sour taste in her mouth.

Elias's grip tightens on my hand, and Cassian's chest begins to rumble with something resembling a growl.

"Is that so?" Joshua turns to stare at the guys, expression decidedly curious. I wonder if he recognizes them as my childhood bullies. As soon as the thought appears in my mind, I dismiss it. I doubt he remembers much of that day. I'm honestly shocked he still remembers me.

"I must insist we perform the memory spell." Darlene lifts her chin snootily into the air. "For the protection of our kind."

"Let's get on with it then," one of the pretty, middle-aged witches says dismissively. All of the men begin to nod, as do most of the women. Only the twins appear hesitant, glancing between me and the guys.

"Maybe we should ask them what they want," one of the sisters suggests.

"Ruby, don't be ridiculous," the old man snarls, and the twin, Ruby, simply steps around him, towards my guys.

She offers us a kind smile, one that reaches her eyes, before taking my hands in both of hers. I can feel Cassian stiffen behind me, hands tightening on my waist as if he's prepared to throw me over his shoulder and run away. But before he can do that, Ruby begins to speak.

"I would like to apologize on behalf of the council for what happened to you," she says softly. "I know that you lost Gabriel in the battle, and I offer you my deepest condolences." I search her pretty blue eyes for any hint of deception, but she appears sincere.

"Thank you," I whisper hoarsely.

"And I'm glad to see you're okay," she adds with another soft smile. She then turns to stare at the Devils. "And as for you four…"

"We want to do the binding ceremony," Karsyn blurts out. When every eye turns to stare at him, his cheeks tint pink. He clears his throat uncomfortably, squeezing my hand tighter. "We talked about it, and…it's what we want. If we have a choice."

I pull myself out of his arms to whirl on them, shock causing my heart to race faster than ever.

"What?" I gasp. "You don't know what you're asking—"

"We understand completely," Elias says gently, with the quiet confidence he always possesses. "Your grandma talked to us about it when you were unconscious."

"Being tied to your hot ass for our entire lives?" Cassian says with a shit-eating grin. "Sign me the fuck up."

Someone makes a disgusted noise from behind me, and I resist the urge to give them my middle finger.

"We're already in love with you," Karsyn continues, blushing slightly. "We know it's new, we know it might not last, but we don't want to give you up. Not after we just got you back."

"You'll have to kill me before I'll leave you again," Lucas says dryly, and I can't help but notice that he changed into his clothes from yesterday. Apparently, he would rather walk downstairs naked than wear clothes belonging to my ex-boyfriend.

"You'll be her slaves," Darlene drawls from behind me. "Her magical slaves. Hers to do with as she pleases."

"That's not true," Joshua cuts in, anger darkening his tone. "If the souls are meant to be together, then it will be a mutual partnership. She will belong to them as surely as they belong to her. They'll be able to wield her magic, just as she can use their energy."

"That's not possible," Darlene protests arrogantly. "There are four of them, and one of her."

"Do you mean like soulmates?" Karsyn interrupts, face scrunched in confusion. One of the witches begins to laugh before she's shushed by my nana.

"Yes and no," Joshua explains as I twist my head to stare at him over my shoulder. He scratches absently at his chin, face deep in thought. "Unlike what you read about in books and see in movies, soulmates aren't destined. They're not written in the stars or whatever. But when you find your equal on this earth, your souls know innately that you belong together."

"And you think that's what we are?" Cassian demands, but Joshua shrugs.

"We'll know for sure once we do the binding spell."

"You can't seriously be considering this!" Darlene screeches.

"Fortunately for all of us," Rose begins, "it's not your choice."

"You guys, are you sure?" I whisper, spinning back around to face them. I know a part of me will wither and die forever if they choose to forget about me, but I refuse to take away that choice. "Once we bind ourselves together...there's no going back."

Cassian's jaw clenches as he turns towards Karsyn and then Elias. Lucas simply meets my gaze, promising an eternity without any words.

"We're sure," all four of them declare at the same time.

Joshua smiles brightly before nodding at Rose. The dark-haired woman moves towards us and places a finger on Karsyn's forehead. Her twin does the same to Cassian, as the old man moves towards Elias. One of the middle-aged women moves to do the same thing to Lucas, but he growls at her, glaring at her finger as if it has grown a head and is now snapping at him.

"Calm, little one," she says, amusement lacing her voice. Instead of addressing her, Lucas stares over her shoulder at me, only me, as if the rest of the world ceases to exist. His shoulders gradually relax, and he doesn't struggle when the woman places a single finger to his forehead, right between his eyes.

Joshua moves to stand in front of me.

"Are you sure about this?" he whispers. "You asked them if they truly wanted this, but is it something you want?"

Lucas's soft smile that he only ever shares with me flashes in my mind.

Cassian's jovial laugh and crude remarks that never fail to make me laugh.

Karsyn's steadfast loyalty and compassion.

And Elias's unyielding strength and confidence.

They're a part of me, a part of my soul, and I'll be damned if I ever let anyone take them from me.

My answer is instantaneous. I don't even have to think about it to know.

"Yes," I whisper.

"Very well." Joshua gently presses his finger against my forehead before leaning forward to whisper, "They're lucky men."

The five council members begin to chant in Latin, and I don't know how else to describe it, but it feels as if pieces of my very being leave my chest. The sensation isn't painful, more like an irritating itch, but I still gasp in surprise, my hands drawing up to rub the spot.

Bright light engulfs my vision as my back arches painfully.

"What's happening?" I whimper, but I don't know if I actually say the words or just think them.

And then, I feel them.

Four bulbs of light materialize in the center of my chest, steadily filling in the missing pieces like a puzzle. I recognizable each of their energies instantly.

Cassian's playful energy, the one bouncing around like it's demanding my attention.

Karsyn's is the one giving me a warm hug. I can practically feel his embrace as if he's actually standing in front of me.

And then there's Elias's, sitting steadily in my chest, loyal and unbending. He doesn't demand my attention like Cassian's does, but I can still sense him keenly.

And then finally, Lucas. A cold brush of air in my chest cavity. Protective. Calm. Fierce.

Slowly, the light engulfing the room recedes, and I come back to myself, shaky and disoriented.

What the...?

I place a hand to my chest where I can still sense my four Devils, as if they truly are a part of me. Right now, they seem confused, slightly frightened, but mostly awed.

"It's true," Rose breathes, eyes wide with wonder as she takes a step back. "You guys are soulmates."

Joshua slowly removes his finger from my head. "Your souls are perfect matches," he agrees with a small tilt to his lips.

"So it worked?" Cassian stares down at his hands in wonderment before turning towards me. I'm shocked to see tears in his dark eyes, even as he gifts me a slow, seductive smile. "You're mine now, baby. I'm never letting you go."

"Stop it with the whole 'baby' thing," I growl, and his smile only broadens.

"Fucking hell, woman!" I'm in Elias's arms before I can even catch my breath. "I can *feel* you. Is that...is that normal?"

I run my fingers through his dark hair, scratching lightly at his scalp. "I feel you, too. All of you," I stress, staring over Elias's shoulder to encompass them all.

I zero in on the brilliant balls of light inside of me, trying to get a sense of how they feel. I don't want to intrude on their private thoughts, but I'm suddenly terrified that they're having regrets. They knew they would be tied to me as my human familiars, but I don't think they imagined *this*.

Cassian is still in shock, but combined with that is something akin to glee.

Elias's emotions are more subdued, though I didn't expect anything else from him. He's happy and excited, but I feel a niggle of fear and self-loathing intermixed. I make myself a note to talk to him about that at a later point. He has nothing to be sorry for, though I'm not sure if just saying that to him will be enough.

Karsyn is a myriad of feelings. Happiness, shock, wonderment, and confusion, being the main ones. I sift through his emotions, wondering if he feels any regret or anger, but I can't find anything.

And then I focus on the cold ball of light. The icy one.

Surprisingly enough, Lucas's is the easiest to read. It's one simple emotion. One emotion that screams at me at the top of its lungs.

Love.

Tears fog my eyes as he meets my stare, and I know he felt me prying. But instead of getting defensive, he opens himself up more to me, his emotions pouring through my body like a summer rain.

"This is fucking ridiculous!" Darlene screeches, rounding the table towards me. Her hand raises, but before it can make contact with my face, Joshua steps in front of her, eyes glacial.

"We did the spell. It's over," he says curtly. But my mother cannot be easily deterred. I watch as her expression turns cunning, malicious. Those red-painted lips twist into something that I can't quite call a smile.

"It's not over just yet," Darlene says like the cat who ate the canary. "I would like to declare something to the council." Her viper-like eyes fix on me, and I brace myself, knowing she's going to officially disown me in front of the coven. What will this mean for me and the guys? I know that we'll still be bonded, but I also know that the ancestors won't allow me to tap into my magic if she disowns me. So what will happen? What does this—

"I would like to officially declare that Darlene Simone is no longer my daughter." Nana's soft voice, nothing more than a hushed murmur, breaks through the silence like a deafening crack of a whip.

Darlene whirls on Nana, red speckles appearing on her face. "What?" she screams.

"Furthermore," Nana continues, ignoring her daughter, "I would like to declare that Peony Simone is now under my care. She will be the witch who receives my grimoire after my death."

"You can't fucking do this!" Darlene shouts, tears in her eyes.

"Think about what you're doing, Cardinal," the older warlock says with a frown. "Once you disown her…"

"The ancestors will no longer grant her access to her magic, yes," Nana finishes. "I am aware."

"Mother!" Darlene bellows. "You can't—"

"You didn't let me grieve!" Nana shouts right back, her own tears flowing freely down her face. "I just lost the love of my life, and you. Didn't. Let. Me. Grieve! Your daughter was just tortured, for fuck's sake, and you still came here for your own malicious intent. All of this power has gone to your head, my daughter, and this is the only way I know how to save you. Maybe in time, you'll figure out how to fix things with your own child. Trust me. You'll thank me for this one day."

"You can't do this." Darlene tries to take a step backwards, but two of the male warlocks are suddenly there, holding her steady. "You can't fucking do this! You can't take away my magic!"

"Get her out of my sight." Nana rips her eyes away from Darlene and focuses on her trembling hands.

"No! Please, no! Mom!" Darlene is still screaming as the warlocks drag her away.

Ryan remains at the table, shaking from head to toe, and only when she's gone does he glance up at me through dark lashes.

"I-I'm sorry," he stutters. "For everything."

I don't want to talk to him. Hell, I don't even know what I'd say to him. He came here with every intention of forcing me into a marriage he knew I didn't want. Uriel's brother or not, I don't think I can ever forgive him for that.

Ignoring his plea, I focus on Joshua, who is speaking softly with my nana. "You know what's going to happen now." It's not a question, but Nana takes it as one, nodding her head slowly.

"You'll need to come down to the council's headquarters and declare to the ancestors and the earth itself that you renounce Darlene Simone as your daughter," Rose adds.

"You're taking away that woman's magic," the older man snaps. "I would think about—"

"I already did," Nana cuts in. "It was either her or my granddaughter. I made my choice, and if you think I don't feel guilt over it, you're wrong. But my decision is final." To Rose, she says, "I'll come down with you guys today. I want this over with." Her voice trembles slightly as more tears cascade down her cheeks. "I want my daughter back."

Joshua places his hand on her shoulder and gives it a squeeze.

"You made the right decision," he whispers to her in reassurance, and she manages a shaky smile.

"So is this over?" Karsyn asks tentatively. "Is this finally over?"

Joshua turns towards us with a brisk nod. "Because you guys are bonded, you'll no longer have to worry about us. Now, I can't promise you that you won't run into any more obstacles. Emmett was only one of many Bloods. And there are still the witch hunters to consider…" He trails off before smiling warmly. "But you no longer need to fear the witch's council. Or your mother."

"Oh, thank fuck," Cassian gripes. "That crazy bitch was giving me a headache."

The rest of the witches and warlocks begin to file out of the house, Nana trailing behind them. I stop her before she can leave with a gentle hand on her arm.

"Nana, are you sure?"

The frown on her face transforms into a timid smile as she presses a watery kiss to my forehead. "Yes, my sweet girl. I've never been more sure about anything in my life."

"We'll look after her," Christian assures me, and he too offers me a wobbly smile. It doesn't quite reach his eyes, I'm not sure if it ever will, but at least it's a start.

Polo gives my shoulders a squeeze before he follows after his brother and girlfriend.

Soon, it's only me, the Devils, and Joshua who remain.

"I'm happy for you, Peony. Truly," the young councilman says softly. His green eyes spark like emeralds in the artificial lighting of the kitchen. "You're not the scared little girl you once were five years ago."

"I'm not," I agree. "And I have you to thank for that."

"Me?" Both of his eyebrows jump up in surprise.

"You were kind to me when no one else was," I confess. "You gave me the strength to fight back."

"I'm glad. You truly are a special girl, Peony. Maybe we'll meet each other again someday."

"In your fucking dreams," Cassian mumbles from beside me. I elbow him in the stomach.

"Oh, and I almost forgot…" Joshua snaps his fingers, and all four of my Devils' pants fall to the ground.

"What?" Karsyn stares confusedly at his jeans around his ankles, while Lucas simply rolls his eyes.

"Fucking warlocks," Cassian grumbles as he struggles to pull them back up.

I giggle, and Joshua's face softens at the sound. He winks at me.

"Until we meet again."

And this time, I actually believe him.

I spend the next week at home, attempting to process all that occurred. Nana tells the school that I've come down with a stomach virus, and since I've never missed a day, they don't question it. I don't know what the guys told the school, but all four of them stay with me.

I alternate between crying, screaming at nothing, and staring blankly into space. Sleep proves difficult for me. Every time I close my eyes, I see Emmett's malicious, cruel smirk as he hovers over me, that damn knife raised in his hand. And then the scene changes, and Gabriel's bloody head fills up my entire vision. Then I think about the people I killed, and it only serves to increase my queasiness.

I usually wake up and vomit into the nearest trash can.

Nana calls me on the fourth day to tell me that it's done. I don't need to be a mind reader to understand her ominous words. Nana officially disowned Darlene as her daughter, and my mother lost all of her magic. I don't know what this means for my family, but I do know that I can never forgive the woman who gave birth to me. I always knew she was cruel and conniving, but this is something else entirely. What she did…it was evil. No amount of groveling will ever get me to forgive her, though I doubt my mother will ever stoop that low. I hope I never see her face again.

Through it all, the guys never leave my side, comforting me when I need them to and holding me when I don't have the strength to stand. One of them always stays next to me, as if they're afraid I'll shatter if they leave me alone. And maybe they're right to be afraid. After all, they can feel my emotions just as I can sense theirs. I'm a tumultuous mixture of pain, fear, anger, and guilt. Mixed in that toxic cocktail is something akin to hope. Happiness. Elation.

The Devils are mine, now and forever. How can I not feel a little happy?

But then the guilt overpowers that positive emotion, and I succumb to my internal darkness once more.

It's on the following Monday when I decide I'm finally ready to head back to school.

"Are you sure this is a good idea?" Karsyn asks softly. Lucas is showering in the downstairs bathroom, while Elias is in the upstairs one. Cassian is still asleep in my bed in the attic.

"I need to live my life again, Kar," I whisper, holding my mug up for him to refill with coffee. The Devils and I...we have become strangely domestic. You can tell that you care about someone immensely when you change your habits a little bit to accommodate theirs. For example, I guarantee you that a week ago, Cassian would've never willingly loaded the dishwasher or cleaned up after dinner. Or Lucas, the silver-spoon baby, would've never cooked dinner for all five of us while Nana and her men were still away.

But they knew what I needed even before I did. So while those two made sure I was fed and the house was clean, Elias held me in his arms on the sofa, while Karsyn put on a stupid romantic comedy. And then the next day, when I had a panic attack because I missed two tests while I was away, Lucas sat with me at the table and helped me with my schoolwork, while Cassian rubbed my tense shoulders and Karsyn swept the kitchen.

I've never felt so loved or cherished before in my life.

"You're the bravest person I know, Simone." Karsyn gives me a cheeky grin, but it doesn't quite reach his eyes. I hate that I'm making him sad, but I don't know what else to do. He's always been the more sensitive Devil, and I know my emotions affect him more than they do the others. I can see it in his pained eyes, his tight smile, and his clenched jaw.

"Back at you, Alder." I shove his shoulder lightly with mine.

He hesitates briefly, staring at his own steaming mug of coffee, before meeting my eyes.

"I went to see my doctor yesterday," he blurts, and my eyebrows raise at his abrupt topic change.

"And?"

"And…" He bites down on his lower lip. "You're right. At least, they think you're right. They're referring me to a specialist, but yeah. There's a good chance that I've been undiagnosed with dyslexia for all this time."

"Karsyn…" I lean forward to place my hand over his. "This a good thing."

His answering smile finally reaches his eyes, making the hazel sparkle in hues of greens, browns, and golds. "Maybe I won't be as stupid anymore."

"Hey." My smile fades instantly as I whack him on the shoulder. Hard. "Don't talk about yourself like that."

"Ow." He makes a face at me as he rubs absently where my fist connected. "What was that for?"

"For you acting like a dumbass," I respond automatically. And then, because I'm still pissed at him, I lean forward and pinch his nipples.

"Ow! Fuck! You crazy witch." He glares at me as he rubs at his nubs.

"Okay fine." I cross my arms over my chest stubbornly. "If this is a 'talk bad about yourself' type of day, then I'll go first. Let's see…

Did you see the scars on my arms? They're hideous, aren't they?" I absently scratch at the most recent one—the one from Emmett's abuse. Nana believes it'll heal with time, but for now, I'll wear it as a badge of honor. "I really am ugly—"

Karsyn growls and reaches forward, pulling up my shirt and bra until he can pinch my bare nipples. Instead of the squeak of dismay that he made, I moan low in my throat, instantly arching towards him like a cat demanding pets.

He pinches my nipples even harder, pulling up my tits and then watching them bounce.

"You're right," he growls. "No talking bad about yourself."

"Tit for tat," I say in response, shoving my breasts further into his hands.

"Did someone say tit?" Cassian shouts from somewhere down the hall. A moment later, he slides into the kitchen in only a pair of loose sleep shorts. His eyes drop to where Karsyn's hands pull and pluck at my breasts, and heat flares. "Oh, fuck yes. I love me some tit for tat." He pushes down his shorts, his cock springing free.

"No more talking bad about ourselves," I tell Karsyn firmly. "Deal?"

"Deal," he agrees.

"Now, how about y'all seal that deal with a kiss," Cassian suggests, and I chuckle.

I don't even care that we're an hour late.

...

The school is already decorated for Halloween. Orange and black streamers hang from the ceiling, and cobwebs decorate the top of each classroom door. Paper bats are placed sporadically throughout the hallway, adding to the aesthetic. It feels strange to be back after a week away. In some ways, life has changed drastically. I'll never be the same Peony Simone I was before Emmett strapped me to that altar. And in others, it has remained the exact same.

My relationships with my mom and the Devils are two of those changes. Some for the worse; some for the better.

And then there are some things that will never change. My friendship with Mariabella being one of them.

She ambushes me when I'm leaving Orchestra.

Felicia, who happens to be standing next to me, raises an eyebrow as the blonde bombshell pulls me into her arms, all but smothering me against her breasts as she rocks us back and forth.

"Karsyn told me you were sick! I've been so worried! How are you feeling? Are you contagious? Fuck, I shouldn't be touching you if you're contagious, right?" Mariabella pulls away from me to give me an assessing once-over. "You don't look too shitty," she concludes with a decisive head nod.

"I'll see you tomorrow, Peony," Felicia says uneasily. Ever since our last conversation, we fell into a truce of sorts. We'll smile cordially at each other in the hallways, and once in a while, we'll even talk.

But as she walks away, hips swaying, it's not me she stares at.

It's Mariabella.

Felicia's eyes drop to my best friend's breasts before snapping back up, her eyes meeting mine. When I raise an eyebrow at her, she runs away from me in panic.

And that's when I understand.

She was never truly jealous about Mr. Tucker's favoritism towards me. She was jealous of my friendship with Mariabella. It's obvious from the wistful, longing look the violist just threw at Mari that she's halfway in love with her.

"Peony, answer me!" Mariabella demands, pulling me out of my thoughts.

"I'm sorry. What?" I reply dazedly, and Mari looks horrified.

"You must have a fever. I should call the nurse. Are you confused? How many fingers am I holding up?"

"Relax! I'm not dying," I say gently as we walk to my third hour. She doesn't have this class with me, but she already made it clear that we're spending every free moment catching up on "girl talk."

"Sorry." She winces slightly. "It's just...you didn't answer my texts, and I was worried..." She trails off once more, scratching absently at the inside of her wrist. "It's still crazy that Emmett moved schools, isn't it? He didn't even say goodbye."

The familiar pinpricks of guilt erupt in my stomach. After a long conversation, Karsyn and I decided that we'll keep the truth about my powers a secret. Mariabella knowing the truth will only put her in more danger, and we both care too much about her for that. That doesn't mean that I don't feel immense, agonizing guilt over my decision. I want to tell Mariabella everything because I trust her more than anyone else in my life, only second to the Devils. She's my best friend, and her heart is pure. Unblemished.

And I intend to keep it that way.

Besides, the less she knows about Emmett, the better. They were friends once upon a time, and I know the truth of what he did to me would destroy her.

"You texted me before...? About having something you wanted to talk to me about?" I press. I've been dying all day ever since I got that cryptic message. I thought she would come out and say it, but she's been tight-lipped, focusing on me instead. But I can see it eating away at her, clawing at her insides until it tears free of her skin.

"I..." A delicate blush detonates in her face. "I told my parents."

I stop walking and turn to gape at her. "You what?"

"I told my parents about...me. The truth." The blush still remains, but this time, she's smiling. A wide, genuine smile, one that makes every guy in the vicinity do a second glance. I've never seen my friend look so radiant.

"And I'm taking it that it went well?" My eyes water with happy tears as she nods her head sheepishly.

"Dad was a little upset about it at first, but only because I kept it a secret for so long. Mom said…" She snorts. "Mom said that she always knew. That she found my collection of Victoria's Secret catalogues when I was in middle school."

I pull my best friend into a tight hug and squeeze the life out of her.

"I'm so fucking happy for you," I whisper sincerely, sniffling.

"Me, too. I mean, I'm happy for myself." She laughs weakly against my shoulder before pulling away and attempting to collect herself. "Now stop crying. You look like shit," she admonishes, and I can't help but snort. "But there was one other thing I wanted to tell you…"

"Don't leave me in suspense, woman. What is it?" I teasingly shake her shoulders as her blush returns with a vengeance.

"You remember that cheerleader Brittany?"

"Oh my god! Oh my god!" I squeal excitedly, jumping up and down and clapping my hands. She shushes me in embarrassment, looking in both directions to ensure that no one's in hearing distance.

"Calm down, you big weirdo," she says. "It was just a date."

"Just a fucking date?" I cock my hip out to the side and level her with my no-nonsense glare. "You better not be holding out on me—"

"And we kissed," she blurts, once more glancing around. "And… other stuff. Naked stuff. No offense, Peony, but she has bigger boobs than you. And her nipples taste like candy."

"You sound as if you're comparing Peony's nipples to this Brittany chick's," Karsyn says as he moves to stand beside me, wrapping an arm around my shoulder. "Are you trying to make me jealous?" The smile fades from Mari's face as she glares up at him.

"Karsyn," she says stiffly, and I can see that her reaction hurts him. If what they told me is true, they were once best friends. I hate that I drove a wedge between them, especially when they're two of my favorite people.

But all I can do is be here for them. They'll come back to each other in time. It might not be today. It might not even be tomorrow. But I have no doubt that Mariabella will forgive him, just as I have.

Hoping to lighten the mood, I jab my elbow into Karsyn's stomach. "Thinking kinky thoughts again, Alder?"

"About your nipples?" He nips at my ear with a playfulness I usually only see in Cassian. "Always."

"Ewww. Don't be talking about my bestie's nipples," Mariabella groans, and Karsyn makes a face at her.

"Wasn't it just a few weeks ago that you loved her nipples?"

"Things change. People change." She turns towards me with a wink. "Unless you want to try it out…"

Karsyn stiffens, tugging me closer to him in a possessive move. I laugh lightly.

"No, thanks. I think four dicks might be enough."

"But zero pussy," she jokes, shaking her head dismay. "That's a sad life to live, Peony."

I twist my head to smile up at the handsome boy beside me. "Yeah. But it's my life."

…

"What the fuck are you doing?" Elias's entire face twists with disgust as he stares at Lucas at the other end of the dinner table.

Lucas glances up from where he's daintily cutting up his hot dog into small bites. As usual, he sits perfectly straight in his chair, the epitome of good posture, with his dark red hair swept away from his face. His icy eyes narrow as he gingerly brings the hot dog bite to his mouth.

"Unlike you Neanderthals, I actually have good manners," he huffs, just as Cassian comes back inside from the back porch, carrying a second tray of grilled hot dogs. One thing's for certain—my guys eat a lot. Honestly, we might need to raid a Costco if they keep this up.

"Good table manners, you say?" With a shit-eating grin, Cassian shovels an entire hot dog into his mouth and then chews in Lucas's face.

I swear Lucas looks one second away from dying of a brain aneurysm.

"Cass, knock it off," I scold with an eye roll, but my amusement quickly transforms into lust when he brings a second hot dog to his mouth and begins to lick at the tip. Maintaining eye contact, he pushes it into his mouth, his teeth grazing the edge, before pulling it back out.

Fucking hell.

We talked just the other night about other...things. We mutually agreed that while the other guys might be comfortable with each other's bodies, none of them would be willing to fuck one another. At least, not with a "perfectly good pussy available." Cassian's words, not mine. But the thought of pegging Cassian...

Molten liquid burns down below, and I rub my thighs in a futile attempt to alleviate the ache.

From his glazed expression, he's thinking about the conversation as well.

"Peony!" Karsyn's bellow has me jumping a solid foot in the air. It's not as if I'm actually scared of him—none of the Devils could scare me anymore, not when they look at me like I hold the moon in one hand and the sun in the other—but the reaction is ingrained within me. Ever since Emmett, I've been jumpy. Fearful. Trembling when I'm alone too long in the dark.

I know this reaction is completely normal, that I went through a horrendous trauma and it's only been a week, but I still fear I'll never go back to normal.

But, then again, what exactly *is* normal? I'm a crazy witch with a voodoo doll, who is in love with four very different and equally psychotic men. Normal is overrated.

"Peony!" Karsyn screams again, barreling into the kitchen. He pauses when he catches sight of Lucas, eyebrows furrowing. "Dude, why are you cutting up your hot dog?"

"Oh for the love of..." Angrily, Lucas pushes his plate away and folds his arms over his chest.

I can't help but tease my stoic lover. "I know for a fact you like some finger foods."

"Ohhhh." Cassian waggles his eyebrows suggestively. "Is this a sex joke? Please tell met this is a sex joke involving his fingers and your food."

"It involves a hamburger," I quip cheerfully, and I swear his dark eyes turn molten.

"And are you the meat in this burger?" he asks huskily.

"I sure hope not," I answer seriously. "Because if I was, then that means he ate me."

Cassian looks less than a second away from pinning me over the table and fucking me senseless.

But...

"Why were you screaming Peony's name?" Elias interjects, leaning casually back in his chair. He's not wearing his leather jacket today, and instead, the muscles of his biceps are on clear display. A tattoo curls around his upper arm, one that I only noticed a few days ago in bed. It's a simple design—a vine interspersed with blooming red roses. I'm a little salty that they're not peonies, but when I told Elias that, he chuckled indulgently.

"You scared I'm going to run off with a girl named Rose?" he teased, hand drifting over the splash of color on his tan skin.

I actually fucking growled at the thought. "If you do, I'm hexing you both," I warned. Completely reasonable reaction, in my opinion.

He simply laughed again, leaned forward, and kissed me senseless.

"Peony, was this you?" Karsyn asks now, yanking me back to the present. At my confused expression, Karsyn waves his phone in the air erratically. "Was. This. You?"

"He called you?" I ask, as understanding finally dawns. I sit up straighter in my chair, a wide smile blossoming on my face.

"He fucking called me, princess!" Karsyn lunges forward, practically shoving me off the chair in an attempt to stick his tongue as far down my throat as humanly possible. I swear I see stars behind my eyelids as he fucks my mouth with that filthy tongue of his.

"Not that I mind the scene," Lucas drawls lazily, still glaring indignantly at the hot dog pieces. "But what are you two going on about?"

"In English, dude," Cassian adds, dropping into the chair beside mine and draping his arm over the back of it.

"State called." Karsyn's too breathless to speak coherently, his words sounding airy and jumbled. He takes a deep breath before trying again, that same infectious smile lighting up his face. "The recruiter from State. He called. Apparently, *someone* delivered footage of me from the first few games of the season and demanded he watch them."

All eyes are suddenly on me, staring at me with varying degrees of awe.

I shrug sheepishly, nervously brushing at my white hair. "It's the least I could do." I glance down at the tabletop, then to the tiles, before finally settling my gaze on the eggshell-colored wall. Anything to avoid the probing gazes I can feel on my scalp. "After what I did…"

Karsyn leans forward to kiss me senseless once more, his tongue tangling with mine before he finally allows me to breathe.

"I haven't told you guys yet," Cassian begins with a faux nonchalance, "but I just received my acceptance letter into State too."

"What?" I screech, whirling on him. His arm drops from around my shoulders as I cup his cheeks in my palms. "Why didn't you tell us?"

Am I mistaken, or does he actually blush?

"There was a lot going on," he mumbles, embarrassed. "It didn't seem important."

"Cassian, *you* are important," I stress, squishing his face until his lips protrude like a duck.

"Youimpotant."

"What?" I ask with a teasing grin, squeezing his face even more. "Can't understand you."

"Youapaninmyass," he tries again.

"Still can't hear you."

"Yeah, man, you need to speak up," Elias adds with a wicked smirk.

When I press down once more, Cassian lunges towards my unprotected stomach and begins to tickle me senseless. I would've fallen off the chair if Karsyn wasn't suddenly there, repositioning me so I'm sitting on his lap.

"Mercy! Mercy!" I squeal, laughing.

"You're such an ass!" Cassian bellows at me, and Elias growls.

"Hey, watch it," he warns.

"Nah. My girl knows she's an ass, doesn't she?" Cassian turns towards me with a wink.

"Is this where you want me to shake my booty in front of your face and have you throw pennies at it?" I ask seriously. "Because I'll have you know, my ass is primed and ready for things to be shoved up there."

At my crude comment, all four of the men groan. Karsyn attempts to reposition me on his lap, eyes closed as if he's in pain.

"I was going to say—before you interrupted me with thoughts of my cock in your beautiful white ass—that State has an amazing music program. And since I can't get into Juilliard because of my grades…" He trails off with a shrug. A pang reverberates through me like cymbals clashing together, but I refuse to feel guilty for what I did. I got a pedophile off the streets and hopefully put in prison. The world will be a much better place without her darkness tainting it.

"You know," Lucas taps his knife to his chin, "I heard that State has one of the best pre-law programs in the country." Without another word, he pulls his phone out of his pocket and pulls up the website, scrolling until he finds the online application. "I'll get in, of course, if this is what we want to do."

"You mean, like, go to college together?" I can barely contain the hope that creeps into my voice. Hope for us. Hope for a future together.

"We're practically fucking married," Cassian drawls, causing a blush to rise to my cheeks.

"Don't be an asshole," Karsyn admonishes, his own face beet-red. He slaps Cassian over the top of the head, and Cassian twists to punch him back.

Only for both of them to freeze when they see their hands.

Tiny flames dance in Karsyn's open palm, while Cassian's fist is coated in a layer of ice.

All five of us stare.

"Well, that's a new development," Elias says after a long, pregnant moment of silence.

Cassian grins broadly, waving his ice fist back and forth. "This is so fucking cool!"

"We were told that we might be able to harness some of Peony's powers," Lucas says dismissively, already turning his attention back towards his phone. When I check in on his emotions, I find nothing but serenity and acceptance. I wonder if Lucas knew that he could do this long before the others. It honestly wouldn't surprise me. Knowing him, he already used his fire power to burn the dead body of one of the people he murdered.

"I'll have to train you guys," I say, my heart lodged in my throat.

"Sexy training?" Cassian asks bluntly.

Both Elias and Karsyn hit him over the head at that one.

"We'll need to be careful," Elias adds with a pointed look at each of his friends. "We can't just turn into human fireballs every time we get pissed or upset."

"Or human icicles, as the case may be," Lucas pipes in, attention still fixed on his phone.

"I wonder if I could turn my cock into an icicle," Cassian muses in contemplation. "The things we could do, Peony. The things we could do."

"I'll go wherever you go," Elias blurts, bringing us back to the conversation at hand. When I turn towards him, his eyes are soft. Loving. "If that's to France, Italy, across the street, the grocery store...I'm following you."

"So we're doing it?" I feel shaky, but this time, I know that it's from happiness and not pain. That's not to say that there won't be some days where I feel like giving up, feel like giving in, but I'll have these four incredible men with me every step of the way. I love them the way the shadows love the light. A way that's pure and desperate and inseparable.

I may go to hell for the things I've done, but at least I'll have four devils to keep me company.

And together, this world will burn.

CHAPTER 57

SIX MONTHS LATER

CASSIAN

"You have a nice ass…and…sass…and…I suck…and…" Scowling, I toss the pen across the room and remove the guitar strap, setting the instrument on the ground. Playing music I can do without a fucking problem, but writing it? Putting your soul into lyrics and notes? Fucking impossible.

"What crawled up your ass and died?" Elias leans against the doorframe of my room, hands crossed over his chest and one leg kicked up. I let out a muffled curse at seeing him. Mom must've let him upstairs while I was distracted.

"Just want to get this right," I mumble, glaring at the offending sheet music. So many scribbles and scratch marks cover the page, it's nearly impossible to see a single note.

Elias's face instantly turns somber as he drops his arms and steps into the room. "It will be."

"This is the most important day of my—"

"It will be," he vows again, bending down to grab a crumpled piece of paper. I actually fucking blush like some sort of pathetic schoolgirl as he reads through one of the many, many songs I attempted to write. His eyebrows shoot up to his hairline.

"And you're going to college for music?" he asks in disbelief, eyes sparkling with mirth.

"Shut the fuck up, you annoying asswipe," I grumble petulantly.

"At least it rhymes," he points out oh-so-helpfully. "Tit and legit. Real top-notch stuff."

I'm across the room in three long strides, ripping the paper from his hand and throwing it in my overflowing garbage bin. "You will not breathe a word of this to anyone."

His lips twitch in amusement. "Does this mean I have new black-mail material?"

I know he's trying to lighten my mood, but my mood refuses to be fucking lightened.

His smile fades as I cross back to the bed, all but throwing myself onto the mattress and staring up at the ceiling. He moves to stand over me.

"Okay, look...I heard your songs before. The ones you wrote, I mean. At the concert in December," he tells me. I can't help but smirk as I remember said concert.

The high school's band and orchestra performed together for some holiday shit show. And while I loved playing with Peony again on stage, the after-show was ten times better. Mainly because it involved her, me, and no fucking clothes.

"Head. Out. Of. Gutter," Elias snaps, emphasizing each word with a kick to my dangling legs. "As I was saying before, I heard the songs you wrote. They're good—really good. So why are they sucking so fucking badly now?"

"Because none of them mattered before," I grumble, bringing my hands to my cheeks and dragging them down. "But this one does."

"Let me see your songwriting journal or whatever the fuck you write them in," Elias demands. Normally, I'll make a smart-ass joke about his bossy tone, but I'm too tired to do anything but point towards my desk, where dozens of old notebooks litter the surface.

Elias grows silent as he grabs one and then another, flipping through the worn-out pages. He's there for fifteen minutes before he freezes suddenly, a slow, beguiling smile appearing on his face. He waves the notebook in front of him enthusiastically as I stare at him with a quirked brow.

"You do realize that you look fucking crazy right now, right?" I ask dryly as he comes back over and drops the notebook onto my chest.

"This one," he says simply. When I continue to stare at him, not moving a muscle, he kicks at my leg again, extracting a growl from me. "Look at it, you dumb fuck."

With a sigh somewhere between exasperated and despondent, I sit upright in bed and pore over the opened notebook. My initial annoyance quickly transitions into shock and then excitement.

"We're doing this?" I ask him, gaze still trained on the notebook page.

I can hear the smile in his voice when he speaks next. "Graduation day, baby."

...

KARSYN

"Where is she?" Mom strains her neck to see over the throng of parents hurrying towards the bleachers.

"She's with her grandma," I placate soothingly. "She'll be here."

Mom clutches the peony to her chest with a huff, even as Dad attempts to calm her.

"You can always give her the flower afterwards," he suggests. And I swear, the look Mom throws him is capable of curdling milk.

"I promise you, Mom, that we'll find you after the ceremony is done," I rush to assure her, squeezing her shoulders. Her eyes, so much like my own, begin to water as she cups my cheeks between both of her hands.

"I'm just so proud of you," she sobs, forcing my head down to give me a slobbery kiss on the forehead.

"Mom!" I murmur in embarrassment when some of the guys from the football team give me amused looks. Though those looks don't compare to the ones I get when people discover I share a girlfriend with my three best friends. But then again, they can all go fuck themselves if they have a problem with it.

"We're going to take our seats now," Dad whispers as he nudges my mother along. He gives me a clap on the shoulder, his eyes watery despite his best attempts to hide it. Pride and love emanate from his gaze as he tousles my hair. "Proud of you, son."

"You'll be even prouder when I play for State next year," I say automatically, my heart gaining wings and fluttering around in my ribcage. State. My fucking dream.

And now, I get to share that dream with my girl and best friends.

In answer, Dad merely reaches into his back pocket and grabs a faded State baseball cap. He places it on his head, mussing his already wild hair.

As my parents drift in one direction with the other parents, I follow the crowd of students towards the small gym where we'll wait until it's time to walk in. We all initially had a huge argument when it was discovered that every girl could only walk with one guy. After a heated—and bloody—game of rock paper scissors, it was decided that Lucas would walk with Peony, I would take Mariabella, Elias would take Mariabella's newest girlfriend, Jennifer, and Cassian would take one of Peony's close friends, Felicia. It wasn't ideal, but we didn't have a lot of choices.

"Karsyn!"

The love of my entire existence runs through the swinging doors of the gym, her white hair billowing behind her like a flurry of snow.

She jumps into my arms, legs twisting around my waist, as she frantically kisses me. She ignores the jealous and envious glares of the other girls, the leers of the men, and the confused glances from the people who don't quite understand our relationship.

"Hey, princess," I say, peppering kisses along the corner of her mouth as she slides back down my body.

"We're doing it," she breathes, excitement dancing in her gorgeous amber eyes.

"We're fucking doing it."

I take a moment to admire her in the cream-colored sweater and form-fitting black leggings. She completes the outfit with a pair of dark knee-high boots. The red graduation gown we're all required to wear is a size too big, stopping just below her knees and hiding her cute little fingers from view. She fiddles with the tassel of her graduation cap as she stares at her fellow classmates.

"We're finally leaving these people behind," she whispers, and I can't quite tell how she feels about that. Mariabella has been accepted into a college a few hours away from State, and though I know that my girl is devastated about the distance, I also know that their friendship will survive. How can it not? Their friendship is one of the most important things in Peony's life.

"You okay with that?" I finally decide to voice my thoughts. After six months of dating, I realized pretty quickly that this relationship will only work if we're all honest with each other. Open. For some of us, like Lucas and Elias, that's harder than others. But as Cassian reminds us numerous times, we're not only in a relationship with her, but also with each other. That second relationship isn't in any way sexual, but it's still important to strengthen the bonds. That's why Peony forces us to hang out without her once a month. It'll take time and energy to go back to the way we used to be five years ago, before she left us, but we're getting there. Slowly and surely, we're getting there.

"I think it's time for a change," Peony states firmly, glancing out of the corner of her eye at a group of girls whispering and pointing. We've been getting a lot of that lately. You would think the novelty would wear off, but nope. People still seem to think that this is nothing more than a fling, that we'll leave her when we get sick of sharing or she'll ditch us.

But then again, most people these days are close-minded when it comes to things they don't understand. I'm just fortunate enough that my parents supported me when we confessed the truth to them. Lucas's parents? Not so much.

Speaking of…

"Where is that little devil?" I question.

…

LUCAS

I straighten out my cufflinks as I survey my reflection in the mirror.

Red hair slicked back…check.

Three-piece, gray tailored suit…check.

Loafers shined to perfection…check.

Watch on my left wrist…check.

Ring…

My eyes widen almost comically as I pat down both of my pockets, sighing in immense relief when I find what I'm looking for.

Taking another deep breath, I shrug the robe on and grab my cap from where I placed it on the sink. And then…I see it. A fucking wrinkle.

My frown deepens.

I almost wish I hadn't been kicked out of the house, if only so my butler, Atkins, could iron my suit.

But alas, Peony's grandmother's house, where I've been staying for the last six months, doesn't even have an ironing board.

"You done staring at yourself in the mirror, asshole?" Cassian asks as he straightens his tie. This is the first time I've ever seen the man in a suit. The dark brown emphasizes his coffee skin and radiant golden eyes. Of course, the asshole completes the look with a polka dot tie, but beggars can't be choosers. I'm lucky I got him out of his basketball shorts to begin with.

"Never," I reply dryly, smoothing out a red lock before putting the hat snugly in place. My lips pull away from my teeth in a grimace. Because this black hat paired with the red robe? Fucking awful. Whoever designed this atrocity must be fired immediately.

"Your parents coming today?" Cassian's voice grows softer than before, almost as if he's afraid someone will overhear us.

I pretend not to understand his question at first as I stride out of the bathroom and into the school's empty hallway. The majority of my classmates are already in the small gym, awaiting the ceremony with bated breath. All of the family members are gathered in the large gym with their cameras and smartphones and beaming, proud smiles.

But not my parents.

Not after they kicked me out of the house without even a backwards glance.

I don't mind. At least, I tell myself I don't mind. They were fairweather friends at best, choosing to be around me on my sunny days and running to high heavens when it was rainy or dark.

"No," I answer Cassian at last, moving briskly down the hallway. I just want to get to my girl and hold her in my arms. "They're not."

"At least they didn't cut you off completely," Cassian points out, no doubt attempting to cheer me up.

I stop abruptly and whirl on him, my cold grin plastered firmly in place. Peony calls it my psycho grin, though I don't know where she got that idea.

"The weekly allowance in my bank account, you mean?" I query before continuing to walk farther down the hall. "You're right. I would much rather have large sums of hush money than an actual mother and father," I finish dryly.

"Your sarcasm has been noted."

We enter the gym, and my eyes immediately seek out Peony, as they usually do when we're in a large crowd of people. It's as if everyone else fades away. No, that's not a good description for what happens. It's almost as if everyone around her turns into dark, indistinct shadows while she remains a bright and blinding light, calling to the darkness inside of me. And one might think a creature like me would cower from her, but I think a part of me craves all that she offers. I've been alone in the abyss for way too goddamn long.

She's laughing with Karsyn and Mariabella, looking more beautiful and ethereal than the paintings I study in art class. Her white hair, the color of pure and untarnished mountain top snow, loosely curls around her shoulders. Even with the garish red robe and black hat, she's a vision of beauty.

For so long, I scoured the earth looking for perfection. True perfection, not something that can be faked. I thought it was unattainable until Peony Simone stumbled back into my life after five agonizing years away. Maybe I sought her out for purely selfish reasons, but all I knew for certain was that I couldn't stay away.

I know that her bitch of mother claimed the spell she placed on us as children caused our hostile reactions towards the stunning woman before me, but I don't think that's entirely true. I think I've always been a monster, and some beasts only know how to impress their mates through cruelty.

Somehow, someway, Peony tamed my beast. I may always be a creature of knives and shadows, but now, I'm hers. My hands will be stained red with blood for all of eternity, and I'll never shed a tear because of it. I still remember a few weeks after I killed Emmett, when Peony confronted me about my fucking feelings.

"Are you okay?" She perched herself daintily on my lap as I sat in my favorite rocking chair in the corner of her bedroom. I wrapped my arms

around her waist and pulled her even closer to my chest, breathing in her distinct scent.

Something about that mouthwatering scent sent my head into a tailspin. I didn't know how to put it into words, so I never did. I just...enjoyed it. Flocked to it. It was something primitive inside of me, something words failed to encapsulate.

"About what?" I asked amusedly. When she began to fidget, my smile, the one I wore only for her, slipped from my face. "Peony, about what?" I gently rubbed at her soft lips, aching to lean forward and capture them between my own. I learned she liked it when I bit down just hard enough to sting.

"We never really talked about..." She trailed off once more.

I slipped my hand beneath her shirt and splayed my fingers over her soft stomach.

"Don't make me spank the question out of you," I warned heatedly, and when her eyes turned into liquid gold, the amber more brown than yellow, I knew she was just as game for that as I was.

Before she could formulate a response, I had her tipped over my knee, her skirt flying upwards until I could see her perfect ass and small red thong. I rubbed my hand over first one cheek and then the other as she whimpered softly.

And then, as if she was suddenly coming to her senses, she sat upright and shifted on my lap until she was straddling me.

"Lucas, I'm being serious. No spankings," she breathed, cupping my face. "We never talked about what happened with Emmett."

My good mood instantly soured, like bloated storm clouds ruining a perfectly good picnic at the park. Any talk of that sadistic fucker seemed to do that to me.

"What about him?"

"You killed a man, Lucas," she prodded gently. And though she tried to keep her face impassive, I could see a glimmer of pain in her gorgeous eyes. Not because she missed him or anything, but because she remembered. Remembered all of the things he did to her before we

arrived. Remembered the feel of his disgusting hands on her perfect skin.

"So did you," I responded immediately, and her face shut down. Shattered. I quickly attempted to backtrack, rubbing my hands up and down her arms to soothe her tense muscles. She wasn't ready to talk about the people she killed, and I didn't blame her. But what she did was in self-defense, and the sooner she understood that, the quicker she could move on. I would be there for her every damn step of the way as she healed from what that sick fuck forced her to do. What he did *to her.*

Emmett's face flashed in my mind.

Anger once more raged a war inside of me, but my love for this woman kept it adequately subdued. I wouldn't dare give in to my primal instincts while she was near.

"Are you asking me if I feel guilty for what I did to protect you?" I questioned gently, and when she nodded, I couldn't help but scoff. "I only wish I had killed him sooner."

"What did you...?" She swallowed. "You never told us what you did with the body. What you did with the bodies." She nibbled anxiously on her lower lip, as the horrors from that night cast shadows in her gorgeous amber eyes.

I smiled at her, one that was laced with maliciousness and darkness. One that had her eyes heating and legs squeezing my thighs in an iron vise.

"You'll never have to worry about Emmett or the other again," I vowed.

I'm pulled from the memory by a soft hand gently squeezing my own.

"You look dashing, Lucas," Peony states softly, eyes traveling across my body. I practically preen at her attention, though I keep my face blank. Even after all of these months, it's hard for me not to keep my cards close to my sleeve.

"You look as beautiful as ever," I whisper, leaning forward to chastely kiss her forehead.

Mariabella stands in front of us beside Karsyn, while Elias and Cassian move behind us. Elias is partnered with Mariabella's newest fling—that girl goes through more flings than Cassian did before Peony—while Cass himself is with Felicia.

I can't help but notice the longing glances Felicia alternates between Mariabella and Peony. I know that over the last six months, she developed a crush on my girl, though her lingering feelings for Mariabella still remain.

Felicia will need to realize, and soon, that Peony will never be hers.

I refuse to let her go.

The thought of someone taking her from me causes me to tighten my grip on her hand. Peony glances over at me in confusion, her brow raised. When I don't immediately explain my caveman actions, she rolls her eyes, though her lips twitch in the beginnings of a smile.

It isn't long until the principal instructs us to enter the gym with our walking partners and take our seats near the stage.

Nerves like I never felt before cascade through my veins, very nearly stealing the breath from my lungs. My heart races as cold sweat drips down my spine.

And I don't fucking sweat.

Ever.

It's like someone is scratching sandpaper against my throat, slowly eroding the skin away.

For the first time in my entire life, I want to run.

But then Peony squeezes my hand and gives me a soft, reassuring smile, and the tension leaks from my body.

"You can do this," she whispers. "You practiced this speech thousands of times in the mirror." When I open my mouth to protest, her grin broadens, and it's the most beautiful thing in the entire fucking world. "Don't deny it. I heard you. Believe it or not, Lucas, you're only human. You're not this unfeeling robot. You're allowed to be scared."

You have no fucking idea.

...

ELIAS

On the stage in front of the graduates and parents, Lucas finishes up his valedictorian speech. He speaks curtly, succinctly, his cold gaze traveling over the people in the room. It's not the impassioned plea I'm sure the school board hoped for, but it's the best they'll get from Lucas Scott.

My eyes drift to Peony sitting in the seat beside me, fidgeting with the sleeves of her graduation robe.

"Are you okay?" I lean forward to whisper, my lips grazing her ear. I take great satisfaction when her breath hitches ever so slightly and her neck arches, like an animal baring her flesh to an alpha.

"We're fucking graduating," she whispers back as Lucas continues to drawl on and on about new beginnings from the raised platform. "It's just crazy how things changed so quickly."

"Are you scared?" I query, because in all honesty, I'm fucking terrified. We're going to a new school, with new people, and new fucking problems. I already know people won't accept this unconventional relationship, but we decided unanimously that we weren't going to hide.

"I know it's silly..."

"There's no reason to be scared," I reassure her.

"It's just with my mother..."

"Whom you haven't seen since your grandma disowned her."

"And your powers..."

I lightly squeeze her hand, pushing a tiny bit of heat into my touch. She gasps, not loud enough to draw attention, and gives me a bland look. I simply smirk at her in response.

"Everything will be okay," I repeat. "Did you know that Cassian and I went to check out the apartment the other day? The landlady reminds me of your grandma. Super sweet. It's only ten minutes away from school and fifteen away from the mechanic's shop."

I decided pretty quickly that more schooling isn't for me. I spent three-fourths of my time ditching class, and I only returned when Peony did. I landed an internship at a mechanic's shop in the area. At first, I worried Peony would be mad at me for not pursuing school, but I shouldn't have underestimated my girl. She was positively thrilled and showed me how happy she was with that perfect body of hers.

"We're really doing it," she whispers dazedly.

I lean forward to claim her lips with my own, tasting her cherry chapstick.

"We're really doing it, baby girl." I reluctantly release her and begin to walk towards the stage, where Cassian and Karsyn already joined Lucas. Whispers break out amongst the students and parents as we stand side by side, staring down at a confused and flustered Peony.

Lucas's lips curl into a grin that isn't entirely pleasant.

"Peony, will you come up here, please?"

...

PEONY

What the fuck are they up to?

My heartbeat increases from a trot to a full-on gallop as I join the four of them on stage.

Unbidden, my mind travels to a different night when they called me onto a stage…

"Good evening, ladies and gentlemen," Lucas begins, his voice drifting over the crowd like an icy wind in December. Cassian, Karsyn, and Elias all wear matching smirks, which only ratchets up my unease and suspicion. "We decided we're going to start a new tradition."

I gape at him—at *them*—wordlessly as they all turn to stare at me. And then, in perfect synchronization, they drop to one knee.

People begin to gasp. Some even begin to scream in shock, crying that this is immoral. I hear someone sobbing in joy, and I don't need to look to know it's Mariabella, eagerly snapping pictures on her phone.

"We made a lot of mistakes in our life," Cassian begins as the rest of the room fades away.

"But loving you has never been one of them," adds Karsyn.

"We promise to love you until our very last days," Elias interjects with a soft smile.

Lucas reaches into his pants pocket and grabs a small ring box, slowly pulling open the lid to reveal a silver band encrusted with four diamonds. One for each of my men.

"Will you marry us?"

Someone shouts that we're going to hell. Another person actually lunges for the stage, before he mysteriously falls to his ass, his pants now on fire. Christian smirks evilly from where he stands with a crying Nana and a beaming Polo.

On the screen that previously displayed the graduates' names, it now plays the lyrics of a song I've never heard before. I recognize the sultry, husky voice as Cassian's.

"*Step by step, it's hard for me to accept. You jumped in my life. And all of the pain melted away. No time. For regrets. Never looking back again.*"

As the song plays through the speakers and tears fill my eyes, Cassian smiles shyly.

"I wrote this the day you returned," he confesses. "I didn't understand why until now. I think a part of me always knew that everything would lead to this."

It takes me a long moment to realize that I still haven't answered

Lucas's question. I don't know how it'll work, a marriage between me and four men, but maybe the hows don't matter, only the whys.

And the why is pretty damn simple—I love these men, and against all odds and reasoning, they love me in return.

A red-faced, furious principal begins to storm towards the stage, the scene almost an exact replica of that night five years ago.

But now, everything has changed.

Now, I have so much love in my life, I'm afraid my heart might actually burst.

"Yes," I whisper. "Yes, I'll marry all of you."

As Lucas slides the ring onto my finger, a wide, genuine smile splitting his face in two, I realize that all of the pain and heartache of my past led me to this moment. To the four of them.

We may be going to hell, but at least we'll be together.

Now and forever.

Just one crazy witch and her four charming devils.

ABOUT THE AUTHOR

Katie May is a reverse harem author, a KDP All-Star winner, and a USA Today bestselling author. She lives in West Michigan with her family. When not writing, she could be found reading a good book, listening to broadway musicals, or playing games. Join Katie's Gang to stay updated on all her releases! Join her newsletter here!

Supernaturalette (Interactive Reverse Harem)

1. Introductions

2. First Dates

3. Group Outing

4. Game Night

5. Exes

CO-WRITES

Afterworld Academy with Loxley Savage (Academy Fantasy Reverse Harem)

1. Dearly Departed

2. Darkness Deceives

Her Immortal Legacy with Elena Lawson (Time Travel Paranormal Reverse Harem)

1. Chasing Time

Darkest Flames with Ann Denton (Paranormal Reverse Harem)

1. Demon Kissed

1.5. Demon Stalked

2. Demon Loved

STAND-ALONES

Toxicity (Contemporary Reverse Harem)

Blindly Indicted (Prison Reverse Harem)

Not All Heroes Wear Capes (Just Dresses) (Short Comedic Reverse Harem)

Charming Devils (Bully/Revenge Reverse Harem)

Goddess of Pain (Fantasy Reverse Harem)

Torn to Bits (Shifter Reverse Harem)